REDUCTION IN FORCE

On the holoscreen glimmered the results of Terachyk's model.

All the people on *Orbitech 1*, all fifteen hundred, would starve in four months.

Brahms felt a drop of sweat trickle in a cold path down his back. Fewer people would be able to survive longer on the same amount of supplies.

He used his thumbprint to unseal one of the compartments in the "Restricted" file. Inside was the duplicate memory-cube containing the confidential results of his Efficiency Study.

He pulled the keypad toward him, saved Allen Terachyk's analysis, then called up the study. As he scrolled down through the names and scores on the holoscreen, he looked only at the rankings, forcing himself not to think of faces, of people . . .

Brahms hesitated a long time before choosing the first name, the one with the lowest score. But once he had chosen the first, the rest came easier.

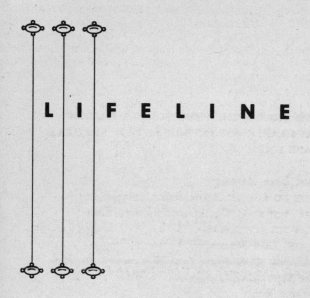

LIFELINE

KEVIN J. ANDERSON
DOUG BEASON

SPECTRA

BANTAM BOOKS
NEW YORK · TORONTO · LONDON · SYDNEY · AUCKLAND

LIFELINE

A Bantam Spectra Book / December 1990

A substantially different version of a portion of this work appeared in
Amazing Stories™ *under the title "If I Fell, Would I Fall," copyright ©*
1988 Kevin J. Anderson and Doug Beason.

ISBN 0-553-28787-7

Published simultaneously in the United States and Canada

Bantam Books are published by Bantam Books, a division of Bantam
Doubleday Dell Publishing Group, Inc. Its trademark, consisting of the
words "Bantam Books" and the portrayal of a rooster, is Registered in U.S.
Patent and Trademark Office and in other countries. Marca Registrada.
Bantam Books, 666 Fifth Avenue, New York, New York 10103.

PRINTED IN THE UNITED STATES OF AMERICA

OPM 0 9 8 7 6 5 4 3 2 1

ACKNOWLEDGMENTS

We'd like to thank the following people for adding their thoughts, expertise, and opinions to this project. Laurence A.P. Moore (and his amazing database!), David Brin, Kevin Mengelt, Steve Homann, Chuck Beason, Stan Schmidt, Betsy Mitchell, Richard Curtis, Michael C. Berch, Walter Williams, M. Coleman Easton, Dan'l Danehy-Oakes, Clare Bell, Avis Minger, Gary W. Schockley, Lori Ann White, Kristine Kathryn Rusch, Lisa Ice, Pat Weber, Pat Price, Pat McGraw Brown, Sally Gwylan, Patti Nagle, Karen McCue and the countless others who encouraged us to keep at it.

To—

    my mother,
    MARTHA GRACE MCCLUNEY BEASON,
    for leading me to books
                  (Doug Beason)

        and

    DEAN WESLEY SMITH
    for being more than just the right place
    at the right time.
               (Kevin J. Anderson)

DRAMATIS PERSONAE

■ *AGUINALDO (L-4)*

RAMIS BARRERA—colonist
AGPALO BARRERA—Ramis's father
PANAY BARRERA—Ramis's mother
SALITA BARRERA—Ramis's brother on Earth
DR. LUIS SANDOVAAL—*Aguinaldo*'s chief scientist
DOBO DAENG—Luis's assistant
BARRETA DAENG—Dobo's wife
YOLI MAGSAYSAY—president of the *Aguinaldo*
NADA MAGSAYSAY—Yoli's wife
DR. PANOGY—celestial mechanics expert

■ CLAVIUS BASE (MOON)

DR. KIM BERENGER—infirmary M.D.
DR. CLIFFORD E. CLANCY—*Orbitech 2* chief engineer
WIAY SHEN—Clancy's chief foreman
PETER HOMANN—*Orbitech 2* engineer

DR. PHILIP TOMKINS—Clavius Base chief administrator
JOSEF ABDALLAH—technician and work scheduler
DR. BILLY ROCKLAND—group leader, celestial
  mechanics
HARMON WOOSTER—*Orbitech 2* engineer

■ *O R B I T E C H   1   (L - 5)*

LINDA ARNANDO—Personnel/Admin Division leader,
  later chief assessor for Curtis Brahms
DR. DANIEL AIKEN—research scientist, biochemist
SHEILA AIKEN—Daniel's wife
STEPHANIE GARLAND—*Miranda* shuttle pilot
ALLEN TERACHYK—Research & Development Division
  leader, later chief assessor for Curtis Brahms
DUNCAN MCLARIS—Production Division leader, later
  acting administrator for Clavius Base
JESSIE MCLARIS—Duncan's daughter
DIANE MCLARIS—Duncan's wife
DR. KAREN LANGELIER—research chemist, polymers
TIM DRURY—Maintenance/Services Division leader
CURTIS BRAHMS—acting director, *Orbitech 1*
SIGAT HARHOOSMA—metallurgist
HIRO KAITANABE—gardener
ROHA OMBALAL—director, *Orbitech 1*
NANCY WINKOWSKI—chemical technician and
  laboratory assistant, later Watcher

■ *K I B A L C H I C H   (L - 5)*

DR. ANNA TRIPOLK—chief biochemist, in charge of
  research
COMMANDER STEPAN RURIK—*Kibalchich*
  commanding officer
ALEXANDROV CAGARIN—political officer
ILLIMUI DANSKOY—activist
GREKOV—technician
ORVINSKAD—technician
SHEVEREMSKY—technician

ORBIT:
L-4 to L-5
Solar Sail Creature
with Earth gravity assist

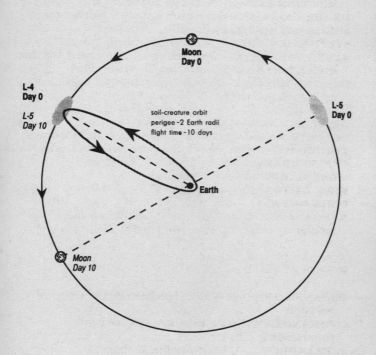

L-4
Day 0

L-5
Day 10

Moon
Day 0

L-5
Day 0

sail-creature orbit
perigee ~2 Earth radii
flight time ~10 days

Earth

Moon
Day 10

AGUINALDO

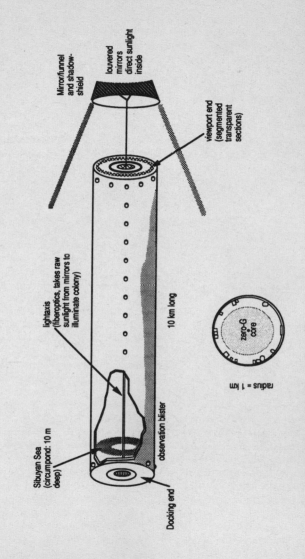

Mirror/funnel and shadow-shield

louvered mirrors direct sunlight inside

viewport end (segmented transparent sections)

lightaxis (fiberoptics, takes raw sunlight from mirrors to illuminate colony)

10 km long

Sibuyan Sea (circumpond: 10 m deep)

observation blister

Docking end

zero-G core

radius = 1 km

ORBITECH 1
1500 people

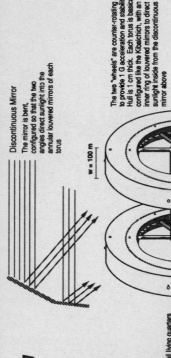

Discontinuous Mirror

The mirror is bent, configured so that the two angles direct sunlight into the annular louvered mirrors of each torus

w = 100 m

r = 1 km

d = 1 km

The two "wheels" are counter-rotating to provide 1 G acceleration and stability. Hull is 1 cm thick. Each torus is basically configured like the Kibalchich, with an inner ring of louvered mirrors to direct sunlight inside from the discontinuous mirror above

The two "wheels" are where all living quarters are, most of the recreational facilities (very few zero-G areas are available — zero gravity space is much valued by Orbitechnologies), and administrative areas. Also, medical facilities, computer centers, "town" stuff (stores, barbers, cafeterias, etc.)

zero G core, for most of the production work. Portions of this core are also at total vacuum. Some of the area is devoted to research & development. An access corridor runs through the core from one wheel to the other.

KIBALCHICH

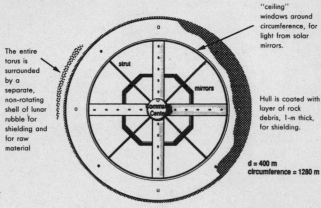

"ceiling" windows around circumference, for light from solar mirrors.

The entire torus is surrounded by a separate, non-rotating shell of lunar rubble for shielding and for raw material

strut

mirrors

Command Center

Hull is coated with layer of rock debris, 1-m thick, for shielding.

d = 400 m
circumference = 1280 m

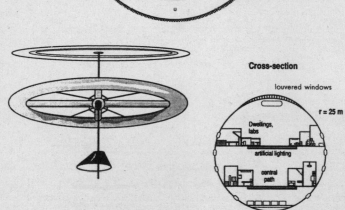

Cross-section

louvered windows

r = 25 m

Dwellings, labs

artificial lighting

central path

Belowdecks, life-support, maintenance equipment, wiring, etc.

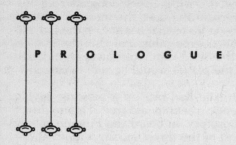

P R O L O G U E

L-4: *AGUINALDO* ■ 5 YEARS BEFORE DAY 1

He thought the experiment would work, but even if it failed, he knew he could bluff his way through. The Filipinos held their Dr. Luis Sandovaal too much in awe for them to doubt anything he did.

Sandovaal ignored the crowd around him. President Magsaysay stood quietly by the airlock, along with the rest of the Council of Twenty. Sandovaal stared past the group, past the habitats and experimental fields, and gazed instead upon the sweeping curve of the cylindrical colony's far side, where Filipino children played floater-tag in the zero-G core.

Sandovaal's whole life revolved around success: taking outrageous chances, working long hours until he felt absolutely sure his experiments would prove out. Admitting to being only "second best" seemed as bad as conceding defeat. The field of applied genetics evolved too fast for stragglers.

That had always made it necessary for Sandovaal to take

certain . . . *chances* . . . with his bioengineering research so he could remain the best, the most innovative. He had come to carry on his researches at L-4, the gravitational stable point 60 degrees ahead of the Moon in its orbit, four hundred thousand kilometers away from Earth —where the rest of the planet would be safe in case anything went wrong.

That self-imposed exile had proven a blessing, giving him unlimited academic freedom and free reign to direct his own research laboratory on board the Filipino colony *Aguinaldo,* the largest of the three human stations at L-4 and L-5. The Filipinos were proud of his presence there, to the point of designating him the colony's chief scientist.

Sandovaal drew himself up to his full five-foot stature and spoke to the crowd in front of the airlock. With his blue eyes and shock of white hair, he didn't look much like the other *Aguinaldo* inhabitants.

"President Magsaysay, distinguished senators. Today the *Aguinaldo* is a mere shell of what is to come. Generations from now the empty fields behind you will be filled with our children's children, and because of the design of our colony, living space will still be plentiful.

"But adequate living space does not imply that there will always be room for growing our food. Plants need open area to grow—area that will be at a premium several years from now. People will not be willing to live in crowded conditions so that their food may flourish. But I have discovered a solution. Although the *Aguinaldo* may be limited in its area, there is a way to tap an *infinite* amount of space in which to grow the crops that can sustain us."

President Magsaysay gave the hint of a smile. "Good, Luis. The Council of Twenty are all proud of you and your accomplishments." He swung an arm around the airlock bay. "But why did you bring us out here, away from your laboratory?"

Sandovaal nodded to his assistant. "Dobo, prepare to eject the organism." It was a hybrid that combined the nervous system and motor capabilities of a Portuguese man-of-war jellyfish with the cellular structure of a plant— a transgenetic organism that extended Sandovaal's research beyond the simple wall-kelp that was even now supplementing the feed for their small population of animals.

Sandovaal turned his attention back to the Council. "This problem concerned me for some time. I tried several ways of genetically forcing plants to become denser, use less light, so that they would not take up so much room. Then I realized that we have all the space and light we need outside the *Aguinaldo.*"

Dobo Daeng ran his fingers over the control panel. A green lightcell changed to red. Sandovaal motioned the Council of Twenty to the viewport. The Filipinos murmured questions in low voices and crowded next to Sandovaal as they peered out the large crystal port. Sandovaal gave a smug smile.

"I have genetically altered this animal to have a dominant survival characteristic that takes advantage of its plant attributes. When it is exposed to a vacuum, the organism will increase its surface area. This allows it to capture more light and increase its ability to photosynthesize. Implanted mineral packets will allow the creature to grow—"

"In a vacuum?" interrupted Magsaysay.

"Yes. That is the point, Yoli. If this proves successful, our next step will be to have this organism grow outside. *Outside!* Think of the food source we could harvest."

Sandovaal pushed through the Council of Twenty and moved right up to the viewport. The organism's cigar-shaped body floated out of the airlock attached to a long tether. Stubby "wings" extended from either side of the meter-long body; lights outside the airlock illuminated the creature. It spun slowly as the line played out.

"By tomorrow the creature's wings will have grown several centimeters. And in two weeks, they will extend for meters. If it survives that long."

Sandovaal pressed his lips together and waited for the accolades. Magsaysay clasped his shoulder as the Council of Twenty nodded among themselves.

Sandovaal did not stay to participate in the political small talk. He had much more important tasks to attend to. He strolled back to the bioengineering lab modules, muttering to himself.

Sandovaal ignored the regular day/night schedule imposed by rotating shutters on the lightaxis. He worked until he had exhausted himself, realizing after several hours that it was Sunday and he could not expect his assistant Dobo to arrive, since Dobo's wife would insist on attending Mass and relaxing with him. Sometimes Sandovaal didn't understand other people's priorities.

He returned to his own quarters and slept for little more than an hour before the insistent ringing of the door chime brought him awake again. He slid open the door, rubbing his eyes and automatically snapping at the short, florid-faced man waiting for him.

"Dobo, why can't you—"

But Dobo seemed agitated and cut off Sandovaal's words. The mere fact that his assistant would dare to interrupt brought Sandovaal to silence. "Dr. Sandovaal, you must come to the viewport end! Quickly! Something strange and wonderful has happened. Perhaps you can tell us what it is. The others are gathering there."

Dobo turned and hurried back to his waiting jeepney before Sandovaal could say anything. His curiosity piqued, Sandovaal joined him. As they drove, he could see other Filipinos jetting or pedaling their way across the core to the cap on the cylinder. After parking the jeepney with the other vehicles at the wall, Dobo cleared a way through the crowd for Sandovaal.

Pressing his face against the hexagonal quartz sections, Sandovaal stared in astounded silence. He saw the familiar sea of stars, the glints of nearby debris at L-4, where the first superstructure for the new station *Orbitech 2* was under construction, the great glare of the gibbous Moon.

But he also saw a giant, translucent wisp of material covering part of the viewport. It seemed extraordinarily thin, yet extended for kilometers. Fragments hundreds of meters across tore away due to the colony's rotation and hovered in the L-4 gravity well, where they would drift under pressure from the solar wind.

Many other people watched the flimsy material, fascinated, possibly frightened. Some looked toward Sandovaal, as if expecting him to produce a comprehensive answer after only a simple glance. He saw President Magsaysay alighting from a jeepney.

Sandovaal turned to Dobo. "Well, has anyone thought to have a piece brought inside for analysis?"

When Sandovaal did complete his inspection in the laboratory—with Magsaysay and some of the senators from the Council of Twenty breathing down his neck—he discovered that the transgenetic organism had grown far beyond even his wildest estimate.

Months later, in a simultaneous announcement to *Nature* and the *New York Times*, Dr. Luis Sandovaal presented his discovery. The original creature looked not unlike a manta ray. It puttered around, swimming in the zero-G core, eating small amounts of wall-kelp and photosynthesizing, completely innocuous. But when ejected into the hard vacuum of space, it underwent a drastic survival measure—a transformation in which its volume expanded to maximize surface area. The tiny flippers in the body core crushed down and smeared out into a layer only a few cells thick. This let it absorb as many solar photons as possible for photosynthesis. The end result was a beautiful, but throughly impractical winglike body spanning scores of kilometers: a giant organic solar sail that could live on its metabolic reserves for perhaps weeks.

Sandovaal did not admit that he had failed to produce a radical new food source—the tissue proved too thin to be of use—but instead played up the basic discovery in the field of transgenetic biology.

The Earth press and intercolony communications dubbed the life-forms "sail-creatures." Sandovaal would have preferred something more elegant, but the name stuck.

CENTER FOR HIGH-TECHNOLOGY MATERIALS ■ ALBUQUERQUE, NEW MEXICO

Colors rippled as Karen Langelier tuned the laser to a different wavelength. The color jumped as it locked onto the new material's resonance structure, glowing a deep red. A long, thin liquid strand of phenolic began to crawl up the beam. She pressed the laser goggles against her high cheekbones to lean over the vacuum vessel. Afraid to breathe, she watched as the phenolic drew out, thinner and thinner, approaching the limit of visibility.

Just as she began to adjust the probe, the delicate strand broke. Globules of pulsating bubbles crashed into each other throughout the vessel, striking the walls.

"Damn!" Karen turned from the vacuum vessel. "Three strikes and I'm out today!"

The new article in the *Online Review of Scientific Instruments* seemed clear enough—laser filamentation was a well-documented process, known for decades. She had arranged the experiment to duplicate the test conditions. It wasn't like she was new at this, either. Maybe there was some problem with the phenolic she had used.

Karen knew she would be a grouch tonight when she got home, and Ray would probably spend the evening talking about the cases in his law office. He wouldn't even notice she'd had a bad day.

"Well, then," Karen said out loud, "I'll just have to make it a good day for myself."

Expelling a breath, she turned back to the three-dimensional holotank. "Let's walk through this one last time." She slapped at the library control panel and called up the article again. "And I've got to stop talking to myself."

As the manuscript popped into the tank, she saw that her fingers had transposed two digits on the recall memory, pulling up instead the backlog of papers from *Physical Review Letters* she still intended to read. Karen leaned forward to correct her mistake, but scanned down the list of contents. Her personal screener program had highlighted everything that matched its preprogammed subset of Karen Langelier's interests. And near the top of the list appeared the title, "Filamentation in One and a Half Dimensions."

She pursed her lips, then smiled. "Serendipity, I suppose."

The author list surprised her. Not content to publish innovative works in only Russian-language journals, Soviet researchers increasingly submitted their most promising work to the prestigious *Letters*. Karen pointed at the article listing and a window flashed open, displaying the contents.

She raised her eyebrows. Published only weeks ago, the Soviet paper presented an elegant yet practical method of constructing one-and-a-half-dimensional strands.

Forgetting her own polymer fiber problem for the moment, she burrowed into the paper and started reading at her "scientific" speed. Lips moving, forehead creased with concentration, Karen began to digest every syllable and equation in the file.

One-and-a-half dimensions. . . . The concept made her mind reel, but with fascination, like wrestling with a paradox.

Karen allowed her mind to wander. Infinity, possibilities. She knew an embryonic answer floated somewhere at the back of her mind. She could access it with careful stroking, off-center concentration. . . .

When she had been a young undergraduate, back when the outside world seemed unattached to her reality, Karen would spend hours contemplating irrational numbers. She felt that her understanding gave her some form of control over them. They weren't infinite where they started—she held one end of the irrational number, the part she could see. A number like pi, simply the ratio of a circle's circumference to its diameter, starting with 3.14159. . . . But the rest of the number rolled away from her, an ever-changing sequence infinitely long.

And she could control that number by knowing what it was. She could hold one end of a magical, mystical sequence that lasted forever.

Back then Karen had realized she was different. Not strange, just different—and content to be. She couldn't relate to the conversations of her dorm mates, the giggling stories, the meaningless concerns. She had a communication problem with them, and she didn't want to take the time to learn their dialect. Instead, she grew to master her own language, a way of communicating with the precise sciences. Mathematics.

One-and-a-half dimensions . . .

She closed her eyes now, imagining that she was part of the filament, floating just outside its structure, like an irrational number. The Soviet paper had elegantly shown the full solution in closed form—and now, as Karen drifted there, it all made perfect sense. The answer was inside herself, inside her capabilities, if only she knew how to bring it to the light of day.

The imaginary strand of molecules extended away from her in an endless line. But instead of being a jumbled sequence of nonrepeating numbers, these molecules were ordered, well-posed in a razor sharp line that had no beginning or end. That was the one-dimensional aspect she recognized.

As she imagined herself moving closer to the filament, she wondered what kept the structure from falling apart, from stretching out and collapsing under its own gravitational weight as it hung in front of her. She considered why it wasn't rigid.

Karen moved around the strand. The molecules stretched down and above, as far as she could see. She approached to touch the apparition and drew suddenly back, her mouth agape.

She wondered if others would call this a mystical experience. It didn't matter if her colleagues laughed at her technique—they couldn't argue with the solutions she found.

Extending radially from every molecule coursed a potential, a force she couldn't see, perpendicular to the strand. The answer tickled the back of her mind, growing stronger, more insistent. Karen didn't push herself, but kept her thoughts flowing, visualizing the strand, imagining herself moving along its length. The potential force remained. The same potential. And hurling herself in the opposite direction, jabbing at every molecular twist, she continued to encounter the identical binding force.

And suddenly she realized. The tickling solution burst into the front of her mind.

When she had first discovered how to master irrational numbers, Karen had wept from the revelation. Now her eyes stung with tears from the knowledge of how a one-and-a-half-dimensional strand—a weave—could grow stronger as it got longer, yet could remain completely flexible. The *potential* bound every molecule, and grew with the number of molecules. The distance between each molecule didn't matter, she realized, because the potential was radial.

The implications overwhelmed her. She blinked and

found herself kneeling on the floor. She stood up and
closed the door, anxious not to have anyone interrupt her
train of thought.

With the laser filamentation technique, she could make
a strand that was, for all practical purposes, an infinite line
of infinite strength and infinite thinness.

Karen Langelier hugged her knees and began to laugh
to herself. No matter what, Ray's caseload tonight could
never compare with this!

Eventually, the single-molecular fiber, woven in one and
a half dimensions with its own potential, became known as
weavewire. Karen would have preferred something more
elegant, but the name stuck.

L-4: *AGUINALDO* ■ DAY 1 MINUS 3 YEARS

Being at the *Aguinaldo*'s Jumpoff was like standing at the
bottom of a garguantuan well. Ramis floated at one end of
the zero-G core; he squinted along the light axis to the
other end, ten kilometers away. Clusters of children
played in the core, punctuated by sail-creature nymphs
darting in and out, genetically programmed to keep the
youngsters away from the central column of fiberoptic
threads. Adults navigated the rim, leaping from bouncer to
bouncer in a race around the circumferential Sibuyan Sea.

Living areas curled around the cylindrical side, snaking
through the fields of taro and abaca, rice paddies, stadiums,
and streams. Experimental sectors of wall-kelp covered
most of the remainder of the *Aguinaldo*'s metallic structure.

As Ramis revolved around the lightaxis, it seemed as
though his whole world might collapse and fall to the center. The sight always made him dizzy. But he smiled.

Ramis Barrera was thirteen, though smaller than others
his age, and he fiercely fought against the perception that
he was younger. He tried to keep aloof, avoiding others to
make himself seem more independent.

Even three years before, back on Earth in the Baguio
resort on the Philippines, Ramis had tried to be tough and
snub his mother when she came to see him and his brother

in the Sari-Sari store. Ramis's parents owned the store, but they spent most of their time at the Scripps Institute with Dr. Sandovaal. Ramis and his older brother Salita often minded the store, and occasionally their mother dropped in to check on them. Salita would hide his newly opened bottle of San Miguel and the blue-seal cigarettes he had been sneaking; Ramis would jump down from the counter and pretend to be businesslike, to impress his mother with how mature he could act. The room would grow quiet, and they would be able to hear the sounds from outside. With only a stern look, his mother would send them back to work. . . .

But now, up in the *Aguinaldo* and floating at Jumpoff, he wished she were here. The exciting but frightening vertigo waited for him above.

Ramis leaped straight up. His momentum bore him high into the zero-G core. Below, Jumpoff grew farther away as he drifted parallel to the lightaxis.

One of the sail-creature nymphs flapped gracefully by as it traversed the core. Ramis fumbled with his pouch and withdrew a hand-sized canister of compressed air. Sending out a quick jet, he changed his direction slightly.

Though it was early in the subjective day, other children had been playing for hours already. As he drifted away from a congregation of them, Ramis twisted himself around and gave a shot of air from the container, slowing his motion. Another burst ensured that he drifted back. The cluster of children showed no sign of noticing him, but he knew he was implicitly included in their game.

Half a dozen sail-creature nymphs moved around the vast core, looking like brownish-green balloons with stubby, finlike "wings." The creatures swam through the air with an eerie and seemingly effortless grace, their flowing wingstrokes calling to mind Earth's giant manta rays. The younger ones frolicked about, some playing with the children and being treated as pets, but most of them were content just to nudge stray children back toward the core.

Ramis played floater-tag with some of the other children. After one breathless chase, he managed to escape being caught by shooting a massive burst of air from his container and flying faster than the girl pursuing him could catch up.

He let himself fly unguided, feeling the breeze rippling his hair as he traveled across the core. Here, his small size didn't hinder him—he was the equal of any of the other children.

He watched the rimbouncing race around the Sibuyan Sea, wishing he had been picked for one of the adult teams. His friend Dobo Daeng had tried out, too, but had withdrawn his application when his work with Dr. Sandovaal had taken a sudden new direction.

Ramis heard faint, distant cheering as the rimbouncing match became more heated. He watched the children playing; bored, he turned to the rimbouncing again, and then looked down.

His heart froze. The rotating wall of the *Aguinaldo* seemed to pull at him as it rushed past. Though it was still meters away, he had drifted much too close to the rim. The Coriolis winds buffeted him.

He pushed down on the compressed-air container. It hissed, then went silent. He had exhausted the air in his rush to win in floater-tag.

One of the colony buildings was rotating toward him. The squat building contained some of the electronics-maintenance equipment. It was only two levels high, but Ramis drifted helpless, unable to get out of the way as the wall swept toward him like a giant flyswatter moving at fifty kilometers per hour.

Ramis tossed the can away, hoping for even a little momentum transfer, and frantically fumbled through his pouch for another container.

Nothing.

He went through his pockets—again, nothing.

He shouted, waving his hands wildly. It would do nothing to change his direction, but he desperately hoped the other players might be able to do something—if he could attract their attention. He had hardly any time. If only he had worn his sandals, he could have hurled them away and caused himself to drift to the side, perhaps enough to let the building slash by without crushing him. But his feet were bare and he wore only loose shorts, a light shirt—not enough mass for any kind of maneuvering.

The sharp corners came closer. Ramis seemed to be falling toward the building. His heart pounded. He felt giddy, helpless. The other children had noticed now. Some pointed at him, some began to move; a scream reached his ears. But it was too late—

Suddenly something firm rammed him from below. He let out a gasp, and then he was struck again, moving away. Ramis whirled in the air, twisting his body. It was a young sail-creature, one with a dark Z-shaped mark on its back. The creature held itself rigid as the broad expanse of the building swept by silently beneath them. Through one of the skylights, Ramis caught a glimpse of several techs working at a table. They didn't even notice him rushing by.

The sail-creature nymph butted him one last time and knocked him toward the center of the core.

Still terrified and shuddering, Ramis drifted as some of the excited children moved in his direction. Only when one of them tossed him an extra container did he fully relax. Twisting, Ramis looked to see the young sail-creature frolicking nearby as if pleased with itself. As it spun in the air, the "Z" marking became visible again.

"Salamat po, Sarat," Ramis whispered in the Filipino dialect of Tagalog: "Thank you, Timely One!"

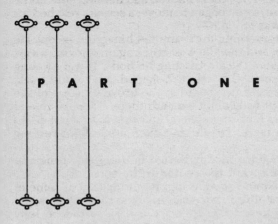

PART ONE

ISOLATION

CHAPTER 1

AGUINALDO ■ DAY 1

The thrill outweighed the consequences—it was as simple as that. He didn't need to show off for anyone but himself.

If Ramis was caught Jumping at night, he'd be barred from the *Aguinaldo*'s zero-G core for a year—until he turned seventeen. But flying across the colony's diameter in the dark made the rush of adrenaline worth the risk.

Ramis had another two hours before the lightaxis came on for the morning period. Two hours to traverse about five kilometers of the *Aguinaldo*'s interior circumference . . . in the dark. Others twice his age could not claim having Jumped all the way around, not even in the light.

He kept his eyes open wide as he flew across the weightless space, hoping they had sufficiently adapted to the dark; but without the danger, it wouldn't be worth doing.

He remembered one night in the Philippine Islands, when his older brother Salita had driven him home down a winding mountain road.

"Watch this," Salita had said, and punched the button that shut off the car lights.

Instantly plunged into the night, Ramis had watched the emptiness around them, the treacherous curves now invisible as the car continued without slowing.

"See how the road glistens?" Fascinated, Salita had accelerated the car. Ramis had gripped the door, but felt some of his brother's feverish excitement. Salita had clicked the lights back on just in time to round a sharp curve. He had shown no sign of uneasiness, but kept smiling in silence as he drove on. . . .

The trampoline surface of the *Aguinaldo*'s bouncer should be coming up now. Straining to see, Ramis caught a glint of light reflected off the circumpond's surface, demarcating his path. Although one hundred meters square, the bouncer seemed no more than a speck in the Sibuyan Sea. And if he missed it, he'd get a dunking, which at the speed he traveled might not be better than slamming into the colony's wall. His entire body felt like a coiled weapon, tense, every cell alive with energy. His lips were curled back in a startling grin.

As he roared toward the bouncer, Ramis bent his knees and shot a blast of air to adjust his momentum. The bouncer grew larger below him. Three, two, one . . . now! He hit the elastic surface and pushed off as hard as he could. He felt his leg muscles cramp from the sudden effort. The bouncer hurled him back into the air. Ramis spun his arms, furiously trying to keep from tumbling.

Finally stable, Ramis exhausted his compressed-air can. He let the empty can float out, fastened to his side by a short cord, as he rummaged through his pouch for another container. The cool, damp wind of his motion rippled his shirtsleeves.

The lightaxis waited out there in the dark, somewhere across his path. The meter-thick array of fiberoptics and titanium structure would smash him like a bug if he hit it.

He had contemplated bringing a small flashlight, but that would have encumbered his hands—and it would also have made the Jump too easy. This wasn't supposed to be *safe*. Now Ramis felt fear building up; the adrenaline roared through his veins. He drew a deep breath. It seemed so much like flying, floating free, drifting . . . and

LIFELINE

he didn't need to be terrified of looking down because he couldn't see anything in the dark.

Ramis squinted, trying to discern a shadow of the light-axis, anything that might warn him. He counted to himself, still searching, as the wind whistled in his ears. He thought he could gauge his speed and direction by the force with which he had pushed off from the bouncer.

When several heartbeats had passed, Ramis relaxed, then turned his concentration on anticipating the next bouncer on the opposite side. He tried to figure in his head the optimum angle at which he'd need to hit it.

Ramis twisted in the air, orienting his feet toward the onrushing wall—

He spotted the lightaxis directly in his path, a gigantic rod stretched out and ready to snap him in two.

The sail-creature nymphs had all been corralled for the night period, where they could feed at their leisure. He couldn't count on Sarat helping him this time.

Ramis shot a blast of air toward the lightaxis, then curled his body into a ball to present the smallest possible target. His course altered, but not by much. The thick mass of optical fibers skimmed by within touching distance. He kicked out, pushing his bare feet against the axis and thrusting himself into safer airspace. In the silent blackness he could hear the low thrum of the vibration he had sent into the lightaxis. He emptied the second air canister to slow himself further.

He floated toward the *Aguinaldo*'s wall at a much safer speed this time. In the darkness, he could barely make out his own location in the air. He checked to make sure he had enough canisters to stop himself from drifting into the rotating deck. He had learned that lesson three years before.

It seemed pointless to finish his circumnavigation now. He was too jittery, and he had lost most of his momentum. The encounter had frightened him more than he had realized at first. He debated if he should tell *dato* Magsaysay about it.

No, then he would have to admit what he had been trying to do. Against the rules, Jumping in the dark—rules designed out of safety considerations, the *dato* had always said.

Of course the other children obeyed, like all good Filipino boys and girls. Obeying rules was part of their culture, part of what they had brought up with them from the Islands. And since Ramis was the foster son of the *dato*— the president of the colony—the others expected him to follow rules better than anyone else. Ramis smirked to himself at the thought. Father Magsaysay did not push him —all the pressure to conform, and to excel, came from within. He could never live up to his parents' names as great martyred researchers unless he constantly pushed himself, proved that he was better than anyone else.

Ramis always pretended to acquiesce to the rules, to go to his quarters during the dark period when the *Aguinaldo* engineers louvered the outer mirrors away from the light-axis port. Then, in the early morning hours, he slipped out to do his Jumps before the mirrors swung back into position again. He was careful. After all, it was against the rules, wasn't it? And he was the best.

Ramis stretched in the air, taking his time to get to the wall since he had more than an hour before the subjective dawn—

Streaks of light shot through wire-fine fiberoptics as the louvered mirrors opened up. Every few millimeters along the axis, a thousand fiberoptic threads frayed outward to illuminate the ten-kilometer span.

On one end, flares of raw sunlight bounced off outer mirrors into the transparent viewing segments. The shielding iris over the viewport end dilated, opening to a vista of space with the Earth hanging off to one side. With the sudden view, it seemed as if the entire end of the colony had sheared off.

Panicked, Ramis squinted at his chronometer in the glare. The lightaxis was on a full hour early. He twisted himself around, trying to see if anyone had noticed him in the air. Luckily, he had drifted far enough away from the circumpond that he wouldn't draw suspicion to himself.

Sounds of shouting came from the inner surface below him; muffled PA announcements echoed in the living units. There was no broadcast over the general colony loudspeakers, Ramis realized, because everyone should have been inside.

A crowd of people began to gather near the curving

viewport end, pressing their faces against the transparent
segments, climbing up the rungs on the wall to get a better
vantage point. Ramis emptied another can of air to increase his speed, then turned around in the air, squirting
short bursts in the opposite direction to slow him again as
he reached the crowd.

Ramis spread his palms to absorb momentum against the
wall. Bouncing, he reached a rung, then hand-walked himself down to one of the elevator platforms. It took him to a
scattered group of people who stood looking out into
space. Sobs mixed with angry shouting.

"What is it?" he yelled, looking for a face he recognized.
"What is happening?"

Behind the broad viewing wall, the Earth hung alone in
space, shining blue and white. Somebody pointed, and
Ramis caught snatches of words. "I cannot see! No, over
there. Look! There goes another one!" It made no sense to
him.

A shaggy, white-haired man pushed impatiently past to
the rungs that would take him up to the observatory alcove. Ramis tried to get his attention over the noise. "Dr.
Sandovaal! What is happening?"

"Are you blind, boy, or just stupid? I am in a hurry!"

"But—"

"I have no time right now."

Sandovaal climbed into the *Aguinaldo*'s observatory.
The toroidal alcove surrounded the lightaxis, jutting out
from the colony. An inertial platform inside the observatory kept the telescopes and instruments pointed toward
their target—Earth, in this case.

Ramis decided against provoking Dr. Sandovaal by following him. He stared out the viewing wall, mystified,
until he heard someone call his name. "Ramis! Over here,
Ramis."

"Dobo!" Ramis flipped over and anchored onto the wall-
handle with his feet. Sandovaal's assistant waved his arms
over the sea of feet. "Dobo, what is going on?" Ramis
called.

Dobo pointed to his ears, then cupped his hands to yell
over the crowd. "Too noisy! Can you get over to me?"

Ramis kicked out into the air and maneuvered to Dobo.
When he got close enough that Dobo could hear him, he

yelled, "Dr. Sandovaal just rushed past me on his way to the observatory." He felt a twinge of anger at the dismissal —after all, Ramis's parents had worked with Sandovaal at the Institute on Earth, and had left everything to come up to L-4 with him.

"Never mind Dr. Sandovaal. He would ignore his own grandmother if she got in his way—especially right now." He hauled Ramis in with an outstretched hand. "Are you all right? Did you come with President Magsaysay? I did not see him here."

Ramis chose not to answer. "He must be around somewhere. But what is all this commotion about? Dr. Sandovaal seemed even more upset than usual!"

Dobo blinked at him. "You have not heard? I thought the announcement was broadcast to every dwelling."

"I am trying to find out, Dobo! Tell me."

Dobo bit his chubby lips, as if reluctant to share bad news. He pushed an elbow away that almost struck him in the eye. "Down there." He took Ramis's arm, and the two rotated in the air, grasped the handholds, and looked out into space. Dobo pointed toward the Earth.

"A war is going on. A big one. Terrible!"

From the *Aguinaldo,* the distant battle was weirdly beautiful. Four hundred thousand kilometers away, nuclear-tipped missiles rose from their silos to draw long streaks across the dark side of the Earth. The plumes were erratic, exploding with a fast sputter-burn through the missiles' boost phase. Opposing defensive systems tried to lock onto the incoming weapons.

American Excaliburs rocketed into space from their scattered hiding places and deployed twigs of x-ray lasers. The beams knocked out delicate Soviet homing mechanisms and disoriented nuclear warheads. A swarm of Brilliant Pebbles searched out any remaining weapon.

Polar-orbiting Soviet space stations spat out kinetic-energy weapons to destroy American missiles. Jittering spots of detonations danced across the globe. Small stations in low Earth orbit exploded as they became targets.

And then it stopped. From the view on the *Aguinaldo,* the battle seemed to last about twenty minutes.

Strategic defenses on both sides of the world had worked

as planned. Even before the first surviving warheads
struck Soviet and American soil, the leaders called a truce.
The war was already over.

Defensive systems had destroyed all but one missile in a
hundred—but that wasn't good enough.

Over four hundred megatons worth of warheads had
survived to do damage. Some burrowed deep into the soil
to destroy the next round of weapons; some exploded high
in the air, the electromagnetic pulse obliterating all communications.

Ramis could not even guess how many deaths he had just
witnessed. He longed for the days of *glasnost*, when the
world had been so different. To him, the war had been
fought in silence—screams of dying people could not be
heard through space. The fires had vanished, but that
could mean either the flames had died out, or simply that
the smoke had hidden them from view.

Quiet and stunned, he floated back from the viewing
wall. Only a damp spot of perspiration remained on the
glass where his hand had been.

Someone in the crowd finally spoke. *"Booto!"*

The curse echoed hollowly. No one stirred. No one tit-
tered at the schoolboy expletive.

At last the people began to disperse. The Filipinos
waited numbly in line for the cross-colony shuttles. A
woman sobbed. Over everything, Ramis could hear the
thrumming sounds of the *Aguinaldo*'s recirculating system.

Ramis remained mesmerized by the delicate picture of
the Earth. He did not yet want to grasp the full implications of the war. Through the churning clouds shrouding
the planet, he tried to pick out the Philippines, letting his
eye roam from the tip of Africa, up the Indian Ocean, past
Indonesia, and out to the horizon where the ocean disappeared into the haze. He searched, but the ten thousand
islands that made up his homeland were just over the
horizon.

His brother Salita still lived there, in Baguio City. He
had stayed behind to run the Sari-Sari store, refusing to
accompany his parents up to the colony. Salita had never

gotten along well with his father. Ramis wanted to think
about his brother, but he was afraid to.

Two of the largest U.S. military bases were on the Philippines, kept in operation and granted a permanent lease
after the Americans had given over the *Aguinaldo* colony
to the Filipino people. The bases must have made the
entire archipelago a major target. . . .

Dobo placed his hand on Ramis's shoulder, startling him.
They both stared into the blackness behind the viewport
wall, watching the crazy cloud patterns on Earth rise and
fall with unnatural speed.

A quiet, warm voice made Ramis turn around. "We have
always been able to find plenty of reasons for war, no
matter how many problems we eliminate."

The *dato*, Yoli Magsaysay, floated alone by the viewport.
He looked thin, with mottled brown skin and flecks of gray
and white peppering his bushy hair. The *Aguinaldo*'s president moved painfully on joints calcified from too many
years of low gravity.

Magsaysay's statement came as a fact, spoken in a mus-
ing tone that asked for no debate. The *dato* seldom talked
in public anymore, but when he did, he bore himself in the
tired, worn-out manner of a man who would not give in,
even after seventy-five years.

"Father Magsaysay—" Ramis caught himself, afraid to
say anything more. After what he had just witnessed, he
did not want to disturb the *dato*'s thoughts.

Magsaysay acted as if he hadn't even heard Ramis. He
said to Dobo, "Please have Dr. Sandovaal prepare an analysis for the Council of Twenty. I will call an emergency
session once he is ready."

He closed his eyes and pulled a deep breath of humid air
into his lungs. "This war will put the *Aguinaldo*'s future in
grave danger. I suspect Dr. Sandovaal is already working
on projections of our existing food supply." The *dato*'s
hand was clenched at his side; the long fingernails were
digging into his palms. "The Council will need that information if we are to select our next course of action."

"I will ask him, President Magsaysay." Dobo frowned
and dropped his voice. "But I cannot promise that you will
like what he has to say."

Magsaysay swept his hand out over the expanse of the

star-filled viewing wall. "If the United States is no longer able to ferry food and supplies to the colonies, then we will face some hard decisions. I want to be sure that we are well informed beforehand."

He went on, mumbling as if to himself. "The Soviet Union might not be as damaged by the war as the United States. We could be forced to open a dialogue with them if it is necessary for our survival—no matter what promises we made to the Americans. All the rules have changed now."

Magsaysay stopped, then smiled down at Ramis. "I am chattering like an old politician. Dobo, I would like to speak with Ramis."

Dobo bowed and moved away from Ramis and Magsaysay, heading for the observatory alcove.

Magsaysay stood in silence. He looked down at Earth, toward the curving horizon where the archipelago of the Philippine Islands would remain hidden under the swirls of clouds. The president spoke quietly.

"Luis Sandovaal and I were close friends many years ago, long before the *Aguinaldo* was even a dream. I knew your parents when Dr. Sandovaal recruited them to come with him up to L-4. I made it a point to know everyone back then. You see, if a leader loses touch with the people, then it is time for him to step down and let himself be replaced." He shook his head. "But today there are so many people I do not know. How can I possibly make these decisions?"

He glanced at his timepiece, then frowned, as if time had no meaning anymore. Ramis remained quiet, unsure of what to say. The *dato* turned to leave, then looked Ramis in the eye, as if he had forgotten to say something.

"The future depends on people such as yourself, Ramis —people willing to take chances." He held up a finger. "We need you, so do not get hurt when you go Jumping alone at night."

Magsaysay stepped onto the stickum of the slidewalk, and rested his hand on the railing.

Ramis watched him, his face feeling flushed. How did he know?

Behind the viewing wall, the Earth was swirled with thick clouds now. Only a few sparse patches of blue managed to peek out from beneath the cover. No land was visible.

Ramis decided against flying freefall along the core to get back home. Though his barrio in the Luzon housing area was at the opposite end of the colony, he followed Magsaysay down the slidewalk. A shadow skittered along the ground in front of him. Overhead, a sail-creature nymph whipped past, released early by the unscheduled dawn. Ramis squinted, but he couldn't make out any markings on the creature's fins. Once on the colony floor, he caught a jeepney to his home.

C H A P T E R 2

The industrial colony *Orbitech 1* hung at L-5 with its supply lines cut—fifteen hundred people, stranded and helpless. They pressed their faces and palms against observation windows, staring at the wounded Earth far below. Still in a state of shock, they had not thought to mourn for their past, for their memories.

Most of the people wallowed in self-protective confusion and shock. They had not yet faced the realization that they would get no more supplies from Earth.

But Duncan McLaris, the Production Division leader on *Orbitech 1,* came to that conclusion not ten minutes after the war started.

He tried to look casual as he approached the shuttle-tug *Miranda.* The *Miranda* was tied down in the colony's docking bay, seeming to glow in the harsh lights reflected from the clean metal walls.

Boxes of *Orbitech 1* export products were tethered throughout the bay area: large, perfect crystals grown in zero gravity, three-dimensional computer chips, super-conducting wires, pharmaceuticals, strange alloys with baffling electromagnetic properties . . . the list of Orbi-technology accomplishments ran on and on.

Rah rah for the company, McLaris thought.

The docking bay seemed deserted. Everyone else was huddling in their quarters or sobbing in the community rooms. The last shuttle looked empty and alone. McLaris called out, "Hello—anybody in there?"

Seconds passed. McLaris started to turn when the pilot, Stephanie Garland, pushed out of the shuttle, wiping her hands on her dark-blue coverall. She eyed McLaris and set her mouth.

McLaris wore a smile as he pushed off the floor, drifting in the zero-G bay until he reached the metal hull of the *Miranda*. Palms splayed, he absorbed the impact and ma-neuvered himself down to floor level again.

Garland's hair was a salt-and-pepper shade of gray, but she didn't give off a sense of being old. "I hope you're not going to give me a pep talk, Mr. McLaris. Save that for your employees. I know what happened. I heard snatches of the broadcast. The Earth has turned into a shit pot and there's no use my going back there."

"Call me Duncan, please," McLaris interrupted. "And you won't hear any pep talks from me. I'm a realist. An 'it'll all come out right in the end' speech would sound kind of hypocritical right now."

McLaris locked his gray eyes with the woman's gaze. He did recognize a well-controlled undercurrent of fear and despair in the pilot's demeanor. He felt for her, was able to put himself in her shoes. He considered that the mark of a good manager.

Wild and contradicting reports were still coming in and being passed along over the *Orbitech 1* PA system; but the *Miranda* was apparently the only interorbital shuttle that had survived the War. The other two craft, *Ariel* and *Oberon,* had finished their runs to Clavius Base on the Moon and out to the L-4 colonies and had returned to low Earth orbit only shortly before the War, awaiting refuel-ing. An extensive fleet of Earth-to-orbit rockets should have brought up more fuel, more supplies, perhaps a change of crew.

The two pilots had radioed back in shock after the War, calling for any kind of contact. They had escaped destruction, but now the two—friends of Garland's—were locked in low orbit, with no fuel and no place to go. Maybe forever.

The two shuttles could not land themselves because the craft had never been designed to withstand the stress of passing through the atmosphere. And they did not have enough fuel to reach the Lagrange colonies again . . . not that it would do them any good. The colonies weren't any better off.

On her last run, though, Stephanie Garland had been half a day late arriving at *Orbitech 1*, and had only just unloaded the supplies. She announced that she would stay an extra day, exercising her option to claim R and R whenever she deemed it necessary to her performance. A coincidence. Otherwise, she would have been stranded as well.

In the docking bay, McLaris took a deep breath. "Why don't we go inside and chat?"

"Why?"

"Well, for one thing, the docking bay monitors can't pick up anything there, right?" Garland looked startled, but then realized—as McLaris had intended—just what he was going to ask her.

"I was wondering when someone would come," Garland muttered. "I didn't think it would be so soon. Zen, it hasn't even been an hour yet!"

McLaris looked around the docking bay, saw the cameras mounted on the walls to monitor operations. It would be just like Curtis Brahms to be watching his division leaders, to see if any of them attempted exactly what McLaris was doing.

"I don't like to waste time," McLaris answered. "Especially now."

The pilot glided into the main cabin of the *Miranda*, hauling herself hand over hand with an ease that testified to her experience with interorbital transit, days at a time without gravity.

"What is it you want?" Garland asked.

McLaris could feel his heart thumping. But when the words came out, when he actually voiced his proposal, he heard himself as if from a distance, wondering how he had found the nerve.

"We have to take the *Miranda* away from here, and we have to do it soon, before anybody else starts putting the pieces together."

Garland started to shake her head, but McLaris added extra emphasis to his voice. "We're all going to starve up here. We're sitting in the last shuttle, and we can't just let it rot."

Garland's fingers tensed on the control panel.

"There's only one place we can go," McLaris continued. "The Moon. Clavius Base can support itself, I think. It's been there long enough. It was established before any of these colonies were constructed."

Garland wet her lips, and her voice sounded very small. "How are we going to get permission?"

"There isn't going to be any damned permission!" McLaris instantly brought his voice under control again. "I'm the Production Division leader on this colony. Since production means everything here on *Orbitech 1*, that makes me one of the most important people here. I can arrange it."

He changed his voice to a quieter, more introspective tone. "No one back on Earth thought about the niceties of being self-sufficient. Survival isn't cost-effective yet for the colonies."

He raised his eyes and folded his hands. "Stephanie, I can get us out of here. You have to operate the shuttle— take us to the Moon. It's going to be me, you, and my daughter. We can survive there."

Garland lifted an eyebrow and asked, "Don't you have a wife? Is she going to come along?"

McLaris felt a stab. "Diane . . . went to Earth before the War all started, on sabbatical. She wanted a few months to wander around the forests and mountains again. She left Jessie here with me."

Words failed him. He avoided looking at the pilot. "Diane could be alive, you know, or maybe not—but there's a chance. One day I'll get back to Earth. I have to survive for her. And for my daughter. But I can't survive here. None of us can. Brahms will see to that."

Garland cocked an eyebrow at him. "Curtis Brahms? I thought Roha Ombalal was the director of *Orbitech 1*?"

"In name only. The parent company stripped him of all duties after Brahms came up and did his Efficiency Study. They left Ombalal in position to save face, but Associate Director Brahms is the one who runs things. Most people here don't realize that yet."

The pilot absently tinkered with her on-board systems, checking things, verifying what the maintenance crews had done to the *Miranda* in the past day. She finally spoke in a low voice. "Fifteen people will fit in the ship. What other twelve are we taking? And how are you going to pick them?"

"There's no way to pick them!" McLaris said, and then brought his tension in check again. "Stephanie, you bring anyone else in on this and we'll have a riot to deal with."

Unobtrusively, he gripped the aluminum brace of the chair back. He hated what he intended to say, but he had to be honest with himself and with the pilot. He had to lay everything on the line, so Garland fully understood what she was agreeing to do. No punches pulled, no ugly marks covered with pretty cosmetics. A guilty conscience could be dealt with later.

"There's no way we could keep this a secret if we needed to plan with a dozen other people. Have you ever tried to get something accomplished by committee? Each one would want to bring a special friend or two—the list would mushroom out of our control."

But Garland kept playing devil's advocate. "Since I'm the pilot, I'd be going anyway. Why should I worry? Why should I pick you?"

"Nobody else has asked, yet. First come, first served." McLaris couldn't stand the uncomfortable silence, so he continued. "And don't be too sure of your own position, Stephanie. If somebody whispered something to the wrong person, we'd have a mob here in a flash . . . and you can bet they'd rather destroy the *Miranda* than let a few, like us, take it and survive."

"That means it's going to be only the three of us," Garland said slowly. "The Moon, huh?"

"That's right."

Garland took a shuddering breath, and looked away

from McLaris to stare at her controls. "I'm worried about landing in a gravity field. I've never done it before—except in the simulator."

Taken by surprise, McLaris blinked. He couldn't think of anything to say.

"Look, what do you want me to tell you? I've been on the same shuttle run, from Earth orbit to *Orbitech 1* and back. Every once in a while I head off to the *Aguinaldo* or the *Orbitech 2* construction site at L-4. That's all I do. When I'm rotated back to Earth, I take R and R. Then I come back and do the same damn run again. I've never landed on Clavius Base—the *Oberon* is the only shuttle that can land there.

"Hell, this ship wasn't designed to land in a gravity field!" She banged her hand on the bulkhead. "Oh, it can take it—contingencies, you know—but when you land on the Moon's surface, even if it is only a seventh of the Earth's gravity . . . it's different, Mr. McLaris. This isn't like driving a limousine."

McLaris drew himself up. "If there's anything I can do to help, I'll do it. But this is our only shot." His eyes pleaded with Garland. "Please? For my girl."

Garland's knuckles whitened on the controls. A long moment of silence passed. Finally the pilot stood up, turning to meet McLaris's gaze. A slight smile came to her lips. "I hear they've got two hundred extra men down there."

McLaris looked puzzled. "Uh?"

"The *Orbitech 2* construction crew. Didn't you hear? They got recalled from L-4 last week, as a diplomatic sign of our displeasure to the Soviet Union. Looks like somebody certainly resented it." The smile left her lips. "You know, they're going to curse us with everything they've got."

"I'm not doing it just for me," McLaris insisted. He felt a flush on his cheeks. It was very important to him that Garland understand why he had to ask this.

"I'm doing it for Jessie. If you could just take her, all by herself, I'd be willing to stay. I'd face what the rest of us have to face. But somebody has to help you. And you need me to get you out of the docking bay—I can double-talk the engineers and anybody else who might be guarding the shuttle. Brahms isn't going to take long to figure this out."

He squeezed his eyes shut and tried to beat down the sickness of guilt building inside him. "Besides, I wouldn't live long anyway if I helped you to escape and then stayed behind. They'd probably throw me into one of the metal processing units or something."

Looking uncomfortable, Garland distracted herself with her equipment. Had he convinced her? McLaris couldn't tell. He kept talking, recognizing that it was partly to convince himself that he was doing the right thing.

"I admit this is a snap decision. I haven't had time to think about it. I'm afraid to think about it too much, because then I might change my mind or lose my nerve. But if I waste time considering the possibilities, somebody else will think of it first, and then we'll lose our chance.

"You don't know Brahms—he's sharp and he's fast and he does not hesitate. He'll be only one step behind me."

"He seemed nice when he came to greet me."

McLaris clenched his hands. "I know him. He might appear to be a nice violin case, but he's really carrying a machine gun inside."

Garland set her mouth. "If we're really going to do this, we'll have to move fast. When do we go?"

McLaris felt a wash of cold sweat break out on his back, as if he had just stepped off a cliff. No turning back now.

"In an hour, if Brahms doesn't seal off the shuttle bay."

CHAPTER 3

As he approached the open-air hall, Ramis realized he had attended only one other Council meeting in his life. Political discussions and tedious plodding through red-tape mazes of motions and countermotions and rebuttals and addenda bored him.

But now it seemed that most of the *Aguinaldo* colonists were trying to push their way into the hall. Their future hung on what the Council of Twenty would decide in the next session.

He had attended that other Council meeting when he had been twelve years old, four years before. Dr. Sandovaal was testifying about the course of agriculture and food production on the colony—about some of the work Ramis's parents had helped him begin before their accident.

Sandovaal had at first seemed a mysterious and frightening man, spiteful for no particular reason, and Ramis's parents were in awe of him. But that Council session—where Sandovaal debated, and defeated, the *Aguinaldo*'s agricultural specialists—had elevated the stature of the unorthodox Filipino bioengineer on self-imposed exile from Earth.

Ramis could still see Sandovaal's ruddy face shaking in rage. "In order to produce a viable food source in space, we cannot just attempt to grow the same old feed crops!"

Sandovaal put an expression of supreme distaste on his face, glaring at the other agricultural specialists and speaking in a mocking voice. "Listen to you—rice and wheat! Corn and abaca! Are you idiots? Do you have tumors for brains? Those crops adapted to *Earth*'s planetary environment—it took them millennia to perfect themselves in that particular ecosystem. Here on a Lagrange colony, plants grow under completely different rules.

"Do you begin to see? Have you opened your eyes? We are not on Earth anymore. It requires us to take a radically new look at how plants and animals are put together. We must first acquire a new feed crop for our animals—a crop high in protein, but without a high overhead to produce. After that, we shall be free to develop new crops for ourselves."

After Sandovaal had stirred their anger, he then smugly presented his first samplings of wall-kelp. Ramis knew that was the way Sandovaal always did things—he made his opponents angry to get their attention, then slapped them in the face with what they should have seen all along.

Sandovaal's preliminary wall-kelp data astounded the Council. The genetically modified kelp, combined with some traits of chlorella algae, had an unheard-of growth rate, incredible efficiency for waste conversion, and—most important of all—a digestible mass of protein. Since the wall-kelp was photosynthetic, it produced oxygen as it grew. It was a starting place, a beginning success for Sandovaal's team. And Ramis's parents had worked with him on it.

Back then, when the Council members and the audience gave Sandovaal a standing ovation for his work, the old scientist sniffed, as if he had expected nothing less. . . .

Ramis smiled to himself at the memory. He came back to the present as Yoli Magsaysay rapped the podium for order. The hall overflowed with people: many squatted on the steps and in the aisles. The noise nearly overwhelmed the PA system. Magsaysay rapped once more. "Quiet, please. Let us begin."

The *dato* cleared his throat. At first, his voice could not be heard, but the president continued in the same low tone. Like his famous namesake in Philippine politics several generations before, Yoli Magsaysay knew how to handle people. The room grew still.

". . . reminded that the Council hall has a tradition for holding open meetings—especially in this instance, where everything will affect us all so profoundly. However, if we are unable to hear each other speak, I will be forced to clear the hall."

Magsaysay scanned the room. Only the rustle of people trying to get a better view disturbed the silence. The air-conditioning hummed, turned to high. Overhead, several sail-creature nymphs drifted near the core. Ramis glanced up, looking for Sarat.

The *dato* spoke again. "Who started the War? Who won? Who survived? All contact has been severed, so we do not know and we may never know. But that is not our problem.

"We may be forced to survive on the *Aguinaldo* without help from Earth. No supplies—only the resources we have here now."

He ticked off the points on his fingers. "That means no food. No clothing. No appliances. We have the Sibuyan Sea, but water is still going to be a problem. We have only leftover Moon rubble for raw materials. Even though the construction site of our neighbor, *Orbitech 2,* is barely a hundred kilometers away, we have no means to get there. We must assume that the *Aguinaldo* has to be totally self-sufficient from now on."

Magsaysay placed his hands on the podium. His big eyes looked very sad.

"I have purposely presented the situation in the bleakest terms. The Council must consider this situation when we make our decisions. If we are too optimistic now, we could doom our entire colony."

Magsaysay raised his gray eyebrows. "Dr. Sandovaal, would you and your staff please brief the Council of Twenty on your projections?"

"Most certainly—you must have named me chief scientist for a reason."

A nervous titter brushed across the hall as Sandovaal led his entourage of assistants on the stage. Dobo Daeng shuffled over to the large-display holotank. Sandovaal cleared his throat and tapped the microphone pad. The speakers squealed as he breathed into the pickup, making him jerk back. He glared at the microphone.

"Mr. President, members of the Council, for the past four years my associates and I have been tracking the progress of my wall-kelp. You will recall that the Council wisely voted to adapt the kelp as the *Aguinaldo*'s main source of feed for our livestock. In addition, the actual crop space the wall-kelp has replaced is minimal."

Ramis wrinkled his nose. The stagnant smell of the wall-kelp had been the basis for numerous insults and expletives invented by the *Aguinaldo* colonists.

"Luis, we all appreciate your work," Magsaysay said from his seat to the left of the stage, "but at the moment, we need to know your projections of *our* ability to survive using our current supply of foodstuff."

Sandovaal's expression grew stormy. Ramis drew in a breath, expecting an outburst from the scientist.

"President Magsaysay, since you ask the question so bluntly, I will answer it bluntly: What are our chances of survival using our current supply of foodstuffs? The answer is none. Zero. No chance whatsoever. It is a simple calculation—anybody can see it."

He stopped and stared around at the faces stunned into silence. His blue eyes looked very cold. Magsaysay struggled to his feet and opened his mouth to speak, but Sandovaal waved him into silence.

"Dobo, display the data. Show them."

Dobo touched the controls. A set of graphs appeared in the giant holotank. The curves rotated, then the window zoomed in on a chart labeled ASSETS—CURRENT CROP PRODUCTION.

Dr. Sandovaal spoke over a growing murmur in the crowd.

"The blue line is our current population. The red curve is our crop surplus, decreasing as we consume more than we produce." He waited a beat, then continued. "As you can see, these two curves intersect at a point not three months in the future. That is when we start getting hungry. Shortly after that, I expect fighting and widespread killing. From that point, we cannot calculate accurately how long the survivors can last—it depends on how many there are after the riots."

A shout rang out from the back. The hall's sergeant at arms scuffled with the person and ejected him. Ramis felt a surge of despair ripple through the gathered people. After watching the War on Earth, this was too much in one day. Ramis no longer felt proud to think of the part his parents had had in Sandovaal's work. Dobo looked up, frowning at Sandovaal's attitude.

Magsaysay looked beaten. He held up his hands. His low voice barely projected over the rising din. "Quiet! Please allow Dr. Sandovaal to continue." When the sounds ceased, the *dato* turned to his chief scientist. "Luis, are your numbers correct?"

"The calculations are simple—you will find no errors. But I was talking about something much more important when you interrupted me. Several years ago we succeeded in producing a highly efficient feed substitute.

"When you tasked me this morning with projecting the *Aguinaldo*'s food supply, you placed ridiculous restrictions on what we are capable of doing. You said 'using our current supply of foodstuff' and allowed for nothing else. That is nonsense. The answer is staring you in the face. Maybe a few hunger pangs will improve your intellect." He cracked his knuckles in front of the microphone pad, making a sound like muffled gunshots.

"Now, this second set of charts is also correct." Dobo quickly changed graphs in the holotank.

Sandovaal allowed the people to study the new curves in silence. He seemed to be forcing down a smug smile. The red and blue lines in the holotank held an uneasy balance, but never intersected. The supply of food remained above the consumption level.

Magsaysay stared and frowned. "What does this show?"

"What do you think? It is certainly not a new idea. A few minutes ago I tried to explain our only way to survive, but you were not interested. You wanted only the bottom line, so I gave it to you. By continuing our present course, wasting too much time and too many resources on inefficient crops, we will starve in a few months.

"We must act immediately if we are going to save the *Aguinaldo*. As you can see from the curves, we have little margin for hesitation or error. If we decide quickly, we can survive—we can all survive."

"What is it we have to do?" Magsaysay asked. "Make it plain for those of us who are stupid."

Sandovaal turned to stare at him. He didn't seem to notice the slight sarcasm in the *dato*'s tone. "Just look at the data! What do the curves tell you?

"We must grow wall-kelp on a massive scale. Use all our available space. Cover the viewport end, the athletic fields, the grazing lands."

The senator from Cebu interrupted. Her accent was heavily Americanized, since she had grown up near the bases. "But wall-kelp tastes like water buffalo manure. And it damn well looks like it, too."

Ramis thought Dr. Sandovaal was going to jump over the table and strangle her. "I presume you have tasted both?" he asked.

Over the snickers, the chief scientist shook his fist at the statistics displayed in the holotank. "We have the means to survive—for all people on the *Aguinaldo*. But we must act now. So what if the wall-kelp's original purpose was animal feed? Will that make you lose sleep at night when you are starving? So what if it tastes worse than tofu or taro? It is protein, and we can produce it fast enough to meet our needs."

The chamber erupted into scattered shouting. Ramis found himself realizing with a half-smile that Dr. Sandovaal had done it again: shocked his audience, then rubbed their noses in the only possible answer.

C H A P T E R 4

ORBITECH 1 ■ DAY 1

Fifteen minutes! Duncan McLaris fought with himself not
to call up the time again. He sat in the plush viewing chair
in the *Orbitech 1* observation alcove. His five-year-old
daughter Jessie squirmed and tugged her hand from his
grip.

"Not so hard, Diddy!"

He had turned all the lights down so that the reddish
glow did not interfere with the panorama of stars. Normally the ocean of space filled him with awe, made him
forget all the trivial problems of being Production Division
leader. Now, those "trivial problems" outweighed anything he had ever endured before.

The first scattered reports implied that a good portion of
Earth's population had survived the War, but most communications were wiped out from the electromagnetic
pulse. As McLaris had guessed, they were utterly incapa-
ble of sending any more supply ships, probably for years.
That didn't surprise him: when only one of the early NASA

shuttles had exploded, the entire nation's space program was grounded for three years. This disaster was much more extensive than a single explosion. Their entire industrial base had probably been knocked to its knees.

As *Orbitech 1* rotated, the great shining ball of the Moon swung into view. It seemed so bright, like a bowl filled with hope. Clavius Base lay on the Moon's surface. The oldest of the space settlements, it had been set up as a stepping-stone for the Lagrange colonies. And since supply shuttles had a vastly more difficult job entering and leaving the Moon's deep gravity well, Clavius Base had been forced to become self-sufficient much sooner than the other colonies.

"Diddy, what star is that?" Jessie's voice interrupted his thoughts.

McLaris looked where his daughter pointed. Her little finger smeared against the crystal, but he had learned to sight along her arm. "That's called Fomalhaut, honey." He wasn't certain, but he knew she'd be disappointed if he didn't come up with some answer for her. "The Arabs named it." She giggled at the strange-sounding name, but seemed satisfied.

She wore her reddish-brown hair in braids. McLaris had never been able to decide if Jessie really preferred her hair that way, or if she just wanted her father to spend the time braiding it.

The first time he had tried it, back when his wife was still on *Orbitech 1*, McLaris had done nothing more than make a tangled mess of Jessie's hair. Taking it upon himself as a father's duty, he sat up late by the light of a small glow-lamp, toying with strings in his hand, studying the diagrams and instructions he had called up on the big screen of his terminal, practicing how to braid hair. Diane slept restlessly in their bed beside him, probably dreaming about hills and trees and fresh air.

McLaris glanced at his watch again in the observation alcove. Close enough. "Ready to go, Jessie?" He tried to sound cheerful, to keep the quaver out of his voice. "Take a last look."

"Ready." She grasped her toy synthesizer/keyboard (she called it her "keeburd") like a teddy bear. McLaris had built it for her from a kit, and she played it relentlessly. He had told Jessie she could take only one of her toys with them tonight, and her decision had not surprised him.

He drew a deep breath and stood up, adjusting the lights in the observation room back to normal. He blinked, waiting to become accustomed to the brightness. Jessie rubbed her eyes but grinned. She didn't look at all worried—she seemed to have a lot of faith in her daddy's abilities.

McLaris didn't want to stop, didn't want to think. He would become frightened if he wasted too much time thinking. This was not the type of decision one made rationally.

The others would realize the implications of the War soon enough. Brahms probably already had, but hadn't yet decided what to do. And if McLaris was to have a chance to save himself and Jessie, he had to do it now, before Brahms decided to act.

McLaris forced his breathing to become even and shallow, though his heart continued to pound. He grasped Jessie's hand, almost dragging her along with his rapid steps. She clutched his fingers and followed as best she could, uncomplaining.

He kept a complacent half-smile on his face. Some of the workers in his Production Division greeted him, but most looked shocked and disturbed, too wrapped up with the very idea of the War itself, the devastation of their home planet.

You're all doomed, McLaris thought. *Have a nice day.*

He and Jessie stepped into one of the rapid-lift shafts that led through a spoke of the habitation torus to the central core. At this end of the colony, the zero-G core contained the docking bay for the supply shuttles.

McLaris squeezed Jessie's shoulder. "Remember what I told you, Jessie. This is very important."

"Yes," she said with a confidence and dignity that made him want to hug her again.

Their survival would depend on it.

As the spoke-shaft elevator took them from the rim to the zero-G core, they felt disoriented as gravity decreased. They fell half a mile in only two minutes. Jessie clung to McLaris's side, quiet and obedient, but wide-eyed with excitement. The doors opened to the docking bay, and

Jessie's face glowed with wonder when she saw the *Miranda*.

McLaris breathed a prayer, relieved that he could see no one else. Though only an hour had passed, Director Roha Ombalal had declared a holiday while he consulted with the division leaders. Unfortunately, McLaris would not be able to make the meeting.

Stephanie Garland floated out of the shuttle, then looked at her watch. McLaris nodded.

"Come on inside, Jessie." The pilot held out her hands.

McLaris picked up his daughter. Jessie giggled in anticipation. He counted, "One . . . two . . . three!" then, bracing himself, tossed her in the zero gravity toward the shuttle-tug. Jessie loved it, laughing all through her brief flight. Garland snagged her, swung her down to the hatch, and took her inside the *Miranda*.

After ensuring they were alone in the bay, McLaris sealed the spoke-shaft elevator door. He heard the forceful hiss as the airlock frame set itself against the impending vacuum of space. Moving surely, he pried off the lift's control panel plate and plucked out the operating wires. As fast as he could maneuver in the zero-G bay, he circled to the remaining five spoke-shaft doors and deactivated them as well.

He launched himself toward the other side of the bay to where the great titanium doors stood closed against the vacuum. Feet drifting from the floor, McLaris fumbled with the control box and activated the bay door sequence. Rotating magenta lights went on at all four corners of the bay, bathing the silver walls with a flickering glow, like a rippling sunrise on Earth. *Red skies at morning, sailor take warning.*

A klaxon sounded twice, paused, then sounded again. A synthesized voice blared from the intercom. "Warning! The airlock sequence has been activated. Please evacuate the chamber at once. The airlock sequence has been activated . . ."

McLaris entered the control code on the wall keyboard. Being a division leader had its advantages. The main computer accepted his command. He set the airlock timer to open in one minute.

When he pushed himself back to the *Miranda*, he

judged his trajectory incorrectly and almost missed—
which would have sent him floating to the other side of the
cavernous bay. Right now, he had no time to lose on clum-
siness. He managed to snare one of the shuttle's struts,
reorient himself, and propel his body feet-first through the
hatch.

He sealed the shuttle door from the inside. With a glance
around, he saw that Jessie had already been strapped in.
She sat rigidly quiet, looking terrified.

"We've got less than one minute," McLaris announced
as he eased himself into the copilot's padded chair.

"One minute! That's not enough time to depressurize
the chamber!"

"We're not going to cycle through. I'm dumping it—
explosive decompression."

Garland's eyes were wide.

"It can be done. Emergency procedure." McLaris
shrugged. "It would take an hour to drain the air out of
here if we did it by the book. We don't have that kind of
time. Somebody would stop us by then. They can replenish
the air from the leftover lunar rocks they've got floating
around here. I'm just worried it'll push the colony out of
orbit."

Garland shook her head sounding practical again. "No
way. The air doesn't have enough momentum. And besides, the Orbitech stabilizer jets would compensate."

McLaris glanced up and saw three faces at the observation windows of the docking bay control room. The figures
gestured wildly at the *Miranda*. Soon they gave up and
pounded on the glass window.

McLaris smiled to himself. He had already disconnected
all the wires from the appropriate control panels. He had
done no damage, nothing that couldn't be fixed—but it
would take them hours to get it working again. By then it
would be too late. The *Miranda*—McLaris, Jessie, and Stephanie Garland—would be long gone.

"I can't believe we're doing this!" Garland said. Her
voice had taken on a panicked high pitch. "It's only been
an hour. What if it's a false alarm? What if things aren't as
bad as we think?"

"Don't kid yourself."

"News reports always get exaggerated in a crisis. What if—"

McLaris glared at her. "Do you have a weapon on board?"

"Yes."

"Then tell them I took it, held you hostage, and forced you to fly out. There, you're ass is covered. Happy now?"

McLaris flicked the external intercom, and suddenly klaxon sounds filled the cockpit of the *Miranda*. The computer voice blared from the intercom again.

"The airlock will open in twenty seconds. You have fifteen seconds to evacuate. Emergency. Evacuate immediately."

McLaris strapped himself into the copilot's chair and reached behind him, extending his fingers toward Jessie, but the straps kept him from touching her. He waved instead. "It's okay, baby. Just be brave."

"I am, Diddy."

"I'm going to lift us up," Stephanie Garland said. She looked beaten and very frightened. "When those doors crack, we'll be blasted out of here with the rest of the air."

McLaris nodded. "The sooner we get away from here, the better."

Garland moved one of the joysticks. The craft hesitated, then jerked free of its moorings. McLaris could hear the attitude jets. The hissing sound cut off, but the *Miranda* continued to drift slowly upward, without gravity to pull it back down.

"Five seconds . . ."

McLaris swallowed, but his throat felt raw. It should be just about—

The giant docking bay doors slid open, and the crack widened like a yawning mouth. The blackness of space spun under them. As the air rushed out, McLaris could imagine he heard the howling wind.

The *Miranda* lunged forward, buffeted from side to side. Like a roller coaster ride, the shuttle-tug burst through the opening doors.

The air froze into a silvery mist of ice crystals that floated around the shuttle. McLaris gripped the arms of his seat, but the acceleration wasn't great enough to cause discomfort.

Garland slapped at her control panel, igniting the thrusters that pushed them away from the colony.

McLaris looked down at *Orbitech 1*—the majestic Lagrange colony he had called home for nearly a year—as it dropped away behind them. The colony looked like two spoked wheels fastened to each end of a thick axle: two giant counterrotating toruses, each half a mile in radius, connected through the center by a mile-long cylinder that did not rotate. The central cylinder provided a large zero-G environment for labs and manufacturing areas.

Floating above the entire colony shone the broad but delicately thin mirror, discontinuous to reflect sunlight to the louvered mirrors on the rims of both toruses. McLaris turned his head away from the colony and looked instead for the Moon. Their survival lay there.

Garland flicked on the radio, and a hubbub of angry chatter burst at them. Disconnected shouting, dismayed and astonished questions: *"Miranda,* where are you going?" "What the hell do you think you're doing?"

McLaris had taken them by surprise. He allowed a satisfied smile to creep onto his face. Relief filled him like ice water, and he felt ready to melt. They were going to make it—they had passed the major challenge. The shuttle was free of *Orbitech 1.*

One sharp voice cut though the babble on the radio. The other voices fell silent. McLaris felt his heart pause with animal fear as he recognized the voice of Curtis Brahms.

"Damn you, McLaris!" He could not possibly have measured the amount of anger and betrayal in the associate director's voice. "Damn you!"

McLaris desperately reached forward and switched the radio off.

Behind him, Jessie cried.

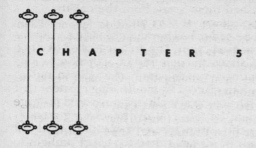

C H A P T E R 5

Curtis Brahms unsealed the desk and withdrew his
bronze-rimmed eyeglasses. He slid them on, careful not to
disturb his precise blond hair. The lenses in the glasses
were blanks, for show only, but they made him look older.
At twenty-nine, the youngest associate director ever,
Brahms felt too self-conscious of his wunderkind status.
And right now he needed to command respect. He insisted
on holding the meeting in his own office chamber.

The actual director of *Orbitech 1*, Roha Ombalal,
slouched next to him in shock. His expression showed little
life. Ombalal had spent half a day poring over the detailed
disaster plan developed by the Orbitechnologies Corporation years before. Brahms had heard him mumbling to
himself, astonished and dismayed because "the plan was
supposed to cover every emergency!"

Indeed, Orbitechnologies had not thought of every scenario. They had not even designed life-support pods into
the station: Brahms felt sure that they hadn't considered it

cost-effective to provide "lifeboats" for all fifteen hundred inhabitants.

Across from him sat the R & D Division leader, Allen Terachyk, who looked little better than Ombalal—a wrong word might bring down his mental house of cards, and Brahms didn't have time for that. He needed Terachyk to help him find the right information. Ombalal could be ignored for the moment.

"Well, Allen? Do you think you can do it?" Brahms added a distinct compassionate tone to his voice. Terachyk was six years older than Brahms, and kept his brown hair cropped very close to his head. Black-framed eyeglasses stood out heavily on his face.

Terachyk blinked at Brahms, his expression as blank and open as a test pattern. Brahms kept his face carefully neutral and reached over to turn on the desktop computer terminal. He swiveled the holoscreen to face Terachyk. Terachyk remained sitting with his hands folded in his lap. Ombalal blinked, but offered no assistance.

Brahms scowled. This was like trying to work with mannequins. He picked up the keypad and dropped it in Terachyk's lap.

"Allen? Hello? Is anybody in there? Come on, you came up through Computer Applications—I *need* that information. Do you still remember how to get it?"

Terachyk squinted at the holoscreen and stared at the keypad in his lap. "Ask me in a couple days, Curtis—I'll be all right then."

"We don't have a couple days, Allen. I have to know now."

"Dammit, can't you have a little compassion?" Terachyk flared up. "What difference does it make?"

Brahms set his mouth. He always worked very hard at showing compassion; he considered it one of his strong points.

Terachyk had been on *Orbitech 1* for more than three years, and he was due to be rotated home in four months. He'd been a model employee, one of the most exceptional workers on the colony. A wife and four sons waited for him in Baltimore.

Or had. From the first scattered reports they'd received, Baltimore had been obliterated in the War.

Two months before, Ombalal's wife and children had been sent home under some sort of cover story that no one believed. On company orders, Ombalal remained on *Orbitech 1*, his self-esteem badly hurt, while Brahms took over the station.

Brahms tapped his fingernails on the desktop. Ombalal knew he had no part in the discussion. "Allen, listen to me. The other people here haven't figured out how desperate our situation is. They're still going to be waiting for rescue ships."

"McLaris figured it out," Terachyk mumbled.

Brahms reddened but maintained his control. He saw bright white light behind his eyes, but he blinked it away. "You and I both know that *Orbitech 1* was never meant to be self-sufficient. We have fifteen hundred employees here —tap into the database, get the exact inventory of our supplies. You can determine how much our gardens will produce right now. Model our consumption rate. Run a worst-case study. Use different rationing schemes."

Terachyk kept his eyes turned away from the associate director, but he seemed to be paying attention. Brahms studied him, made a flash analysis of his reactions—yes, it was obvious. Terachyk would resent being brought back to the real world and its problems. He might turn his despair into anger toward Brahms for pulling him out of his misery.

But Brahms was willing to take that chance. He needed the colony to survive; he didn't give a damn what the employees thought of his methods. *Orbitech 1* had been left in his care, not Ombalal's—Orbitechnologies had made that perfectly clear.

Brahms spoke quietly to Terachyk. "I have to know how long we can last, Allen. And I have to know before people start asking those questions."

A moment passed.

Reluctantly, Terachyk logged on. He flashed a bitter glance at Brahms, then stared at the screen. In a few moments, his fingers picked up speed as he allowed the problem to distract him from his own memories.

Brahms nodded in encouragement. Push the right buttons, and he knew he could get the right reactions.

He watched Terachyk work. Nothing was routine anymore, nothing straightforward. Brahms was being sent through the fire, given an impossible task to manage. He felt himself hardening, rising to the job that had to be done. The people of *Orbitech 1* were lucky to have him—they would have no chance at all relying on Ombalal.

Brahms studied the dark-skinned man. Roha Ombalal had been a brilliant chemist but was an utterly incompetent manager. The tall Indian had a soft, gentle voice with the potential for projecting a great deal of authority. Brahms had envied Ombalal for that, but scorned him for not making use of his gift. He could have been a perfect leader image, paternal and intelligent—all the things that Brahms, with his youth and clean-cut, boyish appearance, did not have.

But Ombalal was not a successful administrator—he had his priorities all wrong.

The Indian chemist had wanted everyone to like him, wanted the *Orbitech 1* people to think of him as a benevolent manager, someone they could talk to.

To foster his image, or maybe just to avoid his other duties, Ombalal had spent a great deal of time wandering through the labs, looking at all the work being done. Occasionally, he would become fascinated with the research, interfering and not getting his own administrative work done. Some of the scientists may have loved him for his genuine interest; others thought he was harassing them, getting in the way.

But what could the parent corporation expect? Orbitechnologies had a consistent policy of "rewarding" brilliant researchers with promotions into administrative posts. Brahms stated his own position frequently: "I wouldn't put a scientist in an important managerial position any more than I would put an administrator in a lab doing research."

When Orbitechnologies finally relieved the director of his duties and ordered Brahms to replace him, Ombalal's family had been sent home, but he had been allowed to stay for a while, as a figurehead, only to save face.

Roha Ombalal had been devastated, wide-eyed and baffled at his misfortune. Brahms could tell that the director had never failed like this before, and he still didn't seem to grasp what exactly he had done wrong.

"Knock, knock?"

Brahms looked up and scowled at the obese man who strode into his office. Tim Drury, the Maintenance/Services Division leader, began to speak, but Brahms held up his hand, indicating Terachyk intent at the terminal.

"Don't disturb him. He's doing something for me."

Drury shrugged. "Question—when are we going to start getting things back to normal? We've told everybody they have a few days off to recover from the shock, but some service parts have already started fizzling. My people are going to have to go back to their maintenance duties before long. It's going to be dregs for their morale if they're the only ones back on the job." Drury threw a glance at Ombalal and lowered his voice. He knew who really made the decisions. "Are you going to restart the production lines, Curtis?"

"I'm just the associate director." Brahms kept his gaze on Ombalal, trying to spark some life in the man.

"Ask me if it makes any difference now." Drury rolled his eyes. He didn't seem to realize what Brahms was trying to do.

Drury had long, curly blond hair and a bushy reddish mustache poised on his upper lip as if it intended to launch itself off at any moment. And he was huge.

Brahms disliked people who had such low self-esteem that they allowed themselves to get so enormously fat. "A lazy body is the sign of a lazy mind" he had always believed. Brahms kept himself in good shape, reveling in the fine-tuned feel to his body. But Drury was always so good-natured it was difficult to be angry at the man.

Ombalal finally spoke. "He is correct, Mr. Brahms. Do not let me hold you back."

Brahms removed his glasses, blinking in the light. "Well we have the raw materials to last us a while. Just no food. Yes, all divisions will return to work. It'll distract them, keep them quiet for a little longer. Until we can think of something."

Drury smirked. "How can the universe bear to go on without a continual supply of our no-smear lipstick? Or airy-but-durable single-molecular weaves for the height of fashion!" He paused. "But what about Production Division? Who's going to fill McLaris's place—now that he's taken, er, a brief leave of absence?" The heavyset man made a maddeningly aloof smile.

Once again, Brahms burned. McLaris's theft of the shuttle-tug was an appalling betrayal of Brahms's leadership—a betrayal of all the good people on *Orbitech 1*. Not only had McLaris taken the last working shuttle, but he had shocked the colonists, called attention to their desperate situation, before Brahms could find a way to solve things. McLaris had stolen their icon of hope, the symbol that allowed them to think they still had a link with Earth. Even now, McLaris was en route to the Moon, safe and free, leaving the rest of them trapped. Trapped.

Brahms threw a glance at Ombalal, hoping that the man might volunteer for McLaris's former position. The station director continued to stare at his large feet.

"I'll take over his duties," Brahms said, sighing. How could McLaris have done such a thing? He eased back, breathing slowly, slapping a mask of composure on his face. Brahms hated himself for these lapses into weakness, these brief moments without control. He had never been so quick to anger before.

"Okay." Drury shrugged. "How about a game of checkers, anybody?"

Brahms bristled. "Fifteen hundred people have their throats up against the razor blade right now—we have to find a way to survive!"

Brushing aside the associate director's retort, Drury spread his meaty hands. "Oh, things'll work out in the end. Positive thinking, Curtis. Give it a whirl."

"Get the hell out of here!"

Waving, Drury left, wandering back out into the corridor of administrative offices. The silica-fiber carpeting muffled his footsteps.

Drury had been with the parent company for the past fourteen years. He was a competent manager, but not truly gifted. Brahms, who had done the numbers himself, knew that Drury had not scored well on the Efficiency Study.

Four months before, Brahms's supervisor back on Earth had spent hours briefing him about what the company expected. The bookkeepers and resource managers looked with glee upon the enormous profits generated from the exotic products created on *Orbitech 1*.

In such isolation the entire political and social structure of the station could be compared to the frontier days of Earth. Orbitechnologies wanted to know how well the colony was doing in relation to how well it *could* be doing. Was it operating at its greatest efficiency? They wanted Curtis Brahms to go up and find out, to make suggestions for improvement. He had a knack for learning things like that.

As the Earth-to-orbit vehicle took Brahms up to rendezvous with the shuttle-tug that would carry him out to L-5, he simmered with excitement. Brahms felt so proud, so sure of himself. He could almost smell something in the air, like a premonition.

Before he had left, *Forbes* ran a small article spotlighting him as an up-and-coming manager, loaded with administrative dynamite and filled with new perspectives and ideas. Prime time had come for Curtis Brahms. Everything would fall into place at the moment he stepped out onto the docking bay of *Orbitech 1* and got to work.

He did not ever intend a vendetta against the former director. Instead, he approached his Efficiency Study with a single-minded insistence to get it done right. Brahms saw this as a great chance to put a gold star on his own career, but he also derived immense satisfaction just from making things work better.

Bright-sounding progress reports and extravagant promises from Roha Ombalal would no longer be sufficient for Orbitechnologies. Brahms had a gut-level feeling that Ombalal was an incompetent director, but he waited until the hard numbers tallied on the spreadsheets.

He developed broad criteria for assessing efficiency. The fifteen hundred people had to fit together as a unit. Productivity must be maximized; waste must be minimized; but the people themselves must remain satisfied as well, which seemed to be the most difficult factor to measure.

Brahms set up an extensive survey form on the *Orbitech 1* computers, which processed the demographic data and scored people on numerous criteria, such as their material productivity, their health, the quality and speed of their work, their ability to get things accomplished by a deadline. Then he rated the "fuzzy" factors, such as their general attitude, their ability to work and live with others as a community so that *Orbitech 1* was more than just a giant factory in space.

Over the months, Brahms dug into every detail of the workers' lives. He studied how happy they were, trying to find which ones wanted to go back to Earth, which ones were still afraid or uncomfortable about living in space, and which ones felt exhilarated and honored to be on the station. He encouraged them to be honest, and thought he had been fairly successful.

Brahms conducted a dozen interviews per day, every day of the week. He watched tapes of the interviews over again to double-check his impressions, then beamed them back to Earth for secondary analysis by one of the company's other teams.

He spent weeks collating information, massaging numbers through a new computer model developed at Orbitechnologies. Looking at his preliminary results, Brahms called about a hundred of the people back again for a second interview. Brahms chose these interviewees carefully and watched their responses as he asked them questions about other colonists. By studying the way they responded to the questions, he gained a second impression about them, and gleaned some information about other colonists.

After four months of wearing himself thin, convincing everyone on the station that he was too cold and too hard, Brahms packaged up the results of his study and transmitted them to Earth. Orbitechnologies thanked him, told him to remain on the colony until further notice, and kept silent for a week while they interpreted the results.

Brahms waited, exhausted but utterly satisfied with his efforts. He was optimistic, hoping that with his background, some lucky breaks, and a hell of a lot of hard work on other projects, he might have a chance as associate director of *Orbitech 2*, the companion station now under construction at L-4.

Then Orbitechnologies unexpectedly relieved Roha Ombalal of most of his duties, and told Brahms to step in as associate director. He drifted in a state of shock for several days, not fully comprehending his good fortune and sudden responsibilities, until the day Ombalal's wife had cursed him, just before she and her children had gone back to Earth in disgrace.

"No." Allen Terachyk broke Brahms's concentration. "We won't last long." Terachyk stood up and turned to leave the office. He hung his head and shuffled down the corridor without speaking further.

Brahms stopped himself from going after him. On the holoscreen glimmered the results of Terachyk's model. His eyes widened at the numbers. With the recent arrival of the *Miranda* they had just restocked all their stores, and Terachyk hadn't spent too much time with various rationing schemes, but in the simplistic, conservative one he had applied, the results still shocked Brahms.

Four months.

All the people on *Orbitech 1,* all fifteen hundred, would starve in four months.

Their gardens were ornamental—bright flowers and the occasional luxury of fresh fruit. *Orbitech 1* was not designed to be self-sufficient.

Earth could never recover in that time. Sixty years before, one shuttle had blown up and stalled the U.S. space program for years. Now the War had driven the entire industrial base to its knees . . . and *Orbitech 1* had only four months until it ran out of food.

Too many people, and not enough supplies. They couldn't all survive. He looked at the numbers again; they were too large and too small. Fifteen hundred people. Four months.

We can't all survive.

He looked to Ombalal. The man stared at the holoscreen, unblinking, as if he had expected nothing else.

Orbitech 1 had its scientists and researchers, whom Brahms respected and admired—but he did not worship them. As part of the big machine of the colony, all pieces had to fit together. The researchers, with their special skills, were just doing their job, as Brahms expected everyone to do.

The colony also had its production people, its workers, its maintenance people, its electronics technicians, its custodians, its medical officers, its gardener, the Personnel and Administration divisions, and they had families. All facets of society were reflected in *Orbitech 1*—they had to be to make it a viable community.

We can't all survive!

How long would it take him to find a way for the colony to live through this? He couldn't do it alone—and he didn't intend to. They all had to make a massive, concerted effort. All of the collective resources of *Orbitech 1* had to pull together as a team to find a way. But how could they possibly discover a radical new means of survival, develop it, and implement it in time to make any difference?

Fifteen hundred. There were still too many people. Four months. The time was still too short. He had to do something—riots would start once people found out they only had four months to live. But how could he stop it?

Brahms felt a drop of sweat trickle in a cold path down his back. His throat went dry. Fewer people would be able to survive longer on the same amount of supplies.

They couldn't all survive anyway.

Brahms closed his eyes and took a deep breath. When he opened his eyes again, the numbers on the screen were still the same.

The associate director got up from his desk. Ombalal had closed his eyes, as if trying to hold back tears. Useless man. Brahms thought briefly about calling for an attendant, but hesitated a moment, then turned instead to the holo unit and punched up a d-cube of Prokofiev's "Kije Suite." The mixed melancholy and optimism of the music would help him think.

As the d-cube played, Brahms used his thumbprint to unseal one of the compartments in the restricted file recessed into the wall. He found the duplicate memory cube containing the confidential results of his Efficiency Study.

Brahms held the hologram memory cube in his hand. It was cold and had sharp corners. He felt as if his insides had turned to metal—bright chrome. He stared at the cube, still reluctant to consider the possibility at hand.

He moved to Ombalal and turned the cube right before the station director's eyes. Brahms said, "Do you know what this is?"

Ombalal blinked. "A data cube, of course."

"Ah, but what's on it?" Brahms squatted down and searched Ombalal's eyes. He whispered, "We can't all survive. But some of our people are more likely than others to come up with a solution—they've shown it by their track record. We might have a chance."

Standing, he pushed the cube into a slot in his desktop, and listened to the quiet whirring as the internal computer read the information into Brahms's private directory.

He pulled the keypad toward him, saved Allen Terachyk's analysis, then called up the results of his Efficiency Study. As he scrolled down through the names and scores on the holoscreen, he looked at the rankings, forcing himself not to think of faces, of people—only numbers and names.

We can't all survive.

He turned to Ombalal. The director's eyes were wide with horror.

Brahms hesitated a long time before choosing the first name, the one with the lowest score. His eyes felt dry and gummy, yet he couldn't secm to find the energy to blink.

But once he had chosen the first name, the rest came easier.

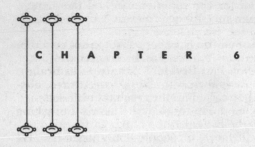

C H A P T E R 6

EN ROUTE TO THE MOON ■ DAY 3

The Moon's blasted landscape swelled below them—craters, mountains, canyons, and black lava flows. The jagged peaks reached up as the *Miranda* swooped in its orbit, homing in on Clavius Base.

Stephanie Garland kept her eyes on the instruments. " 'How to get the whole universe to despise you in three easy steps.' We're good at that, aren't we, McLaris?" Bitterness edged her voice, but McLaris did not rise to the bait.

"Knock it off. It's too late to have second thoughts. You did what you did, and so did I."

He could see Garland growing edgier, uneasier, as they neared the Moon. McLaris stared at the landscape beneath them until his eyes ached. "Shouldn't we be close enough to see it by now?"

"You wouldn't notice it unless you knew exactly where to look. Most of the huts are covered with a few yards of lunar soil for shielding. Everything else is underground. You'll see towers sticking up, maybe a few access doors."

Garland reached for the radio and flicked the switch. "Clavius Base, this is shuttle-tug *Miranda*. We will be landing in a few minutes. Request assistance."

A voice broke in over the speakers. "We do not condone your actions, *Miranda*. You are not welcome here."

Over the past two days they had listened in as Brahms and the intercolony community expressed outrage, condemnation. McLaris had chosen to maintain silence.

"I'm not asking you for the Welcome Wagon—I'm asking for guidance!" Garland snapped.

McLaris gripped the pilot's shoulder to silence her. He spoke into the microphone himself. "Please give our regards to Chief Administrator"—he paused for just a moment as he searched his mind for the right name—"Tomkins. We will explain ourselves to him after we have landed safely. Unfortunately, we are not in a position to turn back, whether you welcome us or not. We are going to be forced to land."

The *Miranda* had carried only enough fuel to take Garland back to Earth orbit, and landing in the lunar gravity field required much more than just maneuvering and braking thrust. McLaris had watched the pilot grow more and more insecure as they neared their destination.

After a pause, the voice on the speakers returned. "We have adjusted the homing beacon. If you've got an inexperienced pilot aboard, we warn you that Clavius Base is close to the crater wall. Watch out."

"Inexperienced, my ass," Garland muttered to herself, then spoke over her shoulder to McLaris. "You'd better suit up. And get Jessie suited up, too. All I have to do is skim a rock, rupture the hull—the suits won't do much good, but let's take all the protection we can get."

McLaris squeezed back to the storage lockers and found the hanging suits.

"Jessie, come here." He looked at the smallest one in dismay: *Oh, great.*

Jessie unstrapped herself and floated over to the lockers. She looked at the bulky adult suit in his hand. "Diddy, that's too big!"

"I know, baby, but it's the only suit we've got. It's just for a little while. I want you to wear it for protection. You don't have to do anything in it. I want you to try to get your feet into the legs of the suit. I'll seal everything else up. You won't be able to see out of the helmet. You're too short."

"But I want to see!"

McLaris took a deep breath. "I can't help that, Jessie. Just think of it like a big sleeping bag. You have to wear it. It'll make you safe." He smiled at her. "This is going to be rough. I told you. But I want you to be brave."

"I am brave."

"Good, I know you are. Let's see if you can keep being brave for just a few more minutes until we land. Then we'll be on the Moon."

"Okay."

McLaris kissed her on the forehead, then playfully tugged at her braids before he made her sink down into the voluminous suit. The suit ballooned as he sealed the helmet. It didn't appear to leak; he hoped the seams would hold.

Dismayed at the way the suit fit her, McLaris lifted Jessie and carried her back to the acceleration seat. He strapped her in carefully and squeezed where he thought her shoulder was.

He brought a suit back for Garland and slipped into another one himself. As he tugged on the thick material, McLaris closed his eyes and thought back to the intense training he had taken before he, Jessie, and Diane had moved up to *Orbitech 1*.

"You'd better hurry—we're coming in," Garland called back without turning her head. "Clavius Base, we're on our way!" She switched off the radio again. "Does Jessie remember any prayers from Sunday school? You'd better have her start saying them."

McLaris went cold. "Let's not get her worried," he said shortly, then sealed his own helmet.

Garland muttered, glancing at the cross hairs on one of the screens as the landscape streaked beneath them. She pulled on her own helmet, and McLaris heard her voice crackle in his headset. "Here we go!"

The *Miranda* dropped in its descent, and its rockets fired to stop the fall. The jagged surface of the Moon rose up toward them. McLaris felt his stomach clench.

The upturned lip of a crater opened before them, and a vast flat plain spread out. Suddenly McLaris could see the blurred forms of the buried buildings on Clavius Base, and the shining, kilometers-long rail of the mass launcher used for catapulting lunar material into orbit for construction of the Lagrange colonies.

The crater Clavius spread out like a giant bowl—it seemed so smooth, a perfect spot to land. But as they came closer, McLaris spotted sharp edges, jutting rocks of smaller craters and fissures.

"Diddy!" Jessie cried, muffled in her suit.

The far wall of the Clavius crater grew visibly with each moment. "It's now or never."

Garland fired the attitude jets in an attempt to slow them down further, to take the shuttle in gently. They still seemed to be descending too fast. The rockets sputtered.

"So much for the safety factor in the fuel supply!"

Garland clutched at the controls, but the shuttle did not respond. A last spurt from one of the engines tilted them sideways at a crazy angle. McLaris squeezed his eyes shut and opened them again, only to see the saw-toothed wall of rock hurtling toward them.

"Stephanie, look out—!"

A ripping explosion tore out the belly of the *Miranda*. The shuttle pitched. McLaris thought he could see stars, then the lunar surface, through a gash in the floor. Ragged metal strips dangled like knives as their air vented out into the vacuum in a cloud of white frost crystals.

The *Miranda* crashed, nose first, half burying itself into the lunar surface. Explosive pain popped inside of McLaris.

The cockpit wall folded up and struck him.

Fighting a red haze, McLaris clawed back to consciousness. Part of him wanted to remain in the floating warmth, in the dark, but another part insisted on returning to life.

He squinted, focused enough to see flecks of blood spattered on the inside of his faceplate. He was hurt. McLaris faced the knowledge coolly, at a distance from himself.

He forced his vision beyond the faceplate, into the distorted wreckage of the shuttle. His eyes began to assess distance and perspective again.

He recognized with a sick detachment the torn remains of Stephanie Garland in the pilot's seat. Frozen, iron-hard tatters of flesh and powder-dry blood hung from the ragged ends of the control panel. Half the cockpit yawned open to space.

McLaris realized that he was now sitting in hard vacuum. He had no idea how long he had been unconscious. He wondered how long the air in his suit would last.

Pain rose up inside his head, and his eyes refused to focus again. Something peaceful called him to come back into sleep . . . back into a blissful coma, away from all pain and worry.

McLaris fought against it. *Jessie!* He had to find Jessie. But movement was much more difficult than opening his eyes. He clenched his hand, feeling the fingers move, touching the fabric on the inside of the glove. He breathed, but it felt as if he had inhaled needles that tore at his lungs with each gasp.

He needed to turn only a little to see Jessie behind him. With each slight motion of his head, the nauseating shadows filled his mind again. He was going to faint soon . . . for a long time. He didn't know if he would ever wake up. But McLaris couldn't fall into unconsciousness again . . . not without seeing Jessie one last time.

He wrenched his head too quickly. Blackness reared, but he did get a chance to locate her, strapped into the passenger seat.

Then he saw the jagged crack down the center of her faceplate.

Darkness filled his head again. He had to save her. He refused to consider that he might be too late, that the decompression and loss of air would be almost instantaneous. His ears began to ring loudly. He couldn't think, couldn't concentrate. The only thing he could feel was horror—and then a baffled, nightmarish thought: why couldn't he see her face? The space suit looked hauntingly empty, vacant, as if her body had vanished entirely.

But then he faded into the off-kilter sea of blackness again.

McLaris woke when they moved him. He blinked back a nightmare of a dwarf sitting on his back, stabbing into his spine over and over again with a sharp little dagger.

Jessie . . . Jessie . . . Jessie!

His eyes focused again, rolling up to reveal a suited man hauling him from the wreckage of the *Miranda*. He couldn't see the man's face or his expression; his polarized faceplate was turned into harsh shadow. But McLaris stared at the name patch on his suit, glowing orange.

CLANCY.

He memorized the name, as if it was something sacred and important. *Clancy*. He couldn't understand why Clancy was wearing the suit of an *Orbitech 2* construction engineer—weren't they supposed to be at L-4?

McLaris tried to call for his daughter, but only a hoarse sound came from his throat—like the sound of air escaping from a cracked faceplate.

Clancy could not understand him, but seemed to recognize that McLaris had returned to consciousness. His words came clearly into McLaris's suit radio, filled with a mixture of anger and dismay.

"You idiot!" Not too gently, Clancy set him inside a rover vehicle. "Do you think we're any better off here?"

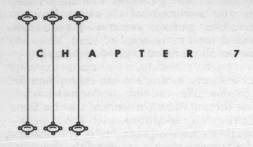

C H A P T E R 7

Pliant green strands, gelatinous and damp. . . .

Luis Sandovaal ran his fingers through the fresh wall-kelp, allowing himself a broad grin since no one else was around. The solarium alcove looked like a lush, primeval forest. Thick fronds dripped from the walls and window plates.

A month ago, ten days ago, his kelp had been nothing more than animal feed. Now the *Aguinaldo*'s survival depended on it. President Magsaysay had told him to find a way to get wall-kelp to *Orbitech 1* and to Clavius Base as well, perhaps even to the Soviet *Kibalchich* station at L-5. It was just like Magsaysay to worry about other people in trouble before he got himself out of the same mess.

The odor of sewage filled the air. Hidden vats circulated the *Aguinaldo*'s untreated wastes for absorption by the kelp nexus. Harsh light from the viewing ports glared into the chamber, washing over the wall-kelp appendages.

Under these ideal conditions, with all the nutrients and

sunlight it could handle, the genetically enhanced kelp grew fast enough to be harvested daily. It was food—unappealing to the colonists, perhaps, but it would see them through. They could treat it, remove all taste, then add their own cayenne and soy and other chemical seasonings. If you were starving, who cared about seasonings anyway?

The other colonies were in much worse shape than the *Aguinaldo,* which the Filipinos had always intended to make into a viable home. The international Clavius Base, the American *Orbitech 1,* and the Soviet *Kibalchich*— they had been caught with their pants down. They had no contingency plans for disasters. Oh, certainly they had backup launch systems on Earth, agreements with other countries, reciprocal treaties with non-spacefaring nations, and even scores of shuttles—but none of that mattered now that Earth's industrial capability had been removed. Even if some industry still functioned, the survivors would use it to rebuild things they desperately needed—not to send supplies to stranded space colonies.

American and Soviet technologies far outstripped what the Filipinos had available to them. With all that skill and knowledge at hand, the superpowers had more than enough ability to survive—but, Sandovaal thought, they seemed to have the wrong mind-set.

The superpowers relied too heavily on high technology —machines—when the key was biotechnology, genetic engineering. Living organisms were more sophisticated and adaptable than anything humans would ever build. The success of Sandovaal's wall-kelp would put the Filipinos in the forefront of all future genetic research. He knew it. Especially now.

But how to get kelp nodules to the other colonies? The *Aguinaldo* didn't have the capability for powered spaceflight, or a facility, or resources to create fuel. All of the stations were effectively stranded on desert islands—like living on the Philippine Islands before the age of boats. Sandovaal was the *Aguinaldo*'s chief scientist. He was supposed to come up with ideas.

He flared his nostrils, wondering how much responsibility one person could shoulder. It seemed the more he did, the more they expected of him.

But then he thought of the others the Council could turn

to. Dobo Daeng? Sandovaal snorted. Dobo was a good assistant, a crackerjack technician, but he had no initiative to head up a research team. Dobo followed orders and did things right, but he had no imagination. Tough times demanded a special type of person—someone who could do what needed to be done. Someone like Luis Sandovaal.

He stood in the alcove for some minutes, lovingly rolling the meter-long strands of wall-kelp with his fingertips. He thought he could sense the wall-kelp growing, hear it moving like bamboo, but a thousand times faster.

Sandovaal brought the strand close to his lips and took a nibble. This substance would etch his name in Filipino history forever, right alongside General Aguinaldo, General MacArthur, and the first President Magsaysay.

Sandovaal winced at the taste.

He dropped the strand and wiped his mouth with the back of his hand. Conceptually, he realized the raw kelp material was edible, but his mouth rebelled at the acrid, unprocessed taste.

Even he admitted that things would have to be very grim before people worshiped *that* as manna from heaven.

Trial and error.

For months their research had followed a dogged routine. Sandovaal's team, including Ramis's parents, Agpalo and Panay Barrera, and Dobo Daeng, clustered in the laboratory units. Using chlorella algae as a genetic base material, combined with two different species of kelp, Sandovaal tried to enhance the salient features of a good food substitute—that it be fast growing, high in protein, and tailored for the *Aguinaldo*'s environment. Sandovaal insisted that the plant be self-sufficient, not tied to the soil by any root system.

After running a series of converging molecular-dynamic calculations, and dozens of trials, the transgenetic algae/kelp survived and increased its mass. Dobo, in a rush of accidental inspiration, suggested they could grow the plant over the *Aguinaldo*'s walls. The idea excited Sandovaal. He grabbed the other man's round face and patted him like a puppy.

The wall-kelp proved to be amazingly versatile—to Sandovaal's surprise as much as anyone else's. It could cling to any freestanding object; a few unsupported spherical nodules drifted in the zero-G core. The fronds of wall-kelp advanced like a green wave over barren sections of the internal hull, producing oxygen and a digestible biomass.

Sandovaal decided he had discovered the panacea that would give the *Aguinaldo* independence from the Americans and their supply shuttles.

Decades before, his grandmother had worked in the rice paddies on the Philippines, tilling the soil and carrying "honey buckets" of human waste to spread as fertilizer. She splashed through the brown water, sweating in the humidity, her hands raw from the rice shoots. Sandovaal remembered seeing a tractor rusting at one end of the rice paddy, but otherwise he might have been imagining a scene from two hundred years ago.

By way of support for the new Filipino government established after World War II, the Americans had shipped in thousands of tons of farm equipment: tractors, harvesters, silos—equipment that should have elevated the Philippines to a true second-world country. The Islands had all the resources; the Filipinos had only to learn to use the new equipment.

But once the tractors ran out of gas or oil, or ground to a halt because of mechanical failures, the Filipinos found it easier just to let them stand in the fields and rust than to fix them.

Sandovaal had heard their excuse: it was Western equipment, built and designed to be run by Western hands.

Sandovaal snorted at the blindness of his own people, their stupidity. Survival was more important than misplaced pride. They should use the tools, the techniques, the discoveries already available. He himself had not felt the need to reproduce all the pioneering genetics experiments Gregor Mendel had performed in his monastery garden. That would be foolish, and Sandovaal had no patience with fools.

The same ingrown resistance to change made the *Aguinaldo* colonists reluctant to accept his wall-kelp as food. They turned up their noses at its taste, though the kelp was nutritionally sound. Sandovaal considered it a direct insult from his own people. But at least they used it as animal feed.

One day, after he had been on the *Aguinaldo* for two years, Sandovaal looked up as daylight streamed into the laboratory from the open door. President Magsaysay stood outside, silhouetted. His bare feet contrasted with the formal barong he wore, but fit his image well.

Sandovaal motioned him inside and indicated the small culture tanks of new wall-kelp strains. The laboratory room carried a spoiled smell from the raw nutrients. He began to jabber about his progress, knowing how important it would be for the Council to learn, but Magsaysay seemed uninterested in the conversation. It occurred to Sandovaal that the *dato*'s eyes were misty and troubled.

Magsaysay stared at his long fingernails, looking very tired. He rubbed his temples, avoiding Sandovaal's gaze. "Luis, that is not the reason I am here."

"I suspected as much."

Magsaysay held out his hands, but said nothing. Sandovaal watched him, growing impatient. "Well, what is it?"

"Agpalo and Panay Barrera were your assistants, correct?" His voice trailed off.

Sandovaal frowned. "Yes. I hired them out of the Baguio barrio, back on the Islands. They were always trying to get ahead. Moonlighting, in fact—running a Sari-Sari store when I found them. They were much too bright for that. Are they giving you trouble?"

Magsaysay set his mouth. "They were killed this morning."

"What?" Sandovaal sat and slumped back in his chair. His face fell slack. "But they were here not more than a few hours ago—"

"They were almost home when—"

"When what? What do you mean?"

"Some youngsters brought a fiberglass plate to the core. They tried to go skimming around the Sibuyan Sea, ride against the rotation. They lost control of the plate—"

Sandovaal sat up straight. "Idiots! If they flew into the rim—" he thought for a moment, calculating. "Why, they could impact at fifty kilometers an hour."

"We found out," Magsaysay said. "The children were

unharmed. But the fiberglass plate flew into one of the walkways. The Barreras . . . I have already talked to their son, Ramis—the one who is here on *Aguinaldo.*"

Sandovaal looked up at him, feeling oddly quiet inside. "Why have you not done anything before this?"

"Luis, how are we going to stop children from sneaking out and playing in the core?"

"Toss them out the airlock if they get caught. That would stop the little terrors."

"We do not have that kind of government, Luis."

Sandovaal hit his hand with his fist. "It should never have happened. Panay and Agpalo did good work." He stopped. "What will you do with their boy, uh—"

"Ramis. This is his home. He will stay with me." Sandovaal lifted an eyebrow at the *dato. President Magsaysay?* he thought. *With a boy to take care of?* But establishing their colony as more than an experimental outpost was very dear to Magsaysay's heart.

"I have not lived with anyone since Nada died. But I have plenty of room—and plenty of time, for that matter. In a country as small as the *Aguinaldo,* even the president is not kept too busy. Ramis has a brother back on Earth, but he may be better off staying here." Magsaysay shrugged. "Besides, I feel responsible for what happened."

Sandovaal still grumbled to himself. "Those idiots should have known better. Humans are supposed to be an intelligent species, remember?"

Magsaysay looked at the floor. "Luis, you cannot convince children what is good for them. You must have precautions and enough safety features to stop accidents. Perhaps we will have to set up a strict patrol, like policemen. No, like lifeguards."

Sandovaal paced back to his desk, pondering. "They are children. They need sheepdogs, not lifeguards." The laboratory seemed silent to him; the vat of maturing wall-kelp emitted a putrid smell.

Magsaysay stood up, brushing the palms of his hands over his barong. "I just needed someone to talk to, Luis. But I should be alone now. Or maybe I should be with Ramis. I will let you get back to your work."

Sandovaal nodded distractedly and walked the *dato* to the door. But long after Magsaysay's electric cart had trun-

dled uphill along the curving rim, Sandovaal remained lost
in thought, staring out at the enclosed world around him.

It was, after all, time to begin the new phase of transgenetic research to follow up on his brilliant success of the
wall-kelp. Take it one step farther. Like that sail-creature
debacle he had pushed.

Sheepdogs. . . .

C H A P T E R 8

The fountain jets in the Japanese garden looked like spurting diamonds. Karen Langelier watched with wonder as each droplet of water rose to its apex, hung there for a prolonged instant, then began its glide back down to the pool. She listened as the drops hit the surface, like a slow-motion rain shower. Her eyes glinted, and she smiled at the beauty that low gravity gave to the downpour.

Karen closed her eyes and drew a deep breath, smelling the air, the moisture, the plants. *Relax, unwind. Then you can get back to work on the new weavewire process.* She moved around the fountain to look at a burst of magenta, button-shaped blooms. The gardener, Hiro Kaitanabe, kept a variety of flowers in bloom, mixing the scents like a master tea blender.

She was glad Kaitanabe refused to label the plants with their scientific names. Karen was a polymer chemist, not a botanist, and had little grasp of Latin names for living species. Scientists loved to name and categorize things, but sometimes it became a little oppressive. She wanted this place to feel like a park, not a plant museum.

She had come to the garden to empty her mind, to get away from thinking. To forget about the War, her work . . . her estranged husband back on Earth. To distract herself, Karen spent too many hours in the lab, surrounded by chemicals, analytical instruments, and polymer spinnerets, using the clumsy techniques of working without gravity.

She could work out her problems, somehow. She was strong enough for that.

Karen wandered along the manicured aisles of bushes, listening to the fountains, the recorded bird song from tiny speakers hidden in the branches. Kaitanabe knew just how much sound and how much silence to add to his garden. Warm illumination glowed from the walls and ceiling, simulating sunlight. Brighter lamps shone out of artificial Japanese lanterns for those plants that required more light.

Karen wore comfortable clothes—stretch jeans and a sweater—under her lab coat, which she rarely removed because she always needed the pockets for her personal paraphernalia, computer, calendar-beeper, black licorice candy. Anything she had to carry consciously, such as a backpack or a purse, always seemed too much bother.

Part of her wanted to hurry back to the lab, to bury herself in work again. She thought she had just made a major breakthrough, found a much faster way to draw out the monomolecular weavewire she had pioneered years before. . . .

No, she would stay here and just let some of the calmness soak in for a while, seek that quiet place in her center where all the ideas originated. She had been consciously teaching herself how to relax, but it was very difficult.

She glanced down at the meandering stream pumped by slow turbines under the floor. She looked a little haggard, but she'd had ghosts of gray in her red hair and laugh lines around her eyes long before the War. Leaving Ray had done that to her—the trial separation to see if they would fare better together or by themselves. A year at L-5 doing her work, giving her time to think . . . and at the end of her assignment, then they could decide what to do.

But the War had decided for them, and she and Ray would never have the chance to find out. Even if he had not been killed in the exchange, they were separated by circumstances more final than any divorce.

Karen did not close her eyes against the pain, but her vision became focused on a faraway place. *Everything will work out the way it's supposed to.* It sounded corny and simplistic, but she believed it.

As she rounded a corner of hedges, Karen came upon Hiro Kaitanabe, bent over a flower bed of cream-colored lilies. She was about to greet the gardener, but stopped as she noticed the tension in his back.

Kaitanabe ripped the lilies out by the roots, crushing the bulbs in his hands. He yanked the leaves off silently and tore the delicate flowers.

Karen took a step forward. "What—?"

The gardener froze, then slowly placed the lilies down on the ground, as if embarrassed. He stood up, brushing his dirt-covered hands together. It took him a moment to place an indifferent mask on his face.

"This entire garden . . . none of it is food." He indicated the plants with a nod of his head. "All this time I could have been growing food."

He padded away, leaving the ruined flower bed and clods of dirt on the path.

Karen stared at him until he disappeared into the foliage. She couldn't even hear him moving. Deep in one of the branches of a sculpted tree, a burst of cheerful bird song echoed in the garden.

The Bifrost Lounge held a dozen people. The chairs, tables, and small holoscreens had been arranged in a haphazard but calculated way. Karen was sure Orbitechnologies had spent a lot of effort on psychological studies to give it just that "homey" touch. Everything was done in earth tones with splashes of green here and there, artificial flowers, real plants.

Three women sat at a table playing a game with a well-worn deck of paper playing cards. Clustered together in the high-throughput ventilation area, four people shared a cigarette. Karen smiled to herself. One of *Orbitech 1's* developments had been an alveoli-scrubber drug—a timed-release capsule that cleaned deposits from the lungs. This made tobacco smoking safe again, but since it cost so much to import tobacco from Earth, few of the Orbitech colonists could smoke anyway.

The lab work waited, but Karen avoided it for now. She needed to be with other people, even if she did nothing more than sit and observe. She was getting tired of hiding with nothing but her problems for company. That was no way to make things better for herself.

She entered the lounge quietly so no one would notice her. A man in a red sweat suit hurried up to her. "The shuttles are going down! Either this orbit or the next one." He looked as if she should be interested, but he went off to tell the others before she could respond.

The shuttle *Miranda* had crashed on the Moon days before. Most of the people on *Orbitech 1* were still furious with Mr. McLaris and the pilot who had stolen the shuttle. Mutineers, some people called them. Some claimed that it was just like upper management to steal the goods and screw the other employees; others chuckled bitterly that McLaris had screwed even the other managers.

But the other two shuttles were a different story. The *Ariel* and the *Oberon* had been trapped in low Earth orbit, arriving at the end of their runs just after the War. At least they hadn't been blasted in the space-based weapons exchange like the Earth-orbiting stations, but now the two pilots had limited supplies and no fuel to go anyplace else.

Every ninety minutes the two shuttles dipped lower in their orbits as the vanishingly thin atmosphere slowed them like quicksand. They had about another day and a half before the craft would hit the ionosphere—not like a stone skipping across the water, but streaking across the sky in a dazzling fireball.

The Colony Communications—ConComm—network between the *Aguinaldo*, Clavius Base, and *Orbitech 1* kept communications open twenty-four hours a day. Occasionally it picked up low-wattage broadcasts from Earth or amateur radio operators, or intercepted transmissions between groups of War survivors, but very few of the transmissions were directed out into space. The colonies were on their own as far as Earth was concerned.

But ConComm also broadcast regular updates of the

situation with the *Ariel* and the *Oberon*. What else did the people have to do but watch and listen to the pilots' gamble for survival? *Heroes—we could use some about now,* Karen thought.

Clavius Base had suggested to the pilots that they maneuver their shuttles together, transfer all remaining fuel from the *Ariel* into the larger *Oberon*, which had been built for landing on the Moon, and kick themselves into a higher, stable orbit. But even if that succeeded, they had only food enough for another week.

The pilots had been more enthusiastic about another suggestion made by someone on *Orbitech 1*. The *Ariel* contained a shipment of tungsten-alloy wire that had been intended for transfer to the *Orbitech 2* construction site at L-4. If the pilots maneuvered close enough, they could lash the two shuttles to each other, strapping one in front to act as a heat shield.

Karen sat down in a chair and thought about dozing, lying back and letting the tension ripple out the base of her neck. Ray used to be so good at giving back rubs. . . .

She must have dozed, because the shuttle pilots broke over the intercom again, ending their forty-five-minute silence. They had successfully attached the two craft together. They were going to toboggan through the atmosphere with the *Oberon* in front as a shield. Karen looked around the lounge and saw that the card game had ended. Several other people had arrived and were listening to the transmissions.

"They're going down!" said the man in the red sweat suit.

Karen closed her eyes, traveling back into her mind and imagining a dull-red glow of plasma forming at the shuttle's ablative front, seeing what it would be like if she were floating along with the craft. The spot of roasting metal grew quickly, heating up until the craft was immersed in a blue-bright bath of light. How long before the bottom shuttle started to melt and crumble?

"Plasma interfer-# # #-communica-# # #." The static in the transmission made it impossible to tell which of the pilots had spoken. "We prom-# # #-say hello-# # #-every-# # #."

All the people in the lounge seemed to be holding their

breath. Karen realized that she had unconsciously crossed her fingers. Smiling at her childishness, she straightened her hands and looked around the room.

The Earth kept its radio silence.

The people waited in the lounge, and kept waiting. After the silence grew too thick, mumbled conversation began to rise and fall in the air.

ConComm remained quiet. After half an hour, the first people started to leave. Karen walked out of the lounge, heading back to her lab.

The shuttles never reestablished contact.

C H A P T E R 9

CLAVIUS BASE ■ DAY 8

The nightmares gave way to consciousness. Duncan McLaris opened his eyes, hoping it had all been part of the dream.

Without moving, he let his body send him messages. He found himself stretched out on a comfortable pallet . . . a bed. He smelled a chemical taint, some kind of disinfectant, and a dusty charcoal smell that hung over everything. McLaris blinked and focused his vision on the clean walls, the white sheets on his bed, the various apparatus in the room . . . the other empty beds. Infirmary.

The *Miranda* had crashed! Memories flooded into his head. He caught glimpses of Stephanie Garland fighting the controls, the lunar surface careening toward them. Stephanie Garland . . . shredded by the shrapnel of the cockpit. And Jessie—oh no, Jessie! He saw a vision of a faceless space suit with a cracked helmet, air hissing out into the vacuum. Jessie!

The figure lurching into view was a narrow-shouldered

Asian woman. Her hair had been smoothed to perfection, like a black silk cap; she wore a white coat and the trappings of a doctor. She narrowed her almond eyes at him.

"You were the only survivor, Mr. McLaris. I thought you'd like to know." Her dark eyes were like cold lava glass.

McLaris worked his mouth, but no words came out. He saw flashbacks of the ruined *Miranda*—Jessie's faceplate smashed . . . unconsciousness . . . pain. Then the rover vehicle, and the space-suited man pulling him out of the wreckage. He had been wearing an *Orbitech 2* suit. Clancy —that was his name.

The doctor busied herself rearranging the gleaming medical instruments in a tray. Finally, she removed a hypodermic needle. "I hope you're satisfied."

McLaris looked at the needle, uneasy, but decided not to ask any questions. He found himself floating, unable to comprehend the doctor's anger, or to respond as intelligently as he wanted to. He felt his body filled with a haze of pain, but it was a distant ache, not sharp and distracting— only enough to tell him that his bloodstream had been pumped with enough painkillers to blunt his awareness.

The doctor maintained her silence. She seemed to be seething inside but not letting much of it show. By the time she turned to leave, McLaris already felt the fuzzy effects of the tranquilizer seep into his head. He noticed a hollow emptiness, horror growing inside his stomach at what the doctor had said.

Jessie was dead. Jessie . . . dead.

He squeezed his eyes shut, and tears started to flow, just as unwilling sleep took him.

■ DAY 9

The sounds around him seemed hushed, snickering in the darkness. McLaris had been awake for hours, staring at the ceiling, or closing his eyes and counting how many times his chest rose and fell. He was alive. He had survived. Was this worth the effort? Now they had a scapegoat to blame everything on.

McLaris winced and felt the sweat itch beneath him on the infirmary bed. As the sheets went from being too hot to too cold, he cast them away from his body or pulled them up to his chin. The pain from his injuries—relatively minor, all of them—had subsided into quiet throbbing. Within a day the doctor, Kim Berenger, had taken him off the painkillers, and now McLaris felt his mind sharpening again, his full capabilities returning.

He liked it better when everything wasn't so harsh and clear. The low lunar gravity showed no mitigating effect on the weight of his conscience.

Nobody had taught how to deal with this in management training classes. *I didn't do it for me—I did it for her,* he thought. But he couldn't explain that to Jessie now. What was it for, after all? His own excuses were pathetic.

You're a survivor, Duncan McLaris! Isn't it great to be alive?

During the day, some people in Clavius Base uniforms had come to stare at him. When the nurses brought him medication or rationed food, they acted cold to him. And Dr. Berenger's frigid bedside manner would have been better suited for a morgue.

"You don't know what Brahms is like," he croaked once in a hoarse whisper. "I know what he's going to do. You'll see. Everything I did will be justified."

Berenger just stared at him.

McLaris could blame nobody but himself. *He* had made a terrible mistake, the wrong choice, acted without thinking. He lay pondering how he could take it and turn it into something he could live with.

He closed his eyes and thought about breathing again. Inhale. Exhale. Deeper, and deeper. He felt the air go in and out of his lungs. He sensed the blood flow through his veins and arteries, detected the faint vibrations of his heartbeat . . . and the spinning wheels in his brain.

Diane was gone, either killed in the War or forever separated from McLaris anyway. He could never get back to Earth.

And Jessie was dead. *I am being brave, Diddy!* He was supposed to take care of her. He had promised Diane.

McLaris tried not to think about it.

■   DAY 10

He got out of bed for the first time, stretching his aching muscles, standing—with only a seventh of Earth-normal weight—on trembling legs. McLaris's body felt like a massive bruise, but the hurt seemed refreshing after the painkiller limbo.

McLaris rubbed the heavy stubble on his chin—about five days' worth—and wondered if he should attempt to shave, to make himself more presentable. He decided against it. He wanted to keep the beard: he didn't think he'd want to feel clean and slick for a long time. He stepped away from the bed, giddy and disoriented in the low lunar gravity. He looked toward the narrow slit window at ceiling height. A sudden memory sliced through him: *What star is that, Diddy?*

The voice in his memory echoed so clearly that he caught himself from turning to see if Jessie stood by him again.

McLaris had delighted in watching her learn things, in seeing the amazed look on her face when she discovered something new. She always wanted him to explain things to her.

Explain things such as how a competent division leader and a skilled pilot could manage to crash a shuttle and kill a little girl?

He heard someone else enter the room, but forced himself not to turn around. It was probably someone he didn't want to see anyway. He tried to catch a reflection in the window, but couldn't see the door from where he stood.

"Mr. McLaris, I am to inform you that Chief Administrator Tomkins wants to see you." The soft, controlled voice belonged to Kim Berenger. "Whenever you think you can face him."

For a moment, the name meant nothing to McLaris, but then he remembered—Philip Tomkins was the head of Clavius Base. Well, he had known it was going to happen sooner or later. He let out a long sigh.

"Dr. Berenger," he said, turning to face the woman. McLaris knew from his reflection how haggard he looked —the half-grown beard, the red eyes. "I was wondering if we might have some kind of—" he searched for a better word, a euphemism, "—service, for my daughter? And for Stephanie Garland?"

Berenger's face remained expressionless. "We decided it was unwise to wait for you to heal. Your daughter and the pilot were interred in a cairn outside after the first day. Chief Administrator Tomkins himself gave a little eulogy."

McLaris drew himself up in sudden anger. The doctor ignored him, instead acknowledging the medical record with her thumbprint. He fixed a haunted gaze at her. "You decided not to wait? What possible difference—"

"Dr. Tomkins insisted on holotaping the service for you. We can rig up a tank and let you watch it at your leisure."

McLaris made his way back to the bed, feeling like the wind had been knocked out of him. He collapsed on the sheets.

"I had reasons for what I did," he muttered.

Guilt rose up in front of him like a mirror, an echo chamber to reflect his thoughts back at him. *Yes, it's my fault. Yes, I killed my daughter.*

Each time he admitted it to himself, he thought the words louder, more forcefully. Reality began to eat its way through the haze of shock and disbelief. *Tomkins wants to see you. Whenever you think you can face him.*

McLaris knew how to handle his own problems. He needed a focus—something to work toward, some goal to achieve. With that as a crutch, he could see himself through this. He lay back on the sheets, the pain in his body insignificant compared to the pain in his mind.

Yes, it's my fault. Yes, I killed my daughter. But no, I didn't intend for it to happen. And, no, I didn't do it for selfish reasons. I did it with the best of intentions. For Jessie.

He would come out of this experience galvanized, a stronger person.

He would make it up to Jessie . . . somehow.

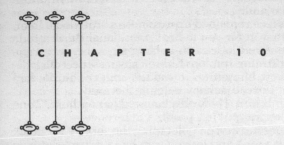

C H A P T E R   1 0

All the tension on the Soviet research station *Kibalchich* had been covered up with an artificial levity, a sense of camaraderie. They held an "end of the world" party to say good-bye to everything that had been lost on Earth—all their friends, all their pasts.

Commander Stepan Rurik leaned back against the wall in the rec room. People came up to talk to him, and he responded with as much interest and encouragement as he could muster. But he focused his attention on the group in general, trying to interpret how they would react.

A day from now all of them were going to leap over a cliff blindfolded, trusting in the skills of their biochemist, Anna Tripolk. They might as well be committing suicide.

Brilliant Anna, lovely Anna—she was so hard and so driven, completely focused on her own goal, and yet so naive about other things. That was part of her charm for Rurik.

Together, all the people had gathered to talk, to party, to

reminisce, to say good-bye to each other. They had drunk up all the remaining alcohol in the stores, then bottle after bottle of illegally brewed vodka and substitute dark beer.

Tired of standing by the walls, Commander Rurik strode out into the crowd, smiling and clapping his crew on the shoulders. He filled the room with his presence, his charisma. The party suddenly seemed sincere. Rurik had brought with him two dark bottles of brandy.

"Georgian brandy? How did you get that up here?" one of the women asked.

"Not Georgian brandy. Real French brandy." Rurik smiled and lowered his voice. "And don't worry about how I got it up here."

Pouring right and left with both bottles, Rurik offered tastes of his brandy until it was all gone—too quickly for most of the people.

As the alcohol seeped into their bodies, restraint dissolved away. After all, they didn't need to be in good shape for duty the next day.

The people began talking in louder voices, some growing brash and daring, saying things they had never risked speaking before. Some bemoaned the loss of the Grand Experiment of *glasnost* and *perestroika* and complained about the harsh backlash, but the Soviet return to conservative isolationism had never quite succeeded because the world economy was too tightly woven.

A few people scowled at the political criticisms, but Rurik knew what types of men and women they really were. He had pegged them long ago. They didn't worry him anymore.

The people sat around in small groups. One woman put on a disc of Stravinsky's *Firebird Suite*, booming the music into the conversation.

Off in a corner, some people compared snapshots in pocket holocubes; others swapped stories, argued over who had the most beautiful spouse or children. But each person looked terribly frightened, and trying to keep distracted from the fear—though it always seemed to keep coming back.

Anna Tripolk joined in conversations herself but drifted from group to group, as if unwilling to become too deeply involved. Rurik watched her, and she kept looking up to meet his eyes. She smiled, looking twenty years younger in a single flash. Anna felt for him, he knew, and he showed her all the affection he could. Rurik was certain he did not love her, though she did prove an interesting secret companion during the night periods.

Tripolk looked lost and empty away from her research. She couldn't seem to find the heart for the feigned cheer the others somehow managed. Rurik knew she felt more saddened at the loss of her life's work than from anything else.

Her life's work.

These last few weeks had destroyed most of their dreams, strained them to the breaking point.

The last coded orders had come up more than a week before, in the heat of battle, when Earth's house of cards was toppling down. The *Kibalchich*'s political officer, Cagarin, had insisted on viewing the orders with Rurik. And because of Cagarin's connections, Rurik could not turn him down.

"You must destroy *Orbitech 1*!" Cagarin kept harping on him, repeating the insane orders. "Or must I do it for you? My authority supersedes your own."

Rurik had had enough of the man. "You are just a minor administrative functionary. Your eleven cronies here are equally nondescript. Do not try to threaten me, Cagarin. Your basis for power has vanished like everything else. I am commander here!"

But Cagarin refused to play along. He raised his thick eyebrows. "Do you wish me to relieve you of your command?"

Rurik sighed, crossing his arms over his chest as if he were speaking to a misbehaving child. "The orders did not specify *when* I was to act. I plan to carry them out—but only when all the other people on the *Kibalchich* are out of the way."

He paused, staring at the other man. "Have you not thought what the others might do when they learn of the orders against *Orbitech 1?* These are scientists, not military troops! Would you like to watch them all revolt? You would bear the brunt of their anger, I fear." He raised an eyebrow, but Cagarin remained silent. "Give me time. It is too late for immediate vengeance. We will carry out the instructions, but when I say the time is right."

Cagarin thrust out his lips in a pouting expression. "I will remain awake with you."

Rurik made a condescending smile. "If that is the penance I must endure. . . . We are supposed to have two monitors anyway."

Now, at their end of the world party, six workers had gone to the zero-G command center at the hub of the *Kibalchich*'s torus. Inside, they had turned the largest external dish antenna toward Earth and begun making calls.

One of the communications engineers tapped into the microwave transmission bands, and together they spent hours trying to call friends they had known. No one answered. They called numbers at random. They laughed and drank and tried again, but the joke had worn thin by the time they finally broke through to a still-functioning recording in French. No one had the slightest idea what it said.

"Someone must still be alive! We know the War could not have been completely devastating."

Rurik answered tiredly, "The electromagnetic pulse from the detonations would be sufficient to destroy most communications substations. Perhaps the equipment is out of commission. But some will still be intact. Have faith."

They continued without success. None of the lines seemed to be working, or else no one felt like answering. "Just like the phone system back in Vladivostok!" one of the men muttered.

They proposed a toast to their commander, but found they had run out of things to drink. Bumping and floating, they made their way to the lift platforms that would carry them back out to the main torus. Rurik moved to follow them.

Turning back, he looked around the command center, where he spent so much of his time. A cylindrical holotank filled the center of the room, surrounding the station axis.

Switching off the vision recorder, Rurik recorded a terse warning in the holotank. In a day or so, when the station was quiet and deserted, he would broadcast the message to the three other colonies on their own ConComm channels, then he would shut down the unit on this end.

"We of the *Kibalchich* hereby sever all ties with other survivors on Earth's space colonies. Do not attempt to contact us; we wish to remain isolated."

It sounded childish and silly to Rurik, but he knew Cagarin would approve. It would keep the other colonies away for a while, at least, and it would give him time alone.

Plenty of time to do what he had to do.

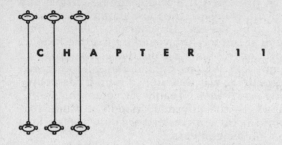

C H A P T E R   1 1

"All right, guys, this isn't going to be like working on *Orbitech 2*. Don't get cocky on me." Clifford E. Clancy surveyed the five space-suited engineers crowded in the base airlock chamber.

"Tomkins wants us to bring back everything that isn't welded to the *Miranda*'s hull. That includes the power pile, if it isn't too hot. We'll be taking both six-pack rovers out, so we've got plenty of room. Any questions?"

Clancy left his channels open, but waited only a beat. His people were never too shy to ask questions. They had worked well enough together on the massive *Orbitech 2* construction project.

"Okay, folks, let's go sightseeing." Clancy activated the airlock that opened out to the Moon's stark surface. A faint hiss indicated that the last of the trapped air had outgassed. Behind them, the mound that covered the base entrance looked like any other hillock in the lunar wasteland.

Clancy much preferred the broad, shining girders and massive wheel of *Orbitech 2*, the most glorious man-made object in the solar system. By contrast, Clavius Base seemed a bunch of tunnels for ground squirrels to hide in.

Clancy heard only breathing on the comm-links; he couldn't see any expressions behind the gold-mirrored faceplates. Something was definitely wrong if his people weren't ribbing each other. "Teamwork communication," he always called it—the informal, friendly attitude that turned them into a real team instead of a bunch of workers with the same job assignments.

He had thought that giving the crew a chance to go outside and get away from the base might let them work off some steam. Clancy himself wanted to see space again, even if it was only overhead and not the full 4 pi.

He could take only five out of the two hundred construction engineers transferred down from the L-4 site. But it gave at least some of his people a chance to do something worthwhile. And the salvage operation would provide a new story for the daily ConComm broadcast. The rest of the crew could watch and stop twiddling their thumbs for a while. After all, they were a construction team—not a bunch of "Lunatics" like the other Moon colonists.

Clancy began a low whistle into the comm-link, a tune his grandfather used to sing to him. After a faltering start, the others picked it up over the communication channels. *Hi ho, hi ho! It's off to work we go!* They even seemed to march along with the tune. Clancy allowed himself a grin. Silence broken. Mission accomplished.

Outside the base, Clancy led his salvage crew out onto the pressed gravel walkway. They followed the path to the two six-pack vehicles sitting on the fused-rock parking area. Stars wheeled overhead, burning with a brilliance that seemed enhanced against the heavy lunar shadows. Still nothing like the awesome drowning sensation of open space, though—here, the ground gave him a frame of reference.

Two weeks ago, they had been up sealing the framework of the second industrial colony, floating by themselves, watching blueprints turn into reality. And then they had all been ordered to return to Clavius Base, to cool their heels while Orbitechnologies Corporation and its consortium of European investors worked out the details to shuttle the crew home. With world tensions heating up, the main contractors thought it best to back away, to hold their breath and wait a few weeks. Clancy hated to see the big project brought to a standstill. He had kept everything close to schedule up until then. What did Earth politics have to do with the peace and silence of L-4?

He'd had a very narrow view of things before the War. Now *Orbitech 2* was going to be on hold for a lot longer than a few weeks.

Clancy sniffed inside his helmet. Dirty socks. *Why does this suit always smell like dirty socks?* No matter how much he cleaned, rubbed, and soaked the tape-wrapped phenolic, he couldn't get rid of the smell. It had never bothered him out in the "open air" at L-4, working and living in the suit eighteen hours every day of the week. A person could get used to nearly anything after that much time. But once he'd been stranded at Clavius Base with the rest of the engineers, he began to notice it.

At first he ignored the smell, trying to convince himself that it wasn't there, that he'd get used to it if he wore his suit more often. But it didn't work. Probably psychosomatic. And if he didn't watch out, somebody would send him to a shrink. Psychiatrists! He didn't trust scientists who couldn't give hard answers.

The gravel path swung hard to the right, bringing them out of the curtain of shadow and into sunlight. His visor darkened instantly, reflecting half of the unpolarized light away from his eyes. Suddenly, the shadows all around them looked like a bottomless black maw. He could read the fluorescent letters of the crew members' names across their chests.

"Homann and Wooster, come with me. The rest of you take the other six-pack and follow. Shen, you drive today."

"Right, boss man," she answered.

"There you go, Cliff, making points with the ladies again." Homann's Arabic accent was barely noticeable.

Shen snapped back, "Open your faceplate, Petey, and I'll give you a big fat kiss!"

The others snickered, and Clancy felt another thread of relief. Banter. He liked that they could tease each other. All of them knew they might never get off the lunar surface. Clavius Base could just about support itself with its five hundred permanent members; but with the extra two hundred engineers who had been unexpectedly recalled from *Orbitech 2*, the Moon base was in just as bad a situation as any of the Lagrange colonies.

One by one, they swung up into the lunar rovers, stepping onto the overinflated wheels. Clancy scooted into the driver's compartment in front of the passenger seats, three in front, three in back. Behind the passenger area a wide cargo platform made the vehicles look like old flatbed trucks created with giant Tinkertoys.

Homann and Wooster strapped into the seats behind Clancy. After the other three had climbed aboard the second six-pack, Clancy gave them a thumbs-up. "Ready to roll?"

Shen's voice came over the comm-link. "Lead on, Mac-Duff."

He reached down and pressed the starter. The rover shook, and Clancy let up on the regulator, easing the six-pack into motion. Like a child's overgrown play vehicle, it lurched around the boulders and sinks on the crater floor, heading out.

After they had left the low markings of Clavius Base behind and begun to work their way across the lunar surface, Clancy switched on the Doppler guidance system. He entered the coordinates for the crash site, then trusted the rover's computer-driven radar to take them there.

Across the great flat sea of the crater glinted the six-mile track of the railgun—the mass launcher that hurled lunar material to the collecting stations at L-2. Under normal circumstances, the rock would be routed off to its rendezvous at L-4 for smelter processing into construction material for *Orbitech 2*. During peak periods, the mass launcher operated continuously, throwing five buckets of rock per second away from the surface, accelerating the material above the Moon's escape velocity so that it would drift precisely toward the catchers in space.

Now, though, the mass driver looked empty and alone, an archaeological relic glinting against the deep-black sky. The single mass launcher had provided the material for all the colonies—*Orbitech 1*, the *Aguinaldo*, the Soviet *Kibalchich*, and most of *Orbitech 2*. Now everything had been mothballed. Before long, the delicate laser gyros and velocity regulators of the induction motors would lose their calibration, making the mass launcher useless.

As they left it behind, Clancy wondered if he should let some of his people work on the mass launcher, just for something to do. They might find it interesting—heck, he might even be interested himself.

He scanned the horizon, which always felt too close, with the Moon's radius being only a third of the Earth's. It all seemed wrong when it looked like you could throw a rock over the edge of the world. And because the horizon was so close, surface detail seemed to leap out at him, even at the guidance system's cautious speed.

A light blinked on the console. "This is it," he announced. "Shen, I've got it about two hundred yards in front of us."

"Can't see a thing but shadows," she answered.

"This is it. I remember."

Three days before, Clancy had pulled Duncan McLaris out of the *Miranda*'s wreckage. He had helped to chisel away Stephanie Garland's mangled and frozen-hard corpse from the cockpit. He had retrieved the body of McLaris's daughter inside her overlarge space suit.

It had been just dumb luck that the rovers had found the crashed shuttle-tug as soon as they had—in time to save McLaris before his own air ran out. Out on the broad and jumbled lunar surface, with its incredible shadows and too-bright sunlight, finding anything so small was difficult.

He saw a glint of reflected sunlight out of the corner of his eye and manually steered to the right. The six-pack bounced, jarring everyone in their seats as they made a straight line for the site. Shen followed in her rover.

When they grew close enough, Clancy flicked on a battery of flood lamps. The ruins of the *Miranda* stood like a haunted house in the rocky desolation.

Clancy spoke into the comm-link. "All right, everybody. Careful. I don't want to have to explain any stupid accidents to Tomkins. Homann, you and Wooster spiral out from the wreckage and comb the surface. Keep going until you're about a hundred yards away—I want to make sure we don't miss anything."

Who knows what we'll need if Clavius Base is going to survive?

Clancy slowed the rover to a halt several yards in front of the shuttle-tug. Twisted metal rose from the dusty lunar surface. Pencil-thin beams of graphite composite jutted from the craft, balanced weirdly in the low gravity. Crushed and shattered crystal covered a large patch on the ground, along with remnants of viewports, astrogator lenses, and infrared sensing equipment. Smears of light from the rover vehicles, along with glare from the Sun and draping pools of black shadows, made the scene look like an overexposed photograph.

Moving stiffly in his suit, Clancy climbed down from the six-pack and jumped the last few feet to the ground. He hit the crumbly surface and bounced another step toward the *Miranda*. The others moved after him like extras in some absurd water ballet.

Homann and Wooster bounded away from the six-pack with recklessly long strides. The Lunatics constantly nagged the engineering crew about the hazards of low-gravity jumping—how even with the lower gravity, they still had a full amount of inertia to deal with. All the workers had seen videos of what happened when faceplates cracked: burst eyeballs, ruptured blood vessels, the dark brown powder of blood streaming out of nostrils and ears, boiling and freezing at the same time, and the awful mummylike desiccation that set in before an hour passed.

But good people got tired of incessant warnings—safety was their own responsibility, and in the isolation at L-4, they knew the dangers of horseplay. They didn't need a mother hen.

Homann jumped too far, let out a distressed yelp at the apex of his flight, and landed unsteadily. A few Arabic expletives sputtered across the open comm-link channel, but he recovered himself. With a smile, Clancy noticed that the two men began to move about more carefully, spiraling away from the crashed shuttle-tug.

Clancy stood in front of the wreckage. The tug's outer hull had been split by the stress of the crash and twisted into three main sections. Clancy stared at it, imagined the shuttle the way it had been, picturing how all the pieces fit together. He rebuilt it in his mind, reconstructing the accident in reverse.

"Shen, take your team and start peeling everything off the outer structure. Some of the ceramic skin plates might be worthwhile, and the precision interlocks are more sophisticated than anything we can make here. Be sure to get the circuit boards in the navigation computers. Let me duck inside and make sure the structure'll hold up before you guys follow."

"Yes, sir." Shen's usual flippant comeback seemed to have been quelled by the sight of the mangled vessel. She had not been part of the initial rescue team.

Clancy picked his way through the ragged opening where he had found McLaris. He placed his hands on the jagged metal edge, careful not to damage his suit, then lifted himself into the craft.

Deep shadows filled the interior. The floodlights from the two six-packs could not reach inside; no atmosphere reflected the light. Only one of the self-illuminated indicator panels glowed, still showing ALARM status.

Through a gaping hole in the main viewing window, he could see a carpet of stars. From his backpack, Clancy removed two trouble lights and set them up, illuminating the chamber. Multiple glares bounced off the floor and walls, like luminous ghosts.

Clancy preferred open space and vast distances with nothing to get in the way. He liked to be able to look in every direction and see infinity. Isolated, the *Orbitech 2* site had seemed to hang at the center of the universe itself. But this place felt like a coffin.

He came to the spot where McLaris had been lying. A broken piece of sharp lunar rock jutted through the floor only a foot away. McLaris had been lucky.

Clancy squeezed through a crushed piece of the bulkhead and the floor. The trouble lights shone on a dry brown stain, darker than the gray lunar dust. Kneeling, Clancy ran his finger through the dry powder. He'd found Stephanie Garland there, as mangled as the *Miranda*. The captain always goes down with her ship, right?

But McLaris had lived. He had to cope with the death of his daughter. Clancy had seen the little girl's last expression, and he would be haunted by it for the rest of his life, but McLaris would have to live with his imagination, and the knowledge of what he had done.

Clancy had no children, not even a niece or sister back on Earth. He'd never wondered what it would be like to have a daughter who depended so totally upon him. Now, after thinking about what McLaris had done, he suspected that the parental instinct must place the rational mind into overdrive. He had seen mother cats jealously protect their kittens . . . and he thought he had read about birds sacrificing themselves to keep predators away from their young.

Still, Clancy found it difficult to imagine how even an overprotective father could have put his daughter into such a hazardous position. Either he was the most devoted parent, or the most abiding horse's ass, in human history.

As he started to stand, Clancy spotted a colorful object trapped under one of the back passenger seats. He had missed it before, but now he ducked under the hatch, squatted, and reached into the darkness. He groped around with his gloved hand, felt the object, and pulled it free.

He hauled it into the full glare of the trouble lights. It was a keyboard with a computer pack in the rear and light synthesizers on a plate on top—a child's musical instrument, undamaged.

Clancy ran his fingertips along the keys. A few streaks of light flashed across the top, but he heard no music . . . of course it would make no sound out in the vacuum, right? Gee, engineers were supposed to know these things.

He grinned at himself in the darkness, embarrassed. He thought he might want to fix the gadget once they got back in the pressurized environment. It might even still play.

Then he realized that it must have belonged to McLaris's daughter. She'd been playing with it during the long escape journey from *Orbitech 1.*

Clancy backed out of the compartment, carrying the instrument with him. On his way out, he banged the flat of his hand against several of the bulkheads to see if the structure felt solid. He brushed past dangling fiberoptic cables and stepped over debris on his way out.

The rest of the salvage crew swarmed over the wreckage, pulling out crushed equipment and prying away sections of the engines to place on the flatbed. Clancy's six-pack was starting to look like a junk truck.

Shen bounced up to him. "Everything all right inside? Can we go in?"

"Uh, yeah—just fine. Go ahead."

"Right." Shen reached out as if to take the musical instrument from him. "Here, I'll throw that on the flatbed if you want to supervise the rest of the team."

"No, I'll take it." Clancy was surprised by his sudden possessiveness. "Go ahead and keep an eye on them. We can't get too many people inside the *Miranda* anyway."

"Right, Doc." She turned and bounced away into the crossed headlight beams toward the shuttle-tug. Clancy made his way back to the rover and placed the instrument on the floor beside the driver's seat.

When Shen signaled for him to bring the flatbed over to the wreckage, he backed it to the north of the crash site. The others unstrapped the winch and crane. Shen and her crew lashed the rear of the six-pack to stakes driven deep into the lunar soil. Slowly, in a meticulous dance in the low gravity, they hoisted the heavy rocket motors onto the platform.

Later, with both rovers loaded, the vehicles lumbered back to Clavius Base. Clancy listened to the silence of his crew, smelled the dirty-sock odor in his suit.

He kept looking at the musical instrument he had found, wedged on the floor between his feet. He thought about McLaris and his terrible sacrifice—all for nothing. The man wasn't any better off here than he would have been on *Orbitech 1*. He couldn't understand what McLaris had been afraid of.

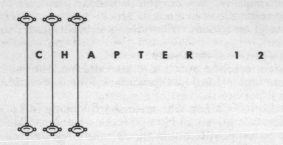

C H A P T E R   1 2

Most of the docking bay lights had been shut down, leaving the chamber in shadow. Curtis Brahms could still see the colored boundary lines painted on the metallic floor as landing guides for the shuttle-tugs. The doors of the six spoke-shaft elevators yawned open like caves.

Brahms gripped a handhold in the upper control bay, looking out the slanted plate glass windows. His reflection stared back at him at an odd angle from the tilted glass. He didn't look fresh and young anymore, not a freckle-faced, overtalented kid who had risen too fast for his own good. Now the bags under his eyes, the less-than-perfect set of his hair, hinted at what he had been through in the past nightmarish week. He had to get this over with.

Brahms scanned the panels, looking for the right switch. "That one." Linda Arnando, the division leader for Administration, pointed beside him, as if she knew what he was looking for.

"Thanks." A bank of concealed white fluorescent lights

lit up, reflecting off the silvery walls and floor. The wash of
light made the entire bay seem harsh and barren, a tomb
lit by probing searchlights. Brahms tried the switches to
the left, but they only activated the rotating magenta
warning lights. He shut them off quickly.

"We'll have to make sure those are disabled," he said.
Linda Arnando nodded and searched for an override
switch.

Brahms glanced at her. She was a hard-looking but attractive Hispanic woman in her mid-forties. Her long, dark
hair was peppered with gray, and the unsmiling I-am-all-
business expression made her seem older still. One of the
top five managers on *Orbitech 1*, Arnando was now dispro-
portionately more important to Brahms since Duncan
McLaris had deserted and Allen Terachyk had started
spending most of his time brooding. Even Ombalal had
surrendered, making little effort even to play the figurehead anymore. But at least he had shouldered his responsibility one last time.

He had made the tape for broadcast, though he had
refused to be present when Brahms played it.

In the control bay, Terachyk sat loosely buckled in a
chair. He had been silent, avoiding Brahms's gaze, his conversation, his questions. "I can't help with this, Curtis."
Terachyk's eyes looked shadowed and deep. "I refuse."

Brahms stiffened and turned to the other division
leader. "Find me another way, Allen—any other way—
and I'll do it. But if you can't help, then shut up."

Brahms had agonized for days, sweated blood, before
coming to the only conclusion. He was terrified he might
break down and change his mind even now, but that he
could not afford to do, not for the survival of *Orbitech 1*.
He didn't want Terachyk to resurrect any doubts. The fate
of the colony rested in his handling of the situation.
Brahms did not relish what he was about to do. But he also
did not want to lose Terachyk entirely. "I'm sorry, Allen.
It's just all the pressure, okay?"

Terachyk unbuckled and turned to leave.

"Allen, I really need your support right now. Ombalal
agreed to tape a message to the station, explaining his
reasons for the RIF." Terachyk raised an eyebrow at the
implication that the director had come up with the idea.

"But that won't help me here." Brahms clenched one fist, hiding it from Terachyk. Linda Arnando glanced at it, puzzled, but Brahms ignored her.

Terachyk hesitated, then pulled himself down again. "I won't help. And I won't watch."

There were a few seconds of silence, which seemed to last hours. Brahms bit his lip. "Okay, if you feel that strongly. I just want you here, that's all." He needed a show of stability right now, not dissent. If the division leaders appeared divided, weak, the other workers would fall on them like wolves.

Terachyk would get over it soon—they all would. Somehow, they had to pull *Orbitech 1* through this.

Brahms looked over the control panel again, trying to memorize every button, each switch. He didn't have much time—the hundred and fifty people would start arriving soon. Brahms knew he was procrastinating again. He needed to master only a few of the controls. All the switches worked now.

It had taken the electronics people two full days to fix the damage McLaris had done. Brahms stared at the shuttle bay. It was empty. The *Miranda* should have been secured—*right there!*—in the central docking area.

Brahms's stomach wrenched with the betrayal again. Somehow, McLaris had suspected what the associate director would decide to do. Somehow, he had known.

Brahms knew he was reacting irrationally, but he had never been stabbed in the back so viciously. He had clawed his own way up the success ladder, but he had fought *fairly*, according to the ethics of the managerial world.

Even the situation with Ombalal being the figurehead—Brahms respected the man's position, though he still made it clear that he, Curtis Brahms, called all the shots.

Yet McLaris had not fought according to the rules—he had allowed his emotions to get in the way. He had hurt everyone, for himself.

Brahms tried to tell himself that the loss of the *Miranda* made no real difference. The shuttle was only a symbol, an imaginary hope that could have no measurable effect on the lives of the fifteen hundred workers. They would still

be on borrowed time. The colony's situation would not be
improved.

The associate director gritted his teeth and clutched the
corner of the control panel. He stared at the white light
reflecting off the metal walls. It was bright, like his rage.
He closed his eyes, seeing Duncan McLaris in front of the
firing squad of his imagination.

He turned to Linda Arnando. She seemed preoccupied.
They were all jittery. In his chair, Allen Terachyk just
glared at them behind his black-rimmed eyeglasses.

Brahms found the intercom button on the panel and
contacted the two attendants at the bottom of the spoke-
shaft elevators. "Send them up."

The attendants acknowledged; they didn't know what
was going on. Nobody else did either—only the three in
the control room and Ombalal, but he didn't count anymore.

A few moments later, the first of the spoke-shaft elevators opened up and ten people pushed out, looking curious
but not afraid. Of course, what could they possibly be worried about? Brahms switched on the public address system.
His voice ran out into the empty docking bay.

"Just move out into the loading area. We've got a hundred and fifty people to come. Let's do this as quickly as we
can. Thanks."

*Yes, let's do this as quickly as we can. But the nightmares
will bother us for the rest of our lives.*

Even with the stress, Brahms kept a cool mask on his
face, a gentle tone in his voice. The workers would believe
him—the calm, benevolent associate director who could
somehow find a way to save them all. They depended on
him. Inside, his stomach turned.

Four women and six men emerged from the elevator.
Brahms recognized some of them, but couldn't attach
names to any. He didn't want to know who they were. He
dreaded the thought of assigning faces to any of the names
on the list. That would make them real to him, flesh and
blood. He might not be able to handle that.

"Keep sending them up," he said to the attendants.

When another load of ten disembarked, people started
to cluster in the empty bay. A few of them knew each

other. They all seemed baffled as to why they had been picked for this special event.

If they had enough sense, they could look around themselves and begin to figure it out. But mediocre workers were likely to fall into friendships with other mediocre workers, and none of them would dream that their performance didn't measure up to standards. Certainly not.

The Efficiency Study did not lie. Brahms had used objective criteria. The workers gathering now in the docking bay had come out at the bottom of the barrel. They had no one to blame but themselves.

But part of him insisted that they were people, nevertheless.

Brahms watched them until he had to turn away. Some of them looked up at him. And Terachyk's accusing expression seemed just as difficult to face. The people in the bay talked among themselves. Brahms switched off the PA system, sick at listening to their chatter.

"I wish I could find some other way," he repeated to Linda Arnando. "I really do." He realized he was beginning to whine. He sounded guilty, childish again. He could not afford that.

"I know," Arnando answered.

On the fifth load, Tim Drury floated out into the bay. Because the Maintenance Division leader was so fat, only six others fit in the elevator with him. Drury hung by the wall. Many of the others didn't seem to know who he was, but some took his presence as reassurance that one of *Orbitech 1*'s upper managers had joined them for the reception.

From above, Brahms stared at the obese division leader through the angled observation windows. Drury looked gray and damp, sickened. He moved slowly with his excessive girth, as if his joints pained him. Drury stared at the floor, jittery. Brahms felt his throat tighten, and he wished he had worn glasses, dark glasses, to hide his face. *He knows!*

Drury glanced up then, and their eyes met. Brahms felt his heart leap. He wanted to run away and hide, but he had to stand strong for *Orbitech 1*. He mouthed "I'm sorry," but Drury broke the gaze too quickly.

Brahms closed his eyes. He locked his feet around the

chair stem and softly pounded the side of the control panel with his fist. "Damn, damn, damn!" he whispered, over and over again.

According to the reports Brahms had received, only three people had declined his invitation and needed to be "escorted" by the guard team. They were the last to arrive on the elevators. Brahms did not give them a chance to worry the other workers when they emerged from the spoke-shaft doors, upset and indignant.

"Would you like us to come up as well?" the spoke-shaft attendant said, interrupting Brahms.

"No!" he said, faster than he could stifle the alarm in his voice.

"Okay. Everyone's up, then."

Arnando acknowledged for him. Brahms nodded to her briskly.

Arnando worked another set of controls. The four spoke-shaft doors pneumatically sealed into their jambs. With a muffled thump, heavy dead bolts shot into place, making the doors impenetrable.

Terachyk glared at her. Arnando turned away from him, aloof.

The people quieted, looking at each other and staring up at the observation windows from the control bay. Some floated up to Brahms's eye level, waiting. Brahms wanted it all to be over with. He wanted them to stop staring at him.

He had sent out a special invitation to all one hundred and fifty of them. It had been printed on formal, official stationery and marked "In Strict Confidence." Brahms had signed Ombalal's name to each one himself: *Come to the docking bay for a special announcement at precisely noon on the indicated date.*

But Drury knew!—and still he took his fate bravely. Brahms felt sick to his stomach. He had *had* to put one of his friends on the list, to make the effort sincere. Brahms had taken the lowest 10 percent of the population—those with the worst scores on the Efficiency Study, the least satisfactory performance. Tim Drury had missed that list— many others had done a poorer job than he had—but Brahms had needed to show his impartiality, his honest desire to remove the deadwood wherever he found it.

Besides, Drury was obese. He didn't necessarily eat any more than his share of food or move any slower than the others, but a fat man looked bad on a starving colony. All the factors had worked against him.

And if he had not needed Ombalal to pull this off, Brahms would have included his name as well.

He switched on the PA system and started playing the tape that would be heard throughout the station. Roha Ombalal's wooden voice boomed over the speakers. The people stared up at Brahms standing behind the plate glass observation windows. He saw all their faces. Many were expectant; some were skeptical. Only a few seemed angry or afraid. Two men hung only inches away from him in the weightless bay.

"Orbitechnology employees—could I have your attention please?" Ombalal's tape said. "You all know that *Orbitech 1* is not self-sufficient. We were not intended to be self-sufficient. We are a commercial venture in space. Long ago, during the planning stages, Orbitechnologies determined that providing the amount of area required to produce enough food to sustain us was not cost-effective.

"And so, the area that could have been dedicated to agriculture has instead been used for material production. You can figure out their philosophy—food can be grown on Earth, but the things we make here can only be made here. We have merely a token capability to provide for ourselves. Orbitechnologies assumed the exchange would be profitable. Understand, I am not condemning their motives—commercial profit is the reason we're up here in the first place."

The mingled faces in the crowd mesmerized Brahms, and his eyes felt gummy. He would never forget them. Linda Arnando handed him a plastic bag of water. He took a sip and swallowed, coating his throat, as Ombalal continued.

"That leaves us in a desperate situation. We have fifteen hundred people aboard *Orbitech 1.* With regular supply shuttles, this number can be sustained. But we no longer have those shuttles, as you well know. Because of the War, we are limited to our supplies on hand and to the small amounts of food we can grow ourselves. We cannot expect assistance from the other colonies. As you know from the regular ConComm broadcasts, they are in the same straits.

"It will take too much time to significantly increase our own food production. We don't have the resources, or the tools, or the experience. It boils down to this—we cannot possibly support the number of people we have. Given our current situation, our current population, we have less than four months left to live, even with strict rationing."

The people muttered at that. Some started crying. Brahms could see it all from the window. Hadn't they thought of this before? Were they still looking for the cavalry to come rescue them?

"Therefore, for the survival of the greatest number possible, I must propose a ten percent reduction in force—a RIF."

Linda Arnando stiffened beside him. Brahms swallowed. There it was—no taking it back now. Allen Terachyk appeared devastated and sickened. On the tape, even Ombalal paused.

Some people in the crowd didn't seem to understand, but Brahms saw Tim Drury drift against the wall, only to rebound. Tears welled in his eyes. *Oh, God, don't come over here!* Brahms didn't know what he would do if Drury came to face him on the other side of the glass. To look him in the eye, accuse him, stare at him. . . .

Ombalal's voice continued. "Before we were thrown into this situation, for reasons purely irrelevant now, our Associate Director, Curtis Brahms, conducted a thorough Efficiency Study of every single employee and family member on *Orbitech 1*. Now that we are faced with a ten percent reduction in personnel, I am forced to fall back on the results of that study.

"I have been obliged to pick the one hundred fifty people who scored lowest on that evaluation."

At last the workers knew why they had been summoned to the docking bay. One man grasped a handhold and pounded on the spoke-shaft elevator doors, but found them sealed and unresponsive. He shouted, kicking at the metal wall. Panic began to rise among the people. Tim Drury floated alone in the far upper corner, sobbing.

"Everyone deserves to live—but everyone won't live. We are faced with a crisis, and I contend that if only some of us can survive, then it must be our *best*—the best of the best. Random selection won't do that."

Brahms worked at the controls, initiating the countdown sequence for dumping the main airlock.

The alarm klaxon shrieked like a beast in pain. Brahms jumped, startled. A metallic voice spilled out from the PA system. "The airlock sequence has been activated. Please evacuate the chamber at once."

Arnando hammered at switches on the control panel. Brahms cursed himself—he had assumed that the warning horns were interlocked with the lights. The PA system fell silent again, but the hundred and fifty workers moved in complete panic. They tried to pull open the spoke-shaft elevators. Brahms thought they might crush each other.

Someone's thrown shoe thumped against the plate glass window; the frame didn't even vibrate. Brahms could see some of the people shouting and shaking fists at him, mouthing obscenities he could not hear. He did not want to switch on the PA system to listen to what they were calling him.

He was tempted to switch off the lights in the docking bay, to make the victims dark and faceless. He did not want to see them, did not want to watch their last moments of life.

But he had to—he owed it to them. He needed to make this action as difficult for himself as he could—such decisions should not come easy. His conscience demanded that he look into the faces of the people he was sacrificing.

Tears filled his eyes as the director's thin voice continued. Brahms doubted if anyone listened anymore.

"You will never know, nor do you care, I think, the depths of my own sorrow at having to do this. It is not fair. It is not just. But it is necessary. This is survival for your friends, your companions, perhaps some of your families. We will hold your memories sacred. You are truly martyrs for all mankind."

Brahms felt Linda Arnando put her hand on his shoulder.

He triggered the explosive bolts that opened the huge docking bay doors. The air rushed out like a hurricane, dragging everything with it. He thought he could hear a haunted collective scream of terror, of betrayal. He watched their faces, each one drowning in horror.

The hundred and fifty men and women of *Orbitech 1* swirled out into the black mouth of space.

Brahms pushed himself backward to his chair, missed the seat, and continued to the cubicle wall. He shook violently, as if in the grip of a seizure. He knew they had only passed into the eye of the storm.

Allen Terachyk threw up in the rear of the control room. Globules of vomit sprayed throughout the air.

But, eyes closed, Brahms felt a strength growing in him —a white-hot steel band, newly forged.

He had done it. He had found the strength. He had accomplished what needed to be done.

Next time, he thought, *it will be easier. It has to get easier than this.*

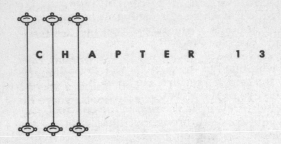

CHAPTER 13

AGUINALDO ■ DAY 11

The orbits displayed on the holoscreen made no sense to Luis Sandovaal, but he wasn't going to admit that to anybody. He cracked his knuckles and leaned back in his seat. He understood little about celestial mechanics, but enough not to believe it when something was supposedly "impossible." Besides, once he knew even a little about a subject, it was easy to convince others that he was an expert.

Plodding along and optimizing its own parameters, Sandovaal's computer model had found a way to send his wall-kelp to the other colonies, using only the magic of gravity. His kelp would save the lives of thousands. President Magsaysay would like that. But Sandovaal had to understand the orbital principles enough so that he'd seem knowledgeable when he made the proposal to the Council. The next meeting would be within the hour.

Orbits, ellipses, perturbations, a slow-moving tug-of-war with gravity . . . he had difficulty conceptualizing the rules. He wondered if this was how other people felt about

biology and genetics. But then, everybody had genetics
inside them. Sandovaal's distinctive pale hair and blue
eyes set in a round Filipino face had caused his own fascination with the subject.

The son of a Danish diplomat and a Filipino woman, Luis
Sandovaal had grown up in the expansive diplomatic
household of his grandfather. They had found a special
exemption to get Luis into the embassy schools, where he
studied voraciously—especially the natural sciences.
Later, the old Danish ambassador had arranged for his
grandson to study at Cambridge.

Luis's mother had pulled him aside the day before he
had boarded the Philippine Airways flight from Manila to
London, begging him not to desert the Islands forever, to
come back with what he had learned.

Sandovaal logged off the computer and made his way
out of the lab complex, onto the *Aguinaldo*'s main floor
level. Sandovaal pressed a taxicall by the stairs and waited
for one of the electric carts to find him. His thumbprint
would trigger a priority call and ensure a speedy dispatch.

Above him, children played in the zero-G core, squirting
compressed-air out of cans to maneuver themselves. A sail-
creature nymph and an older boy played a game of crack-
the-whip. Sandovaal squinted, then snorted to himself. *The
Barrera boy—Ramis,* he thought. *Always up to something
dangerous.* Ramis flew past the nymph until the rope grew
taut, then snapped them both about. With the colony's
crisis, President Magsaysay had been far too busy to keep a
close watch on his foster son.

The taxi's arrival startled Sandovaal from his thoughts.
He climbed in, directed it to the main Council chambers,
then craned his neck to look out the taxi's wire-mesh window. Ramis and the sail-creature nymph still frolicked in
the core. An old woman slowly made her way along the
axis on a pedal-kite. Other nymphs guarded the children
playing in the core, as they had been conditioned to do.

Like sheepdogs. . . .

Years ago the colony animals had accepted the wall-kelp as
a substitute feed, once it had been dried and processed.
Sandovaal and Dobo Daeng, along with the technicians
who had replaced Agpalo and Panay Barrera, worked on

the next step in their experiments. Sandovaal had been stifled on Earth, unable to get permission to do some of his research because it was too unorthodox, and therefore considered "risky." Here on the *Aguinaldo,* the Filipinos trusted his judgment.

Sandovaal expanded on the technique of gene grafting he had developed for the wall-kelp. At times he felt like a Filipino Frankenstein; at other times he conceived of himself as a chromosomal gourmet chef.

Most of the time the recipe failed. The failures usually died immediately, but some survived into the embryonic stage. Only rarely did a hideously distorted patchwork "thing" manage to grow to maturity.

Then they succeeded in creating the first proto-creature —robust and strong, featureless. The creature had both mitochondria and chloroplasts within its cell walls—it was plant and animal. Somehow, everything had worked exactly right—everything fit together, everything functioned as it should.

Sandovaal would never admit that it had been an accident.

Dobo kept staring at the proto-creature with wide eyes, astonished. The other assistants crowded around.

"It is still a plant, so it functions as a plant. It needs nutrients, sunlight, water." Sandovaal felt smug. "We grew its lungs and digestive system, but they were superfluous. Like our appendix: everyone has one, but it serves no purpose. A baby can be perfectly happy in the womb, unaware of its lungs, until we take it away from the mother and force it to breathe the open air."

"Mother Marie, it is a miracle, I think," Dobo whispered.

Sandovaal made a rude sound. "Since when does a thousand trials, breaking your back for months and months, qualify as a miracle? We did not create life, Dobo, we just rearranged it."

Sandovaal thought of what Magsaysay had said a year before, and smiled to himself.

Sheepdogs!

The twenty senators were settling into their seats in the Council chamber when Sandovaal strode in. He knew they did not expect him, which would heighten the effect. The senator from Leyte—a thin woman who needed the simplest things explained to her several times—scowled at his intrusion.

Magsaysay sat up straight and blinked his large eyes, then smiled. "Welcome, Luis. Feel free to join us."

"I have learned something important. As your chief scientist I am required to point it out—" He stopped. Sitting cross-legged in a chair against the back wall was the Barrera boy.

Sandovaal blinked in surprise. Only minutes before, Ramis had been playing with the sail-creature nymph up in the core. Sandovaal's taxi had encountered only the typical delays—how could the boy have gotten here so fast? Had he somehow directed the nymph where he wanted to go?

"Yes, Luis?" Magsaysay said, raising his eyebrows.

Sandovaal turned back to the Council members, trying to mesmerize them with his bright blue eyes. They would survive, thanks to him. And he was about to pull another rabbit out of his hat.

"You asked me to see if we could somehow help the other colonies—get wall-kelp to the lunar base and to the American Orbitechnology colony. You must decide if we should assist the Soviet *Kibalchich* as well. If they had a nexus of the wall-kelp, the other colonies would be able to grow their own supply. They would survive. But we have no rockets, no shuttles. How will we launch these packages to them?"

Sandovaal went to the display holotank in the center of the chamber, activated it, then logged on. He accessed the files he had just been viewing in his laboratory, and displayed the results. The Moon, the Earth, and the Lagrange points appeared on the screen.

"The concept is simple, and the celestial mechanics models say it will work. You will have to discuss details with one of our orbital specialists, but I am confident we have the ability among our distinguished engineers and physicists to implement my idea." He scanned the senators' faces again. Ramis stared at the tank, fascinated.

Sandovaal tapped his fingernail on the glass in front of the display. "Reaching the Moon is relatively simple. We can, in effect, just toss the wall-kelp there. We can sling a

ORBIT:
L-4 TO MOON
with tether assist

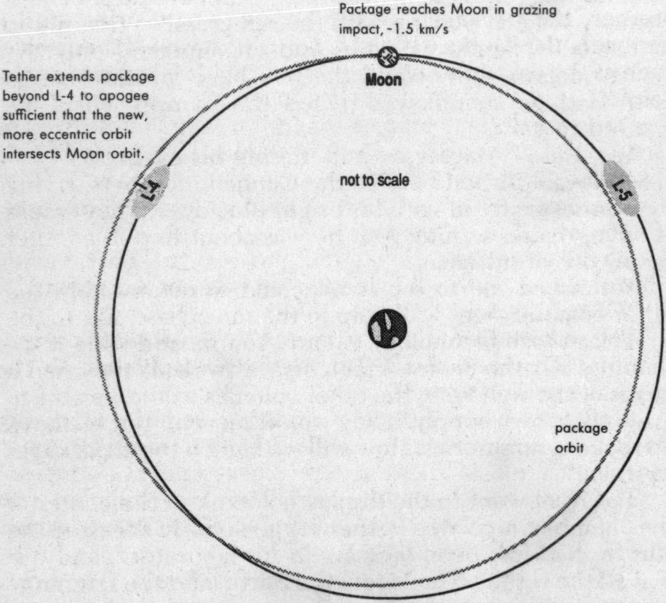

Package reaches Moon in grazing
impact, ~1.5 km/s

Moon

Tether extends package
beyond L-4 to apogee
sufficient that the new,
more eccentric orbit
intersects Moon orbit.

L-4

L-5

not to scale

package
orbit

package there by attaching it to the end of a tether. According to the diagram, if we make the tether long enough and reel the package away from the *Aguinaldo,* then the package and our colony will be in different orbits."

He worked with the keyboard on the podium and animated the display. "If you think about it, the concept is clear." He flashed a glance at the thin senator from Leyte. "The length of the tether determines the package's orbit. We can calculate an orbit that will intersect the Moon's and adjust the tether's length to match it. Once we release the tether, the package will travel in the new orbit until it impacts the Moon. Think of children slinging themselves across the core, playing crack-the-whip. It is the same principle.

"It is possible to impact the Moon with a velocity less than one kilometer a second. If we package the wall-kelp properly, it should be able to survive the shock."

Sandovaal smiled at them, satisfied. "My results are open to confirmation, of course."

Magsaysay stood and clapped his hands. "That is wonderful, Luis! My confidence in you was not misplaced."

"Of course not."

The senator from Leyte stood up. "Why all these complications, Dr. Sandovaal? Can we not simply launch the package at the Moon?"

Sandovaal raised his eyebrows and gave her a withering look. "Madam, we are trying to deliver a fragile package, not shoot a missile that will strike the ground like a bullet!"

The *dato* seated himself again. The other senators nodded and smiled. The senator from Leyte muttered something and sat down as well.

"Reaching L-5 will be much more difficult." He didn't want them to get complacent.

Ramis spoke from his seat. He studied the curves on the holotank, taking no notice of the others in the chamber. "How will you get there?"

Sandovaal raised his eyebrows at the interruption. Magsaysay waved Ramis into silence, but waited for Sandovaal to answer the question.

He turned to the group. "Conceptually, we could use the same technique, I suppose. But with the Moon we have an entire planetary body as a target. Given the right parameters, it is not a challenge to get there. The Lagrange well is more subtle, though, and the colony itself is so small we cannot expect to hit it. The uncertainties are too great."

Magsaysay pressed his fingertips together, overlapping his long nails. "And your solution?"

"We will have to guide the package, of course—deliver it ourselves."

The other senators muttered. The senator from Cebu raised his hand. "How do you propose this, Luis?" Magsaysay said, ignoring the senator's question.

Sandovaal smiled. Now it was time for his gamble.

"Given an optimum orbit, which I am certain our mathematicians can provide, ten days should be enough for a sail-creature to travel from here to *Orbitech 1*." He changed the image in the holotank to recordings taken years ago of the first sail-creatures, their gossamer wings stretching kilometers across as they were slowly swept away by the solar wind.

Ramis sat up abruptly. The other senators fell silent as they watched the pictures; the senator from Cebu put his head down on the table. Magsaysay opened and closed his mouth several times, but no words came out.

"And how will we steer the sail-creature as it rides the solar wind, you ask?" Sandovaal continued. "Our experiments showed that even after its drastic physical rearrangement, the creature's body core is still responsive to stimuli. An irritation at the right spot will cause the creature to reorient its sails."

Sandovaal closed his eyes and drew in a long breath. In his mind he could picture a sail-creature tacking from one Lagrange point to another.

The president finally found his words again. "A *sail-creature*? Steered by remote control? I am still trying to grasp the idea."

"No, we do not have the proper equipment to achieve that." Sandovaal averted his eyes, but he kept his face calm, confident. This was the part Magsaysay would object to the most.

"Someone must ride along. Inside."

Sandovaal cringed at the Council's outcry, but he shouted his explanation above their noise.

"You must listen! With the correct injection of hor-mones, we can create a cavity inside the sail-creature's body core—a cyst or a blister, a place for someone to ride. This person can then irritate the sail-creature's inner membrane and reorient the sails. The rider would have to be small. We could then fill most of the cavity with wall-kelp, perhaps even some sail-creature embryos."

Magsaysay stood up, looking angry. The chamber qui-eted. "I am afraid we cannot accept this proposal, Luis."

"Then you are condemning the Americans to death. You asked me to find a way. I have found one. It is up to you to implement it."

The *dato* shook his head. "But who would volunteer for a mission that could only lead to certain death?"

"Myself! Who better—"

Magsaysay dismissed the idea with a wave. "Have you lost your mind, Luis? You are too valuable to us. Even if your sail-creature managed to get to the other colony, how would the rider ever return to the *Aguinaldo*?"

The Council members sat in silence as the reality sank in. Sandovaal kept his gaze locked on Magsaysay's. "I can-not give you a solution without risks."

The president nodded slowly to himself. "We will begin work on your tether idea. That sounds feasible. Perhaps we will not be able to help the American L-5 colony after all."

A young voice rang out. "I volunteer."

Magsaysay leaned forward, startled. Sandovaal grinned.

Ramis Barrera stood up straight and pushed away from his chair. He was small for his age, but his eyes held an intensity that Sandovaal had not noticed before.

"I volunteer to ride the sail-creature."

Magsaysay motioned for the boy to sit down, as if in dismissal. Ramis remained standing, with his hands clenched at his side. The Council looked stunned. The *dato* frowned. "Ramis, this journey is not a game."

"I am well aware of the consequences." Ramis stared at his guardian defiantly. The senators stirred at his tone. "You must realize it, Father—I am the only person quali-fied to undertake this trip. Dr. Sandovaal just said that the rider must be small and light. An adult will be too large to go. And I know the creatures better than any of you. In-cluding you, Dr. Sandovaal."

Sandovaal growled.

Ramis looked at each of the Council members in turn. "You all know that I am best qualified for the trip."

Magsaysay shook his head, stunned. "You are still just a boy—"

Sandovaal felt angry. He knew the boy was right. Besides, Ramis was always doing crazy stunts like this, especially since his parents had died. "You cannot call him a boy, Yoli. Ramis is of age—sixteen, I believe. By the *Aguinaldo*'s own laws he is old enough to vote, old enough to attend Council meetings."

"Luis—" Magsaysay's eyes seemed haunted.

"Look at him." Sandovaal held out an arm to Ramis. "He is an expert in zero-G gymnastics. Everyone knows about his nighttime acrobatics in the core. Do you wish to deny the best-qualified person on the *Aguinaldo* his right to go? Think! It could be our only chance to save all those people." He knew that tactic would work best against Magsaysay.

Sandovaal breathed heavily, his nostrils flaring. The Council members watched the two men. Ramis stood unflinching, as if in the eye of the storm.

Sandovaal spoke again in a quieter tone. "You must not allow your feelings for Ramis to keep thousands from living, Yoli. Agpalo and Panay Barrera would have wanted it this way. I knew them well. They would not have stopped their son. Your son."

Magsaysay's shoulders slumped. He looked suddenly older than the seventy-five years he carried. The colony's low gravity had been kind to him, keeping age at arm's length. But the thought of Ramis leaving seemed to bury him.

Seconds passed; no one spoke.

The *dato* straightened. "Dr. Sandovaal, I accept your conclusions and direct the following actions: your tether idea to send wall-kelp to Clavius Base will receive the utmost priority. Your research team will also prepare one of the sail-creatures for a journey to our sister Lagrange point. As chief scientist, you will have all the resources of the *Aguinaldo* at your disposal."

Magsaysay lowered his eyes, his voice barely audible as he turned to the rear door of the chamber. He avoided looking at Ramis. "For now, I wish to be alone. The special Council meeting is adjourned."

C H A P T E R   1 4

CLAVIUS BASE ■ DAY 11

His slippers scritched on the polished rock floor as he made
his way from the infirmary. McLaris had decided not to
don a Clavius Base uniform. He still wore his robe, still
brandished his bandages, hoping to divert some of the
anger of the other base inhabitants.

Sharp pains stabbed his side from the cracked ribs. His
eyes were puffed red, and his beard had grown to a rough
stubble. All of him ached, but that was a sign of healing.

Dr. Berenger had declared McLaris fit enough to walk
about, and McLaris had decided it was best not to avoid
the issue any longer. He had to face the chief administrator
of Clavius Base.

McLaris knew virtually nothing about Philip Tomkins,
except that he'd been running the lunar base for several
years. He had contacted Tomkins, who had said he'd be
delighted to chat and had given him directions to the communications center.

McLaris decided he'd make no mention of his injuries,

try not to show that he was aware of them at all. He didn't want to come across as looking for sympathy. But neither did he want to appear completely unscathed by the crash.

Fluorescent lights glinted off the lumpy fused rock of the walls. The air smelled damp and dusty, cavelike. He saw no windows, only occasional narrow slits at eye level. He thought the lunar tunnels would get oppressive after a while.

He didn't know what Tomkins and the others would do. Would they sentence him? Punish him? Would Tomkins himself be the judge and jury? Had the chief administrator already made up his mind? Everyone else on Clavius Base seemed convinced of McLaris's worthlessness.

But he walked straight, keeping his face set. He had spent days wallowing in guilt, reliving what he should have done and what he had done. He'd passed through that now, though. He felt tempered, stronger.

McLaris regretted his actions. He was guilty—no question about it. But he couldn't take it back, couldn't return the *Miranda*. He could only move forward, changed, and hope that he could work his way back to acceptance.

McLaris paused at the communications center doorway, took a deep breath, then entered the room without announcing himself. Three large holotanks protruded from the white tile walls. A pair of technicians argued over data flashing in the units; another lounged back and spoke to her computer with her eyes closed. A long, narrow window ran at eye level along the far wall.

Beside the window stood a big-boned black man with his back to the door, staring out onto the lunar surface. Philip Tomkins: McLaris recognized him from a picture he'd seen.

"Excuse me, Dr. Tomkins. I'm Duncan McLaris—" He tried to speak calmly, businesslike, but his vocal cords clenched so that no sound came out until the third syllable. He forced himself not to clear his throat—that would seem a nervous gesture.

Tomkins turned around. The chief administrator was heavily built, a massive man. He looked as if he had been well-muscled once but had slacked off his exercise routine in the Moon's low gravity, allowing himself to soften. His skin was a warm chocolate brown, smooth, with wrinkles around his eyes and throat. His tight, woolly hair was thinning, scattered with white and trimmed close to his head. He looked to be in his early sixties.

Tomkins nodded toward the technicians, who had stopped when McLaris spoke. "Why don't you three take a break? Thanks."

McLaris felt the technicians staring as they left the room, but he refused to look at them. Tomkins was the one who mattered here.

Now he was alone with Tomkins, but he could not guess what the chief administrator intended to do. He felt tense, wary, expecting something terrible. *Go on, get it over with!*

He pictured Tomkins pronouncing sentence, condemning him to be executed for crimes against humanity. They would take him outside in a suit, march him across the flatlands to the middle of the crater, tell him to kneel down. He would bend to his knees in the loose rock and powder, not feeling it in his padded suit. He would look up at the deep pool of stars one last time, and then someone would ritually bash open his faceplate with a club. . . .

"So, Mr. McLaris,—" Tomkins stared at him, "about this business of stealing the *Miranda*. That was rather a selfish and ill-advised thing for you to do, don't you think? On a par with one man in a lifeboat drinking all the water when everyone else is asleep." His voice was rich and well controlled, as if from a lifetime of speaking in large auditoriums.

McLaris tried to keep his expression from changing. He wanted to cringe, confess his guilt, beg for forgiveness. He forced himself to count to five before he answered, to make his voice steady.

"My daughter has already paid the price for my selfishness. So has Stephanie Garland." He swallowed, but found he couldn't wait any longer to ask. "What are you going to do to me? Saying I'm sorry just won't—"

"You're going to be punished, of course," Tomkins interrupted. McLaris felt cold.

"You are not going to get a free ride—no lounging around some padded cell, wasting your time watching the holos. I'm going to make you pay, put you to work." He paused. "From now on, you are going to do some of my tedious administrative duties. Input the daily logs, study work force and resource allocation sheets. Deathly boring stuff. Worse than working on an assembly line."

McLaris blinked at the administrator. It all seemed so absurd. "That's it?"

"It's been punishment for me—I can't stand doing those things."

The chief administrator turned back to stare out the narrow window at the tread-marked lunar dust. He sounded tired. "Mr. McLaris, if I ordered your death, what would that accomplish? What good would it do? The difference between human beings and machines is that we learn from our mistakes."

Tomkins extended a large hand toward McLaris. "Welcome to Clavius Base."

McLaris walked carefully forward and gripped the administrator's hand, feeling as if his own would be swallowed up in the other man's broad palm. His first impulse was to be intimidated, but as he watched Tomkins move and talk, he picked up subtle hints. The chief administrator looked massive but gentle, and he was not as comfortable as he tried to appear.

"Besides, I'm afraid you've been vindicated. You can now say 'I told you so' and have people believe you."

McLaris felt an ice ball forming in the pit of his stomach. "What do you mean?"

Tomkins closed his eyes and spoke without looking at anything. "On *Orbitech 1* your director, Roha Ombalal, just ejected a hundred and fifty people out of the airlock. Ten percent of the population. He called it a reduction in force."

McLaris sat down, blinking hot tears from his eyes. "Ombalal doesn't have the spine to do something like that. Brahms was behind it." He hung his head. "Now do you see why I had to get my daughter out of there?"

"I didn't ask you for any explanations, Mr. McLaris. Our official response was outrage. We broadcast a direct communiqué to *Orbitech 1,* breaking off all contact."

McLaris couldn't seem to focus on what Tomkins was saying, or why it mattered. "What good is that going to do?"

Tomkins looked flustered. "Since we're completely cut

off from each other anyway, there aren't a lot of things we *can* do. Think of it as a symbolic gesture."

Tomkins motioned for McLaris to join him at one of the tables. He walked to a wall unit and came back carrying two steaming cups, then shoved equipment aside to make room on the tabletop. "Tea," he explained. "No nutritional value, but we can manufacture the water and synthesize the flavoring. More substantial food is in shorter supply, I'm afraid." He took a sip, slurping on the edge of the cup.

"At least there's no shortage of personnel—not with two hundred extra construction people from *Orbitech 2*. I'm keeping everyone at low physical activity to reduce caloric consumption. I don't know how much good that'll do."

The chief administrator set down his tea, stood, and paced back and forth. Tomkins seemed starved for conversation, and McLaris let him speak. Tomkins had a faraway look in his eyes.

"I wanted to attend the Air Force Academy and be an astronaut—my father worked for NASA at Langley—but I was too tall. Six foot ten. Silly reason, huh? Instead, I went to the Hampton Institute and studied astrophysics. I got here eventually, though. Been chief administrator three years now."

Tomkins turned his gaze away, staring into the rising steam from his tea. "But I'm no administrator, Mr. McLaris. We don't have a genuine manager on this entire base—we're all scientists. My passion is radio astronomy, not red tape and paperwork."

McLaris sighed, sensing what the man needed. "Please call me Duncan. I'd like you to."

Tomkins walked back over to the narrow window in two long strides. Tapping his fingers on the thick glass, he indicated the shadowed surface of the crater's basin.

"Do you know what Arecibo is, Duncan? The radio telescope in Puerto Rico? It's the largest single radio telescope in the world, laid down in a perfect bowl-shaped valley. You don't find many natural locations like that, so radio astronomy spends most of its effort on aperture synthesis, adding up the signals from an array of smaller dishes instead of a single big antenna."

Tomkins's voice took on a tone of delight. "But look out there! All those craters, hundreds of kilometers across, perfectly round. Think of how easy it would be to construct mankind's most magnificent radio telescope—just a little excavation on the crater floor, then lay down wire mesh that we can make here, attach some receivers . . . it would be so simple! So glorious. I'd call it Arecibo II or something appropriate."

McLaris wondered at the man's priorities: cut off from Earth, two hundred extra people on his base, food in short supply—how could Tomkins dream about building a new telescope? McLaris kept his face carefully neutral.

The chief administrator returned to sit at the table again. He slurped his tea. "Ah, but that project is put on permanent hold now, I suppose, because of the damn War. Why can't politicians ever think with a broader perspective?"

Tomkins touched McLaris's arm. "Come here—I've been compiling all the snippets from the War. Since we're run by the U.N., Clavius Base keeps close watch on all events on Earth—we always have. We can filter through some of the confusion, since we've got a good perspective here—a view from a height, you might say."

He went to one of the computer consoles, then indicated the main holotank set into the white-tiled wall. The tank was tuned to ConComm. Tomkins pursed his lips and spoke to the computer. "Assemble hyperstack. Header: The War, in serial." He shrugged apologetically at McLaris. "Couldn't think of a better title."

The tank blinked once, then focused on laserfax transmissions of various news reports. Tomkins pointed to a geopolitical world map shimmering in the tank.

"Someday, if mankind ever has historians again, they'll go back and find all the preliminary influences. Remember the MacKenzie Treaties? Those wonderful days of *glasnost*, before the backlash? The U.S. gave up its expensive space-based weapons systems, then cut just as much money on conventional forces."

Tomkins flicked from one photo to another, skimming past story after story so rapidly that McLaris could do no more than glean highlights.

"What we didn't know was that the U.S. had deployed its super-Excalibur pop-up defensive weapons anyway. Nuclear-driven x-ray lasers—one of their 'black' programs.

Now they can say it was justified, I suppose. The Soviets had also publicly claimed to be giving up space-based weaponry, as they armed their space platforms in secret. Disguised as polar-orbiting 'scientific research stations,' of all things!"

Tomkins snorted. "But you can't hide a space-based laser while you're using it. We've got actual footage from the War, computer enhanced."

The chief administrator talked the way a child would at show-and-tell—like Jessie trying to explain things to other children. McLaris felt a twinge of grief.

"Up until about a week before the outbreak, the squab-blings between the United States and the Soviet Union bubbled along as they always had. But the discovery of a well-entrenched Soviet battalion in the Turkish foothills outraged the U.S., and all Soviet officials were expelled from Washington."

Tomkins frowned. "Since Orbitechnologies Corporation was going to allow some Soviet production work to take place on *Orbitech 2*, the U.S. pressured the company to withdraw all construction engineers and delay completion of the station. All two hundred men and women from L-4 were brought back down here for a few days. Supposedly, they were going to be shipped home, but I honestly think it was just a bluff."

Tomkins showed some videotapes of the transports landing, all the construction people disembarking and finding cramped quarters on the base.

"So, Clavius Base suddenly had seven hundred people instead of five hundred. The construction crew brought some supplies, but most of their stores are still sitting at L-4, totally out of reach. Remember what I said about them expecting to go right back? Makes you wonder, doesn't it?"

Tomkins grew philosophical, running his fingers along his chin as he spoke. "It's all political games—everything working according to murky rules that nobody seems to understand."

The chief administrator looked like a storyteller at a camp fire. A grainy satellite photograph showed a blasted urban area: buildings had toppled, fires burned from gird-ers and trees, but the skyline in the distance appeared to be undamaged. McLaris thought he recognized Washington, D.C.

"Then a wild card was played and blew the game all to hell. A terrorist built a crude nuclear device and detonated it in an apartment building less than two miles from the White House. The weapon barely worked, but he still wiped out a good section of urban Washington and contaminated a portion of Maryland and Virginia. Both the president and the vice president were killed in the blast.

"But that's not all of it. In his transmission just before the detonation, the terrorist claimed to be doing this to free the world from . . . let's see," Tomkins flipped through screen after screen until he froze on a transcript. " 'From American democratic oppression, to pave the way for a peaceful and equal communist world.' "

McLaris stared at the picture of ground zero.

"Who knows if the Soviets put the terrorist up to that or not? It sounds stupid to me. It seems more likely that some Third World country backed him, just to implicate the Soviets."

The chief administrator shrugged. "As you can probably guess, the first things shot down were the Earth-orbiting stations. Since nobody knew which ones contained weapons, every Soviet 'research station,' every U.S. spacelab module and shuttle, the ESA space station, the *Heinlein*, even most of the big communications satellites—all went down."

McLaris thought about the Soviet station sharing the L-5 point with *Orbitech 1*. "What about the *Kibalchich*? We haven't heard anything from them."

"As far as we can tell, they played no active part in the War, but the L-5 colonies are too far away to be in a strategic position. Your own colony would have been the prime target if they did have any weapons, I suppose. But we haven't received any word from them except to keep the hell away. They aren't participating in ConComm with the rest of the colonies."

Tomkins looked pensive again. "We are now citizens of Clavius Base and will likely die here. The old political boundaries were wiped out in the nuclear exchange." He blanked the holotank.

"We don't know the current situation on Earth. Most of

its communications capability is gone. We've got a few reports from amateurs, other broadcasts we picked up from scattered sources, but the puzzle has plenty of pieces missing. Even though it was only a limited exchange, we think the War may cause the deaths of about sixty percent of Earth's population—that includes indirect deaths from long-term fallout. There's no way to guess the fatalities that'll result from starvation, lack of medical care, and housing.

"We can be certain the industrial base is effectively gone. All manufacturing has been knocked to its knees, and what's left will no doubt be used exclusively for survival of the remaining people. The Earth has been knocked back into the nineteenth century: no electricity, clean drinking water, sewage treatment, or local communications."

The chief administrator squeezed McLaris's shoulder with a massive hand. "You realized it before anyone else, Duncan. You knew it immediately. Earth can't possibly afford the technological effort to come up and rescue us. And with all those casualties in the War, how can the people left down there worry about a few thousand of us left stranded in space? No, our numbers are already written in their books. We're on our own." Tomkins bumped his plastic teacup, knocking it over. He scrambled to pick it up, but the cup was empty anyway.

In his mind, McLaris ran over the scenario. It wasn't a role-playing game, it wasn't a newsreel from World War II —it had actually happened to him, to everyone. Diane had been down there, in the middle of it.

He felt his calm expression melt away like candle wax, and he jerked his head around so that Tomkins would not see. Under the table he clenched his fist, trying to squeeze out some of his tension.

Orbitech 1 had discarded 10 percent of its people.

After an awkward pause Tomkins stood up. "Why don't you get some more rest? After you're all healed, come back to me. I've got some things you can help me with."

The two men shook hands again before McLaris turned to leave. His slippers scritched on the polished floor as he shuffled back down the corridors toward the infirmary.

C H A P T E R   1 5

ORBITECH 1 ■ DAY 12

He had always considered himself a benevolent director.

He cared for the people on *Orbitech 1*. Roha Ombalal went to see them; he listened to their concerns; he wanted them to think of him as a gentle leader, a "papa" for them all.

For more than a full day, though, he had isolated himself in his quarters, shivering, having nightmares about the reduction in force. He made sure his porthole remained sealed, terrified that accusing corpses would drift by and stare at him through the quartz. He kept seeing a finger—Brahms's finger, but it might as well have been his own—pushing the explosive release button, over and over again.

Ombalal had made the tape. The entire colony had heard him explain the reasons, give the order. He wondered what his wife would think of him now.

What would she tell his two girls, his precious children? Ombalal stood in front of the mirror, trying to wipe away the horrified look on his face. His deep black hair seemed to have more silver strands in just the last few hours.

But he couldn't hide any longer. He was the director of *Orbitech 1*. He had to show the people he still cared, he still thought of them. He had had to make a horrible, difficult decision . . . but sometimes even a "papa" was faced with painful choices like this.

A part of him cursed Curtis Brahms for forcing him to act so quickly. Brahms had been persuasive—and he did hold the ultimate authority, according to the Orbitechnologies Corporation. But no matter how much sense the RIF decision might have made, Ombalal hated Brahms for making him select that course of action. Now there could never be any turning back.

Ombalal dressed in his formal uniform with the insignia of *Orbitech 1* at his breast. The people would remember all the good things he had done, all the times he had chatted with them, kept his door open for anyone.

They would forgive him.

His throat felt dry. His hands were shaking. But he drew himself up with dignity. He would earn their respect.

In cafeteria complex five, people had already started muttering before Roha Ombalal entered. *Orbitech 1* had begun rationing immediately after the War; but this was their first day on further restricted rations. They stared at the small quantities of food as the fear sank in that they would get no more than this for a full day. The server stood behind the line, looking harried and frightened. Beside him stood one of the security men, but he looked just as disgruntled. They had been taking the brunt of the complaints, Ombalal realized. He felt sorry for both of them, but they would all have to deal with hard times from now until . . . whenever.

At least the people would survive, though—those who had died in the RIF had not made their sacrifice in vain.

When Ombalal stepped into the cafeteria complex, the temperature in the room seemed to drop.

Conversations stopped. Faces turned toward him with expressions molded into bleak despair or vengeful anger. Suddenly Ombalal felt a thread of fear, which he tried to push away. These were his people; he had been among them for years. But he had lost all their names—he couldn't remember any of them! They seemed completely faceless, strangers to him.

Ombalal looked around. He drew himself up. His voice was soft. He meant it to be consoling, but instead it came out like the words of a frightened rabbit.

"I . . . I cannot tell you how sorry I am for the decision I have been forced to make. We must all stick together. Things will get better. I pray I never need to order such a thing again."

It was the wrong thing to say.

Out of the corner of his eye he saw someone move. A plastic beverage container bounced off his shoulder blade.

"Stop!" Everyone stood still for just a moment.

Then a woman stood at the table in front of him and dumped her tray of steaming beef-flavored noodles into his face. Ombalal let out a cry of pain and brushed them away from his eyes. All the while, he wanted to shout, *Don't waste food like this!*

A third person threw another beverage container, which struck him on the side of his head. He heard shouts. Where was the security man? Why didn't he stop them?

But when Ombalal looked up, he saw the man standing with narrowed eyes and his arms crossed in front of his chest.

"Please—" he said, then choked.

Someone hit him on the temple with a serving tray. Ombalal fell to his knees. Astonishment reared up in him so fully that he had no room for fear.

He heard more shouting. Fists began pummeling him. He heard only the voices, felt the pain—he saw no faces. Part of him imagined that they were the faces of those hundred and fifty people he had ejected out the airlock.

In his mind, he watched himself give the order.

This was what it cost him. Ombalal squeezed his eyes shut and tried to keep from whimpering. The fight in him drained away. With a hand over his head to fend off the blows, he cried how sorry he was, over and over.

From behind the counter, the serving man brought out a tray of knives.

* * *

Curtis Brahms sat in his own office with the door sealed, allowing absolutely no one to enter. Outside he had stationed two guards, but he didn't necessarily trust them, either.

He squeezed his eyes shut and saw the bright light of anger inside him. Roha Ombalal was so stupid! How could a man manage to live for so many years and understand so little of human nature? Even after the RIF, he had still considered all the people on *Orbitech 1* to be One Big Happy Family. Idiot!

Not that Brahms condoned what they had done to him, but in a way, Ombalal had asked for it. When you do stupid things in space, the universe makes sure to punish you for it!

Brahms had sat in anger for longer than an hour after the riot. Everything was falling apart—the chief administrator of Clavius Base had issued a pretentious statement, breaking all contact with *Orbitech 1*. In an apparently unrelated move, the Soviets on the *Kibalchich* had ceased all transmissions, leaving only a warning that they were not to be disturbed. The last centers of civilization seemed to be disintegrating.

Brahms couldn't afford to remain silent anymore. He needed to stop even a hint of mutiny. *Orbitech 1* was his station now.

He activated the intercom, speaking simultaneously with the security crew and the maintenance staff. "I want cafeteria complex five scrubbed clean, all traces of the disturbance removed. But first, I want every square inch of the place documented. Lots of graphic stuff." He drew in a deep breath, forcing back the anger.

"I want to show the blood. I want to show these people—everyone on this station—what they have done!"

Brahms snapped off the intercom, but continued grinding his teeth together, thinking of the people, the simmering mob, on his own station.

He realized that was the part that concerned him—keeping the people under control—since he was now the true director of *Orbitech 1*. No longer did he have to pander to Ombalal's incompetence just to save face for the Orbitechnologies Corporation.

Another part of him, a tiny but insistent voice, kept Brahms wondering if that's what he had really wanted all along.

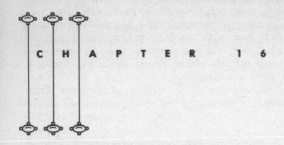

C H A P T E R 1 6

All the reckless I-won't-care-until-tomorrow singing had stopped. Anna Tripolk wondered if she would ever hear it again. The others stood silent now, shifting uneasily. A few of them broke into forced jokes or flat conversation, but that quickly petered out. Tripolk smelled a haze of nervous sweat in the *Kibalchich*'s recycled air.

The big lab space had been converted into a giant infirmary and medical center. At another time, a better time, they had done delicate engineering work here—precision laser applications. None of that mattered anymore.

Tripolk raised her eyes as the line moved forward. *Standing in line again,* she thought. *Even to the end, we must stand in line for everything.* High above in the curved ceiling of the research station, she could look through the slitted windows. The suspended saucerlike mirror hung over the rotating torus of the *Kibalchich* like a giant silver dinner plate. The two lower decks were lit by yellowish artificial light, but Rurik had decided that this was best done in sunlight. Tripolk agreed with him.

The station's walls were metal, cold, sterile—fabricated from Moon rock, but with no concessions made for the appearance of comfort. All the rooms had been enameled a dreary eggshell white—walls, floors, ceilings, doors. It hurt the eyes after a while.

A few months ago, one of the other researchers, Danskoy, had painted a broad mural along one wall in the recreation hall. It broke up the *Kibalchich*'s monotony in a startling way.

Danskoy had been sent home soon afterward. Tripolk couldn't figure out how anybody Earthside had learned of it.

As the next man in line stepped forward, Tripolk took another clean syringe and filled it with the vile-looking yellow chemical. She smoothed her doctor's uniform, tried to look professional and strong. She, of all people, had to show confidence now. The testing phase had ended; this was for real.

Tripolk didn't want to look at the man shuffling up, but she did anyway. He had mouse-brown hair, cut too short to be attractive; two days' growth of beard bristled on his chin. A week before, that lack of attention to personal hygiene would never have been tolerated.

A name patch sewn to the man's uniform said *Sheveremsky*. Tripolk had never bothered to learn the names of all five hundred people on the *Kibalchich*. She could have done it, of course, but it had not seemed a necessary effort . . . and her own work kept her busy enough.

Tripolk started to say something inane, something encouraging, out of habit, but the man cut her off. "Just get it over with. No speeches." Sheveremsky stared at her. "We all know what we are doing."

Tripolk clenched her teeth, resenting Sheveremsky's attitude. Did he think she enjoyed this? The Party wasn't paying her a bonus for it. It was nothing she wanted to do. She hated to be pushed into such a desperate situation. But this was their only hope, and necessary things had to be done.

"What do you want me to say, then?" She held the syringe in her hand and locked her eyes with Sheveremsky's.

"Do you want me to say everything will be all right? Yes? So—everything will be all right. Now, give me your arm."

She grasped his bicep and jabbed the needle into his arm. Deep behind the man's eyes, Tripolk could see a startled wince, but the man himself did not cringe.

The next person came up, a thin woman, silent and looking very frightened. Tripolk gave her the injection.

At the other end of the wide, echoing room, several people looked groggy and disoriented—the first visible effects of the drug. A team of de facto orderlies wheeled them out of the room before they could grow cold and still.

More workers came and went, each receiving an injection, not daring to let pride slip while in the presence of comrades.

Tripolk looked down at the medical cart beside her. She had known of a slaughterhouse just south of Moscow; as a child she had often thought of the lines of animals marching in ignorance to their deaths, trusting and unconcerned. Now, the *Kibalchich* seemed like that slaughterhouse to her: lines of workers in the vast infirmary, waiting for a pinprick to send them off on a single hopeless chance.

On the supply cart, she saw so many vials left, so many people. A film of tears flashed across her eyes and she looked down, not daring to meet anyone's gaze. She drew a deep breath and tried to burn the moisture away with determination.

As the hours ticked by, the numbers of people in the infirmary room diminished. She knew this was going to require more than a day. She and two assistants had been working without a break, but the strain was growing. Tripolk found her hands shaking. The large chamber began to take on a funereal air.

When a tech named Orvinskad went into convulsions after receiving the injection, Tripolk found herself startled and scared. *That was not supposed to happen,* she thought. *It is supposed to be peaceful and painless.* But considering the circumstances, how pushed to the edge they all were, there were bound to be surprises.

Two men wrestled Orvinskad to the ground and held him still until the seizure left him drained and motionless. They hauled him out. After a few nervous moments, the remaining people fell into an uneasy quiet again, and shuffled forward to face Tripolk's needle. She wished they would start singing again.

The war on Earth had put an abrupt end to her project, her life's work. It had vanished, never to be completed. Tripolk felt like a starving man who'd had a fine roasted chicken snatched out of his grasp.

ARES 2 would be indefinitely postponed now. Tripolk might never see cosmonauts land on Mars. She had wanted to watch the live transmissions, to shake her fist in triumph and know that she, Anna Tripolk, had helped her people get there. But not anymore. Patriotic accomplishments for the pride and glory of the Soviet people had fallen by the wayside.

Mars—how she longed to go there. But that would never happen.

The first Soviet manned Mars mission, ARES 1, had been launched seven years previously, before Tripolk had become involved with the program. But that first mission had ended in disaster.

Though the flight time was long, Soviet cosmonauts had spent many times that duration alone in orbit in their own stations. No one expected the isolation to be a factor. But when the small crew of ARES 1 had reached interplanetary space, they had crumbled.

It seemed that in an Earth-orbiting station or in one of the Lagrange colonies, people still had a sense of perspective, a feeling of home. They could look out the window and see the Earth sitting there in space, filling a huge portion of their view. They could still see the Moon, accompanying them.

But in the deep space between Earth and Mars, the cosmonauts had no such landmark. Earth shrank to a bright blue-green light, with the Moon a much smaller dot beside it. Mars itself was only a reddish disk. Even the Sun itself grew smaller, while the blackness of space grew bigger. Everything seemed a yawning ocean of vacuum, infinity itself staring them in the face—with no place they could go to get away from it all.

Transmissions had grown sporadic and baffling, hard to interpret. The ARES 1 crew had severed communication. The captain's final transmission, accompanied by nervous laughter from her crew mates, had said that they were abandoning their ship. . . .

But the Soviet Union still needed to put a manned mission on Mars—for their own glory, for international prestige. It was mankind's next logical step, and the United States had never bothered even to make the attempt. The Soviet people would be the ones to push forward, to take that step.

Tripolk, a biophysicist, had thrown herself at the task. Somehow, the trip to Mars had to be shortened—either the distance, the actual flight time, or the time perceived by the cosmonauts. The mission planners could not screen candidates for the disorientation and pick psychologically stronger crew members; that held too few guarantees.

Tripolk had made great progress in the suspended animation process. She had found a workable solution, and had developed almost everything they needed. Only a few tests remained to prove its feasibility.

And then the War had put an end to everything.

Now, fewer and fewer people remained in the infirmary room. They came, Tripolk gave them an injection, and other workers took them out to the waiting area. *Waiting area*, she thought ironically. *What a ridiculously poetic way to think of it. We are going to be waiting a long time.*

Tripolk realized with a kind of uneasy horror that she was doing this mechanically, by rote. Doing this to people, to human beings, had become run-of-the-mill? She was not even certain it would work for all of them! She tried to swallow, but her throat was too dry. She drew a deep breath, and motioned for the next man to come forward.

Only seven remained now—herself, Commander Rurik, the political officer, Cagarin, and the four men who had acted as orderlies to cart away the groggy and listless men and women. Her assistants had given each other the injection an hour before and were now resting quietly, she hoped.

"Should we all go off to the big room now?" Rurik suggested.

Grekov, a big Ossetian—like Stalin—stood up. His hair was thick and full, but even so, his head looked too small for his broad shoulders. "If you please, Commander, Doctor," he said in his heavily accented voice, "I don't want to see them all . . . there. I would like mine here. Please."

He thrust his arm toward Tripolk. The doctor gathered up the remaining ampoules, filled a hypodermic needle, and as gently as she could, injected Grekov.

"How long will it take for me to feel it?"

"It is different for everyone." Tripolk shrugged. "You can feel it as soon as you want to. Don't worry."

Rurik paced back and forth. "Thank you all for what you have done. You are being very brave."

Tripolk admired him more than ever before. She didn't know how Rurik could be so stoic, so optimistic even now.

"Shall we go?" Rurik stood up, took a deep breath, and marched toward the door. Tripolk gathered the four remaining hypodermic needles and looked at the mess she had left behind—wrappers, empty ampoules, discarded needles, the stained and dirty cart. Cleaning up didn't matter. In years, when the next generation of Soviet survivors finally made it back to the cold and silent *Kibalchich*, they would have to take Tripolk to task for the poor housekeeping. For now, she wouldn't let it bother her rest. It was easier to think of it like that. Perhaps Rurik would clean it up or, better yet, he would have Cagarin do so.

Rurik and Cagarin each draped one of Grekov's arms around their shoulders and helped the Ossetian walk out of the empty infirmary room. Tripolk followed, flanked by the remaining two orderlies.

They walked down the wide, barren-looking corridor. Overhead, the fluted windows let sunlight and starlight in. Many of the louvers had already been closed, scaling down the *Kibalchich* for its dormancy. The station was already looking like a tomb.

Rurik and Cagarin were going to be very lonely and very bored. They didn't even seem to like each other in the first place. Anna Tripolk wished Rurik had allowed *her* to remain with him.

Down the hall they reached the other main lab room. The doors were propped open into their sockets, but the inside of the room had been dimmed to thick shadows. Tripolk felt thankful for that at least. The orderlies themselves had perhaps been spooked from looking at all the bodies lined row upon row, each in its neat enclosure.

Rurik and Cagarin carefully laid Grekov's body inside one of the empty cubicles, straightened his arms and legs, then inserted another needle into each brachial artery.

The two orderlies looked around themselves uneasily, then pulled crucifixes from their jumpsuits. Rurik glanced at them, but said nothing and turned away. Cagarin scowled and seemed about to snap at them, but Rurik grabbed his arm. Tripolk could see how hard he squeezed.

Tripolk removed her three hypodermic needles and looked at them in odd fascination. She blinked. "Are you ready?"

Sullenly, the first man put away his crucifix, then bared his arm. The other received his injection as well, and they went to lie down in their glass compartments. Tripolk waited for them to grow somewhat groggy, then hooked up the artificial circulatory system, jabbing needles inside their elbows.

Cagarin scowled and walked out, leaving Tripolk and Commander Rurik alone.

Tripolk had one hypodermic needle left, for herself. "You will take care of everything else?"

Rurik squeezed her shoulder. "You know I will."

"And there is no way I can talk you into joining us?"

The commander pressed his lips together and shook his head. "Later. It must be later. You know that two of us must remain to watch the station."

"But why Cagarin?" she asked, unable to suppress a whine in her voice. "Why not me?"

"He is the one I chose." Rurik refused to raise his voice, which upset Tripolk.

"Are you sure you're not just being a coward?" Tripolk surprised herself with this comment, and realized that she didn't mean it—she was just trying to provoke Rurik into changing his mind.

"Anna. Let us not debate who is making the bravest choice. The answer is not clear-cut. I do what I must, and you do what you must. Only the future will tell how we are all remembered . . . if we are remembered at all."

Rurik smiled a little, as if trying to lighten the air. "Without me, you would be the acting commander of this station."

Tripolk forced a smile of her own. "And without me, you

would be in charge of a station without a purpose!" She dropped her voice to a whisper. "Mars was so close."

Rurik pursed his lips. "Anna, the *Kibalchich* has strategic uses beyond mere scientific research. That point has not been lost on the military or State Security. You know as well as I that some of our 'assistants' are KGB."

She smirked, annoyed to hear the reactionary paranoia she had encountered so often, but never from Rurik. "You and Cagarin will have to go under. There aren't enough supplies to last even the two of you."

"Enough for a while," Rurik said.

"Not long enough."

"Enough . . . for a while."

Tripolk stared at the long silver point of the last hypodermic needle, then turned her head away. She injected herself with the yellow drug.

She had stepped across the line now. No turning back. Onward, ever onward—even to this. She couldn't call for help.

Her body began to feel as if it were turning to ice water, flowing away from her brain stem. She felt dissociated, apart from it and drifting. Her arms and legs flopped listlessly, like mannequins' limbs.

Rurik gently helped her to lie down in the glass-walled cubicle. He smiled down at her. "I saved one bottle of brandy for myself. Tonight I will drink a toast to you— without Cagarin."

"Thank you," Tripolk managed to whisper. She found it hard to move her lips.

Rurik reached down and brushed a strand of hair away from her forehead. "Yes. No need to worry. Everything will be all right."

Yes, she thought, *everything will be all right.* It would take years and years for anyone to come up and find them. She wondered what it would be like.

Her vision began to grow black and she couldn't tell if she had closed her eyes or not. With a twitch, she moved her arm and bumped the smooth glass wall of the cubicle. *At least I'll have a coffin if anything goes wrong.*

Then the cold of space seemed to reach through her veins, through her limbs, and into her heart.

Maybe she would dream about Mars.

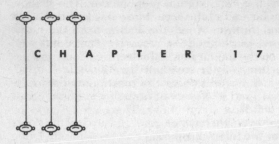

C H A P T E R 1 7

AGUINALDO ■ DAY 13

The crystal observation blister opened to the *Aguinaldo*'s exterior. Stars wheeled overhead, making a complete circuit every ten minutes as the colony rotated.

Standing on the translucent, segmented floor of the blister, Ramis kept his attention on the view below him, trying to stay out of Dr. Sandovaal's way. He felt as if he were in one of the glass-bottomed boats a man had used back in the P.I. to take tourists around on the inlets.

Sandovaal fidgeted like an overeager child. Ramis held his breath as the scientist touched a finger to one of the micro-earphones on his head.

"They say everything is ready, Yoli."

Magsaysay nodded, hands behind his back. "Tell them to proceed." Sandovaal snapped an order into the transmitter. Magsaysay had let him command the mission, since the tether idea had been his and since it would keep him from complaining.

Ramis splayed his fingers on the crystal viewport, trying

to peer down the long edge of the cylinder. The shadow shield on the far end of the *Aguinaldo* blocked the harsh solar radiation. Smears of light, reflected from the Earth and the Moon, splashed off the smooth external hull, but most of the colony lay in black shadow.

Ten kilometers away he could see the *Aguinaldo*'s opposite end drop off. Scattered glints of metal a hundred kilometers distant marked the construction site of the giant wheel of *Orbitech 2.*

From his perspective he could not see the docking doors swing open or the team of suited engineers drift out. Dobo was supposedly directing operations down in the docking area. Ramis suspected that the engineers knew what they were doing, and he hoped Dobo wasn't just getting in the way.

The other people clustered by the transparent ring around the end cap had a better view, but Ramis preferred to be with Magsaysay and Sandovaal, in the heart of things.

The viewport veranda remained quiet as they waited. He forced himself to be patient. Ramis knew how long it took for people in clumsy maneuvering suits to complete a simple task.

He caught a glimmer out of the corner of his eye. He paused a moment to make sure, then pointed it out to Magsaysay. "I can see the package of wall-kelp, and one of the suits, I think." He squinted. "The tether is too narrow to make out."

Sandovaal ducked his head down to Ramis's level. Ramis refused to move, but the scientist did not seem to notice. He pressed his finger against the pane, indicating where a glimmer crept into view. In the dim Earthlight, Ramis found it difficult to see the compact package drifting deeper into space, reeling out from the *Aguinaldo.*

Sandovaal moved to one of the joysticks controlling the exterior-mounted telescopes. "Come on, slowly now . . ." he muttered to himself. He located the package with the telescope and focused the image on the console's inlaid holoscreen. Sandovaal squinted at the package, down at his timepiece, then at the package again before he jabbed at the transmitter. "Dobo—tell them they are playing the cable out too fast! Slow down or it will rebound!"

"Is the cable going to break?" Ramis asked.

Sandovaal scowled. "The engineers assure us it can take the strain. It is tape-wrapped carbon something-or-other. But they are playing it out too quickly, I think. If the wall-kelp reaches the end of the tether, it will rebound back to the *Aguinaldo*."

Ramis doubted the small package striking the docking end would do much damage—but they would miss a chance to send food to the lunar colony.

"I am sure they know what they are doing, Luis," Magsaysay said, then tugged on his lip. "Though the backlash could kill somebody."

Sandovaal blinked into the telescope. "Yes. Yes, it very well could."

The president paced across the veranda and stared out the wide window plates. "It looks as if the package is slowing down."

The wall-kelp crept away until they could no longer resolve the dim point of light against the grainy background of stars. Ramis joined Sandovaal at the holoscreen.

Sandovaal muttered, "Nineteen point eight eight three kilometers—not quite twice the length of the colony. It is trivial distance compared to the size of the orbits here. But the tether length must be exact, and that will bring my kelp to the Moon. Amazing subject, celestial mechanics—like witchcraft."

Magsaysay turned from the window plate and smiled at Ramis with a look of satisfied relief. "We have already informed Dr. Tomkins at Clavius Base over the ConComm network. He is a bit skeptical, but anxious to try it."

"And it will give us a chance to see how the wall-kelp fares in a planetary environment." Sandovaal transmitted again to Dobo in the docking bay, double-checking everything.

After more than an hour, all of the cable had been reeled out. Dobo informed them that the tether was taut, holding the package twenty kilometers away from the colony by means of a small compressed-air container.

Sandovaal fondled the transmitter button. "We will wait a moment to be sure the tether has stabilized. We have a rather large time window, if the initial orbital trajectory is correct."

"It is correct on this end, Dr. Sandovaal," Dobo's voice

answered. "But if we wait too long, the cable could stretch."

"I will not wait too long." Sandovaal pursed his lips. He looked at Magsaysay.

Magsaysay closed his eyes as if in prayer, then nodded. "Send it to them, Luis."

Sandovaal turned back to the radio and gave the order. A charge severed the other end of the cable from the *Aguinaldo*, and the bobbin and cable were ejected from the bay. If it had remained secured to the colony, the twenty kilometers of cable would have gained angular momentum from the *Aguinaldo's* rotation, turning the tether into a corkscrewing whip.

Ramis could see no change in the package, but over the next few hours it would drift away as the wall-kelp and the L-4 point continued along different orbits.

"In two weeks, the Moon will have a new food source." Sandovaal looked pleased with himself. "Dobo, tell the engineers they can finish up now. Make sure the doors are sealed properly. We can do no more now—only wait. It is in the hands of God . . . and the laws of physics."

"I will ask the bishop to say a special prayer at Mass," Dobo replied over the speakers.

Magsaysay looked out to where he could no longer see the tiny package of wall-kelp. "Do you think we just saved the people of Clavius Base, Luis?"

"We have given them a better chance. They must save themselves."

Ramis cracked his knuckles. "When are we going to help the Orbitech colony? They are probably in more serious trouble."

"We have not heard from them in several days—they claim trouble with ConComm," Magsaysay answered, avoiding Ramis's question. "And we must also think about the Soviets—if I can convince the Council of Twenty to extend goodwill."

Sandovaal switched off the holotank and used controls to retract the external telescopes into their casings. "Getting to L-5 is a much more difficult problem. We must use an exotic orbit, swing around the Earth. But we must first grow the sail-creature outside the *Aguinaldo*. You should order the preparations to begin soon."

Magsaysay set his mouth, making lines stand out in his dark skin. His gaze drifted out the observation window, focused on infinity. He seemed to be avoiding Ramis, who sat holding his breath.

Magsaysay spoke without turning. His knuckles were white against the window. "Luis, you are forcing me to use Ramis."

Sandovaal grunted. "I am trying to send food to save fifteen hundred people. If anyone can accomplish this mission, the boy can. We will make it as safe as possible for him."

Silence, then, "Very well. You and Dobo do what you must. Prepare one of the sail-creature nymphs." He closed his eyes, then looked directly at Ramis. He seemed to be pronouncing a death sentence, no matter how much Ramis wanted to go. "And I am very sorry, Ramis."

C H A P T E R   1 8

O R B I T E C H   1 ■   DAY 14

The mass spectrometer did not give the results she wanted. Karen Langelier felt tears of frustration brim in her eyelids. It was so difficult to work in fear.

After five years of testing and development, the weavewire she had developed at the Center for High-Technology Materials proved a growing success. Indestructible garments woven from the monomolecular fiber had just started to gain popularity before the War, first in protective clothing and then in expensive items of high fashion. It had nearly unlimited potential: surgical knives, new types of construction and engineering, materials processing. But drawing the weavewire out a few kilometers a day in their precious L-5 industrial complex was not economically feasible for Orbitechnologies Corp. Karen had been sent up to *Orbitech 1* only a few months before to work on a scheme for accelerating the extraction process. In theory, the weavewire should be able to form along its laser guide beam as fast as molecules could react.

In theory.

Karen felt frantic with pressure to perform. Perhaps the spinneret had been too small this time. Her hands had been shaking during the attempt.

In her anger, she tossed the Pyrex flask across the lab. It tumbled end over end, striking the curved wall and ricocheting back. The specimen hardened into a lump inside the flask. Karen scowled at it. *Give me the right answer, dammit!* Her thoughts brimmed with hysteria. *Do what you're supposed to do!*

Polymer research in zero gravity had so little history that everything was new. When a technique worked, they tried every variation, attempting to improve the process, or at least to understand it.

The complex had been a bustling outpost, with dozens of other chemistry team members working at their own brainstormed experiments. The laboratory bay contained imaginative apparatus with odd adaptations for zero-G: heating units were self-enclosed and mechanically stirred, since convection did not occur; gas-jet burners had been supplanted by high-intensity electrical-resistance heating units—without gravity, open flames remained spherical and extinguished themselves from lack of oxygen.

But the lab cubicles were without friendly banter after the RIF. Two of the testing stations stood painfully empty. A few of the other researchers looked up at Karen's outburst and watched, but most kept working.

Primary researchers and their assistants sweated over their own projects, as if they could bring them to fruition by sheer force of will. Others, like Karen, worked independently, hoping for that one breakthrough, whatever it was, that might turn things around.

Everything will work out the way it's supposed to, Karen thought to herself. It had always sounded good to her before. *But what if it doesn't work out?*

She swallowed back her fear, pretending not to look affected. It would work next time. She would just try again. She needed to make a significant breakthrough.

Nobody competed for Nobel prizes anymore—this time, the reward was simple survival. And Curtis Brahms was the only judge.

Brahms had suggested they all work together, to cooperate more than ever. But Karen knew the teams would prefer to tear each other apart, gladiators in a scientific coliseum, squirming to climb on top and give themselves a few more moments of survival.

And only two weeks had passed since the War. What would they do when things began to get worse, much worse?

She thought again of Ombalal's RIF—a hundred and fifty people dead, without warning. She had been in her quarters, reading *Soviet Physics JEPT* online, when the announcement had come over the PA system.

Ombalal's words were slow and precise, as if he was reading from a prepared statement. It took a few moments for her to realize exactly what he was *saying*. Nobody questioned the orders of the director . . . why should they? Karen remembered dimming the light, switching off her book, and lying back in bed as she listened to the growing horror.

Her mind filled in all the details, over and over again, as she scrambled to a viewport, wondering if she even wanted to look. She had caught a glimpse of frozen bodies drifting along with the station, and her imagination showed their faces fixed in a scream, bloated and petrified in the frozen vacuum.

Everything will work out the way it's supposed to.

Karen gave Ombalal credit for the resolution to admit his actions, rather than let rumors go wild. Viewed through cold logic, the way he presented his case, Ombalal had perfect justification for doing it, too. Karen wasn't that cold—but she wouldn't want to be in his place.

She had stood in the hall beside two other people and watched the low-res holotank announcement of Ombalal's death. Brahms did not seem comfortable in the transmission, and kept moving from side to side, out of the best-focus zone.

"I want you all to see what you have done." Brahms's face dissolved into the awful images of the blood-spattered cafeteria complex and Ombalal's body. "We are supposed to be civilized. We are supposed to be human beings—*not animals!*" A hint of horror seeped into his voice, but he spoke with absolute conviction.

"I have looked through the personnel files and selected a

group of 'Watchers' who will supplement our minimal security force, since our security has proven itself inadequate. They will also assist in implementing new rationing schemes.

"It is not a measure I enjoy taking, but this appalling episode of violence has made it necessary. Now, as acting director, I must do everything I can to hold off another RIF as long as possible."

As long as possible.

Karen and the other two workers stared at each other as if wondering whether they were really awake. Up and down the hall other doors slid open as people gawked in sick amazement at the acting director's words, at the images of Ombalal's slaughter. Karen felt a sudden urge to hide, to go someplace where Brahms could not find her. But on the sealed colony, no one could hide anywhere.

Brahms continued his careful explanation. Karen listened, trying to convince herself of what he was saying—that Ombalal had acted on his own, without consulting his division leaders. Watching the holotank in the hall, a middle-aged man started to grumble angrily, but Karen and the others hushed him.

"We are on our own," Brahms said. "You all know that Earth will not rescue us. We are trapped with only our abilities and whatever resources remain here. If there is a way to survive, we have to find it without outside help. We must drive ourselves, work ourselves as hard as we can."

Brahms turned his head, swiveling the picture around as if he were trying to stare down the entire population of the station. Karen shuddered.

"I respect science and I have a firm faith in human ingenuity. We have incredible technological resources here on *Orbitech 1*—we must find a way. We have raw materials of Moon rock outside the station—enough to supply us with air and water for years, but we can't live on that alone.

"If we don't come up with a new way to survive, then we'll all be dead in a few months. This isn't just a pep talk. Station Director Ombalal tried one solution with the RIF; let's not allow the untimely deaths of our friends to be in vain. Turn your creativity loose, unlock the fringes of your imaginations. I want us all to live."

Brahms swallowed hard, and his three-dimensional image wavered for a moment.

"To this end, I am assigning a team of assessors to oversee your work, to inspect what you are doing, and assess the importance of your research—how well it is done, how hard you are working.

"Naturally, we will be looking for new modes of food production and transport to the other colonies, or perhaps back to Earth—but we cannot be narrow-minded. A single discovery does not exist in a vacuum. Cooperate with each other. If one researcher creates a new alloy, then perhaps someone else can use that alloy for some kind of vehicle to get us out of here. I leave it to your imaginations. The assessors will report to me the importance of the new developments.

"My first two appointments are my remaining division leaders, Linda Arnando and Allen Terachyk. I will issue a formal statement describing their duties and responsibilities."

Brahms scanned the screen once more. His eyeglasses seemed to be an absurd attempt to make him look serious.

"We must strive harder. We must find a way to save ourselves. We need to share the results of our work, so that others may use your discoveries in tandem with their own. Save us . . . you have to save us." The image of Brahms faded into the gray, neutral pattern of the holotank.

Karen and the other researchers buried themselves in their work, frantically trying to make breakthroughs as fast as they could. They never said anything aloud, but they knew a useful discovery would keep their name off the RIF list.

The once-homey touches in the labs now seemed pathetic. A spider plant drifted in the corner near a workstation, growing in random directions, sending streamers straight up into the air and sideways in search of gravity. Over by the lounge area, colorful personalized coffee containers, some with lids hanging open, bobbled untouched against the wall. The times when anyone could casually drink or eat throughout the day had passed, leaving nothing but harried work and restrained hysteria.

Karen Langelier did not want to know how well she had

done in the Efficiency Study. When Brahms had collected his data, she had just separated from Ray, and she had taken too long to adjust to work up here . . . if she hadn't been riding the coattails of her weavewire discovery, Karen might have joined the first hundred fifty.

The airlock door at the end of the laboratory complex opened and a chunky young woman drifted in. She wore a pale green jumpsuit with the insignia of *Orbitech 1* prominent on the left shoulder—the work outfit that had become the uniform for Brahms's watchers. Karen kept a scowl from her face. She looked away, feigning concentration on her work.

Nancy Winkowski grabbed hold of the handbars on the wall and pulled herself across the room. Her hair was carrot orange, and she had a carpet of freckles on her arms.

Winkowski stood still for several moments, hovering close beside her. "Hello, Karen."

Karen watched her, lips pressed together.

Winkowski floated up and steadied herself on the table. "Thinking about new lines of research? Are you going to save us all?"

Karen turned her gaze away. She resented how easily she felt helpless and intimidated. "That's the general idea. But it's hard to concentrate with distractions."

Winkowski glanced at the mass spectrometer; somehow, she even noticed the bobbing flask near the wall where Karen had thrown it. Her sarcasm grew stronger. "Well, I'm sure it's going to be something big and exciting."

Nancy Winkowski had been Karen's laboratory assistant. Never terribly helpful, Winkowski had always carried a grudge, angry that she had been with Orbitechnologies Corporation for years and had not advanced beyond technician, while newcomers from Earth, like Karen Langelier, just walked into important positions.

But that had all changed, now that Brahms had picked her as one of his watchers to look for ways to make the colony run more efficiently. It seemed so patriotic, and logical at first—after all, with everything so scarce, hoarding and laziness could not be tolerated. And now Winkowski apparently felt she had to get back at Karen, to harass her as much as she could.

Karen expected it, in a way, but she was still disappointed in her former assistant. Winkowski was not stupid. She was ambitious, but impatient, and she preferred to have her way directly rather than take the trouble to earn her position.

Karen glared at her, then snatched her Pyrex flask from the air and began to reheat the polymer batter. She worked her jaw, keeping her face turned away from Winkowski. "If you'll excuse me, Nancy, I'm doing important work here."

Satisfied at Karen's reaction, Winkowski turned and drifted along the laboratory areas, puffed with her own importance.

Winkowski left through the opposite airlock, leaving it open so that one of the technicians had to drift over and close it. The other teams in the lab looked at Karen sidelong, trying not to be too obvious with their stares. They seemed relieved that Winkowski had chosen her, instead of one of them, as a scapegoat.

Karen found it difficult to breathe. *Orbitech 1* seemed dark and forbidding—a prison with no escape, where jailers and prisoners all waited side by side on Death Row.

By habit, she shut down her equipment, ran through the checks, and secured her experiments. It would be only a matter of time before the researchers started sabotaging each other's work. The idea made her feel sick inside.

She needed peace. Quiet. And escape.

The door of the Japanese garden sealed behind her, and she stood in silence, breathing the humid air. She leaned back against the camouflage-painted wall, smelling the plants, listening to the artificial bird song. She heard no one else. Few people took the time to relax anymore.

Karen wondered how long it would be until the colonists were driven to the point where they would break in here and strip the garden bare to eat the plants. Some of the leaves and stems were probably toxic—would starving people care?

She already felt weak from low rations. She could picture herself, gaunt and sunken-eyed, haunted by hunger. Would she pause a moment to think of the beauty in the garden before she tore flowers off the shrubs?

First Ombalal and then Brahms had cut back their food.

Hunger was a dull ache now: nothing intolerable, but knowing that it was only the beginning made it much more difficult. The nightmare would spiral deeper and deeper into darkness, and people would begin to do irrational things.

She stared at the splashing fountain with such an intensity that her eyes dried out, though she felt like crying. Her vision grew blurry as she tried to focus on the droplets of water hanging in the air and drifting slowly to the pool.

She ran her fingers along the tips of the leaves.

What if Brahms did another RIF? She could not hide anywhere on *Orbitech 1*—not even here in the garden.

To her disappointment, the garden looked . . . run down. Leaves floated in the fountain pools. The path had not been swept. The flowers themselves looked untrimmed and in disarray, with dead blooms unsnipped.

The place was empty—nature holding sway without the presence of man. Would the garden continue to grow, she wondered, even after all the inhabitants had died?

Irregular bird song burst cheerfully from hidden microphones in the foliage. The muted skylights, the precision of the rows and sculpted shrubbery, showed the deft but obvious hand of the gardener.

Karen did not see Kaitanabe; in fact, she had not seen him the last two times she'd been in the garden. She thought that with Brahms's plea for everyone to work twice as hard for survival, Kaitanabe would have turned the garden over, tried to cultivate some fast-growing edible plant. She didn't know anything about the station's biological stores, but she assumed they must have some sort of seed stock.

Karen wandered along the pathways looking for him. "Hello?" she called, not wanting to speak too loudly. The silence of the place made it seem like a cemetery.

Then she remembered the storage and maintenance cubicle set into the wall, hidden behind a row of hedges. Karen doubted anyone else cared whether they saw the cubicle door or not, but the precision of Kaitanabe's garden would not have allowed such an anachronism to be seen.

She broke through hedges of magenta oleanders and found the door. She called out again but heard no response. The cubicle door was ajar, and she wondered if he might be sleeping. A heavy, acrid odor of chemicals hung in the air.

Several of the random speakers rang out at once, making the garden sound as if it were filled with raucous birds.

Karen pulled open the door to a gagging stench. Containers of fertilizer and plant nutrients, growth hormones, and caustic treatment chemicals had been spilled on the floor.

The blotched and bloated corpse of Hiro Kaitanabe lay sprawled out in a frozen spasm on his thin cot. His lips were cracked and stained, and dribbles of colored chemicals had dried on his chin. Somehow, he had managed to keep his hands primly folded across his chest, even though his spine was twisted upward in mid-convulsion.

She looked at the spilled containers on the floor and stared at him in horror, but he could not look back. It had taken him a very long time to die.

Karen took several steps away from the cubicle, leaving the door open. She bumped into the hedge and it seemed to reach out and grab her. The rustle of the branches dislodged one of the hidden speakers. She swallowed a scream.

Would the others mourn, or would they consider it one less mouth to feed without worrying about who would be chosen for the next RIF? Karen shuddered.

What are we becoming?

Out in the garden, the cheerful bird song continued.

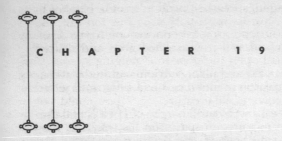

CHAPTER 19

Ramis floated in the core, alone. Sail-creature nymphs dodged among the children playing floater-tag. None of the other nymphs bore the splotchy "Z" marking of the creature that had saved Ramis's life three years before.

Sarat would never be there to play with him again.

Ramis closed his eyes as he drifted. The core seemed empty without Sarat. . . .

The bioengineers had made three attempts with the oldest sail-creature nymphs. Dobo stood by Sandovaal as they attached a coupling harness to the first of the disoriented creatures.

They had anesthetized the nymph before ejecting it from the airlock; Dobo argued that was the humane way to conduct such experiments. But the anesthetized nymph had exploded from its own internal pressure, unable to compensate fast enough. Dobo had refused to come to work for a full day afterward.

On the second attempt, with Sandovaal looking smug,

they did not drug the nymph. Exposed to the vacuum, it grew and expanded, spreading itself in a wide blanket to absorb sunlight. But its metamorphosis was too fast, too violent for the restraining hooks connecting it to the *Aguinaldo*. The newborn sail-creature tore free and drifted away into space.

Ramis had been there, peering out the window plates as two engineers wearing manned maneuvering units jetted after the still-growing sail-creature, but they could not turn it around again without damaging the sail's cell-thin membrane. The engineers looked like tiny dolls as they floated side by side back to the docking bay, with the green-tinged sail moving behind them against the stars.

As the second attempt failed, Ramis felt his heart sink. The next nymph would be Sarat—his companion, his . . . pet.

Ramis kept to himself and said a silent prayer and good-bye when the bioengineers came to remove Sarat from the weightless core. Sarat drifted along with them, complacent, unaware. They had been force-feeding Sarat for the past day, "hyperfueling" the creature, the bioengineers called it, to make the sail survive as long as possible in space.

The nymphs had no awareness, according to Dr. Sandovaal. It had been a lucky coincidence that Sarat had kept Ramis from crashing into the *Aguinaldo*'s rim—a programmed reaction, that was all.

But Sarat had always found Ramis in the core. The nymph had recognized him, played with him.

The bioengineers led Sarat away as Ramis floated in the air, watching. He kept his eyes dry. *Help me out one more time, my friend. We have a long journey together.*

Sarat survived the accelerated metamorphosis. Ramis did not watch. He went back to the *dato*'s dwelling and dimmed his own rooms, pretending to sleep in the middle of the day. After an hour or so had passed, he heard Magsaysay return home and shuffle across the floor to his closed door. He listened, waiting for Magsaysay to knock, to say something, but the president walked away and left him alone.

Ramis loved him for it.

The bioengineers performed the procedure in space, tending the sail-creature like a baby. They oriented Sarat's proto-sails edge-on to the Sun to keep it from the light pressure before the process could complete itself. They injected concentrated nutrients into the body core to make it grow faster, larger. For two days the sails expanded. Sarat's fins spread out into vast, cell-thin wings, scores of kilometers to a side.

Sarat's main body core became rigid and exceedingly tough, an organic "hull." But the creature could still metabolize, using the hard solar radiation for direct photosynthesis. With the metamorphosis, the sail-creature switched over to the plant attributes in its cells, becoming an immobile receptor of solar radiation.

Ramis watched the creature out the window plate and thought about the process, the right and wrong of it. Sarat had had no choice. It knew nothing of the people who would be rescued by its sacrifice. It could never turn back, could never come back inside to play in the zero-G core of the *Aguinaldo*. The creature's course had been set. Sarat had no future except to become a dead and drifting sail, used up, battered about by the solar wind.

Ramis rubbed his fingers on the window plate, but the coated quartz showed no smudges.

"What we want to do is this, so pay attention, boy." Sandovaal rapped on the surface of the holotank with his old-fashioned pointer stick. The image in the tank jiggled, then focused again into a diagram of the Earth–Moon system.

Magsaysay spoke up. "Luis, Dr. Panogy should be explaining this. She is the *Aguinaldo*'s celestial mechanics—"

"Too long-winded," snapped Sandovaal. "Ask her what time it is and she will tell you the history of timepieces, starting with sundials. I will explain just enough so as not to confuse the boy." He turned his attention to Ramis. "Now. When we release you from the *Aguinaldo*, you will turn the sail so that it faces the Sun, taking the full momentum of solar photons. Never mind what that means."

"I know what it means," Ramis muttered, but Sandovaal did not hear him.

"You will then be moving 'backwards' in orbit, relative

Lagrange points and colonies
(not to scale)

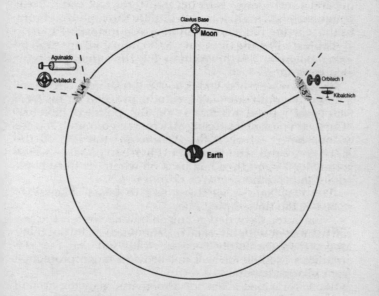

LAGRANGE, J.L. (1736–1813)—French mathematician who discovered stable points in a planetary orbit. These locations, known as "Lagrange points," are ideal for the placement of space colonies, especially the points L-4 and L-5, which occur 60° ahead of and behind an orbiting body, the Moon in this case.

to the *Aguinaldo*. In about three hours, this will provide enough braking to slow you from our orbital velocity at L-4 down to three kilometers per second. You must then turn your sail edgewise. This will help you drop like a stone toward Earth, skim past it at a distance of about an Earth radius, and then head back up to where you started."

On the holotank a dotted blue line appeared, tracing Ramis's planned trajectory. "But while you have been going down and coming back up, the Moon, L-4, and L-5 will have continued in their own orbits. By the time you return to the starting point, L-5 will be there instead of L-4."

Ramis studied the diagram. "So I am just killing time by going down to Earth? Waiting for the other points to change position?"

Magsaysay watched Ramis, looking troubled, but Ramis ignored the *dato*, keeping a calm expression on his face. Sandovaal tapped his fingers on the polished tabletop. "Correct! Think of it as being on a merry-go-round. You are on one horse, which is the *Aguinaldo*. You hop off the merry-go-round, wait for the next horse to pass by—which is the Moon—and then hop back on when the third horse comes into position. That is *Orbitech 1*."

"But how long is all this going to take?" Magsaysay stared at the dotted blue line.

"Nine or ten days, depending on how accurately the boy can maneuver with the sail. We cannot leave him out there longer than absolutely necessary—his suit and the sail-creature's exoskeleton will not provide much protection from solar radiation."

Ramis remained silent for a moment, glancing around the empty chamber. The room was large, dominated by a long meeting table surrounded by unoccupied chairs. Overhead, shadows of pedal-kites and playing children crossed over the skylights. Ramis set his mouth. "And Sarat must die in the vacuum."

Sandovaal faced him with a puzzled expression. "What?"

"Sarat," Magsaysay said quietly, "is Ramis's name for the creature. In the core it was his . . . pet—a plaything. It will die, now that the metamorphosis has taken place?"

"That is correct." Sandovaal blinked his eyes at Ramis, as if wondering at the relevance of the comment.

Ramis swallowed. "Then, how long will Sarat live?"

"We cannot implant you too soon—the creature's physical structure is still hardening, you see, forming a rigid sheath to keep the 'cargo' in place. But the timing will be close."

"You already told me that. I want to know how long Sarat will live?"

Sandovaal switched off the holotank, letting the images fade back into the murk. As the lights came up, Ramis watched Magsaysay nod to Sandovaal. Sandovaal pursed his lips.

"The sail-creature might die after a week, or possibly longer. We have too little data to be confident. However, we will provide you with hormone injections that you can use to induce nerve reactions, so you should still be able to move its sails. If the sail ceases to respond before you reach *Orbitech 1*, you will not be able to tack. And then you will be trapped."

Magsaysay's shoulders sagged and he started to speak up, but Sandovaal cut him off. "It will be close, but it is still possible. I am confident."

The president did not look greatly consoled. He turned again to Ramis, as if pleading with him to change his mind. Ramis stood, his face expressionless as he pushed away from the meeting table. "Thank you, Dr. Sandovaal." He strode from the room.

AGUINALDO ■ DAY 15

Sandovaal's eyes widened at the recording. He whispered to Magsaysay. "Who else knows of this?"

The *dato* switched off the holotank and sank to a cushioned chair. "The control room crew and the ConComm personnel. I have decided to keep this quiet until—"

"Until the boy leaves?" snapped Sandovaal. He fidgeted in his chair. "Has Clavius Base seen this?"

Magsaysay dismissed the question with a wave. "Yes, yes. They have refused to make further ConComm broadcasts to *Orbitech 1*—their equivalent of severing diplomatic ties. But it is a useless gesture, meaningless, because it will

not solve the problem. People are still starving on
Orbitech 1, still dying."

Sandovaal thought for a moment. He said slowly, "What
are you going to do, Yoli? Still send the boy over—to a
bunch of savages? From that announcement it sounds as if
they would rather eat Ramis than welcome him."

"All the more reason why he *must* go!" President Magsaysay raised his voice, then fell silent, tapping his fingertips together. It sounded to Sandovaal as if the *dato* was
rationalizing things to himself. "Ramis will still insist on
going, even after he learns of this."

AGUINALDO ■ DAY 16

The wall-kelp vats were usually deserted—the unpleasant
smell deterred the curious. Thick foliage thrived on
the bath of reflected light from the crescent Earth and the
gibbous Moon that swept by every ten minutes with the
Aguinaldo's rotation. Ramis came upon President Magsaysay there by accident.

In the past two days Ramis had spent much time staring
out the window plates, ignoring other people. Magsaysay
had gone out of his way to spend time with him, but Ramis
had made it clear that he wanted to be by himself, to think.
He was concerned about Sarat.

But now, when he entered the chamber to be alone,
Ramis saw the *dato* staring out the greenhouse window
plate, squinting at the image of Earth. The crescent was
like a cupped hand, immersed in thick smoke. Ramis felt a
deep pang grab at his heart and he thought briefly of his
brother, on Luzon. *Salita, are you still alive?*

Engulfed by shadows, Magsaysay looked thin. In the
years since the death of Ramis's parents, the *dato* had tried
to treat him like a son. But Ramis was a loner, very independent. Maybe it was because of Magsaysay's advanced
age, or his position of power, but he had never filled the
void that was left.

But now, when Magsaysay thought he was unobserved,
Ramis saw how distraught he seemed. He looked old.

The *dato* muttered to himself, as if in deep thought.

"What if this starts the process snowballing again? What if we allow it to happen once more?"

Ramis decided to speak up. "Father?"

Magsaysay turned abruptly. "Ramis! I did not know you were here."

Ramis pushed aside a strand of pliant wall-kelp and stepped forward. "What do you mean, starting the process snowballing again?"

Maysaysay looked out the observation window. He sounded afraid to turn around. "We are surviving, Ramis. Dr. Sandovaal projects that even with an increase in population, the *Aguinaldo* will manage. The Filipino people have succeeded and our culture will endure. With Luis's wall-kelp, we have won, truly won, perhaps for the first time."

"But *Orbitech 1*—"

Magsaysay looked back at Ramis and put a hand on his shoulder. "You are doing a brave thing, Ramis. If you are successful, *Orbitech 1* will be able to pull through this crisis as well. With food, they have the resources to rebuild things. They have capabilities far beyond ours." He tightened his grip.

"And that is what frightens me. How long will it take them to forget? How soon before we on the *Aguinaldo* go back to being their 'little brown brothers,' forever relying on the West? Even though we outnumber them twenty-five to one, it is hard for me to tear away from the past.

"For years we lived in the shadow of the Americans. We were content to let them keep their military bases on our soil, to respond to their whims. The Filipino culture nearly died out as we tried to imitate the United States. Even on the *Aguinaldo,* Tagalog is rarely spoken anymore. You know it because I have insisted you learn. The others know it, but we are enamored of English when we speak. Listen to me—even me." He shook his head.

"Only when the Filipino people put their foot down did things change. When we declared war on Switzerland and forced the Swiss to open their financial records and divulge the whereabouts of our country's lost fortunes, then the world took notice. Only after we kicked the Americans out and allowed the Soviets into our country did the United States take us seriously." He swept his arms around. "And look what we got for it: this shining, expensive colony—a bribe, to allow the Americans to retain their status quo."

Ramis could see tears of anger in the president's large brown eyes. Magsaysay's hand trembled, and he withdrew his grip. He flexed his fingers and looked at them wonderingly.

"This colony was to be our new beginning, our hope for a future that we could never realize on Earth. The War severed all ties, and now we have proved that we can overcome the obstacles from the past." He shook his head.

"In some ways, it would be better if you did not go. I am very afraid of what the Orbitech people might eventually do if they survive. Already, their half-finished *Orbitech 2* sits in our backyard here at L-4. What if they want more and more, as it always happens?" He stared at Ramis.

"What if *I* am to blame for all that happens, just by allowing you to go?" He was silent for a long time. He placed a hand on Ramis's shoulder. "We have been keeping something from you—something you need to know before you get to *Orbitech 1*." The *dato* seemed to have trouble continuing.

"Something terrible just happened on *Orbitech 1*—one hundred and fifty of their people have been killed, by decree of the director. And now, apparently, the director has been murdered as well."

Ramis spoke without hesitating. "Was it rioting? What happened?"

Magsaysay squeezed Ramis's shoulder. "They were apparently sacrificed to save the colony. A ten percent reduction of personnel to make the remaining supplies last longer. The associate director of the station has now taken over—Curtis Brahms. I know little about him. He has been there only a few months. Orbitechnologies seems to have thought highly of him.

"They are desperate, Ramis. They are starving. It is worse than we thought. You . . . you are stepping into something much deeper than we expected. If you want to change your mind and not go, no one will blame you." His eyes searched Ramis's.

Ramis was at a loss for words. "Surely you cannot let all those people starve—"

Magsaysay dropped his hands to his sides and took a

deep breath. He forced a smile. "No, no—it is an old man's nightmare. To do nothing would be unthinkable, both for them and for us. You must save *Orbitech 1,* Ramis. And I must pray my fears for you are false."

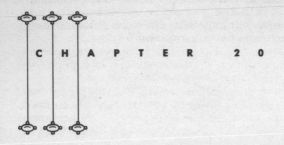

C H A P T E R   2 0

When the time came to go, Ramis participated in the ceremonies with self-contained indignation. Solemnly, he attended a special Mass held for him and managed to recite Saint Christopher's litany without stumbling.

Dobo Daeng helped him suit up as Magsaysay watched in silence. Ramis turned around to take a yearning look back at the *Aguinaldo.* Several adult Jumpers sped around the circumference of the cylinder or bounced across the Sibuyan Sea. Ramis realized he had never completed his nighttime Jump, and now he'd probably not have another chance. *They will miss me*, he thought, knowing it was true.

The great cylindrical core, with wall-kelp, dwellings, small buildings, and recreational areas wrapped around the axis, rotated on.

Ramis followed Dobo to the airlock. President Magsaysay held out a slender hand. "Your father and mother would be proud of you this day, Ramis. Our people are proud."

Sandovaal scowled, fidgeting where he stood. "Hurry, boy. The creature is dying as you waste time."

Ramis set his mouth. He knew if he spoke, tears would flow. And if that happened, they would not let him go—*he is only a boy!* they would say.

"If I am doing this, Dr. Sandovaal, you can please stop calling me a *boy*." He lowered his gaze, mainly to keep Sandovaal from seeing the smug expression on his face.

Dobo gave the boy an unexpected hug. "May God be with you." He crossed himself.

Turning, Ramis snapped his faceplate down so no one could see the tears in his eyes. He entered the airlock and stomped his boot on the floorplates, to feel solid ground beneath him perhaps for the last time.

A bioengineer met him as the airlock outgassed to the vacuum. Ramis pushed out from the airlock, and the spectacle of the unbounded universe took his breath away. The stars, black space, the rich river of the Milky Way pouring across the sky.

Moored to the *Aguinaldo,* Sarat's bodily core ballooned in a fat cigar shape. Three space-suited figures worked at a cavity at one end of its body. Ramis felt nauseated. *What have they done to you, Sarat?* he thought. One of the space-suited figures motioned for him to hurry.

Approaching, Ramis saw wispy-thin sails, like gigantic butterfly wings, spreading out from Sarat's body core. They were stretched farther than he could see, more fragile than anything seen on Earth.

He drew in a breath. The air echoed in the confined chamber of his helmet. The suit pressure made his movements stiff and difficult. The thin sail-membranes reflected little light toward him. But they haloed Sarat in a glorious majesty—a crown for the sacrifice the creature would make for the survival of *Orbitech 1.*

A gloved hand touched his elbow, guiding him closer to Sarat's main body. Ramis closed his eyes, not wanting to look. Through the careful application of irritant chemicals, the bioengineers had caused a cyst to form in Sarat's expanding core—a cramped and hollow blister to house one small rider, some packages of wall-kelp, and three sail-creature embryos. The wall-kelp would grow inside the cyst, providing oxygen and food for Ramis to survive the journey.

Swimming through open space, Ramis reached the end of the tether holding Sarat to the colony. With the help of the others, he worked his way into the cavity, pushing against Sarat's skin, elbowing into the darkness inside. It was cramped but flexible, like a giant womb. Through the material of his gloves, he felt Sarat's body. It seemed different—tougher, thinner. Not like the gentle, harmless beast he had played with in the core.

He tucked his arms and legs in, moving his elbows to see how much room he would have—pitifully little for a ten-day journey. The bioengineers floated in front of the opening, blocking his view of the *Aguinaldo*'s long cylinder. Together they worked to join the edges, using cellular sealant to close the cyst. Ramis was completely enclosed, safe—trapped.

He moved his legs to get more comfortable. He reached out a hand to touch the inner wall of the sail-creature and imagined Sarat exposed to the cold nothing of space.

"Boy, are you all right?" Sandovaal's grating voice came over the radio.

"Yes." Ramis switched his receiver off. "Stop calling me *boy*," he muttered to himself. He methodically unpackaged the wall-kelp nodules and set them against the membrane wall. Even here, the kelp would grow rapidly, tapping into Sarat's metabolism and filling the cavity with oxygen. Ramis also knew the kelp would drain Sarat's energy reserves, further shortening the sail-creature's life.

While Ramis waited, the bioengineers hooked up the external video camera, allowing him to see his destination. He could hear nothing in the vacuum, but he felt occasional vibrations through Sarat's skin. Testing, Ramis used the joystick controls wired through the cyst. He swiveled the camera around, panning the ten-kilometer length of the *Aguinaldo*. He wondered if he would get homesick.

Through the camera, Ramis watched a suited figure move his arm rapidly up and down, signaling that everything looked good. The sail-creature started to slowly rotate, orienting its sails to the sun. He turned his receiver back on and listened to the chatter. The movement seemed to take forever.

"Prepare for release when the sail-creature is fully turned."

"I am ready," Ramis said.

When the bioengineers released the tether, Ramis did not even notice the slight acceleration. Inside Sarat, he imagined motion, knowing that he would start falling again—this time swooping toward Earth. He stared at the video monitor, but found it disorienting.

"Safe journey, Ramis. Travel swiftly." He recognized Magsaysay's voice. Then, in Tagalog, *"Good luck, my son."*

Solar photons struck the creature's vast sail surface and increased its momentum, little by little. Pushed at an ever-accelerating snail's pace, Sarat drifted down toward Earth.

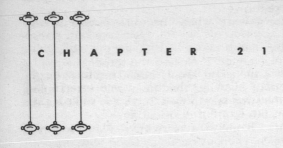

C H A P T E R   2 1

CLAVIUS BASE ■ DAY 26

Damned dirty socks again.

Clancy tried to ignore the smell, but the suit refused to cooperate. Lunar rocks, their edges razor sharp in the direct sunlight, stared him in the face as he stepped around them. His foot slipped. Cursing, he kicked up a volley of pebbles and caught himself before falling in slow motion.

From up on the wall, he could see Longomontanus Crater unfold before him—sixty miles of unbroken smoothness. A five-mile-long track ran through the dust from the point where the wall-kelp had hit the lunar surface. The Filipino scientists couldn't have aimed the package any better: the container had struck at one and a half kilometers per second, nearly tangential to the ground. Maybe it was even still intact.

"The Lunatics think we're a bunch of rednecks, Cliffy," Shen's voice came over the suit radio. "But look who gets to go out on a two-day wild-goose chase for a package of space seaweed?"

"Gives you a chance to stretch your legs. Nice legs, too." Clancy grinned inside his helmet. She gave him a raspberry over the suit radio. "Is that beeper still going strong?"

"Intermittent now—the battery must be almost dead."

"Doesn't matter, Cliff," Homann's voice interrupted. "We can see the track now. Piece of cake. It's like a giant arrow pointing straight to the pot of gold."

"I thought it was rainbows that pointed to the pot of gold," Shen said.

"Can't get any rainbows here. No atmosphere."

"Well, let's just find it and get back to base," Clancy interrupted them. "Wooster's probably screwing up my score in the docking simulator."

At Clavius Base the *Orbitech 2* engineers kept to themselves. Once in a while Clancy had to step in and bash heads together, but in general the engineers were well-behaved. The other Lunatics resented the unwelcome guests, though, begrudging them the precious supplies they consumed.

But while the Lunatics sulked, Clancy's engineers had taken over the mundane grit work that the Clavius Base scientists had to do—hydroponic gardening, ice mining, equipment repair. It was "busywork" for the engineers, Clancy knew—and so did they—but it kept them from being bored silly.

Left to his own intuition, Clancy would have suggested some sports activity, maybe a regular jaunt outside—it did no real harm, and the oxygen tanks were readily replenished from processing lunar rock. But Dr. Tomkins had suggested low levels of physical activity to decrease food consumption. He expressed optimism at the hydroponics teams working to increase productivity in the underground garden tunnels.

"Aww, Tomkins can't even make up his own bed, not to mention his mind," Shen had complained. "He's so wishy-washy, he'll have things in complete disarray before long."

Clancy held up his hand, cutting short any echo of her complaints. "Tomkins might not be the most outstanding administrator around, but he's been in charge of Clavius

Base for years. If he wasn't capable, NASA and the U.N. would have canned him years ago. Let's see how he does with this kelp stuff."

Spirits had lifted noticeably around Clavius Base when the container had hit the Moon. Most of the Lunatic scientists had been dubious about the slingshot scheme—especially after they found out the idea came from the arrogant and unpredictable Luis Sandovaal.

The Filipino scientist's thick white hair stood out in the holotank. His blue eyes blazed; his face filled the unit as he shouted.

"What do you take us for—idiots? Of course we plotted the trajectory. Ten days and the package will intersect the Moon, but you will have to locate it yourself. We put a homing beacon on it. The wall-kelp is our gift to you. And once you see its growth characteristics, you will think it is manna from heaven."

Tomkins had done his best to appease the temperamental scientist. "You have our thanks, Dr. Sandovaal. We will be in contact if we have any questions, and to describe the progress of your wall-kelp."

Clancy felt warm in his suit, but all the gauges read normal. He wanted to find the package and start the journey back. After two days moving out in the rovers, he was getting a little tired of the tedium. The smell of dirty socks seemed to grow stronger. It had never felt like this up at *Orbitech 2.* There they at least had modular living quarters, so they could take off the suits after a long day's work. He was tired of sucking on the suit nutrients, of using the piddlepack. He desperately wanted a shower.

Below him, the team of six-packs spread out and moved along the popcorn-powdery floor of the crater. Their big wheels rolled along, grinding the surface to dust in silence.

The second lunar rover lay fifty yards away on the crater floor. The rest of the crew was hidden by jutting rocks. He activated his chin mike and hoped the others were within line-of-sight transmission.

"Any luck?"

"The beeper's pretty much useless now, Cliff. Just a ping or two. It's more confusion than help." Shen's voice sounded loud in his helmet.

"Find anything, Homann?" He could see the silver of the other man's suit as he bounded ahead.

"You'd hear the hollering if I did."

"Get to a higher spot so you can see better—but be careful." The skipping track of the package's landing had been obvious from a distance, but on the jumbled crater floor it was indistinguishable. Clancy worked his shoulders back and forth to reach an itch on his back. Comfortable again, he looked up at the crater walls towering over him. They jutted into the star-filled sky, hiding their fissures and jagged edges.

"Looks like it skidded into the crater wall and bounced back," Homann said. "Five hundred pounds of packaged seaweed. Blooey! So much for 'Fragile—handle with care.' Ever see any of those classic Roadrunner cartoons? I wonder if it's Acme wall-kelp."

"Okay, okay, just direct us to the terminus of the skid path. Come on, Pete, I'm getting tired of being out here." Clancy tried to keep the impatience out of his voice. *There's got to be an easier way to find this stuff,* he thought. He'd calculated enough scattering cones at MIT to be able to guess where the package would land.

"I'll give you a nice long back rub when we get back, boss," Shen said.

"Ooooh!" Homann broke in. "You could give me one!"

"Quit clowning, you guys."

Homann directed them across the crater floor. Even from the inconvenient vantage point, now Clancy could see the skid tracks from the impact. "X marks the spot!" Homann radioed.

"Shen, listen for beeps."

After a few more minutes of searching, Clancy brushed fine lunar dust off the pitted surface of the package. Buried under three centimeters of dust, the desk-sized container was bashed on one end from its collision with the rock, but the outer wall seemed to be unbreached. The kelp was intact.

He radioed, "Merry Christmas, everybody!"

"Easy, easy!" Philip Tomkins hovered over the construction workers like a mother hen. Duncan McLaris stood on his tiptoes away from the crowd, watching. The rest of

Clavius Base observed through personal holoscreens. The ConComm link to the *Aguinaldo* showed the Filipino Council of Twenty, with Dr. Sandovaal in the foreground.

Clancy pried at the container until the seal suddenly burst open. "Ooof." He went sprawling backwards.

Shen caught him and propped him back up, patting his shoulder. "I told you you'd be throwing yourself at me after a year, boss."

Clancy ignored her and motioned to Dr. Tomkins. "All yours, sir."

Tomkins straightened and peered into the hololink with the *Aguinaldo*. "I sincerely thank our Filipino friends for this gift of food, this opportunity. If it fulfills only a fraction of your expectations, Dr. Sandovaal, it will indeed save our lives here at Clavius Base."

With Sandovaal nodding sagely in the background, Tomkins cracked open the main chamber of the container. "It appears to be intact!" Tomkins turned to the holotank. He grinned, and his big body seemed to be filled with a greater excitement than Clancy had ever seen him display.

Sandovaal's voice came across the three hundred thousand kilometers from the *Aguinaldo*. "When your lunar tunnels are filled with wall-kelp, just remember me." He moved out of sight of the holotransmitters, the bare hint of a smile on his face.

Clavius Base got its first look at the wall-kelp. Clancy sniffed the air, frowning, and looked into the wet, green receptacle of wall-kelp.

Perhaps this substance was going to save them, but for now, it smelled even worse than the dirty socks in his space suit.

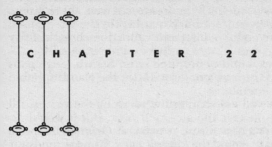

C H A P T E R 2 2

Encased in the vast solar sail-creature, Ramis watched through the monitors, studying his course. The awesome face of Earth seemed like an oil painting below him, reaching up to swallow him in its oceans.

"You were always there to catch me when I fell, Sarat," Ramis muttered. "Are you there to catch me now?"

Sarat's orbit approached closer than two Earth radii at its nearest point, before they swooped back out again on their way to L-5. He wondered if anyone on the planet could look up and see him blotting out a swath of stars against the night sky. Or if anyone would bother. He wondered if his brother Salita was staring up into the Philippine darkness right now . . . or if the Islands had been swallowed by an even greater darkness.

Leaving the planet behind, Ramis and Sarat climbed toward *Orbitech 1.*

Ramis shifted his legs in the cramped cyst-cavity. He had no room to move, no place to stretch—and sitting here in the same position had begun to drive him insane with boredom after a week. He took extreme care not to bump the three sail-creature embryos at his feet.

Ramis removed his helmet and took a deep breath of the humid air. He didn't want to leave the helmet off long—hard cosmic rays still penetrated even Sarat's tough exoskeleton—but fresh oxygen drove back the claustrophobic dankness for a while.

By now the wall-kelp had grown all along the inner sides of the cavity, making the air smell rank. But it would be enough to start a new forest growing in *Orbitech 1,* and it gave him food to eat on the long journey. Unprocessed and raw, the kelp tasted awful, but his stomach kept it down. He knew, conceptually at least, that it provided him with necessary nourishment and moisture.

Ramis groped around the spongy cyst until he found the joystick controls for the external video. Swiveling the camera, he focused on the bright pinpoint of the L-5 colony waxing larger and larger. A week ago the colony had been invisible against the stars. Now, under extreme magnification, he could just make out the two counterrotating wheels of *Orbitech 1.* Also at L-5, the Soviet station *Kibalchich* revolved slowly into view on the fringe of the Lagrange gravity well.

Time was growing short for them, for him. He found it difficult to think clearly.

"Calling *Orbitech 1*!" Ramis squinted at the screen in front of him. Why weren't they answering? "*Orbitech 1,* come in please." Maybe his transceiver was too weak. Maybe he was trying the wrong frequency. Maybe they had stopped listening for messages entirely after Clavius Base had cut off communications.

A thought struck him—what if the new director, Curtis Brahms, had done something else? Brahms did not scare Ramis; it was the uncertainty that made him uneasy.

Ramis muttered under his breath. He had been talking to himself too much in the past few days. "How am I supposed to rescue you if you won't answer?" He snapped the helmet shut.

Maybe the radio's gain was too weak. Maybe he had used the batteries too much over the past week, chatting with people on the *Aguinaldo* just to quell his loneliness and isolation. As he swung close to Earth, he had scanned the radio bands. Briefly he caught a burst of hysterical shouting, but it had faded into static before he could tune it.

There was nothing to do. No way to notice that time was passing. Sarat continued to drift on course, to waste away and die.

Keeping himself occupied, Ramis squinted at the cross hairs barely visible on the video screen. The camera angle had been offset enough to account for the American colony's orbital motion. By centering the image in the cross hairs, the sail-creature would tack ahead and arrive at the right position to intercept the colony in its orbit.

He saw that Sarat was off course by only a fraction of a radian, but with thousands of kilometers left to travel, he would miss *Orbitech 1* with room to spare.

Time to steer again. Ramis withdrew a small knife from the equipment pouch. He looked at the cross hairs and judged the angle from inside the cyst. With the sharp point of the blade he poked Sarat's sensitive internal membrane.

"Sorry, Sarat."

The cyst tightened. Ramis felt a tension, a ripple, as the vast creature's reflexes turned it away from the knife's prick. The lumbering movement seemed to take years, but the L-5 colony finally drifted into the center of the cross hairs again.

He tried counting stars, then making up rhymes, reciting Bible passages he'd had to memorize for catechism years before—anything to make him forget the boredom for a while. And to forget about his slim chances for ever returning to the *Aguinaldo*. He would give anything just to stretch his legs.

Inside Sarat, looking at *Orbitech 1*, Ramis felt as if he were falling down toward the station. The old fears began to come back. Space gave him no reference, no horizon, no gravity. The direction *down* was where things fell when you dropped them . . . but out in space, everywhere was down.

As the colony loomed closer, Ramis groped out to touch the walls of the cyst, searching for stability, trying to fight off the sickening vertigo. He would be falling forever because there was no place to land.

Sarat had always saved him from falling before . . . but

would Sarat still be there for him, even as Ramis killed him?

Ramis was cramped, hot. The air in the cyst was stifling. The pain in his elbows and knees ached without relief. He felt dizzy most of the time now, sick to his stomach.

Dr. Sandovaal had warned him that the suit might not protect him enough from the hard radiation. They had given him some kind of medication before departure, something that had made him uncomfortably queasy for more than a day, that would supposedly help him fight radiation damage. Now he just considered himself lucky that no solar flares had occurred. He would be a long time recovering from this journey . . . if he survived at all.

Sarat hardly responded to Ramis's course-adjusting maneuvers anymore. Reluctantly, Ramis had had to resort to vicious jabs with the knife to get the sail-creature to turn even a little.

The L-5 colony filled most of the viewscreen, like a rotating dumbbell with two wheels spinning on a central axle.

Ramis reached out and stroked Sarat's inner membrane through the thick jungle of wall-kelp. He didn't know if the creature could feel him, or respond, but he continued his caress. It kept his hands occupied.

Ramis conserved the batteries in his transceiver, using it only occasionally to send a signal toward the American colony. He had long ago passed out of range of the *Aguinaldo*. Magsaysay had promised that they would continue to transmit to the people on *Orbitech 1*, telling them what to expect, telling them how they could receive the lifesaving supplies Ramis was bringing them. But Ramis had no way of knowing if those messages had been acknowledged, or even received.

Was anybody even alive on the Orbitech colony? The wheels' metallic surfaces glinted in the sunlight, causing bright flares and smears on the video screen. The colony's observation windows glimmered with light from the inside, but they were devoid of any wall-kelp, naked. It looked strange to Ramis, but he could not focus the video camera enough to see inside.

What if he found no one at all? What if they were all dead, a result of some rampage by the director, or some

riot by the other colonists? How would he ever get back?
He couldn't even get inside unless someone caught the
sail-creature, freed him, and took him in.

And Sarat was almost dead, which left Ramis with no
way back home.

"*Orbitech 1*, I am almost to you."

A loud meaningless crackle returned, but Ramis kept
trying. He hated these line-of-sight, energy-conserving
units. The Americans had to know he was coming. No one
could mistake the sight of the giant organic solar sail drifting closer every day. He kept trying and almost missed it
when a weak voice came from the receiver.

"# # #tech here# # #. Ready# # #receive you."

As Ramis stroked the inner membrane of the sail-creature, he willed Sarat to remain alive just a short while
longer.

They rapidly closed on the L-5 colony. Ramis's stomach
wrenched because he knew what that would mean for
Sarat. In order to slow down enough to impact the colony
without killing himself, Ramis had to collapse Sarat's broad
and beautiful sails—draw them in to cushion him from the
crash.

Orbitech 1 gleamed on the monitor. He knew which end
would have the docking bay, where people would be waiting for him—he hoped. Ramis watched the wheels turning, one clockwise, the other counterclockwise. Floating
above, the discontinuous, near-invisible mirror hung
where it could direct sunlight inside the colony. With each
rotation of *Orbitech 1*, Sarat drifted nearer. Ramis swallowed. The picture on the monitor screen blurred, but it
was just his eyes watering.

Moving slowly, like someone preparing to give a eulogy,
Ramis withdrew the pressurized vial from its cellophane
pack, along with the tiny explosive-driven carrier pellets.

He had to judge when the time was right. He had to
know, and he could not hesitate.

Ramis had to rid himself of all sentimentality now, because he would not have time for it when the moment
came. If he botched this up, he'd sacrifice Sarat for nothing
—and make a martyr of himself, as well.

And he would have snuffed the last hope of survival for everyone inside the American L-5 colony.

He could see the details of the giant docking bay now, the Orbitechnologies logo, the viewing windows studded on either side of it. The colony swelled to fill the entire video screen.

Out here, somewhere, floated the hundred and fifty bodies that had been ejected from the airlock.

Ramis noticed the sweat of his fingers inside his gloves. He held the vial of pressurized trigger-hormone; it felt slick against the mylar of his suit. He remembered Sarat, years ago, saving him from the building that came rotating toward him at deadly speed, when he drifted too close to the *Aguinaldo's* rim.

And later, finding the one sail-creature nymph with the "Z" mark on its back—the one that had been more special than any other.

He remembered playing with Sarat, as they both grew older, and Sandovaal assuring him that sail-creatures were not intelligent, that they only responded to stimuli.

Falling toward the curved, kelp-covered inner surface of the *Aguinaldo,* stranded and helpless as the wide wall rushed toward him. Ramis felt the fear burn in his lungs. But Sarat was there, stopping him, pushing him to safety, saving him.

You were always there to catch me when I fell, Sarat. Are you ready to catch me now?

Ramis rammed the hypodermic cartridge inside the sail-creature's membrane and ejected the vial's contents.

Minutes passed. Ramis began to wonder if it would even work.

Reacting with incredible slowness, the cell-thin sails collapsed. They drew in toward Sarat's body, lumbering together as a butterfly might bring in its wings. They stretched dozens of kilometers out in front of the cyst. With the sudden movement, wispy fragments tore away, rippling like the shrouds of a ghost.

Sarat's crumpled body struck *Orbitech 1,* pushing against the tattered ends of its sails. Ramis felt the impact ripple through the creature's flesh, but he was padded by the curtains of wall-kelp and kilometers of sail. The minute-long collision dragged on; it seemed to take too long.

He felt himself drifting back again, rebounding. Suddenly, panic burned through him. If he drifted out of the colony's grasp, then he would be stranded again, without even the sails for maneuvering.

Sarat was dead; Ramis knew it, but he refused to let the journey be wasted. Sarat could not have died for nothing.

The video monitor was dark. Outside, the cameras had been covered up by folds of the collapsed sails. Ramis sealed his helmet, made certain that the sail-creature embryos were protected in their airtight canisters, then took out his knife.

He had to get out; he had to do something before it was too late. Ramis shouted again into the transmitter. Nothing. He saw that he had left it on, and the battery was dead.

He hesitated only a moment out of respect for Sarat, then plunged the knife into the tough membrane, trying to cut his way out of the cyst. When the blade broke through to the outside, decompression tried to rip the knife out of his hand. Outrushing oxygen tore the gash open wider. Ramis continued to saw with the knife edge. Crystals sparkled as the humidity inside the cyst flash-froze, layering everything with a thin coating of ice. One of the wall-kelp bladders burst and froze in the same second.

Ramis could see through the opening in the cyst, then he felt a tug on the carcass of the sail-creature. As he peered out, he saw several figures in space suits near him, attaching a tether to keep Sarat from drifting farther away.

Ramis felt drained with relief, but he could not yet relax. He kept hacking with his knife, trying to make the opening wide enough for him to emerge. One of the suited figures swam up in front of him, face-to-face, nodding.

Ramis was startled to see behind the faceplate a man who bore a look of excited hope and wonderment that seemed to cut through weeks of despair.

As he emerged from the hulk of the dead sail-creature, Ramis turned back, feeling like a newborn coming out of a womb. He looked at the shriveled remains of Sarat. The once-magnificent sails now looked as if someone had crumpled up a gigantic wad of paper and tossed it aside.

Sharp needles of pain struck his joints, and uneasy tremors raced through his muscles. But it felt wonderful to move again, to stretch, to be free. He stared down and saw only an infinity of stars, not the curved wall of the *Aguinaldo*. If he started to fall, he would keep falling forever and ever. . . .

Dizzy, he looked up at the large observation windows on either side of the *Orbitech 1* docking bay doors. Pressed against the observation windows were scattered faces. They appeared as gaunt and anxious as the face he had seen inside the suit.

One of the suited figures wrestled the knife from his hand. Ramis was too weary to struggle, so he released it and kicked it toward the airlock. He tried to make motions to show them what they needed to get from the cyst. Apparently they used a different frequency in their suit radios, and he didn't want to waste time figuring it out. That was one more detail they should have firmed up before his departure.

He saw the others removing the sail-creature embryos, then the wall-kelp nodules. The wall-kelp would survive for some time in the vacuum, but they needed to bring it inside as soon as possible.

As he drifted through the maw of the towering docking bay doors, he could see the empty hangar where the shuttle-tugs would have docked, back when everything was normal. He could see a control bay up above with slanted transparent windows. He saw several forms behind the windows.

Another space-suited figure took his arm and directed him to one of the airlock doors at the wall. He supposed it was an elevator shaft. His legs continued to tremble, and he felt ready to dissolve inside his suit. He wanted to get *out*, where he could breathe again. He had exerted himself too much all at once. He was not anxious to be back inside a gravity environment.

Behind him, he saw the suited figures cutting at Sarat's crumpled sails, getting at the creature's body core. The severed, tissue-thin sails drifted away as the L-5 colony continued to orbit.

Though he felt weary and dizzy, he waited by the spoke-shaft elevator and watched to make sure the colonists brought in the wall-kelp and embryos. The frozen kelp strands were still edible, and the central nodules would

LIFELINE 177

survive. His escort seemed impatient and urged him to enter the elevator.

Ramis floated inside the elevator chamber as the other figures carried Sarat's hard, elongated body core into the bay, pushing it toward one of the other elevators. He felt a moment of shocked indignation and anger as he realized they were probably recovering the meat for distribution among the colonists.

One more sacrifice for Sarat, one more debt owed.

As the spoke-shaft elevator descended, the chamber filled with air. Ramis could feel his weight increase as the elevator traveled out to the rim of the torus, picking up artificial gravity along the way.

Ramis's suit lost some of its stiffness as the elevator pressurized. His escort cracked open his helmet and indicated for Ramis to do the same. As the elevator reached the bottom of the shaft, Ramis lifted up the faceplate and took a deep breath of the warm, stale air of the industrial colony. He heaved an exhausted sigh. The man beside him clapped him on the back.

A potpourri of odors wafted past, very different from the dank, stifling air of the cramped cyst. The smell was metallic, scrubbed clean—more artificial than the *Aguinaldo'*s. But Ramis felt numb, unable to take it all in at once.

A buzz of people surrounded him. Arms reached out to embrace him, and he almost collapsed in their grasp. He looked around frantically. The men with the embryos must have gone into one of the other elevators, down a different spoke into another part of the wheel. Ramis stood on his tiptoes and called out, wondering what he should do.

"Wait—the sail-creatures! They are my only way back! I need to tell you about the wall-kelp!"

A man pushed through the mass and grabbed Ramis's elbow. He was tall and forceful, with blond hair swept back from his forehead. At first glance, he seemed too young to be in charge, but the dark bags under his eyes made him look old beyond himself.

"—Curtis Brahms, Acting Director of *Orbitech 1*." He seemed to be out of breath. "Welcome to our colony. I hope you've brought a miracle with you. We could sure use one. We must have a meeting with my assessors as soon as possible."

The people grew silent when the man spoke. Their faces smiled back at Ramis, but their eyes looked dead, beaten.

Ramis studied Brahms, trying to quell the urgency he felt. He did not look as forbidding as Magsaysay had led him to expect.

Ramis wanted to see the embryos, make certain they were not mishandled or injured. "I must show you how to grow the wall-kelp, raise the sail-creatures. It is a chance for you all to survive."

"We can't thank you enough for helping us." Brahms gripped Ramis on the shoulders. "We had only . . . unpleasant options left." Brahms steered Ramis through the crowd. People stepped out of their way.

"Let me show you your room. We've got good quarters for you—they used to belong to one of our division leaders."

Ramis stumbled along, feeling weak. He tried not to think of Sarat, of the *Aguinaldo,* of the time he would have to live here until the sail-creature embryos reached maturity—nor of the unpleasant options to which Brahms had referred.

"After you clean up, we need to have a talk." He flashed a smile that made Ramis uneasy.

The people appeared glad to see Ramis, but somehow he felt more stifled than welcome. He would be walking a tightrope, balancing everything he knew against what he understood of the grim situation on the American colony.

Orbitech 1 seemed to hold many secrets.

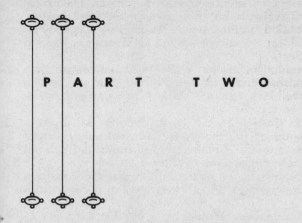

PART TWO

INCENTIVE

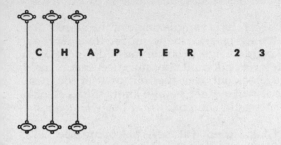

ORBITECH 1   ■   DAY 30

Chief assessor on *Orbitech 1*—she liked the sound of that. Linda Arnando brushed at the shoulders of her clean green uniform. She felt tired but exhilarated, like a marathon runner who had finished an impossible race and won by the barest of margins, but won, nevertheless.

She'd have to see if Brahms would let her wear some sort of badge to denote her rank.

Linda knew the game. Much of it had been unpleasant, but she had played along and followed the rules, because getting ahead was The Most Important Thing. Too many women balked at the harsh world of corporate politics, refused to let themselves be used, and then whined that they had never gotten a chance. But being named chief assessor made up for all the humiliation.

If *Orbitech 1* didn't get out of this mess, then at least she had finished up on top.

Speaking of finishing up on top. . . . She allowed her eyes to wander over some of the men in line—men who had never noticed her before, but did now. It was a marvelous switch.

Linda stood in cafeteria complex nine of the administrative torus, watching people queue up for their daily rations. A hand-painted sign proclaiming "Alferd Packard Memorial Cafeteria" adorned the entrance. She made a mental note to check out what that meant after the meal. She didn't like it when other people knew things she did not. As Chief Assessor, she could find out whatever she wanted.

Brahms had his armed watchers patrolling the halls, dressed in spring-green, nearly indestructible weavewire jumpsuits that had been destined for Earth before the War. The watchers supposedly kept everyone calm after the riot that had killed Ombalal, but people still seemed uneasy. Someone had used one of the permanent no-smear lipstick tubes from the Orbitech cosmetics labs to scrawl graffiti on the clean wall of one of the corridors:

"REDUCTION IN FORCE? Why not *streamline* the management structure instead?"

And thanks to the wonderful polymer base of the lipstick, someone would have to use sandblasting equipment to remove it from the wall.

Behind the counters in the cafeteria complex, four other watchers scanned ID cards to make sure no one tried to get a double allotment. The computerized distributors monitored rations to the nearest few grams per person.

Brahms had selected the watchers from their profiles in his precious Efficiency Study. She'd never seen a man squeeze so much out of one set of data. Linda frowned, but accepted it. She knew what Brahms was doing—it wasn't a pleasant thing. It wasn't an easy thing. But he was doing what he had to.

In one of their meetings, Linda had suggested a rationing methodology she thought would increase the incentive of the workers—rations would start out at some minimum and then be increased on the basis of productivity, as a kind of reward system.

Allen Terachyk sat silent and brooding in the meeting, as usual. Brahms raised his eyebrows at Linda's suggestion and removed his unnecessary eyeglasses. He glanced at her, then at Terachyk, then back at her. With his face naked and open, Linda thought he appeared fragile, like a wounded child. His cheekbones shone smooth from where he had rubbed them, but his sharp blue eyes looked active, ready to pop out of his face and flit around the station where he could watch everyone.

"I'm not sure we can get any better incentive than the implied threat of another RIF." His teeth were very small when he smiled.

Now, at the head of the ration line, one of the watchers stiffened and yelled at the man handing him a card. The red light on the ID reader blinked on and off. Linda recognized the burly, red-haired watcher as a former researcher, but she didn't know his name. For show, she knew she should go over and make herself visible by the commotion.

"Don't try to pull one over on me," the watcher said.

"But it's not for me. My wife is in our quarters and she's not feeling well. I want to bring it to her."

"She'll have to come herself."

Exasperated, the man in line put his hands on his hips. "But if you'd check, you'll see that she hasn't used her card yet today."

"Then bring her card here."

"And waste a trip to the other torus? I'm just trying to make things more *efficient*." The word carried a stinger of sarcasm.

Linda Arnando stepped up and scowled at the man. He had a quiet intelligence about him and neatly trimmed brown hair that was thinning on top. His hands were pale and very clean, as if he scrubbed them often. His name badge read "Daniel Aiken."

"You may think you have a perfectly valid complaint, Mr. Aiken." Linda felt herself taking charge, wielding her authority. The watcher looked relieved. "But we had equally valid reasons when we decided to allow *no exceptions*."

She lowered her voice, speaking to him only.

"Morale around here is low enough without you causing a fuss. Just do as you're told, or I can see to it that your rations are cut off entirely for a few days, all right? None of these people would mind if you don't get your share."

Daniel Aiken shook as if unaccustomed to losing his temper. He remained silent and finally turned to depart. He moved out the door, awkward, seething with anger and helplessness. Linda placed a strained smile on her face, motioned for the rest of the line to proceed, and then she too left.

Food was tight enough, and getting tighter. As chief assessor, Linda Arnando could alter some figures, but since Brahms was such a stickler on "being fair" to everyone, she couldn't do it for just anybody, no matter how indignant they became. She increased her own rations only when she felt particularly weak, when she couldn't function properly.

Linda went back to the office and set about planning which research teams she would investigate next. On her desk an electrostatic "perpetual motion" toy clicked away, silver balls whirling in orbits that wouldn't decay for five years.

She ran her hands over her desktop, then activated the inset terminal. She and Terachyk had divided up the various laboratory efforts, the administrative groups, the performance appraisals.

Linda Arnando didn't know much about the detailed research. Her specialty was management psychology— how employees worked together, how they got the job done. She was good at finding out who the most useful employees were.

Linda logged in to the confidential employee data base and used her Assessor password, which gave her access to all levels of information. Whether she understood the details or not, she had a sixth sense that allowed her to cut through the extraneous stuff, get a good feel for what was useful and what was BS.

Tapping a fingernail on the textured metal surface, she called up the file on Daniel Aiken. She wanted to see about this man who was trying to do things so much more efficiently.

The list identified Aiken as an organic chemist specializing in photosynthetic processes. His wife Sheila worked as an electronics engineer with a focus on communications. Daniel Aiken had an average score in the Efficiency Study; Sheila had done a bit better.

Aiken's stated primary project was investigating ways to synthesize sugar molecules using the raw elemental materials available on *Orbitech 1,* which could chemically create basic foodstuff for them out of the remaining lunar debris left in the stable Lagrange point. *An admirable project,* Linda thought—and Aiken seemed to be making rapid progress, too. According to the available log summaries, he had made several amazing breakthroughs since the first RIF.

There we go: incentive in action.

But Aiken had run up against the same problem many other *Orbitech 1* researchers had encountered. The lunar rocks sent up by the mass driver on Clavius Base were rich in some materials, yet had the Moon's own limitations in others. Mainly they were hindered by lack of hydrogen, the lightest element, which had escaped away into space because of the Moon's small mass and low gravity.

Aiken needed elemental hydrogen to fill in the blanks in the sugar molecules. Other researchers needed it to develop rocket fuel to help the colonists escape.

Linda smiled ironically. For want of a nail the shoe was lost, for want of a shoe the horse was lost . . . for want of hydrogen, the colony was lost.

She looked at some of Aiken's results. Impressive. She scanned the dates of his test runs, accessed his log entries, and called up the times of his data manipulations.

Something didn't look right. Linda stepped back.

She accessed the rough files in his personal directory, not just the summaries he would expect people to look at. She read the last entries, wondering what he had done to some of his results. She could not understand the science, but she could spot the gaps in his entries.

Many of his test runs had not been impressive at all. He showed some progress, but nothing to get excited about. He had logged his results, mentioning a few directions he might wish to pursue.

And then the RIF had happened.

The following day, Aiken had opened his old data files again and changed some of the numbers. He had tried to wipe out evidence of his tampering, but Linda could call up the original tags on the files, the coded dates and times of input.

She knew how to do such manipulation—she had done the same type of thing at times to get herself extra rations. But she knew how to cover her trail; Aiken didn't.

She frowned. The data points he had changed were the outlying values—the ones that put his results into question. Everything looked nice and pretty once he brought them in line.

"Tsk, tsk, tsk," Linda said to herself.

She made a mental note of his office number and the location of his living quarters. Then she smiled. It felt good to be on the other side, for once.

"Now then, Dr. Aiken." Linda drifted back in a net chair in his laboratory cubicle. She turned her head, and rich dark hair moved in front of her face, then upward. She brushed it back down, keeping herself neat. Her lips were bright red from the sparkle lipstick she had applied.

She smelled chemicals—an acrid mixture of experiments not sealed entirely in fume-confinement zones. The strange scents changed from moment to moment as they crawled through the air on currents stirred by the ventilators.

Orbitech 1's successful zero-G pharmaceutical production processes had been developed in this section. Other designated laboratory areas were defined in a three-dimensional matrix throughout the colony's nonrotating central cylinder, color-coded to research topics.

Daniel Aiken nodded at her, looking tense. That would make things easier.

He was middle-aged, reasonably fit. Linda found him attractive in a puppy-dog sort of way. She studied her fingernails, drawing out the silence. She had applied some of the garish Orbitech cosmetics to make her nails swirl with changing, oily color.

"As chief assessor, it is my job to look into all these different projects and find the ones with the greatest merit —the ones that have the most bearing on our survival. Your work could have very important implications. I'm sure you realize that, Dr. Aiken." She paused. "Actually, I think I'm going to call you Daniel." She said it as a statement, not asking permission.

"I remember you from the cafeteria. Tell me, what does the name Alferd Packard mean—from the sign by the door?"

Aiken allowed a thin smile. "I did my graduate work at the University of Colorado. The main cafeteria is named after him." To Linda's blank stare he continued, "Packard led an expedition up in the Rockies and they got trapped in the snow. The next spring he was the only member to return. He was accused of cannibalism."

Linda set her mouth in distaste. "That's rather sick humor for a cafeteria."

Aiken blinked and avoided her eyes. "Since the RIF, I think we've all been a little morbid around here." He muttered something else noncommittal, and she slid her hook in deeper.

"But back to your research. I found it very interesting, with most impressive results." Linda glanced up at him. "In fact, the numbers were even more impressive after you altered your data."

Aiken's eyes widened. His shock could not have been more absolute if she had suddenly pulled out a knife and slashed him. Linda's smile was brittle, glistening red from the lipstick.

Aiken tried to stammer something, but she made a shushing motion that sent her drifting away in the net chair. Linda could see him squirming—it made her feel light-headed.

He could no longer restrain himself. "I just needed more time! My project is going to work, but I've had a small setback, and I . . . didn't think it was fair. If I get a little more time, I—I could make this breakthrough so we can all survive."

"Of course, I understand." She kept her voice even, her rigid smile in place. Poor man. He had it so difficult. If only he had a little more time . . .

She wondered just what he'd had to go through to get to his position, what he'd had to do to get his biochemistry degree. How did he have to degrade himself? Where did he have to crawl? Whose back did he have to stab? Whose rear end did he have to kiss?

Linda Arnando thought of the men she'd slept with, all the condescension she had taken from supposed "equals," the ways they had abused their positions of power, tried to crush her down.

But she had come through it all, and now the shoe was on the other foot, wasn't it?

"You realize, don't you, that when I tell Director Brahms about this, he's likely to have you thrown out the airlock as an example. At the very least, he'll put your name at the top of the next RIF list."

She raised her eyebrows and waited, trying to predict what he would do next. Aiken stared at her, baffled. She opened her palms to him, waiting.

Finally, he got the idea. "All right, Ms. Arnando—"

"Chief Assessor Arnando!"

"Chief Assessor Arnando." He drew out each word, refusing to meet her eyes. "What do you want? What is it I have to do?"

She thought of all the times she had been in Aiken's position. Perhaps it didn't have anything to do with lust or sex. It was power—the ability to make someone do something he didn't want to do.

She leaned forward out of the net chair, got to her feet, and moved around behind him. Aiken sat stiffly, afraid to move. He gripped the edge of his work surface. Around him the details of his lab—the enclosed petri dishes, the culture flasks, the fermentation locks—stood clean and quiet.

He jumped when she touched him.

Linda rubbed his neck, ran her fingernail down the side of his face, lingered on his lips, then traced down to where a few curly chest hairs stuck out from his lab smock.

"I think we could come to some . . . sort of agreement."

Aiken sat perfectly still. It excited her. There was something like a rabbit about him. He swallowed, then spoke in a whisper, "My wife—"

Linda smiled. That made it even better; she had forgotten about his wife. "I think you can work something out, Daniel—considering the stakes."

She moved to leave, but at the door of his cubicle she paused and turned. "You can find the location of my quarters. I'll expect you there, oh, let's say, twenty-two hundred hours?"

She knew from his schedule that he always spent time at home then.

Before he could stammer anything, she left.

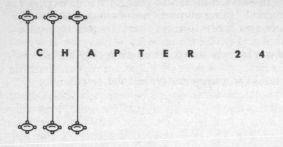

C H A P T E R   2 4

ORBITECH 1 ■ DAY 34

The American colony was full of strange smells, odd
sounds, subtle changes that continually reminded Ramis
that he did not belong there. This was not his home. The
Aguinaldo might as well have been a million kilometers
away.

He saw a lot of metal here—ordered cubicles, color-
coded sections. He missed the natural chaos that made the
Filipino colony seem more a world than a construction
project. *Orbitech 1* was like an office building, precisely
arranged and cold, not a place to live. Even the occasional
"living walls," showing holographic scenes from Earth, did
not help. A smattering of angry graffiti marred the pictures, taking away from the forced naturalness.

Ramis felt exhausted, impatient, and depressed all at
once. He had focused on the challenge, the mission, the
risk of flying the sail-creature through open space against
all odds, to arrive here.

Ramis spent two days resting under medical observation, being treated for radiation exposure and having his blood checked. Brahms allowed him to use the *Orbitech* communications center to radio back to the *Aguinaldo*, where he spoke of trivial things with Magsaysay. It wasn't until partway through the conversation that Ramis realized Brahms had put him on the ConComm, broadcasting the conversation to everyone on the other colonies.

Dr. Sandovaal asked him several specific questions about Sarat—how long the sail-creature had survived, how difficult was steering, and so on—which Ramis answered as best he could. He had checked on the care of the sail-creature embryos he had brought with him. Everything seemed to be fine, but it would be nearly a year before they reached maturity. He was stranded here until then.

Now that things had settled down, he felt as if he were waiting for something else to happen. He had nothing to do, no place in this industrial research station. He could speak formal English, but the American colloquialisms confused him and made him feel inadequate. He had brought the wall-kelp, they had thanked him, and now they wanted him to . . . ride westward? *Ride off into the sunset*—that was the right phrase. He shook his head. He felt trapped here, isolated from the things he had taken for granted.

Ramis couldn't Jump in the zero-G lab spaces. The cubicles were too regimented, serviceable rather than livable. Even his clothes were uncomfortable: an Orbitech-issue jumpsuit made of some sort of superfiber—weavewire, they called it. He remained barefoot in a small effort to imitate life on the *Aguinaldo*.

His new quarters seemed alien, too, as if he had trespassed in someone else's room. Some personal possessions had been removed, but much remained from the previous occupant. The quarters were spacious, with a window plate, a large bed, and a small entertainment center. Posters of famous Earth restaurants covered the walls: the Brown Derby, Antoine's, M&J's Sanitary Tortilla Factory. Brahms told him that it had been the suite of Tim Drury, one of the division leaders on *Orbitech 1*.

When Ramis asked the director what had happened to Drury, Brahms had stared at the wall for a long moment. "He was a victim of our first reduction in force."

Only after Brahms left did Ramis realize what he had meant. *Orbitech 1* suddenly seemed too small for him.

Ramis spent the next two days wandering the colony. He went to look at the sail-creature embryos in their monitored incubators; he watched Orbitech workers attach nodules of wall-kelp to prime spots around the station.

He roamed free. A few people tried to touch him, as if to bless themselves with his optimism, his brighter outlook toward the future. Then one woman with a long, gray-blond ponytail shouted at him for disrupting her train of thought, and continued shouting long after he had left.

Not everyone viewed him as a savior. Some saw only the extra mouth to feed. His fears and loneliness increased, making him want to run and hide.

He found himself in the Japanese garden.

The foliage brought back memories from home. The enclosed acre lacked the lushness of the greenhouse alcoves on the *Aguinaldo*, and the humidity was not as high. Still, it seemed more peaceful here than anywhere else on the colony, away from the brooding paranoia in the corridors, the signs of restless frustration, the lowered voices of the other workers.

Bright stars shone like ice picks through the crystal port above, and light the color of melted butter seeped from banks of lamps at the intersection of the wall and the ceiling. Recorded bird song broke into the air at regular intervals.

As Ramis wandered about, a fountain splashed slow drops through the canopy of green. He saw traces of cleared vegetation, bare spots in the imported soil, furrows that had been scooped deep enough to expose a gash of the metal deck.

The small harvest from the Japanese garden could never sustain *Orbitech 1.* Even Ramis could see the scope was all wrong—too much food needed in too little time.

Along the periphery swelled several masses of wall-kelp, recently planted and growing well. The thick strands of coarse greenery were reaching up the wall toward the crystal port that allowed sunlight into the atrium. Ramis wondered if the wall-kelp would eventually dominate the other plants in the garden, swallow them up.

He found himself walking by the fountain again. Droplets of water curled from the apex back to the stream, falling in slow motion. He felt serene, quiet and peaceful, as the fear faded back like fluttering wings on the edges of his thoughts. The garden insulated him from the crowds, the horror of the RIF the people had gone through.

His thoughts turned to home, then to Earth, to the place he had lived before coming to the *Aguinaldo*. His memory of the Philippine Islands grew dimmer with each passing year.

Salita . . . was he still alive? His last evening with his lanky older brother rose like a ghost to the front of his mind—the Philippine president's reception at the Hotel Intercontinental for all the departing *Aguinaldo* colonists, the throngs of people lining Manila's boulevards. Though he was only ten years old, Ramis had managed to sneak Salita into every whirlwind event. No longer barefoot, dressed in the finest barongs, the two had stayed up most of the night before Ramis left, chatting and drinking San Miguel in their hotel room. Ramis felt tough and mature to have his own room, to drink beer with his brother, to sit and talk with Salita as though they were men.

Salita had squirmed back and forth on the bedspread, mussing it, then running his fingers over the red fabric nubbins. His skin was creamier than Ramis's, and his brown eyes looked like weak coffee instead of having irises so deep they swallowed the pupils.

Ramis took a long drink of his beer. The inside of his head already seemed to be ringing with a TV test pattern from the alcohol. Salita pocketed the packs of matches in the hotel ashtrays. Ramis took off his stiff, polished dress shoes and thumped them on the floor.

When Salita frowned at the wall, unwilling to look at his younger brother, Ramis could see the angular contours emphasized on his face. For a moment he could clearly see what Salita would look like as an old man.

Ramis said, "I wish you were coming up with us."

"I do not want to go." Salita wiped his mouth and cradled the beer bottle between his thighs. "I will be glad to untie myself from our parents. They never loved me much anyway—not like you."

"You talk like a crazy water buffalo." Ramis shuffled his bare feet on the carpet, wiggling his toes. Outside the door he could hear rowdy attendants running down the hall. "They let you do what you want, Salita. They do not hover over you. You are free. They will allow you to stay here, and you are only sixteen. I think you must be the special one, not me."

The expression on his brother's face didn't change. Salita stared at the wall. The inactive stereo tank in the corner remained a neutral gray, absorbing all light from the room. "And you, my little brother, would not know a fact if it rose up and bit you on the butt." He drew moodily on the San Miguel bottle.

They heard more sounds from the celebration below, but Ramis was wrapped up in his own little world. He stretched his hands over his head and yawned, uncertain how to distract his brother from his depression.

"Come on, Salita—finish your beer. I need to sleep." With the first planeload of colonists leaving for the Australian launch site the following morning, the shouting and merrymaking outside would soon be over as well.

Salita threw back his head and gurgled the remaining beer, but reached into the ice pack for another.

"Salita, I said I'm tired—" Ramis heard a whine in his voice. He had wanted it to sound like a stern reproval.

"Sit down, little one." Salita motioned with his new beer, and Ramis dropped back to the floor with a scowl. Salita took a pull on the bottle before speaking. Ramis had to lean forward to hear his words.

"You are tough, Ramis, and I am proud of you. But sometimes you do not look at what is right in front of your face. People will think you are stupid if you fail to notice the obvious. I was your age when I realized why I was always treated so coldly at home. Just look at me!"

Ramis fought back conflicting emotions. Salita was proud of him!—but he did not understand what his brother meant. The silence in the room was broken only by the low humming of the air conditioner. Salita stared at him, then frowned in disgust, partially drunk himself. He took the bottle of San Miguel with him and went to the door. When he opened it, the sounds of the music and people grew suddenly louder.

He turned and locked eyes with Ramis. "Have a good trip, little one. Take care of yourself, and learn how to be brave and strong. I will look up at the stars and think of you. Maybe I will even wave."

He turned his back and closed the door behind him, muffling the outside sounds again. Ramis got up off the floor and lay on the bedspread Salita had wrinkled. It was still warm.

He had never seen his brother again.

Now, his parents were both dead in an accident on the *Aguinaldo,* and the War had probably destroyed the Islands, and Salita as well.

It had taken him years to figure out what Salita had meant. He was tall for a Filipino, with lighter skin and eyes. His features looked different, softened. His birthday celebrations had always been subdued. Their father had always treated Salita with something akin to resentment. Ramis could not remember when he had realized that his mother must have been pregnant before she and Agpalo had been married. That would have been enough to shame them, with their strict Roman Catholic upbringing.

But he wasn't sure that was enough to explain everything. Both parents had been students at the University of the Philippines. His mother had lived in Angeles City, where she had grown up, near the American military base. But before graduating from the university, both Agpalo and Panay had dropped out, married, and left Angeles City. With a promising future there, they had moved north, instead, to run a Sari-Sari store in Baguio.

They had ignored all their biochemistry training until Dr. Sandovaal had tracked them down for the *Aguinaldo* assignment. Ramis's father had seemed afraid to leave Baguio, afraid to go near the Americans, whom he often cursed at home.

People will think you are stupid if you fail to notice the obvious.

After all he had been through—the flight through space, killing Sarat, being trapped here where a hundred and fifty people had died because of some administrative order —why did this still upset him so much?

One of the recorded bird songs rang out next to him, and he whirled, ready to yank the speaker free and step on it, even with his bare feet.

Then he recoiled in shock as he saw a woman standing

behind him, smiling with deep empathy. Ramis rubbed his eyes and tried to regain his composure.

She spoke softly. "Are you all right?"

Ramis started to answer, but his voice caught in his throat.

The woman continued to speak in a controlled, warm voice. Her eyes were brown but bright, quick to move and focus on anything that captured her interest. A few dark freckles dusted her cheeks and forearms, like tiny splashes of tan from a melanin experiment gone wrong.

"You're the Filipino boy." She held out her hand. "I'm Karen Langelier, one of the polymer chemists here."

Ramis took a deep breath. "My name is Ramis. I am sorry —I was thinking."

She smiled. "I come here often, too, and I think I know how you feel. If you want to talk later, I'll be here to listen." She turned to go. "Look me up."

Ramis studied her face for a moment. A few crow's-feet spread from her eyes. She looked old; but then, at sixteen, everyone over twenty looked old to him.

"Thank you," he said. "I have not made any friends here yet."

She smiled again, and for a moment Ramis thought she was going to hug him, and he didn't know if he wanted that or not. He was afraid to let himself feel vulnerable on this foreign colony.

"Come to my lab and I'll show you what I'm working on. It'll be nice to talk to someone who isn't paranoid."

Before Ramis recognized the fear in her own eyes, Karen had walked away. All he could hear was the cool rainfall of the fountain.

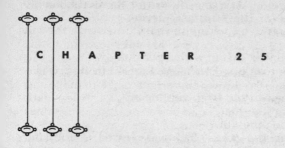

CHAPTER 25

CLAVIUS BASE ■ DAY 35

The man who stopped in front of McLaris was frowning. "Is Dr. Tomkins around?" The question came as a demand. He tried to peer around the desk to the chief administrator's chambers beyond.

Sitting in the outer office, McLaris had heard the visitor approach down the muffled corridors. The visitor rolled when he walked, taking each step carefully on the balls of his feet, as if not trusting low gravity. His cheeks showed a gray wash of unshaven stubble. His manner hinted that he was someone who got things done with no nonsense.

"Dr. Tomkins is busy at the moment. May I help you?" He had been reorganizing some of the administrative work in the outer office, but he didn't like to be treated as a receptionist. He glanced at the name tag sewn onto the jumpsuit's right breast pocket: CLANCY. He had seen that name before, on another name tag.

McLaris blinked, then smiled to cover his surprise. He stood up behind the administrative desk and console, extending his hand. "Are you the one who pulled me out of the wreckage of the *Miranda*? Thank you. I'm Duncan McLaris. I guess we couldn't see each other with the suits and all."

Clancy squinted at him with a puzzled expression, then his eyebrows rose up. "You're McLaris? I'm surprised to see you here."

"Rather than in the brig, you mean?"

"Something like that."

"I'm just helping out."

The desk in the outer office was cleared of Tomkins's scientific potpourri; only an empty cup remained, stained with a brown rim of tea. McLaris hadn't dared to get himself a nameplate for the desk, or even to request an official title. He was happy enough that Tomkins let him do something productive at all.

The rest of Tomkins's outer office was cluttered with stacks of d-cubes, holo pictures of stars, drawings of radio telescopes, and a few old-fashioned paper textbooks.

McLaris waited for Clancy to take in the situation. He had watched the scene repeat itself over the past week as Tomkins spent less and less time doing administrative duties, leaving McLaris in his place.

He flattened his hands on the desk. "Is there something I can do for you, Mr. Clancy?"

Clancy set his mouth. "My people are still working in the tunnels, on the chief administrator's orders." McLaris thought he detected an angry overtone to the last phrase. "I need to show Tomkins something."

McLaris moved around to the front of the desk with a take-charge expression on his face. "What's the problem? Is this an emergency?"

Clancy bristled and stared at the left well, covered by a panoramic photograph of the Milky Way in Sagittarius, taken by the Hubble Space Telescope. McLaris could see he was upset about something, frustrated and losing control.

"I'd really rather discuss it with Dr. Tomkins. If I'm going to lose my temper, I might as well do it in front of the right person."

McLaris smiled. "Maybe it would be better if you did lose your temper in front of me, and saved a little diplo-

macy for the chief administrator." He waited a beat. "Why
don't you let me go with you and see what this is all
about?"

Before Clancy had a chance to answer, McLaris had
started easing him out of the office. It felt good to be managing people again, dealing with their problems and acting
as arbitrator—not for any sense of power it gave, but to see
things work together.

McLaris motioned for Clancy to lead the way. "Dr. Tomkins left me with explicit instructions not to bother him
unless there's an emergency. I've been helping him out
with the paper pushing and stuff like that. He hates it—he
says it's my punishment."

Clancy grunted something noncommittal. The engineer
seemed uneasy, not sure how to treat McLaris. He kept
conversation to a minimum as they walked. "I heard what
happened on *Orbitech 1*."

McLaris didn't respond.

They left the office complex behind and entered the
smooth rock tunnels that connected the administrative,
laboratory, and living areas. Their boots clicked down a
long passageway. "Where are these tunnels your men are
digging?" McLaris asked.

"My *people*, you mean—almost a third of them are
women."

McLaris chuckled. "Touché! I haven't slipped in years, I
don't think. But that doesn't answer my question."

"They're the far tunnels, away from the main complex."

Several turns and some minutes later, Clancy stopped
before a newly installed airlock, jerked open the door, and
stepped into the tunnel. McLaris sniffed the spoiled wet
smell of growing wall-kelp. They stepped inside.

Incandescent lamps ran down the length of the murky
tunnel. Cut-up pieces of the wall-kelp had been mounted
in the brightest yellow patches under the lamps. Looking
tiny against the immense volume of the new catacombs,
the shreds of wall-kelp grew as fast as they could metabolize.

Clancy extended his arm to show where the incandescent lights disappeared around a bend in the tunnel. "My crew spent the last week tunneling down here.
My guess is that we've scooped out at least as much volume

as was dug for the entire base in the first place. Here, see our chart."

Clancy took out a pocket flatscreen and punched up a base map, then added an overlay plot of the *Orbitech 2* engineers' additions.

"We took the debris over to the rubble processor. Don't ask me why, since we haven't been doing materials processing anyway—not with construction shut down. And it'll be a while before the base itself is hurting so much that we need to scale up production again."

McLaris interrupted. "Mr. Clancy, you're not giving me very many hints about what's bothering you. I don't picture you as the type of man who enjoys playing mind games." The image of Curtis Brahms flashed across McLaris's mind, leaving a cold line of fear in its wake; he wondered how Brahms had convinced Ombalal to do his dirty work. "Please tell me what the problem is."

Clancy put his hands on his hips. McLaris watched his expression change from annoyance to resignation, and then to grudging pleasure at the directness of the question.

"You're right—I don't like to beat around the bush. The fact is, McLaris, that I have a highly trained team of construction engineers here. If we weren't the very best at what we do, we would never have gotten the contract for *Orbitech 2*.

"We dug out these tunnels because Dr. Tomkins told us to. Whenever we send him a progress report, he just tells us to keep at it. He doesn't have any idea how much we've done. I wanted to show him all the room we've got already. Granted, we needed better quarters for my people to live in, since we're now permanent inhabitants of the base. And we needed a lot of extra space for that kelp that came from the *Aguinaldo*.

"But we've gone far past the point where it's useful anymore. We all know this is just more pointless busywork. That's worse than just sitting around."

Clancy met his eyes, and McLaris saw a depth of emotions in them—genuine concern and insight—that he had not expected. He learned from that glance not to underestimate Clifford Clancy.

"Things are going to start getting very restless around here," Clancy continued. "I don't want that. We've got

enough problems just living from day to day. I thought I
should let you know while it's still fixable."

McLaris knew Clancy was right. Once the initial problem of short-term survival was addressed, the futility began to become more and more apparent. He nodded.
"And what would you like to do about it?"

"I don't know." Clancy seemed alarmed; he scowled.
"You're the manager type—we just build things."

McLaris scratched his chin. His beard hardly itched at all
anymore, though it still looked patchy and thin in the
mirror. "Come on. Let's go talk to Tomkins."

McLaris went through the antechamber into the chief administrator's office. Clifford Clancy followed a step behind
him, but an invisible balance had shifted.

McLaris was in charge now.

Around his office Tomkins had pasted up photographs,
spectral strip charts, and false-color radio telescope images
—so many that McLaris had no idea which were for deco-
ration and which were part of his ongoing work. Coming
to Clavius Base should have been an astronomer's dream,
but Tomkins had been frustrated by the amount of time he
had to spend bean counting and paper pushing.

Now that McLaris was taking care of most of the tasks,
Tomkins buried himself in research again. McLaris wondered if it was just a defense mechanism to keep him from
thinking about their situation.

They disturbed Tomkins running a computer simulation
and comparing his results to the actual spectra of Wolf-
Rayet stars. He frowned and barely looked up when they
entered.

"I think I've come up with something peculiar—either a
flaw in our existing theory of these things or a new way of
interpreting the data."

"Dr. Tomkins, we need to speak with you. Mr. Clancy is
here with me."

"Ah, Mr. Clancy."

"That's *Dr.* Clancy. My degree's from MIT and every bit
as good as yours."

Tomkins changed one of the parameters in his study. He
stood up, a full head taller than either of them. He looked
somewhat perturbed at the interruption.

McLaris spoke quickly to defuse any anger from the head engineer. "Dr. Clancy and his crew have been digging new tunnels for the past week—"

Tomkins held up a dark brown hand and spread his fingers. "I know that, Duncan. I instructed them to do it." His normally gentle voice carried an edge of strain. "You may think I've lost touch with everything, but I still keep tabs. Those tunnels are vital to our survival and our ability to expand here."

McLaris met the chief administrator's eyes. He knew Tomkins had been working for hours at his computer problem, frustrated, hunched with a stiff neck in front of the holotank and jabbing his fingers at the keypad. This was not a good time to broach the subject, but they couldn't turn around and walk out again.

"My people are going to stop digging those tunnels, Tomkins," Clancy said. "Enough is enough. If you'd bother to check, you could see that we already have more than enough room to last us for a century or so."

The tall black man blinked his eyes, surprised and then angry. "Mr. Clancy, I think you are forgetting which of us is the chief administrator of this base."

"If my people keep digging those stupid tunnels, they're going to go crazy. They're engineers, not ditchdiggers! If you want to turn this base into an ant farm, your personnel can drill those tunnels as well as my crew can."

McLaris tried to interrupt as their voices rose higher, but Tomkins blanked his holoscreen in cool anger and turned to stare at the head engineer.

"Clavius Base was built as a research station, and will continue to function as one. I will not force research physicists, geologists, and astronomers to dig holes, Mr. Clancy."

"*Dr.* Clancy!"

"I think that may be at the heart of our problem, gentlemen!" McLaris stepped between the two men. Both Clancy and Tomkins looked at him with raised eyebrows.

McLaris allowed himself a brief smile and then continued. "Dr. Tomkins, you should not treat the *Orbitech 2* crew as simple laborers."

"That's right!" Clancy sputtered. "These are highly trained construction engineers—mechanical, thermal, and structures people. Not rock pile workers."

"And you, Dr. Clancy," McLaris said, turning to face the engineer, "must remember who's boss. Your people are effectively guests here on the Moon, just like I am. Dr. Tomkins tells you what to do, and you do it. If he says keep digging tunnels, then you keep digging tunnels."

Clancy grumbled and lowered his eyes. Tomkins still looked like a statue, unmoving, which made McLaris uneasier than he would have felt if Tomkins had been fuming with anger.

McLaris sat down, where he could look up at both men. He steepled his fingers, a gesture he realized he had picked up from Brahms.

"But I don't think Dr. Tomkins is going to tell you to keep digging tunnels. It's just make-work and it serves no purpose."

He turned his gaze to Tomkins. "We're starting to see something that may become a very grave problem for us here at Clavius Base. The frustration Clancy's engineers are feeling is bound to be growing among all the people. It's cabin fever. We're all going stir-crazy."

Tomkins placed his hands behind his back in a Napoleonic pose, but his towering height dissolved any such comparison. "Survival is my prime motivator. My people are working just as hard as Clancy's."

"That's not at issue," McLaris said. "I've got a different idea." Then he ignored them both for a moment as he went to the tea dispenser and poured himself a cup. He offered one to each of the two stone-faced men.

"We've got the *Aguinaldo*'s wall-kelp. If that grows as rapidly as Sandovaal promises, then it should tide us over when our primary supplies run out a few months from now. It will take even longer for our greenhouse gardens to start producing noticeable amounts of food—and most of that will have to be returned as seed stock so we can start planting sizable crops. It'll be tight, but the curves show we should be able to make it."

He sat back down in the chair; the other two men remained standing. McLaris tried to take advantage of the momentary calm.

"There are only a limited number of things we can do to help it along. We just sit around and let the stuff grow.

Clancy's engineers aren't the only high achievers—none of us wants to mope around twiddling our thumbs."

McLaris could see impatience growing in the two men. Here he was, giving a lecture, just like a manager at a staff meeting. He drew in a deep breath and decided to cut the background patriotic stuff to a minimum.

"We need to take on a new project—a big project. Look forward—spit in the face of our bad situation. We're sitting on all the industrial resources we could possibly want." He stamped his foot on the floor. "Maybe we can't make food, but we can process just about anything else."

Tomkins stared absently at one of the pictures on the wall. Clancy waved his finger in the air. "Rah rah! But what's the point? What do we need here?"

"This is what I propose: We should start construction of something that will set the stage for our eventual expansion—something that will provide a foundation for growth. At the same time, this project has to have utility. It can't just be make-work; there's plenty of that around as it is. What we do has to impact not only Clavius Base, but the future of the human race. It has to be a Holy Grail for us, if you want to think of it like that. Imagine what it would do for morale—not just here, but everywhere, once we broadcast it over ConComm."

McLaris stood again, pushing the chair behind him. Tomkins looked as if his interest was piqued, and Clancy seemed intrigued to see what the challenge would be. McLaris thought rapidly, *Okay, so what next?* He'd taken them this far in the hopes that they would both jump in, come up with a solution. Instead, they waited patiently for him to continue.

"Okay, first we'll have to get the automatic processing plants stepped up again. Someday, with all the brainpower combined on the three colonies—or four colonies, if the Russians ever decide to break their silence—we might be able to design a bargain-basement spaceship that'll take us back to Earth. Also, we need to have the mass driver functional. *Orbitech 1* and the *Aguinaldo* will run out of the raw materials they've got up there eventually, and they'll be asking for more."

"You're assuming that we're all going to survive," Tomkins said.

McLaris looked at him until the big black man broke the gaze. In a determined voice, McLaris answered him. "Yes. I am assuming we're all going to survive."

Out of the corner of his eye, McLaris caught a glimpse of Tomkins's sketches hanging on the wall. He remembered his initial meeting with the chief administrator, back when he first left the infirmary. And then it hit him. He smiled.

"If we're ever going to leave the Moon again, if we ever hope to grow beyond these tunnels, we've got to keep our Golden Age alive. Dr. Clancy, your crew can construct just about anything, am I correct?"

"Within reason," Clancy said. "If you're thinking about that spaceship, though, forget it. It would take years to gear up for that, not to mention the lack of hydrogen and nitrogen for chemical fuels, or even atomics."

"No, no." McLaris shook his head. He perched at the edge of his chair. "Maybe in a decade we'll be willing to tackle something like it, but not right now. This is a precursor to all that. If we can pull it off, this could be the largest solo construction project since *Orbitech 2*."

He took a deep breath and turned to the chief administrator. "Dr. Tomkins, how would you like us to build your giant radio telescope—your lunar Arecibo?"

"A radio telescope?" Clancy flopped back in his chair. "What in the world do we need a telescope for?"

But Tomkins's dark eyes sparkled. "Didn't you hear him, Clifford? The largest construction project since *Orbitech 2*. Wouldn't that excite your men?"

"My *people*. But what's it going to be used for?"

Tomkins shushed the head engineer. "What does it matter? Isn't the challenge enough? That's the beauty of it."

Clancy ran a finger over his lips. "I thought you did radio astronomy with aperture synthesis now? There's no need for a giant telescope—you just hook a bunch of smaller receivers together along a big baseline."

"You need two ends of a baseline for that to work," Tomkins said. "And our Earth end is no longer communicating."

McLaris spoke up. "If you need a different reason, Dr. Clancy, then how about as a communications focal point? The ideal would have been to place the telescope on Far-side, away from Earth's noisy radio environment." He hesitated.

"Well, that isn't a concern anymore, but it just amplifies my point. We can place it here at Clavius-B to probe Earth, to look for the milliwatt home transmitter that someone built, trying to raise communications with the rest of the world."

Tomkins's smile seemed filled with unspoken ideas. "Or we can use it as humanitarian aid, to supplement the geosynchronous navigation satellites knocked out during the War, when the people on Earth get back to that stage again." His voice grew quieter. "Or maybe even use it as an anchor back to our solar system if we head out for the stars."

Clancy struggled to his feet, and McLaris saw clearly on his face the point when he dropped his skeptical resistance to the idea and embraced it. "We'd need to completely revamp our technology base here on the Moon. Upgrade the mining and smelting facility—"

Tomkins broke in, smiling. "Refurbish the machine shops, electrical labs."

McLaris nodded, ticking off items on his fingers as they occurred to him. "The welding capability, generators, power supplies, control panels, diagnostics. I think you get the idea. Dr. Clancy, do you think you could convince your crew to take on this project?"

"You're wasting time, McLaris!" He stood with his feet wide apart, looking ready for action.

"All right. Dr. Tomkins, do you think you'd be willing to oversee this project? Coordinate things?"

Tomkins straightened and towered over both McLaris and Clancy. "I'm the chief administrator, so I'm supposed to be good at delegating responsibility."

He placed a massive hand on McLaris's shoulder. "I think I've found my niche—and yours, as well. I'm officially appointing you base manager. That'll involve some restructuring, but I'll turn my daily responsibilities over to you."

McLaris sputtered. He hadn't intended that at all. "I can't do—"

"What do you mean, *can't*?" asked Clancy, waving the protest away. "Practice what you preach, McLaris."

Tomkins steered McLaris over to where Clancy stood beside the photograph of the original Arecibo telescope on Puerto Rico. "Clifford is absolutely right. I told you I was a scientist, tied down by a bureaucratic job. You've got managerial experience, you've proven you can handle the job, and you actually like the horrible stuff. No excuses allowed. This job is your punishment, remember?"

McLaris stood quiet for a moment, unsure what to say. Things seemed to be moving too fast. After all, it had only been a month since he had left *Orbitech 1*, since killing Jessie. He had to do his best, to make up for what he had done. He had fled *Orbitech 1* because he had known what Brahms would do, and he had turned coward when perhaps he should have stayed and used all his skills to convince Brahms to follow a different course of action. While lying in the infirmary bed feeling the anger of the other people around him, McLaris had sworn never to step aside again when an opportunity presented itself.

"I'll do it."

For the first time since the War, McLaris felt as though he had a purpose, a future. And he could sense it in the other, as well.

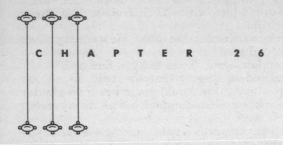

C H A P T E R 2 6

Curtis Brahms sat up straight behind his desk as Linda Arnando walked in. He had made her wait in the corridor while he combed his hair, dabbed cool water on his red eyes. Now he appeared a model of composure. He brushed his hands across the flat desktop and stared at her.

Linda looked at him, puzzled.

Brahms kept his voice neutral as he spoke to her. He intentionally made no greeting. "Close the door behind you, please. And seal it."

As the silence lengthened, Linda began to appear actively uncomfortable. "You asked to see me?"

Brahms took no pleasure in watching her squirm. He drummed his fingertips on the desktop, then straightened his eyeglasses. "You've been caught. I took Dr. Aiken under restraint an hour ago."

Her eyes widened.

"You're just as guilty as he is." Brahms felt his voice grow heavy. He seemed very tired, without energy, though he

had been trying to get enough sleep despite the nightmares that plagued him of the RIF, of obese Tim Drury
looking betrayed.

He lurched forward across the desk. "How could you act
like this? I trusted you!"

Linda bowed her head. "How did you find out?"

Brahms realized in disgust that the only reason she
wanted to know was so she could cover her tracks better
the next time. His shoulders slumped, but he saw no reason
to keep it to himself.

"You don't hang around scientists, Linda. We know you
better than that. You just don't. I had Terachyk check
Aiken out. Once we looked, we saw what you found—yes,
he had manipulated his data and, yes, he had greatly exaggerated his results.

"And then, you know what? I had a strange idea. Call it a
hunch—that's what I'm supposed to be good at. But when
we looked into *your* records, Linda, you know what we
found?" He felt hot and feverish with his anger, as if sweat
prickled and boiled up under his scalp. "We found out
you've been using your computer access to increase your
own allotment of rations."

Linda sat up straight, indignant. She brushed her dark
hair back. The sparse silver strands seemed to be getting
more prominent. "My job is important. I didn't do it very
often, only when I really needed—"

Brahms closed out her words. He felt anger rushing up
inside, and he lashed out and slapped her across the face.
Then he strode around the desk. "How dare you! How
dare you claim that you're better than anyone else on this
station! How dare you imply that your job is more important than anyone else's here!"

Linda looked stunned. A red splash of flushed skin
showed where he had struck her cheek. Brahms hooked
his fingers together and clenched them.

"Four division leaders, and I killed Tim Drury because
his score was lowest. It was a show of my faith, of how
honest I was trying to be under the circumstances."
Brahms felt the blood pounding in his temples. Fury made
it difficult for him to see straight.

"McLaris . . ." Brahms ground his teeth together.
"Stealing our shuttle! You—a traitor!"

He turned away, feeling his face flush. He was losing control. He took a deep breath, let it out slowly. "And Allen—he's so wrapped up in his own misery he can't even pay attention to what he's doing."

Brahms stood stiffly. He didn't know what to do. This wasn't supposed to happen. Curtis Brahms *never* lost control.

Linda brushed at her uniform, as if trying to regain a semblance of dignity. "It won't happen again."

The anger surged back behind his eyes again, making him so outraged he could find no words. He threw his eyeglasses down at the desk; one of the flat lenses shattered. Brahms looked at the glasses as if they were a strange animal, then brushed them onto the floor. He stared at Linda, eyes blazing.

"You're damn right it won't happen again!"

She shifted in her chair, avoided his gaze for an instant, then looked back at him, refusing to retreat. But that didn't make any points with Brahms. He lowered his head as the bright anger backed off a bit. His voice dropped to a sad whisper.

"You really don't understand, do you? You really don't get it?" Brahms tapped at the intercom link. "Send Dr. Aiken in." He pushed another button, which unsealed the door.

Linda maintained her silence, puzzled, looking uneasy. He heard footsteps on the thin carpet, then two Watchers in spring-green jumpsuits came to the doorway, holding Daniel Aiken up between them.

The two watchers—an older man and a sour-looking woman—held Aiken's hands behind his back, but he seemed to be in no condition to struggle.

He had been beaten badly. His upper lip was smashed into an angry, blood-coated wound that had been cleaned and tended but not bandaged. His hair was rumpled, his eyes bloodshot, his skin scuffed with new bruises that would soon turn purple. The way he acted made him look like a lost animal, utterly helpless.

Linda looked at Aiken, and her false repentant expression dropped away like a sheet. She stared, then whirled to gape in horror at Brahms. He waved away her accusation before she could say anything.

"Two of the watchers . . . misinterpreted my instructions. They have been reprimanded, don't worry. You'll be getting punishment enough, both of you."

Now Linda began to look very afraid. Brahms watched it creep up on her: Her skin became pale and grayish, and a sheen of sweat appeared on her forehead. Brahms turned away from her. He began to talk in a low voice as he stared at a picture on the wall. It was a reprint of an old Russian masterpiece by Ilia Repin, a dramatic portrait of Ivan the Terrible in the moment of shock after he had accidentally killed his own son, his only hope for the future of his dynasty. Now the tsar's problems seemed trivial and melodramatic.

Brahms's words were low and ominous, but they built in intensity.

"I trusted you, Linda. And I don't trust people lightly. You were supposed to be concerned for the safety and the future of this colony. You were not to use your position for your own ends. You have let me down. Do you realize that? Do you even know what you've done?"

Brahms glared at her, then at Aiken, with undisguised disgust. "If I can't trust my own assessors, we're all doomed. You know the magnitude of trouble we're in, and you still think you can do whatever you want, that your actions have no consequences.

"You and this . . . worm of a scientist who tried to bankrupt our hope—you are lower than any of those who went out the airlock first. I can't have it."

He shook his head stiffly, like a ventriloquist's dummy that could rotate only a little from side to side. He clutched his fists, then released them. His whole body stiffened. He felt his muscles locking.

"I can't have it!"

Then it all ran out of him. He let his voice drop to a dead, uninflected tone. "You, Linda Arnando, and you, Daniel Aiken, will be RIFed. Tomorrow.

"It will be broadcast live. Everyone on this station will be given the full story. Everyone will know what you have done, how you betrayed us. All of us. It's your fault entirely."

Linda blinked her eyes, absolutely astounded.

"But you . . . can't. I'm one of your division leaders, for Christ's sake! How can you—"

But Brahms was not even listening. Aiken seemed to collapse in on himself. He made no sound, did not beg for his life or plead for mercy. He just shook with silent sobs. His puffed eyes were shut tight. Tears streamed down his bruised cheeks.

Brahms pushed the intercom button again. "Come and get them."

The two watchers came back in and escorted Linda Arnando and Daniel Aiken out.

"See that they stay in their cabins. Seal the doors."

One of the watchers lifted an eyebrow. It was the woman, Nancy Winkowski. "There's nowhere for them to go, Mr. Brahms."

"Seal it anyway." *There's no place for any of us to go,* he thought.

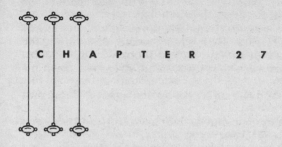

C H A P T E R 2 7

To Ramis, Karen Langelier's lab seemed like a toy store, filled with remnants of American industrial technology that in light of their disaster were alien or even nonsensical. The lipstick fabrication section seemed especially ludicrous.

Karen showed him how she extruded her weavewire, making it zip up the laser guide beam into a fiber so fine that it couldn't be seen—and though two rockets couldn't snap it in half, it could cut through titanium. Even to touch a single strand of the fiber would have sliced his fingertips off.

And when Karen pointed out that some of the garments on *Orbitech 1* were woven from the monomolecular fiber, he was even more astonished. He listened to her explanation of how the manufacturing prototypes spun together hundreds of kilometers of thread—thereby making it safe—into a single piece of indestructible clothing that could be worn like any other shirt.

Over the last two days, he and Karen had spent hours together. They found in their loneliness a friendship that transcended the quarter-century difference in their ages.

Now he sat and watched. She wanted to talk, but he knew she couldn't afford to give up more time from her research, not with the assessors watching over them all. Karen's lower lip was drawn back, held between white teeth in an expression of concentration. Her red hair was tousled.

The air stank of escaped chemicals from burners and polymer melts. His eyes stung at first, but he got used to it. The other polymer chemists worked on their own projects, and Ramis knew how dangerous it would be to interrupt them.

He could drift in the zero-G labs, float from cubicle boundary to cubicle boundary, though he could not Jump here. They didn't have the wide-open spaces. He thought of the *Aguinaldo*'s core.

Here, only the wraithlike spider plant, sealed vials of chemicals, and empty spheres from drinks bobbled and drifted in the air currents. The zero gravity offered them freedom, so they caged everything.

After a burst of static, the "attention" tones sounded from the PA holotank column in the center of the lab cubicles. Karen sat up with a start and turned to look, focusing back in on her situation. The neutral gray of the holotank resolved into colored speckles that congealed into a three-dimensional representation of the face of Curtis Brahms.

"May I have your attention, please?" His voice warbled and his face moved, as if he was working the controls himself and didn't quite know what he was doing.

"May I have your attention, please?" The voice became stronger, firmer. "I must make an announcement of the greatest importance to all on *Orbitech 1*."

The other workers in the lab complex snapped to attention. "Another RIF already? My God!" someone said. Ramis drifted closer to the curved face of the holotank.

"You all know the desperate plight the War has brought us to. You all know how hard you're working to help save us from starvation, to rescue us by using our technical excellence to make up for the few resources we have on hand."

Brahms lifted his chin and swallowed, as if opting not to continue his morale-building speech. His face had a haunted look. Ramis noticed he was not wearing his eyeglasses, and he appeared too young for the burden he bore, too boyish.

"I am sorry to say that two among us have been traitors to that mission. They have tried to sabotage our survival by lying and cheating, to improve their own situation at the expense of the rest of our people. This man—"

The scene dissolved, and a camera swiveled to show a man being hauled along by two of the watchers. His lip looked wounded, and his eyes were sunken and dark with bruises.

"—is Daniel Aiken. He altered research results to make his work seem more important, to make us seem closer to survival than we are. His lie has stolen a valid hope from all of us. He sidetracked and wasted valuable resources."

"Look, they've beaten him up!" one of the polymer chemists cried. "Brahms beat him up!"

"Linda Arnando is also part of this," Brahms continued. "She worked with Aiken. She was our chief assessor—one of my division leaders. But instead of reporting Aiken's falsified data, she used it to blackmail him. She also used her administrative position to steal our rations—to take more than her share."

Arnando looked broken. The view pulled back to show her and Aiken inside the empty shuttle bay. Several of the researchers muttered; someone in the background began to sob.

The armed watchers let go of their charges and then pushed toward the spoke-shaft elevator, sealing it behind them. Aiken stood looking battered and stunned, but Linda Arnando gathered herself and bounced for the sealed doors.

The camera flicked back to Brahms again. "These two do not deny what they have done. They are guilty of cheating us, of hurting our chances for survival. I hope to God these are the only two in our midst.

"Director Ombalal did not try to hide his reduction in force from you, and you killed him for it. But these two are not innocents, and I will not hide this. Their guilt is cut and dried, and clear. Linda Arnando and Daniel Aiken have forfeited their right to live on *Orbitech 1* while others have sacrificed themselves.

"Therefore, these two will add their numbers to those who have already gone to reduce our population."

The camera showed a full view of the shuttle bay now. Ramis could see where he had come in, drifting with the carcass of Sarat, the colored lines painted on the floor where a shuttle would land—a shuttle like the *Miranda*, which Duncan McLaris had stolen.

Aiken floated upside down, cross-legged, above the bull's-eye with his head in his hands. Linda Arnando bounced off the walls, shouting something, but the picture carried no sound. A magenta warning light flashed by the outer airlock doors, but Ramis could hear no klaxon.

The other people in the lab complex were quiet, terrified. "This is going to backfire on him," Karen whispered out loud, but she seemed to be talking to herself. "The first RIF was for survival—this one is for revenge."

The camera pivoted down the length of Brahms's arm to where his hand rested on a red button on the control panel. He had already removed the interlocks.

As the camera focused on his hand, he pushed the button.

Karen drew in a single gasping breath. The holotank showed Brahms's face again. He looked drained.

"I don't want you to think of this as a reign of terror. Our future lies in the people of *Orbitech 1*, on our skills and our abilities. There is no prejudice in survival—all are equal here.

"You have the ability to prevent another RIF, but you cannot prevent it with lies." He paused and swallowed. When he spoke again, his voice sounded dry and cracked. "We're all in this together."

The picture of him winked off, to be replaced by the gaping starlit maw of the open shuttle-bay doors and the empty, empty chamber where Linda Arnando and Daniel Aiken had been only moments before. A patch of smeared frost stood out on the polished floor.

Ramis watched, appalled and sickened. He stared at the vastness of black, cold space where Aiken and Arnando had now set their sails, but they had no Sarat to catch them. A giddiness swirled up around Ramis, and he muttered quietly, but loud enough for Karen Langelier to hear, "I do not want to stay here anymore. I want to go home."

Karen went looking for Ramis after he fled the lab complex. The Filipino boy moved stiffly, reeling and uncomfortable, as if he couldn't believe what he had just witnessed.

Karen knew the shock the other people on *Orbitech 1* were feeling—the stunned resignation and growing fear that the nightmare would never end. But Ramis seemed worse off. He had not been there for the first RIF; he had not suffered the horrified astonishment that the rest of them had. He had heard about it, but that was not enough.

Karen felt sorry for the boy in an almost maternal way as she searched for him. She smiled at that. She and Ray had never had any children, which was no surprise—they couldn't find enough time for each other in the relationship, so how could they possibly have introduced a wild card like a child?

Karen had wanted children, though. She and Ray had discussed it, but always conditionally. We'll talk about it after this. Or we'll wait and see how that turns out. After they had been married for five years, Karen had had the estrogen implant on the inside of her left arm removed, theoretically making her fertile again, but nothing had happened.

She looked for Ramis in the Japanese garden, the obvious place for him to have gone to find peace. But watchers were there, planting some confiscated plants and inspecting the progress of the wall-kelp.

Karen found him on the darkened observation deck in one of the plush lounge chairs, staring out into the blizzard of stars. The smoky belt of the Milky Way swept across the view along the Galactic plane, but the spatters of outlying stars were impressive even in the dimmest areas.

Karen didn't see him at first, with his dark hair, sitting so still in the chair. "Ramis?"

He didn't get up. He must have heard her approach. "I'm just looking at the stars."

She lost her voice, and had to cough before words would come out again. "Is there anything I can do?"

"I can't stay here anymore." His words sounded sad and devastated. "The embryos I brought with me will not be ready to go for a year. I cannot return to the *Aguinaldo*." She didn't know what to think, or if she should humor him. "I have found where I want to go."

Then Karen saw he had raised a hand and pointed out the window. With the broad sea of stars, it was difficult to follow exactly where he pointed, but she knew he meant the brilliant point of light, brighter than anything in view.

"Look in the observation scope," Ramis said.

She stepped forward and pressed her eyes against the cushioned eyepieces. The shining torus of the silent Soviet *Kibalchich* burst into view.

"Ramis, you can't get over there—you can't go over there. I don't think they've made contact with us since just after the War. They warned everyone to stay away."

He didn't look at her, didn't move in his chair. "I can get there. It is only a hundred kilometers. I can Jump."

For the first time, Karen realized that Ramis was serious, not just fantasizing. Then a deep fear for him struck her. She put her hand on his shoulder; he flinched, then relaxed.

"Ramis, that's too dangerous. It's foolish! You can't—" She cut herself off and remembered that Ramis had indeed flown by himself all the way from L-4.

"It can't be any worse than here." His next words were spoken in a soft, cold whisper. "The most frightening part is going to be asking Brahms for permission."

ORBITECH 1 ■ DAY 37

In the director's office, Ramis tried to remain still. He sat up straight and met Brahms's gaze. Karen Langelier remained beside him, giving him moral support, but Ramis knew this was his show—the confrontation would be up to him.

Curtis Brahms smiled and steepled his fingers across the desktop. It was an annoying gesture he seemed to make often. He appeared warm and welcoming to his visitors, but he made Ramis's skin crawl. Ramis had watched him eject two people from the airlock the day before. He could sense the anger, the violence of this man hiding behind his cool, efficient facade.

The acting director was cordial now, though, as if all those terrible things had been done by someone else. By bringing the wall-kelp, by distracting all the people on *Orbitech 1* with his heroic mission, Ramis had earned Brahms's gratitude—at least enough for him to see the two of them when Ramis had asked, and to listen attentively to the *Kibalchich* proposal.

Brahms pondered the idea in silence. Karen said nothing, but Ramis was glad she was there.

Brahms took a deep breath. "Ramis, that is a fascinating proposal. I don't know why none of us thought of it." Brahms flashed the briefest of sharp glances at Karen, as if she were a scapegoat for all the researchers on *Orbitech 1*.

"But listen to this last transmission from the *Kibalchich*, broadcast on the open band about three weeks ago." His fingers spent a few moments working at the keypad, linking to the communications center log. Ramis and Karen remained silent, waiting for him. Brahms found what he wanted and played it over the set of desk speakers. "It's voice only. We can't even see for sure who was talking."

He sat back and listened.

"This is Commander Stepan Rurik of the Soviet research station *Kibalchich*. We hereby sever all ties with other survivors on Earth's space colonies. Do not attempt to contact us. We wish to remain isolated."

Brahms drew his mouth tight. "We haven't heard a word from them since. I've had my communications people try to contact them daily, but no one ever answers. I can't tell if they're just being stubborn, or if something's happened to them."

He frowned again. "And you want to go over there and investigate. My automatic inclination is to say no, it's too dangerous. But then secondary thoughts kick in, and I come up with many different reasons why I *should* let you go."

He held up his fingers, ticking them off. "First, I think it's important for us to find out what happened to them, why they've broken off contact. Even if we were adversaries in the War, we could find some way to work things out, now that we've got so much to lose.

"Ah!" He smiled as if another thought had just occurred to him. "And you'd be going as a Filipino citizen, not as a representative of *Orbitech 1*. They won't be able to hold anything against us.

"The second reason—if they all did die, it happened much too quickly for them to have used up all their supplies. Even though we now have the wall-kelp, the *Kibalchich* could have lots of other provisions just sitting there for the taking. Hmmm, although getting them back over here will be another problem."

Karen spoke up. "I have an idea about that, Mr. Brahms."

He looked at her and nodded. "Let me finish my reasons first, then I'll ask."

Karen nodded, then sat back. The words sounded like a reprimand to Ramis, but he could detect no negative tone in Brahms's voice. The director held up his hand and ticked off a third reason, as if he didn't want to lose his train of thought.

"Also, the Soviets were working on many different research items. They were very close-mouthed about everything, but we were able to watch them constructing the *Kibalchich* through our telescopes. All we know is that it was a research station. Now, if they are indeed gone, perhaps they left something behind that we can use. We can take their technology for our own benefit.

"Fourth—and this may be more important than you realize—by undertaking such an adventure, you will give a tremendous boost to our morale here. I'm not too stupid to admit that we're in bad shape. Our researchers are too frightened or too depressed to do their best work. This mission of yours would give them something to hope for, something to watch. We could even hold a competition for designing the best apparatus to assist you in getting over there.

"After we broadcast it over ConComm, you'll also be a hero, twice over—to Clavius Base and to your home, *Aguinaldo.*"

He smiled, looking boyish all of a sudden without his eyeglasses. "And, finally, what have we got to lose?"

Ramis grinned back at him, but in a corner of his mind he thought of another reason, one that Brahms no doubt had been reluctant to say out loud. *If I don't come back, that's one less mouth you have to feed from your precious supplies.*

Brahms cleared his throat and turned to address Karen. She jumped at the sudden attention and averted her eyes.

"Now then, Dr. Langelier, I'm interested in hearing your ideas about bringing supplies back."

"Well, I don't know if your assessors have been keeping you up-to-date on my work."

Brahms flicked his eyes to the console screen on his desk surface. He brushed his fingers over a few keys and stared at the words scrolling up. "Ah, yes, your weavewire. But that was years ago, and in New Mexico yet. There haven't been any new developments that I can see, unless you count those garments you've made."

Karen wet her lips. "Let me explain, Mr. Brahms—put this in perspective. The weavewire is only one molecule thick and held together by an unusual type of potential. It won't mean anything to you, but it's called a one-and-a-half-dimensional material. It's so thin you can't see it, but it won't break except under conditions so extreme we can't even create them in the laboratory. And since it's only one molecule thick, it requires very little raw material and weighs almost nothing, in addition to being extremely flexible."

"And?" Brahms tapped one finger on the desktop with the first signs of impatience. "I'm sure that's all summarized here."

"Well, up until lately, I've only been able to draw out a couple hundred kilometers a day under stringently controlled laboratory conditions. As I draw it out I have to electromagnetically braid the fiber into a macroscopic weave so it will not be dangerous. Being one molecule thick, it can slice through anything—steel, people, the colony.

"Anyway, I've perfected a new process to draw out tens of thousands of kilometers a day without being under those stringent conditions. That is, I can make the weavewire on demand, anywhere and any time. Since the weavewire doesn't even exist until it's drawn out, we don't have to

222 KEVIN J. ANDERSON AND DOUG BEASON

store it—we can use it as an indestructible cable. When Ramis goes, he can trail a double wire behind him. If he reaches the *Kibalchich,* our two colonies will then be connected by a very thin and very strong cable—a lifeline, like they used to have between rescue ships. We can use it as a ferry to haul things back and forth, like a big pulley."

Brahms watched her. "I thought you just said the wire would slice through any material—"

"Any material except itself! We could construct a harness made of weavewire that rides along the length of the line, use that to haul supplies back from the *Kibalchich.*"

Brahms got a far-off look in his eyes. "Yessss." He stood up and nodded to them with his decision. "Ramis, as soon as Dr. Langelier has everything ready for you, I want you to go to the *Kibalchich.* I will announce the project and have a competition to design the best method for getting you there. That would certainly raise the colony's morale."

He pointed toward the door in an obvious gesture of dismissal. Ramis felt so uncomfortable at being near the director, he lost no time getting up from his seat.

"I can't tell you how much of a pleasure it is to be able to make this kind of announcement instead of something much more unpleasant," Brahms continued. "Good luck, and Godspeed."

Relieved, and trying not to run, Ramis fled the acting director's office.

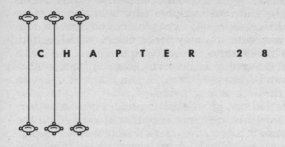

C H A P T E R 2 8

CLAVIUS BASE ■ DAY 39

Leaning back on his bunk, Duncan McLaris stared at the
gray-brown rock of the textured wall. Some of the rooms
were finished with white ceramic tiles; others had been
sealed and left *au naturel*. McLaris preferred the latter.

He tilted his gaze up to the narrow strip of thick glass
that formed a window for him to look out at the lunar
surface and the stars beyond.

With the new catacombs and the extra quarters dug in
them, Cliff Clancy's engineers had spread out. Many of the
other Clavius Base personnel had moved into newer and
more spacious quarters. Since he was now base manager,
McLaris himself laid claim to one of the biggest new rooms
—one close enough to the surface to have the lip of a
window.

From where he lay on the cot, he noticed smudged fin-
gerprints on the clear plastic from the many times he had
pulled himself up to see better.

The window was important to him. His wife Diane had

always insisted on being where she could stare outside. In their quarters on *Orbitech 1* she had grown a small pine seedling in a pot under a UV lamp. McLaris had left the seedling behind, with so many other things, when he had escaped from the station.

He had left those others behind to die, a hundred and fifty of them, in Brahms's RIF.

But the satisfaction and pride of what he was now achieving for Clavius Base did much to chip away the leaden weight of his conscience. McLaris could honestly say he was doing his best work now. He saw some results quite plainly. He was getting things done—things that Tomkins had long put off out of disinterest.

Now that Tomkins had absorbed himself in his Arecibo II telescope project, he had come back to life; he was dynamic and enthusiastic again. He should never have become an administrator in the first place.

And the Clavius Base personnel did not shun McLaris quite so much. Though he hated even to consider it, McLaris had been vindicated by Brahms and his RIF. It had shown that McLaris wasn't being an alarmist, that he had known exactly what the acting director would do.

And just three days before, Brahms had ejected Linda Arnando into cold space. They had mentioned that as only a footnote to their daily ConComm broadcast, but McLaris had heard. He had not known Linda Arnando well—she had seemed too much of a climber, always pushing to get ahead and looking to turn things to her own advantage. But the thought of her thrown out into space made him sick inside. Brahms was turning worse than even he had imagined.

Restless, McLaris got up and went to his computer console. He didn't feel like sleeping, though it was ostensibly the base's night period. After life on *Orbitech 1*, the crazy journey on the *Miranda*, and now the Moon base, all three with distinctly different periods of day and night, his body's circadian rhythms had given up in despair.

He called up the electronic memo pad and accessed his crossheadings. A glance at the "Things to Do" window displayed four items McLaris felt he had firmly in hand. He was making progress.

Chimes rang at his door. McLaris called for the visitor to

come in, but after he spoke he sat up, startled, realizing how late it was. He wondered who would call on him now.

The door slid open and Clifford Clancy stood outside, carrying a package wrapped in a silvery reflecting blanket from one of the lunar six-pack rovers.

"Dr. Clancy, what are you doing up this time of night?"

Clancy blinked and looked at his wrist chronometer. "Oh, sorry. I lost track of what time it is, as usual. Did I disturb you? You don't look like you were asleep."

"No, no. I was just scheduling things. Come on in. And by the way, I think you can call me Duncan. Anybody who's saved my life has the right to do that."

Clancy waved his hand in a gesture of dismissal, but McLaris could see he was hiding a broad smile. "Doesn't do much good to have only one of us on a first-name basis. You might as well call me Cliff. We seem to be stuck here for the duration."

"And with our jobs, we'll be crossing paths once in a while," McLaris added. He watched Clancy, and soon he could detect a strong undercurrent of nervousness in the head engineer's actions.

"So, Cliff, what have you got? Is everything going all right with the Arecibo II project? Do you think Tomkins knows what he's talking about?"

Clancy chuckled. "When it comes to telescopes and stuff, Tomkins is tops. I have no qualms with him there."

But that wasn't what Clancy wanted to talk about. McLaris sat back and waited in silence. He decided that banter would only put off what Clancy wanted to say, make him even uneasier.

"McLaris—Duncan, I mean—I just wanted to say that I'm . . . I appreciate the way you handled the, uh, problem between me and Tomkins. Some of my engineers were skeptical about building that telescope, but they're all for it now. They were just so damned antsy with nothing to do—and this is a big enough project that it's going to keep us all occupied for a long time. I've got one crew tuning up the mass driver, another bunch at the smelting processors.

"You were right. With the wall-kelp and our botanical stuff, we've already done what we can to survive. It's just wait and see for now. You gave us something to keep our hopes up, to keep our minds active in the meantime. And I really appreciate it. That comes from me and all my men."

"All your *people*," McLaris said, grinning.

"Touché." Clancy set down his package on McLaris's rounded tabletop and unfolded the blanket.

"I found this in the wreckage of the *Miranda*. I didn't know what to do with it and I sort of forgot about it until the other day. It must have been your daughter's . . . and I thought you might want it back."

McLaris stared down at Jessie's computerized music synthesizer. Smudges of lunar dust marked its polished black sides. His eyes filmed over with a wet sheen of tears.

Clancy saw him and stepped backward toward the door, embarrassed. "Um, I just wanted to give that to you. I have to go." He left McLaris's quarters rapidly with his half-balanced, rolling gait.

Distracted, McLaris closed the door and stared at the dead instrument. He had given it to Jessie for her birthday —or was it Christmas? She had played it on *Orbitech 1* over and over again, in their quarters, in the lounge. Jessie had also played it in the cramped cabin of the shuttle as they fled *Orbitech 1*. She had made up her own songs, or followed along with the flashing colored lights to play pre-programmed tunes.

He remembered trying to braid her hair, trying to explain things to her that she couldn't possibly understand, though she nodded sagely and accepted what he told her.

He had sat in the lounge with her, pointing out at the universe and tracing the constellations for her. Jessie had been intrigued by the idea of connect-the-dots with the stars, and had made up her own constellations, drawing a chair and a tree, and in the majestic form of Orion, she had drawn her "diddy."

Jessie had cried when her mother had left for that short sabbatical on Earth, to see trees again, and mountains. . . .

Once again, like the shark's mouth of a nightmare, McLaris remembered Jessie's cracked, empty faceplate with the air hissing out. And though he tried and tried, he couldn't move in his own splintered agony to help her.

He had told her to be brave. He had told her she'd be all right.

McLaris activated the keyboard. The instrument played
back the last song in its memory—a crystalline, synthesized version of "Twinkle, Twinkle, Little Star."

McLaris remembered the three of them sitting in the
Miranda as Jessie pushed on the follow-along keys when
they lit up, playing the tune as the computer guided her.
McLaris and Stephanie Garland sang along, laughing to
drive away their fear and nervousness. Jessie giggled and
played the song over and over, until McLaris thought he
never wanted to hear it again.

But now, in his quarters, the song came out of the keyboard. Jessie's fingers had played that song into the computer's memory. It was like a ghost of his daughter coming
back to haunt him. Or to forgive him.

Duncan McLaris sat back on his bunk and tilted his head
to look through the window near the ceiling, seeing far
beyond the stars. Then he closed his eyes, squeezing out
warm moisture to run down along his temples as he lay
back.

He kept crying, because there was no one to see him.

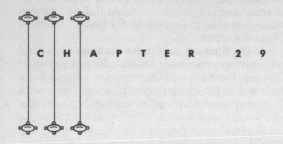

CHAPTER 29

The *Kibalchich* hung in the silent blackness fifty miles away. Even outside of *Orbitech 1*, suited up and floating without any curved walls to block her view, Karen had to squint to discern the Soviet station. It looked like a brilliant point, smeared into shapelessness by reflected sunlight. She couldn't even tell if it still rotated, much less if it displayed any signs of life.

She knew she would see some of the frozen bodies from the RIF. The Lagrange gravity well encompassed a huge volume of space, but they were still out there, desiccated by the vacuum, frozen solid, their final expressions intact.

Karen had never been outside before. She didn't like listening to every breath echoing in her head. The air pressure in her suit made her feel stiff, like a knight in rusty armor. During history's first space walk, Alexei Leonov had found it impossible even to bend over enough to get back inside the airlock of the *Voskhod 2*; if he hadn't risked a desperate vacuum decompression maneuver he would have died in space, a few inches away from safety. Sometimes Karen wished she had limited her Russian background to being able to read their technical journals, as she had originally intended.

She waited quietly, floating next to Ramis as he prepared himself for the journey, checking his suit, looking around with practiced ease. Karen was accustomed to zero-G from her lab space, but this felt colder somehow, blacker, with the whole wide universe waiting to gobble her up. She couldn't think of any word to describe the absolute opposite of claustrophobia.

Hour after hour, Brahms had his communications people attempting to contact the *Kibalchich*. They sent greetings, messages of peace; they announced that Ramis was coming over. No reply. They asked to know why the Soviets had warned them away, why they had stopped sending radio transmissions. Karen could have understood the Russian language herself, but no one had asked for her to respond to any contact.

"There's nobody over there," Brahms had said.

"Then how is Ramis supposed to get inside?" she had asked. Brahms looked at her as if she had interrupted his thoughts again.

"Do not worry, Karen," Ramis had said. "They have emergency-access airlocks studded around the hull—all the colonies have them left over from construction. The crews had to be able to get inside quickly if a disaster happened, or if somebody detected a big solar flare. Maintenance people still use them to go out and inspect the hull. Those airlocks are all over the *Aguinaldo* and *Orbitech 1*. I can get in even if the Soviets do not answer when I knock."

Karen didn't think it made any sense for the Soviets to break off contact, especially now, when they would all have to pull together and pool resources. The *Kibalchich* was the smallest of the space colonies; perhaps they had run out of supplies already.

Karen's stomach felt queasy, though she wasn't the one going across the gulf. Were they all dead over there? What was Ramis getting himself into?

Brahms's competition had resulted in some innovative designs for Ramis's passage. It was only after the director had realized that some of his brighter engineers might use their designs personally that Brahms had called a halt to the contest.

Ramis's space suit made him appear much larger than he was, insectlike. He was dwarfed by the Manned Maneuvering Unit strapped to his back and the harness carrying the half-dozen air bottles he would need for the long journey.

In case he couldn't find any food on the Soviet station, Karen had helped him lash some supplies and a sealed container of wall-kelp to his waist. Despite Brahms's sour protests, Ramis had insisted the gift from the *Aguinaldo* was for both L-5 colonies. Mounted on the center of his chest, Ramis wore a small two-dimensional video camera to record the journey and whatever he found inside the *Kibalchich*.

Aided by the MMU, Ramis would Jump the fifty-odd miles of deep, bottomless space across the L-5 zone. The idea didn't seem to bother him, and that concerned Karen. The *Orbitech 1* telescopes had pinpointed several of the *Kibalchich*'s manually operated emergency hatches, so he could get inside without other assistance—but after the warning the Soviets had issued, what if they had active defense mechanisms against such an entry? Ramis was resilient, maybe even reckless. That could be dangerous.

If nothing else, Karen hoped she had managed to impress on him the extreme danger from the trailing weavewire on his back. The single-molecule-thick strand was sharper than the sharpest razor in the world. A nick could just as easily cut off an arm or a leg, or sever an air tank in two and make it explode. The other Orbitech engineers were scared silly of the lifeline fiber, and they had been reluctant to help Ramis prepare, though Karen had made the first hundred feet of fiber a million braided strands thick, so it posed no greater danger than any fine wire.

Finally, Karen had volunteered herself, though she hated to suit up. She felt obligated to give him the best possible safety factor. The odds against him seemed bad enough to start with.

Karen felt herself sweating inside the snug, temperature-monitored environment of her suit. But Ramis's

LIFELINE   231

breathing came over her headphones—slow, measured
breaths, with no sense of excitement. She knew his greatest emotion right now would be relief at escaping the
sharp eyes of Curtis Brahms, if only for a time.

Karen scanned the diagnostic on the outside of the dispensing cavity mounted to the hull of *Orbitech 1.* Using
absorption resonance, the unit kept track of the total mass
of weavewire that had been drawn out. High above, the
thin, discontinuous mirror that directed sunlight into the
colony's two toruses looked black and filled with stars, reflecting the universe back into itself.

Ramis tugged at the belt that connected the weavewire
fiber to him. "Is it all ready for me?" He pushed closer to
the dispensing outlet, moving slowly in his huge suit, and
studied the apparatus.

The thick, braided weavewire trailed from Ramis's belt,
which had also been woven from the fiber to give an
anchoring point. The tail-end of the weavewire showed
thin and faint, Day-Glo orange but visible only when she
knew exactly where to look. The remainder in the dispensing cavity would be completely invisible in its double
strand when Ramis reeled it out behind him.

Karen still felt the tightness in her stomach, but she
forced herself to speak. "It's ready to go. Just be careful not
to start spinning. If you get tangled in it—" Her voice
trailed off.

"I will be like a fish that has been filleted!" Ramis said,
then laughed over the intercom. "But I want you to think
good thoughts, Karen. Your fiber is making this journey
possible. If I needed to bear a steel cable behind me, I
would have so much inertia I could never stop my Jump. I
would be a yo-yo between these two colonies."

She wasn't sure if she should feel proud or guilty.

Ramis spoke optimistically, as if he knew that Brahms,
and most of *Orbitech 1,* were listening in on their conversation. "This will be a much simpler journey than my trip
from the *Aguinaldo* here. This time I have a margin for
error, and I am in control."

Before Karen could say anything, another voice cut in.
Brahms. "Ramis, the entire colony is anxious to hear what
you find in the *Kibalchich.* Is there anything more Dr.
Langelier can do before you attempt your jump?"

Ramis swung around to face Karen. By his cautious movements, she knew he remained conscious of the weavewire. He held out both his hands, as if to ask a question. Karen shook her helmet slowly. Seemingly satisfied, Ramis spoke over the radio, "I am ready, Mr. Brahms."

Karen reached out and grasped his space-suited arm, but the padding was so thick she couldn't tell if he felt her reassuring squeeze. *You're our only hope to get out of here, Ramis.*

Ramis took an unsteady step. The MMUs held him back momentarily, adding to his inertia. He turned to face the *Kibalchich* and bent his knees, planting his feet firmly against the metal hull of *Orbitech 1*.

Karen caught herself holding her breath.

"Do not worry," he radioed to her.

Ramis pushed off and drifted out into space toward the distant Soviet colony.

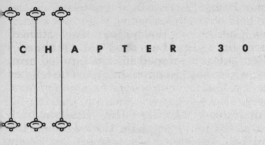

C H A P T E R   3 0

Dobo rushed into the laboratory, red-faced and short of breath. Sandovaal looked up from what he was doing and growled. "This had better be important, Dobo."

Sandovaal released the red grips of the microwaldoes he used to guide the nucleus-sized needle tip into a cellular mass. On the holotank image in front of him, an electron micrograph showed his work surrounded by a dashed bull's-eye pattern. Without his guidance, the tiny needle slewed off to the side of the target.

"I thought you knew by now not to disturb me. You could have ruined this entire series."

Rising from the lab bench, Sandovaal wiped his hands on his white apron. He was annoyed, but not overly so. The experimental grafts had been successful, and Dobo's entrance served to release the tension in his neck—yelling at someone always made him feel better.

Dobo shifted his weight from one foot to another, as if standing on a hot plate. "It is about Ramis! *Orbitech 1* has decided to allow him . . . I mean, Ramis has asked the *Orbitech* director for permission to—" He gulped a deep breath.

Sandovaal tapped his fingers together. "Well, out with it!" He waved for his assistant to take a seat. "Is Ramis in trouble again?" Sandovaal eased himself into his chair, which was far more comfortable and lower than the lab bench.

Dobo could barely keep his excitement to himself. "He is going to Jump from *Orbitech 1* to the *Kibalchich*!"

Sandovaal straightened in his chair. His long white hair fell into his eyes, and he flipped it away with such force that it dropped back into his face again. "What nonsense are you talking about?"

"It is true! Ramis has volunteered to cross the distance and see what has happened to the Soviet colony—"

"A hundred kilometers by Jumping?" Sandovaal snorted. "If he is only a little off course he will float forever! No, he will probably carry air tanks with him for maneuvering. Hmmm, I thought his journey in the sail-creature would make him grow up."

"Ramis is ready even as I speak. *Orbitech 1* is broadcasting it over the ConComm."

Sandovaal rocked forward in his chair and sprang up to pace across the room. He punched up the *Aguinaldo* communications center on the holotank. A man's face came into focus, startled at Sandovaal's override.

"What is this nonsense about Ramis Jumping?" Sandovaal said.

The face in the holotank blinked at him. Behind him, the nerve center of the *Aguinaldo* went about business as usual: safety operations in the zero-G core, housing emergencies, micrometeorite drills. "We are monitoring the *Orbitech 1* transmissions over ConComm, Dr. Sandovaal. They are beaming us a view from outside their colony. Ramis has attached himself to some sort of wire and will secure it to the *Kibalchich* once he completes his journey."

Sandovaal raised his hands and shouted at the communications officer. "Now I know the Americans are insane. They have so polluted their bodies with pizza and nachos that my wall-kelp must have sent them over the brink."

The officer's image faded, and was replaced by a starry view outside *Orbitech 1*. Dobo leaned forward to mutter to him. "I believe the Americans are using a new type of wire. It is very dangerous, I think."

"New type of wire?" Sandoval turned away from the holotank, raising his bushy eyebrows. "A hundred kilometers of wire? Do they have enough material to make a wire that long, or a place to store it?""

The holotank's picture rotated around Ramis, taking in the giant Manned Maneuvering Unit strapped to his back and resting on a small orange canister mounted to the colony's surface. Trailing from the canister, a thin Day-Glo orange strand was barely visible against the colony, enhanced for the broadcast. The image focused on the strand, and a voice started describing the wire in English.

"That is the stuff they make clothes out of!" Sandovaal made a deprecating sound with his lips. "I thought they could only draw that out a few kilometers a day."

As the explanation grew more detailed, Sandovaal frowned and leaned forward in his seat. "Turn the volume up." The footage took on the air of a documentary, with only Ramis's breathing to punctuate the background as the broadcaster's voice continued. It seemed rehearsed. At least the Americans would leave a good record of the efforts they had made, in case they did not survive.

Sandovaal strode to the holotank, squinting. "Magnify the image, Dobo. There, where it connects to Ramis's suit." Seconds later the weavewire filled the holotank; the sharp image warbled at the edges with the intense magnification.

Sandovaal's voice rose imperceptibly. "Do a data search, Dobo—request all information *Orbitech 1* will give us about how they draw out this fiber of theirs."

Poking his finger into the hologram image, Sandovaal tried to touch Ramis. "And make a note about those tactile-response holotanks. Times like these are when it is worth putting the damned things together."

Sandovaal traced the thin orange line from a belt around Ramis's waist. Another space-suited person floated in and out of the recorder's view. The narrator's voice grew quiet as another voice came over ConComm. "I am ready, Mr. Brahms."

The holotank swelled with the vision of Ramis. He squatted on *Orbitech 1*'s surface with his knees bent deep. The bulky MMUs looked as though they were going to make him topple backward.

Then Ramis sprang from the hull. The holocamera followed him as he receded from the colony. The view swung down for a parting shot at the unit reeling out the weavewire. A space-suited figure stood by the mechanism, stroking its surface as if it were alive.

Sandovaal remained quiet, staring into the holotank. The fiber seemed mystical to him.

"Dr. Sandovaal?"

Sandovaal waved Dobo quiet. A full minute passed before he whispered, "I must speak with Yoli Magsaysay."

The *dato* did not share his enthusiasm. Sandovaal blew his nose and spoke slowly, controlling himself. His impulse was to explain again, as if to an uncooperative child. But he knew that would annoy Magsaysay more than anything.

"The weavewire is the key, Yoli. I did not know they could produce useful quantities of the stuff. But apparently this is a new discovery. We must have this weavewire—it is the only way."

Magsaysay studied him before answering. "The only way, Luis? That sounds like a dangerous assumption from the outset."

Dobo relaxed beside Sandovaal, and thankfully kept his mouth shut. Magsaysay drummed his fingernails on the table and continued. "We are doing well now, are we not? Your projections show a sufficient distance between ourselves and starvation. This weavewire is the only way for what?"

"The only way for us to exploit the *Orbitech 2* site—all the resources left there."

He kept a smile off his face as Magsaysay reacted. Sandovaal continued. "Did we not learn from our pigheaded ancestors, who were so enamored of the old ways that they refused to accept help, to consider more efficient methods of production?" A sudden vision of tractors rusting in rice paddies filled his head.

"Yes, we can survive and live forever in our little colony. We will keep the status quo and never achieve anything else. And when the Americans survive and reach higher and higher, we will be their little brown brothers again, even if we outnumber them two hundred to one. Look what happened to the Chinese, and they outnumbered the Americans by a thousand times!"

Sandovaal narrowed his eyes and leaned across the table to the president. "We sent Ramis to *Orbitech 1* because we believed in helping people. It is time now to help ourselves. With the weavewire, we can safely Jump to the construction site and ferry all the supplies back here. The American crew left plenty of things there, including superior computers, materials, tools. With that, perhaps we can maintain our position as equals."

Magsaysay shifted uncomfortably. "Improving our way of life is one thing—changing our culture is a different matter."

Dobo seemed about to say something, but Sandovaal jutted out his jaw. "If we are growing antibiotics, then it is all right! But using the processing plant left at *Orbitech 2*, that is forbidden? This is like a race. Everyone else is riding a horse. We should not insist on walking because we are too lazy to look in the stable."

The two men stared at each other. Sandovaal had known Yoli Magsaysay for scores of years. They had butted heads often, but they shared the goal of bettering the Filipino people. Down Magsaysay's path, the Filipinos would keep to themselves, and the wall-kelp would see them through —just barely. But down the other path, they faced the danger of losing themselves and their culture, becoming ensnared with the Americans' obsession with breakneck progress. Or what was left of it.

But the *Aguinaldo* also had the opportunity to hold its own, to be equals instead of patronized "little brothers."

Sandovaal smiled plaintively. It was all an act, and he knew it. Magsaysay knew it, too. "Yoli, I followed you into space because I believed in your dream for us. Now I am asking you to follow *my* dream."

After some moments, a grin came to Magsaysay's lips, then he sighed. "You, my friend, have a point. But tell me —how will we get the weavewire to the *Aguinaldo*? Assuming *Orbitech 1* will even give it to us."

"We gave them the wall-kelp, did we not?" Dobo interrupted. "How can they refuse our request?"

Sandovaal shot a sidelong glance at Dobo. "Ramis used a sail-creature; so can we. And if we carry other sail-creature nymphs with us, and launch them at appropriate times during our flight, we can complete the circle and sail back to the *Aguinaldo*."

Magsaysay looked puzzled. "Who is 'we,' Luis? Only a few of us have Ramis's tenacity to survive the journey."

Sandovaal looked surprised. "Why, Dobo and myself, of course. Who better to ensure that the sail-creatures will make it back?"

A chair tipped over and clattered to the deck. Both men turned, startled at the sound. Dobo lay crumpled on the floor.

Sandovaal shrugged. "You see, Yoli? He has fainted with the excitement."

CHAPTER 31

Ramis felt regret the moment he Jumped from *Orbitech 1*. He knew the measured burst from the MMU added to his velocity, but he could not tell the difference. He was always bouncing from situation to situation, afraid to stay in one place too long. He always felt he had to show off, to take risks, to push himself to the edge.

The glaring metal hull of the industrial colony rushed away from him, rotating slowly around its axis. The weavewire trailed behind him, drawn out of its chamber on *Orbitech 1*'s nonrotating section, dangling him like a lure on a long fishing line. This time he felt vulnerable and alone without the protective womb of Sarat around him.

Relax, he told himself. This journey would not be as long as his previous one. Depending on how much force he had used to push himself away from *Orbitech 1* and the extra thrust from the MMU, it might take him six hours to cross the gap, or it might take a full day.

The *Kibalchich* looked so far away. It would be a long

time before he would notice it growing any closer. He drifted with absolutely no sense of motion. The Soviet colony, Earth, the stars, even the gibbous section of the Moon, seemed to hang like props in a silent movie. The stars did not help; cold and bright, they peppered the vast darkness with an immovable reference frame.

Twisting his head around, but careful not to pull the weavewire across his MMU pack, Ramis assured himself that he was indeed receding from the American colony. The video camera on his chest would record everything he saw.

He tried to estimate how fast he was drifting. His depth perception grew worse the farther he moved away, making it harder to judge.

A voice from the *Orbitech 1* control bay came over the link, answering the question before he could ask it. "We've got him at a velocity of four point eight meters per second—"

Ramis finished the calculation in his head: that was about seventeen kilometers per hour. Divide that into a hundred kilometers to the *Kibalchich*. The trip would take him six hours. Not as good as he'd hoped, but he couldn't change now without jetting from his MMUs, and he needed to reserve the fuel there for corrections. For good or bad, his course had been set.

Ramis could hear Curtis Brahms and Karen speaking to each other. Karen wanted to remain outside for as long as possible, ostensibly to monitor the weavewire dispensing cavity. Ramis knew she felt as much urgency to get off the claustrophobic colony as Ramis did, but she didn't seem willing to admit it to herself.

Ramis tuned out the radio chatter in his helmet, the babble of reassuring comments, good wishes, redundant instructions. He was by himself now, in control of everything in his own small environment. Despite the constant sensation of falling, he felt somehow at peace.

He let his arms and legs dangle loose. The closed environment of his suit felt huge and bulky, but not uncomfortable. As he sweated, the temperature controls of the suit cooled his skin. He felt nothing—nothing to touch, nothing to feel. He sensed the mass of the air tanks, the MMU pack, the sealed boots, but none of that mattered in weight-lessness.

He was swimming in the ocean of space, tethered by a line so thin it was invisible to the eye. He'd have to hang there for hours, vulnerable.

The thought of a solar flare spewing out deadly protons and x-rays gnawed at the back of his mind. If that hap-pened, he would be drilled by high-energy particles, fried crisper than a "dog on a log" back home on the Philip-pines.

He wished he could use the MMU again to add to his velocity, speed up the trip. Maybe he could use one of the air tanks. With nothing else to occupy him, Ramis began to run through mathematics in his head. If he doubled his velocity and finished the trip in half the time, he'd need only half as much air. And he could use compressed air from his tanks as easily as he could use propellant gas in the MMU. A couple of blasts from the nozzle of an air tank, and he could double, maybe even triple his speed. And if he did get inside the Soviet station, he could recharge his tanks. That meant he really only needed enough air for one way, not two.

He pursed his lips. He vowed not to be like the bickering senators in the *Aguinaldo*'s council meetings, endlessly considering options until the problem got around to resolving itself. And besides, what did he have to look forward to if he returned to *Orbitech 1*?

It sounded like a good enough risk to him.

Ramis took a few moments to rig one of his spare bottles, pointing the emergency bleed nozzle directly behind him over his shoulder. He wondered why none of the Orbitech theoreticians had come up with that solution.

He had to be extremely careful not to send himself into a tumble that would get him tangled in Karen's weavewire; the first hundred meters were thick multistrands that wouldn't cut him, but a tangle could still cause him big difficulties.

He blasted a jet of air behind him. In the padded suit, he felt the jerk of sudden acceleration, then rapidly lost all sensation of movement again. The *Orbitech 1* monitors would probably lecture him for altering his plans without letting them know.

Let Director Brahms come give me a spanking, then, he thought. *I can make my own decisions.* As if in defiance, he let out two more bursts from the air tank.

"—Ramis, what in the living hell are you doing out there?" He clicked off Brahms's voice, leaving his helmet in silence.

He decided he should try to get a little sleep. He could do nothing else. Newton's first law—or was it the second? —would keep him drifting until something made him stop.

Ramis jerked his eyes open. Stars rotated around him in a slow drift. Waving his arms in panic, he tried to see what was happening. The *Kibalchich* was nowhere in sight.

Fumbling with the controls on his suit's forearm, Ramis squirted the MMUs to compensate for his rotation. He felt the vibration of the hissing attitude jets. The bright wheel of the Soviet colony centered itself in his visor again.

The sound of breathing filled his helmet. He kicked on his heads-up display and scanned the suit diagnostics as they were bounced from the control panel below his chin into his front view plate. His air tank supply and the propellant in the MMUs looked good. The carbon dioxide count was a little high in the suit, but that made sense with his recent burst of rapid breathing.

He kicked back on his radio.

"—detected a click. We've got him back on line. Someone get the director."

A minute passed but no other sounds came over radio, until, "—Ramis, Curtis Brahms here. We lost you there for a while. How are you feeling?"

"Fine." His voice came out rough from sleepiness. He cleared his throat. "I am fine. I took a short nap—"

"We know," said Brahms. "We were monitoring your vital signs, and we show your breathing rate greatly increased. Is anything wrong?" Brahms paused a beat. "Why did you turn your radio off, Ramis?" His voice had an edge to it.

Ramis scowled to himself. *Even here, he is watching me.* "I started to rotate, but I have made the appropriate correction with the MMUs."

Karen Langelier's voice broke back into the conversation. "Diagnostics show the weavewire has twisted but is not now rotating. He's doing just fine."

"Good. Good job, Ramis." Brahms's voice still sounded tight. Ramis closed his eyes and scowled. "I'm leaving now. You will follow directions, won't you, Ramis?"

"Of course." Ramis cut the transmission short.

Hours passed as the universe coasted beneath him. Karen occasionally broke in to chat, and Ramis was glad of the company. Off and on he tried to signal the *Kibalchich* himself, but received no answer.

Now, it was less than thirty minutes away. The station's outer sheath of rubble hid the rotating living quarters. He could make out the giant mirror suspended above the colony. Unlike the *Aguinaldo*, which was built as an immense rotating cylinder, or even *Orbitech 1*'s dumbbell of counterrotating wheels, the Soviet colony looked like the classic doughnut-shaped space station conceived by Willy Ley more than a century before.

As he grew close, though, the station took on an alien look: jutting struts, weirdly placed objects on the exterior, even the paint scheme looked dark and brooding. The silent Soviet colony looked dormant, devoid of life. Tiny darkened portholes dotted clear patches on the outer hull.

Ramis remembered his approach to *Orbitech 1* while riding in the organic solar sail, watching as the flatscreen broadcast the view from the external cameras mounted on Sarat. He had been half an hour away from the American colony when he had injected Sarat with the hormone that collapsed the huge, beautiful sails. He had been half an hour away when he had caught sight of faces in the colony windows—weary and frightened faces, watching him with hope.

Now, thirty minutes from the *Kibalchich*, he saw nothing.

"I will use the maneuvering units to guide me in," he said into the radio.

"Be careful—every time you punch those MMUs, you're adding some component to your forward velocity," Karen said. "It might not seem like much, but remember how fast you're already going."

"I will manage." Ramis thought to himself that with all her concern, Karen did not know of his experience flying in the *Aguinaldo*. He had hit the Jump squares peppering the Sibuyan Sea going twice as fast as he was moving now.

The *Kibalchich* should have had two hundred people aboard, waiting to greet him. But instead, the colony refused any contact. It hung dark, like a giant empty house in space.

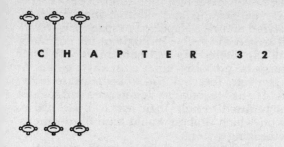

C H A P T E R   3 2

Drawing in a breath, Allen Terachyk looked both ways down the corridor. He was all alone, yet he had a feeling that someone was watching him. Air coming from a ventilation grate made a whispering sound in the silence.

Of the four division leaders on *Orbitech 1*, only he remained. Duncan McLaris had stolen the shuttle and escaped to Clavius Base; Tim Drury had been killed in the first RIF; and three days ago, Linda Arnando had been murdered. And now, Terachyk was the only one who knew that Brahms, not Ombalal, had ordered the RIF.

He did not feel comfortable in his exclusive position.

When his home city of Baltimore had become one of the first slag heaps in the War, his family had gone with it. He had had a wife and four sons. Their names haunted him: Helen, Josh, Jon, Cameron, and Danny. For a moment, he couldn't remember their faces, their voices—only the motionless family portrait he kept in a holocube in his quarters.

Brahms had never given him time to grieve.

Under a clever disguise and sidetracking of blame, Brahms had styled himself a Napoleon in space. His watchers remained armed and visible throughout the corridors. Brahms had not appointed any replacements for the other division leaders—he probably didn't trust anyone else. As the only assessor left, Terachyk had to keep aware of everyone's work. He had to judge its significance and suggest how it might be used to help their survival. He had to provide data on which Brahms would base his decisions, his efficiency ranking system.

With the wall-kelp giving them a small amount of breathing space, Terachyk didn't know why *Orbitech 1* still required Brahms's brutal crackdown measures, but the director refused to hear any argument about it.

The spoke-shaft elevator to the docking bay stood directly in front of him, like the closed metal doors of a coffin. The light on the elevator door blinked without a sound, signaling it was ready to be boarded. Terachyk clutched the d-cube he carried and closed his eyes.

A recurring nightmare haunted him. In the dream, the elevator seemed to beckon him, drawing him inside for a silent journey to the bay. He stepped out from the dilated opening, floating up to the high bay window. He heard the sound of the elevator whisking shut, leaving him alone . . . only to see Brahms watching from the control panel, self-righteously playing Ombalal's recording on why it was so important for Allen Terachyk to die for the survival of the colony. Nobody else knew that it had been Brahms and not Ombalal all along.

Beads of sweat formed on his forehead and he felt hot, scared. He lurched down the corridor. It was getting more difficult to move past the elevator each time he had the nightmare. He wondered if anyone had used that elevator since Brahms had RIFed Linda Arnando and Daniel Aiken.

RIF.

Reduction in force. What a wonderful euphemism.

Duncan McLaris had figured it out ahead of time. He had stolen the shuttle and escaped.

Terachyk was trapped on *Orbitech 1* with the rest of them. After the loss of his family, his life and the lives of others had become doubly precious to him. That made everything harder about his own job as assessor and the implications of his results.

And who would believe him if he revealed that Brahms had been behind the first RIF? They would tear him apart along with Brahms, for how would they know who was telling the truth?

He tightened his grip on the d-cube, wishing he could crush the information out of the three-dimensional memory module. Terachyk knew that when they manufactured the d-chips in vacuum, once in a while a cosmic ray plowed in and ruined the matrix; he could use that as an excuse. But even if he did, if the performance information were somehow lost, Brahms would find out again. Terachyk had been head of the Computer Applications branch of *Orbitech 1* before being promoted to division leader. He knew that nothing was truly erasable anymore; ways existed to resurrect deleted information.

Linda Arnando had discovered that fact the hard way.

He could do nothing but deliver the information, and somehow talk Brahms out of another RIF.

He turned the last corner and stood in front of Brahms's main office. The darkened offices of the other two division leaders looked painfully empty and ominous. Brahms had put the Filipino boy Ramis in Tim Drury's private quarters, where Drury had held open checkers tournaments for some of his friends, but the offices themselves remained vacant. Terachyk reached out to rap on the door.

"Come in, Allen." Curtis Brahms stood from behind his desk and reached for his glasses. He grasped the wire-rimmed frames, and as he swung them up, his eyes met Terachyk's. One of the lenses had shattered, but Brahms did not acknowledge it. He tossed the unnecessary glasses back down on the desk and motioned for Terachyk to take a seat.

Behind the director, a holotank showed a starscape. Brahms glanced toward it. "Ramis is well along on his journey. That's footage we're seeing from his camera. The colony's morale seems to have improved remarkably already!"

Terachyk felt his face grow warm. He forced his eyes away from the acting director.

Acting director . . . Terachyk wasn't sure he could convince himself that their situation was only temporary, but he held onto that hope for the strength to play this through until things really were better on *Orbitech 1*.

"I take it your efficiency study is complete?"

"The second study." Terachyk leaned forward and pushed the d-cube across the table.

"That's what I meant." Brahms raised a brow at Terachyk's tone.

Flipping the black solid around, Brahms inserted the d-cube into his desk unit. A series of graphs appeared in the holotank—statistics underscored by explanations. At the touch of a nested menu, tiny portraits sprang up next to the data to fill the image.

"You'll need time to study it, of course," Terachyk said.

"I trust your conclusions, Allen. That's why you're our main assessor."

Terachyk shook his head. "It's not that simple. I've taken days to compile this. There are some extenuating circumstances and they need to be looked at carefully before you start pronouncing death sentences."

Brahms looked up sharply. "I have not said there will be another RIF! This is just a precautionary measure."

Terachyk felt afraid, but maintained his position. "Of course."

Brahms lounged back to take in the display. A descending list, numbered from 1,247 to one, appeared in the tank. Next to the names and numbers floated another set of scores: FIRST EFFICIENCY SURVEY RANKING.

As Brahms digested the rankings, Terachyk stared stonefaced at the bottom 10 percent. Many of the names at the bottom of the list had received the same ranking in both the first and second efficiency studies; Brahms highlighted those names in red. Other names, higher up on the list, he marked in yellow—still low, but showing some improvement. As Brahms took in the names, Terachyk felt sickened and giddy.

The rankings were so cold—they showed a quantitatively correct, business-school evaluation of what Brahms had chosen as the most critical factor of survival: efficiency. But how could you compare the tasks of a maintenance electrician with those of a pharmaceutical chemist? It didn't matter what hard luck the person had run into—physical illness or broken equipment, even sabotage by other workers. All of the soul of human experience was missing from this evaluation—no mercy, only judgment.

And the part that made Terachyk most afraid was that Brahms himself believed in it.

Terachyk broke the silence filling the office. "So you are not even considering . . . ?" He let the question hang in the air.

"Another RIF?" Brahms sounded on edge. His body looked stiff, but his voice came out cool, modulated. "That's something we'll always need to consider, Allen. You were there. You saw how people reacted. It wasn't easy, but we've survived this long. The wall-kelp is helping us, but you know as well as I that our colony is not static. We are standing on the razor's edge of survival. It will be a long time before we can be sure of our balance."

Brahms sat up in his chair. Terachyk kept his eyes on the tiny pictures of the low-ranking people sorted out by the arbitrary scores Terachyk himself had assigned.

He recognized one of the men: Sigat Harhoosma. His wife was a sickly woman with a muscular disease that required her to live in the low-gravity environment. It had taken two people—a physical therapist and a nurse—to monitor her condition. Brahms had placed her on the first RIF list, and she was gone now.

Afterward, Terachyk had heard some people muttering that Harhoosma's wife had deserved to be chosen for the first group—as if they condoned Brahms's madness! That left her husband saddled with their two children and his high-pressure job as a metallurgist. Harhoosma was a hard worker, but he was trapped in the ranking war, and would probably never pull himself up. He had too many factors against him.

Brahms could always argue that people were going to die anyway, so it might as well be the ones pulling down the rest of the colony—like Sigat Harhoosma. And to make things worse, other people were beginning to believe as Brahms did. He had fooled them. Otherwise, they would have revolted against him a month before.

Unless no one was willing to stand up and organize the rebellion.

Terachyk spoke as Brahms continued to stare at the data. "I'm not sure how valid those rankings are. I did my best, but you shouldn't just take the results at face value. They know they're being watched, and they'll only make adjustments to do better when I'm around."

Brahms waved a hand at the holotank. "You can get statistics from all over—how many times they access their computers, how many times they call up entertainment on their holotanks, how many hours they spend with their families compared to how many hours they spend at their jobs. There are dozens of ways to get around them."

"And dozens of ways to be fooled," Terachyk shot back.

Brahms sat up straight in his chair. "The efficiency survey can't be fooled. It has too many safeguards built in."

"You can't be absolutely sure."

"Yes, I can. I know. It was my master's thesis at Harvard. It passed all of its beta tests."

Terachyk nodded at the holotank. Data still floated, names highlighted with a blood-red glow. "I see an error right now—look at Sigat Harhoosma. Your Efficiency Study didn't take his particular situation into account."

Brahms studied the statistics. He came back quickly—too quickly. Terachyk realized that Brahms must have prepared a justification for every single person on the potential RIF list.

"You've pointed him out before, Terachyk. Harhoosma wasn't hit any harder than anyone else. He is unable to perform under pressure. In fact, he gets worse. This shows that our efficiency ranking does work. Tough times demand tough people."

Brahms rocked back in his chair. He lifted an eyebrow. "Any other examples?"

Terachyk's stomach burned. He needed to get out of there. He stood, shaking his head. "No." The response sounded lame.

Brahms smiled tightly. "I'm glad you approve of the technique, then. I wouldn't want my chief assessor having second thoughts."

Terachyk felt Brahms's voice closing in around him, like the metal doors of the spoke-shaft elevator carrying him up out of his nightmare and into cold, empty space. He turned toward the door, feeling dizzy.

"You should keep track of Ramis's progress, Allen," Brahms called. "He might find something over on the *Kibalchich* that'll help us all."

Mumbling a good-bye, Terachyk backed out of the office and let the door close by itself. He saw Nancy Winkowski lounging outside the door, dressed in her spring-green watcher jumpsuit. She stared at him without emotion. Terachyk mumbled a greeting to her as he turned down the corridor. He didn't let his face show any worry, although he wondered why Brahms had seen fit to station one of the Watchers outside his own door. Was he afraid of other colonists? Or did he not trust Allen Terachyk?

He drew in a breath to clear his thoughts. The air smelled stale and cold. He walked past the elevator, feeling trapped.

He was going to be sick.

He quickened his step.

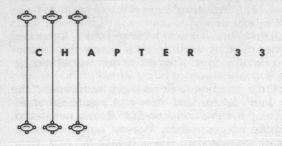

C H A P T E R 3 3

KIBALCHICH ■ DAY 40

As Ramis approached, the torus of the *Kibalchich* turned in front of him like a colossal windmill. It astounded him that it had been just a point of light seen from *Orbitech 1*.

Karen's voice came over the radio. "Ramis, the Doppler has pegged you five hundred yards from the *Kibalchich*. You'll feel some tension in the weavewire as we help slow you down."

Ramis mumbled an acknowledgment but continued to stare at the giant construction.

The Soviet station looked like a huge doughnut with four thick spokes radiating away from a small central sphere— the command center, most likely, which would be at zero gravity. Thinner support struts extended between the thick spokes.

Above the center of the torus, connected by a long, cylindrical shaft, floated an aluminized mirror, nearly invisible except where it reflected a smear of sunlight down into a central network of angled mirrors that, in turn, directed light into the station. The central shaft seemed able to swivel and point the mirror in different directions, perhaps to focus incoming energy toward different spots on the *Kibalchich*. In the zero-G environment, it puzzled Ramis that the Soviets would expend so much unnecessary mass and reinforcement on a structure that would hang in place by itself.

The central shaft extended through the hub and out the bottom in a long, antennalike prong. *A rotational stabilizer for the mirror and the colony?* Ramis wondered. Large masses hung hundreds of meters "below" the central hub sphere, centered on the prong; at the end of the prong, a broad inverted cone pointed toward the Sun like the *Aguinaldo*'s shadow shield.

Slag left over from the *Kibalchich*'s processing of lunar rock had been encrusted on the sides of the hull for additional radiation shielding, and another sheath of rubble drifted around the main torus. Ramis saw wide swathes where the rubble had been stripped away, as if the Soviets had needed to salvage more raw material for their own purposes.

Cyrillic characters stood out in one of the clear patches, black against the silvery metal background. Ramis assumed the characters spelled out the name of the station, though he couldn't read the language or even the alphabet.

As Ramis drifted in, he made his way toward the central hub sphere. He had to attach the weavewire where it would not be wound up like a fishing reel by the *Kibalchich*'s rotation. And from the telescope photos back on *Orbitech 1*, the hub would also be the most likely place for him to get inside through one of the emergency access hatches.

Orienting himself to the relative positions of *Orbitech 1* and the Soviet station, Ramis shot another spurt from his MMU. He seemed to be moving in faster than he expected.

Karen's voice broke the silence. "Ramis, we have you at approximately one hundred yards from the *Kibalchich*. How are you doing?"

"Fine. I doubt I can miss it now."

He had reserve fuel in the MMU, but he had greatly increased his forward velocity by jetting with the air tank early in his Jump. Without bothering to tell *Orbitech 1,* Ramis turned toward the *Kibalchich* and kicked on the MMU braking thruster. A force hit his chest as the maneuvering unit pushed in the opposite direction, slowing his motion.

Gyrating once more about his center of gravity, he saw with some satisfaction that he had slowed himself enough, but now he had veered off course.

"Ramis, are you all right? The video showed you rotating." Karen sounded worried.

"I am just preparing to land."

No problem, Ramis thought to himself. *This is getting easier.* He made a quick estimate and, trying to hold down his breathing rate, he gave two more squirts on the thruster. He found himself drifting toward the *Kibalchich*'s giant mirror support. The flat reflecting surface grew closer, like a tilted plate filled with stars. Everything seemed to be in slow motion, inexorable, like a dream.

Holding his breath, Ramis reached out and grabbed onto the approaching mirror support girder as he started to sail by. His feet swung around, slamming his upper body into the mirror's surface. He let out an audible "Ooof!" The reflector rocked back and forth, wobbling with the impact.

"Ramis! We've lost you on the visual. Have you reached the *Kibalchich*?"

Ramis pushed backward, hand over hand, down the girder. It was made of a dark, porous material—some sort of composite manufactured from lunar soil. He eyed the central hub and caught his breath for a moment. "I am here, but I need a few moments to position myself."

"Keep in contact," Brahms broke in.

Ramis did not bother to answer. Looking above him at the mirror's surface still oscillating from his impact, he continued crawling down the support structure. The dish mirror did not appear to concentrate light, as the *Aguinaldo*'s did, only reflect it. Then the conical light collector below the station probably provided for their energy needs, he thought. So why bother with the big reflecting mirror above?

Ramis keyed his mike. "Karen?"

She came back instantly. "Yes? Are you all right?"

"I am right above the *Kibalchich*. It is rotating quite rapidly. I intend to move down to the hub and try to enter from there."

"That's just what we were going to suggest," Brahms said.

"Be careful," Karen added.

"By the way, the Soviets have sent no welcoming committee. I see no one so far."

"I didn't expect anything," Brahms said.

Making sure that he kept the braided part of the weavewire away from the superstructure, he climbed down the *Kibalchich*'s central axis, careful to have a good grip each time, until he reached the point where the support column intersected the hub sphere. His feet touched the metal surface. He let out a long sigh of relief as the magnets in his soles clanked against the hull.

Karen and several of the other engineers had constructed his braided weavewire belt so he could unfasten it from around his waist and use reinforced clamps to anchor it to the *Kibalchich*. Ramis tugged on the fiber behind him and felt a slight tension.

Fumbling, he managed to unfasten the belt, still holding it tightly. He turned, extending his arms and stepping away from the fiber. The lack of resistance and the bulkiness of his suit made his movements awkward, contrived. He started to sweat.

The support shaft rising from the command sphere looked to be an ideal place. He wrapped his feet around it and fastened the belt around the shaft, anchoring it with clamps. He plucked a self-sealing tube from his belt and squeezed liberal amounts of vacuum cement over the connection. In less than a minute the polymer resin would harden from the cold and the vacuum into a bond more powerful than the metal of which the *Kibalchich* was constructed.

Smiling inside his helmet, Ramis turned and looked at the tiny Day-Glo orange thread extending a hundred meters from the support column, then vanishing abruptly into its single-molecule thickness. Ramis could not see the remainder of the weavewire, but frozen in space, it pointed directly to where the bright spot of *Orbitech 1* anchored the opposite end of the strand.

The bridge was established. The two colonies were joined. He tongued his radio mike. *"Orbitech 1.* I have successfully anchored the weavewire to the *Kibalchich."*

Throughout the maneuver he had remained silent, debating whether to keep in constant, step-by-step contact with *Orbitech 1.* But he decided against that. If they wanted to know exactly how it was done, they could come do it themselves.

"I am now standing on the outside of the central sphere. I will search for an entrance."

Free of the line and able to be more versatile in his movement, Ramis scrambled along the hull of the hub sphere, planting one foot in front of the other. Following the rotational axis, he tried to orient himself with "up" and "down."

He clunked along the outside of the sphere until he found the markings of a man-sized emergency hatch recessed into the hull. He made his way to it, then stopped and stared. Strange symbols, painted in a deep dull yellow, covered the hatch. He could not understand the writing, but the mechanism itself seemed obvious enough. He flicked on his radio mike again. *"Orbitech 1,* I have found one of the access hatches." He pointed his chest camera toward it. "I will attempt to enter the Soviet colony."

Then he turned to face the sphere and, after a moment's thought, spoke toward the metal wall. *"Kibalchich,* I hope you give me a happy welcome." After all, he thought, perhaps their radio was just broken and they could not respond. Maybe it was that simple. But then why hadn't they come out to meet him?

He fitted his bulky fingers into the red-painted lock mechanism and turned it counterclockwise. Bolts around the seal kicked back, and the door slid out and over, leading to a cramped airlock chamber. It looked like a great black mouth; he halfway expected to see fangs around the edge.

"Orbitech 1, the outer door has opened. I am stepping inside. This will be your last contact from me until I find a working transceiver inside. If something happens—" He paused, then shrugged. "The cable is connected between the two colonies. The next step will be yours."

Brahms's voice answered back, echoing in his ears.

"Ramis, we wish you the best of luck. Our hopes ride with you. Your transmissions are being broadcast over Con-Comm. Everyone is cheering for you."

Ramis shut off the mike. "Thanks," he muttered.

When he closed the outer door, the chamber was dark, with only a red strip of phosphors on the ceiling for dim illumination.

He punched a sequence of buttons that he thought would fill the chamber with air, but his suit was so insulated he could hear no hissing. The light on the panel turned from red to green, which looked more like white to black in the reddish background light, and Ramis hesitated. His suit had relaxed, lost most of its stiffness.

He cracked open his faceplate and drew a deep breath of stale, sour air. It had a rotten smell to it.

Fear crept up his spine again. If the Soviets' radio wasn't broken and if they had all died, perhaps they had succumbed to some kind of disease, a plague. Genetic research gone wrong? That was the ostensible reason Dr. Sandovaal had come up to L-4—so he wouldn't have to worry about unleashing a plague on Earth if his experiments went awry. And if the Soviets had contaminated their colony with a deadly virus, Ramis had just breathed a lungful of it.

He let the air out of his nostrils and swallowed hard. *No good now—it is too late. I have already exposed myself.* He took another breath, turned to the interior door, and pushed the release button. It slid open with a grating hiss.

Directly in front of his face was the purple, bloated body of a dead man, drifting in the disturbed air currents.

Ramis gasped and choked. The stench was powerful.

The man's eyes were wide open, his face swollen and distorted. He was a large man, clad in a dark uniform spangled with military insignia.

Ramis backed up in horror, but he could go no farther. The back wall of the airlock chamber stopped him. The body drifted in, as if it were following him.

He screamed *"Help!"* in Tagalog.

He stopped, felt his pounding heartbeat, calmed his own breathing. The stench continued to seep into his pores, into his lungs. He forced himself to relax.

It was only a dead man. Someone had died on this colony. He had been prepared for that. Perhaps the entire Soviet station had turned into a huge tomb in space. Without gravity, the body had been drawn over to the door when Ramis had filled the inner airlock.

He stared at the bulging, jellied eyes of the corpse. The man's hair was neatly combed, fixed into place with hair oil. The insignia on the dark uniform showed him to be someone of importance—a commander, perhaps—left here untended to rot.

Ramis forced himself to move. He had to bump past the bobbing corpse to enter the main command center. He touched the body with his shoulder, shielding it with the most padded portion of the space suit. He felt his skin crawl. As the firm, weightless mass moved aside, the arm bent at the elbow and the gray-green, blotched hand drifted up and down, as if waving good-bye. Ramis's stomach flopped.

He closed his eyes and reached out with gloved fingers, grasping the corpse's torso. He felt a rush of sweat inside his suit. He gave the body a shove toward the airlock chamber. After it obligingly floated inside, Ramis sealed the door, closing the body out of sight.

He expected to see more corpses there, all sprawled out and ripe with decay, but the command center stood empty. He swiveled his head to stare at the large, spherical room. From "floor" to "ceiling" ran a cylindrical pipe, embedded in a holotank; he realized the pipe must be the support strut for the mirror overhead and the solar shield below. The pipe would not be noticed when the central holotank was functioning.

Lighted screens and input pads covered the curved walls without any regard for standardizing the direction of up or down. Mounted chairs jutted out from beneath the control panels at odd angles to each other to maximize the working arrangement, though Ramis thought it must be disorienting. The chairs had Velcro straps to keep the workers from recoiling across the room every time they punched a keypad.

Ramis kicked off the wall and drifted in, looking at the buttons and readouts, everything in indecipherable Cyrillic characters. The individual panels were unfamiliar to him. The station seemed to be functioning still, but he couldn't figure out how to control anything.

He searched for the radio, but the controls made no sense at all. He had taken a tour of *Orbitech 1*'s communications center to familiarize himself with the general layout of what the Soviets might have, but this place seemed totally alien.

He flipped on his suit radio. *"Orbitech 1,* are you there?" He turned off the radio at the static; the signals could not propagate out of the metal-covered hull.

He decided to try the computer, hoping that it was voice-activated. There was nothing around to indicate where the computer was, so he spoke as loudly as he could. "Computer, transmit on ninety-four point one megacycles: *Orbitech 1,* do you read me?"

The pounding silence around him made him feel uneasy and vulnerable. He didn't like being where he was. When the voice of the American communications officer burst back at him, he jumped, startled enough that he had to catch himself on the corner of the chair before he drifted out to the center of the room.

"This is *Orbitech 1.* We are receiving you—"

Brahms's voice broke in. "Did you get in all right, Ramis? What did you find? Have you seen anyone?"

Ramis cleared his throat. "I am inside at this moment. I have found a man. He is dead. It appears he was alone in the command center. I do not know how he died. I must inspect the rest of the colony. I will communicate with you when I have further information." He hesitated. "Computer, end transmission."

He did not feel like speaking with Brahms at the moment.

He saw four prominently marked pneumatic doors at perpendicular points, each with bright red frames. These must be the *Kibalchich*'s spoke-shafts—conduits from the outer ring of living quarters up toward the central hub.

The other Soviets must be somewhere out in the main torus. He stared at the curved wall and pushed over to the nearest airlock. "One spoke should be as good as another," he said to himself.

The spoke-shaft door was much larger than the small emergency hatch he had used to enter the station. He played with the mechanism for a few moments, then waited, wondering if it was broken. Each set of buttons seemed different; he thought he had pushed the right ones, but it was hard to tell. Then the indicator light changed from red to amber. Some sort of elevator was making its way up the shaft from the torus to the center. The light changed to green, blinked twice, and the door slid aside with a hiss of hydraulics.

A vertical platform stood in front of him, perpendicular to his orientation. Ramis realized that if he rotated himself and stood on it while the platform traveled toward the rim, he would definitely feel that he was heading down, and the platform beneath his feet would become the floor.

He stared at the lift platform for a few moments, feeling the jitters again. He wasn't sure if he wanted to see what had happened to the other Soviets.

In his bulky suit he felt sluggish and clumsy, unable to react in an emergency. He paused, weighing the decision. Taking care to complete each step properly, he removed his helmet, unfastened the connections at his waist, lifted off his MMU pack and spare air bottles. Over the course of fifteen minutes, he managed to pull himself out of the suit.

Ramis stood, breathing comfortably again. He flopped his arms back and forth, loosening the muscles. He felt small now, agile, ready to face challenges. Staring at the enormity of the empty suit, he was amazed that he had been able to move while wearing it.

The *Kibalchich* felt cold and empty. He had dressed lightly inside the suit, wearing the old tan barong he'd brought on his long journey from the *Aguinaldo*. He had laundered it and taken great care to mend everything. One of the production designers on *Orbitech 1* had offered him a silky weavewire shirt, but it just didn't feel the same to him.

He took a deep breath of the stale air, then buckled his equipment around a chair support to keep the pieces from drifting about while he was gone.

Bending over, Ramis slipped off his booties and socks and pressed his bare toes against the smooth, cool metal of the lift platform. He felt adrenaline pumping, bringing him to a new pitch of awareness. Without all the padding

and external protection, he could be part of his situation,
not sheltered from it.

He held onto a side rail to keep his balance, then pushed
the activation panel. He was growing confident of his
knack for these machines.

The lift platform plunged downward. Ramis held onto
the rail to keep from drifting away. But as he dropped
toward the outer torus, he grew heavier and heavier
against the floor.

At the bottom of the shaft, the lift platform stopped,
then a set of doors opened in front of him. He stepped out
onto the textured metal floor of the *Kibalchich*'s main
body.

He took a few steps forward. The floor felt icy against his
feet. The lights were dim, reduced to emergency illumination only. Someone had shut down the systems on the
entire station—mothballed it, as if in preparation for a
long, long wait.

In the dim glow, Ramis could see faint wisps of his breath
—the station was that cold. He shivered and ran his palms
up and down his wiry brown arms. He was not used to chill
like this. Looking straight ahead, he walked faster.

He shouted hello, but his voice came back explosively
loud, like a thunderclap. The echoes shattered up and
down the hall like accusing screams. He shrank back
against the wall.

He decided not to call out again.

Above him, on the curved band of the ceiling, a strip of
louvered windows let in some reflected sunlight from the
inner ring of secondary mirrors. But the louvers were half
closed, and the giant mirror overhead did not direct the
sunlight in. The stars themselves looked distorted and
haloed with diffraction from the slanted glass.

Ramis walked along the curving main corridor, which
was wide enough for several people to walk abreast. Dark
scuffs on the floor showed tracks from where little three-
wheeled carts had moved along the thoroughfare. A faint
tracing of mildew stood in patches against the wall, across
one of the window plates.

To his right and left, vertical walls blocked off sections of
private rooms, looking odd against the smooth arcs of the
torus. He tried several doors; most were unlocked. Ramis

poked his head in but found no one, only darkened spaces that seemed to be administrative offices, meeting rooms. Some looked to be rather plush living quarters all clustered in a row—probably for the high-ranking Soviets.

Inside one room he saw the soft, greenish-yellow glow of an aquarium module. The aerator bubbled in the silence, humming with insolent noise. Half a dozen fish floated belly-up in the tank.

Ramis kept walking. The constant tension was starting to wear on him. He jumped at little noises.

The walls ahead of him ended abruptly on either side, opening into a large section of the torus. Long tables were lined up—a mess hall for the two hundred men and women aboard the station. It was clean, yet something about it conveyed a sense of disarray.

Ramis noticed medical supply carts, packages neatly stacked, five used hypodermic syringes on a stainless-steel counter. He sniffed, but the air had been long purged of any odor that might have hinted at what the inhabitants had done with themselves. They had left no signs, no notices, nothing to indicate where they had gone.

At the end of the mess hall the side walls appeared again, enclosing additional private work spaces. The inner curved wall showed a bright red hydraulic door that marked another of the spoke-shaft lift platforms. He had traveled a quarter of the way around the station, and had still found no sign of people. In the air in front of his face a cloud of fruit flies flitted like static in a faulty holotank; they must have escaped from some biological experiment.

Ramis walked ahead. On the floor he found several access hatches. When he stomped his feet, he heard a hollow echo. Looking at the ceiling and where the floor met the curved wall, he realized that there must be another entire level below him.

The next set of rooms appeared to be laboratories cluttered with experimental paraphernalia. Sketches and equations were scrawled on magnetic-imprint boards. The markings had not been degaussed, but were beginning to fuzz out from the passage of time.

He passed another section of living quarters, this one more austere than the others. In each cabin the beds were neatly made and empty. On some of the bureaus, he found stereocubes with pictures of families, which had been left activated. Beside them he found occasional messages or data cubes. In one instance he even picked up a note written by hand, but he couldn't read any of the Russian.

Everything was silent. The *Kibalchich* held its breath.

As the curve continued, the side walls dropped away again. A red cross on a field of white signified that the large room ahead would be the infirmary.

By now, Ramis had grown accustomed to the dim light. He moved as if he were one of the shadows, not an enemy of them. His eyes were wide. His bare feet made no sound as he crept forward.

The walls opened up around him, and the infirmary ahead seemed like a vast empty space, broader and colder than the gulf between the two colonies. The soft light glowed, and he blinked his eyes, staring and trying to gather in as much detail as he could. He took a deep breath.

Spread out in front of him lay all the Soviets, row upon row upon row.

His throat was dry. He stood still.

They looked like legions from an ancient Roman army, all lined up side by side, motionless and cold. Each body was encased in a glass coffin, a crystalline chamber flecked with frost on the inside and lit up by a mixed glow of monitor lights.

The cubicles lined the entire infirmary, crammed together.

He took a step forward and placed his hand on the top of the nearest coffin. The man inside looked waxen, expressionless, at peace. The glass felt cold.

Ramis raised his eyes and stared in front of him at all of them. They had all come here. Forsaking hope, had they all just given up and died?

He moved forward between the cubicles, feeling numb and awed. He didn't know what to think or do, but part of the fear had melted from him.

He had found the inhabitants of the *Kibalchich*.

PART THREE

INTERACTION

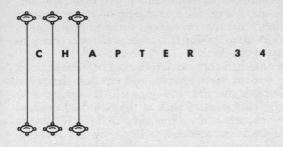

C H A P T E R   3 4

Clancy's job-site headquarters felt more like a locker room than a survival hut. Stuffed with ten people in a space meant for five, the airtight shanty provided Clancy's crew a chance to take a break from the excavation and construction. It reminded him of those quaint little Quonset huts the old British soldiers had used in India or Africa. Another team had set up similar huts out by the mass driver.

Clancy stared outside through the quartz inset plate. He could make out three other enclosures in the distance; the job site had fifteen units total—half again as many as necessary to house his crew. But that margin didn't seem like much when everybody crammed in the central dwelling— the powwow tent, Shen called it. Clancy felt as if he had to breathe in whenever anyone breathed out. But he insisted on having an open door policy during any construction operation. He wanted his people to feel free to talk over problems and share ideas.

The radio-telescope project was about to take off, big

time. Clavius Base had systematically provided all the necessary items—air, water, food, and now housing. At least now they didn't have to worry about funding problems or maddening permits—the Earth bureaucracy was one welcome casualty of the War.

Clancy's people had constructed the huts in record time, ferried them out on the six-packs, and erected them just outside the crater, where the gigantic telescope dish would sprawl. The Lunatics back at the base had reacted with such enthusiasm to the expedition that it had Clancy convinced they wanted his construction crew out of there.

Tomkins had come up with a name for his baby. He had proudly announced that the crater-sized telescope would be dubbed "Arecibo II." Clancy and his people thought the name sounded much too pretentious, and decided to call it "Bigeye" instead. The engineers and the Lunatics insisted on using their preferred names whenever referring to the project, each side hoping the other would give up.

Clancy tried to push his way through the crowd in the headquarters hut. The regular ConComm broadcasts of news from the other colonies always generated a lot of interest, but this time, *Orbitech 1* seemed to be up to something spectacular. All the senior engineers had gathered in the powwow tent to watch on the portable holotank there, normally used for communicating back with Clavius Base.

Laughter rose around him as three of the excavation crew related an incident that had occurred earlier in the day. As Clancy squeezed past, a hand snaked out and grabbed him around the waist.

"Hey, boss." A body pressed against him.

"Hello, Shen."

"Kind of tight in here, isn't it?" She rotated him around until they faced each other. He felt off balance in the low gravity; he preferred either full-G or nothing—none of this fractional-weight ballet. The top of Shen's head came just to the middle of his chest. He had to look straight down to see her. Long black hair framed her face.

Clancy nodded. "See what happens when I call the foremen together. Can't expect them to work now, can I?"

"You'll have to have these meetings more often."

Clancy overacted a grimace.

Shen pushed a finger in his stomach. "Come on, Cliffy—you love it. How else could you get a group of intelligent, talented women to throw themselves at you?"

"Thanks a lot, Shen."

"Wiay," she corrected him. "After all this time—my first name is Wiay. Some compassionate boss you turned out to be."

"All right . . . Wiay. Thanks a lot."

Wiay Shen had started to retort when the room grew quiet. People crowded around the holotank image. Clancy steered Shen toward the receiver. He stepped up on the single-cast table to see above people's heads, and pulled Shen up to join him.

When he was finally able to look down on the three-dimensional image, he saw pitch black around the edges. Seconds passed before he could make out stars. Suddenly, the view swung around to encompass a space suit and a stretch of gleaming surface on which the figure stood.

"Where's this coming from?" Clancy asked.

"Orbitech 1," someone said. Someone else shushed him. Clancy scowled.

A sober voice from the tiny speakers described Ramis's heroic journey from the *Aguinaldo* and his odyssey to the Soviet colony. Coming over the ConComm, it sounded like a propaganda film. As Ramis bent to start his fifty-mile Jump, Shen slipped her arm around Clancy's waist.

Clancy dwelled on the narrator's explanation of the weavewire. One of the hopes of zero-G manufacturing had always been the development of a true monofilament—a fiber held together by a force stronger than the covalent bonds of the atoms themselves. The garments produced by *Orbitech 1* had used this monofilament—a frivolous waste of good science, in Clancy's opinion. Until a way was found to efficiently and rapidly draw out the filament, it would continue to be a toy. But if somebody had found a way. . . .

The others listened to the announcer's speculation on what Ramis might find on the silent *Kibalchich,* what might have happened to the Soviets. Clancy kept pondering the weavewire, though. They could draw out unlimited lengths of this fiber, which required negligible raw materials. The possibilities sparkled in his imagination like champagne.

The holotank faded to neutral gray, with the announcer promising updates at regular intervals. In the last scene, Ramis appeared no more than a flickering dot, contrasting with the stars that burned steadily through the darkness. In typical fashion, the engineers debated why Ramis's image would shimmer. Someone pointed out that he must be moving his arms, randomly reflecting the sunlight, for the scintillation to appear.

Clancy became aware of other sounds in the room. An idea had flashed through his mind—a vision. The implications almost struck him down. He grinned like an idiot.

He was still standing on top of the table. As he started to move, he met resistance. Glancing down, he discovered Shen's arm had been around his waist throughout the holocast. He muttered something unintelligible and helped her down from the table. Her hand was warm and damp.

She looked up at him, her eyes bright. "What do you think?"

"About what?"

"The Jump—that kid flying fifty miles across space!"

His voice grew quiet, lowered conspiratorially. He didn't meet her eyes. "I just had this crazy thought—"

Shen stood on her tiptoes and searched his face. "After that, nothing could be crazy. What is it?"

Clancy shook his head. "Later. I want to check it out first." The crowded room had become as humid as the tropics, but Clancy felt drained, dehydrated, with his excitement. Searching the hut, he spotted his crew scheduler, Josef Abdallah. Clancy raised his voice to be heard over the crowd. "Josef—over here. When's our next six-pack heading back to base?"

Abdallah answered around a mouthful of fried wall-kelp. "Tomorrow morning."

"Great," muttered Clancy to no one in particular.

Shen pressed back against him, but not as close as before. Her voice was low, as if she were sharing a secret. "What's up?"

"Nothing. I just need to check something out."

"I can get you back to base."

He shook his head. "This can wait."

"If it's really important, I'll drive the six-pack. They won't even notice one of them is missing."

"And have the top two people away from the crew?"

"Josef is a big boy, and the crew can get along fine. It's only a six-hour trip. Besides, you're the boss. Do what you want—otherwise, there's no point in having the job."

Clancy looked her in the eyes for the first time since the holotank had switched off. Her dark eyebrows contrasted sharply against her skin. Her space suit was oversized for her petite figure and lay against her in soft folds, giving her an exotic look, like a nymphet wearing a mattress.

On impulse he asked, "Do you know anything about celestial mechanics?"

"No, but I can set up an orbital program that'll blow your socks off. Is that what you need to check out?"

"I need an expert." Then he quickly added, "Not to take away from your offer."

"Well, you up for a six-hour jaunt, then?"

A pause. "You're right, as usual. Sometimes that six hours makes it seem we're a thousand miles away."

"It's the inconvenience that matters. Come on. If we head out now we'll be back before the end of next shift."

Clancy answered by pushing through the crowd and collaring Josef Abdallah. After Josef complained about rescheduling and juggling who would need what and when, he nodded his approval. Clancy motioned to Shen.

Seconds later they were in the airlock, prepping for the trip outside on the lunar surface.

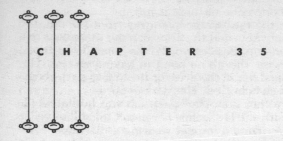

C H A P T E R 3 5

Ramis leaned back in the *Kibalchich*'s command center, trying to relax as he held onto one of the protruding chairs from the transceiver deck. The air still smelled rotten. His feet drifted like a slow pendulum in the zero-G.

"Please hold on a moment," the *Orbitech 1* communications chief said. Her face turned away from the holotank in the center of the chamber. "I'll get Mr. Brahms."

Ramis steeled himself to see Brahms's face. He had remained in the Soviet command center, testing various functions using the computer. It also gave him time to marshal his thoughts and consider how he would describe his discovery to *Orbitech 1*. He downloaded his videotape from the camera he carried and prepared it for broadcast back to the other station.

The curved image in front of him flickered, winked out, and switched to the giant face of Curtis Brahms in the central holotank. The director grinned; light glittered in his eyes. Ramis thought he looked like a wolf.

"Ramis, we've been waiting to hear from you! What have you found?"

Ramis took a deep breath. With meticulous detail, he described what he had seen, step by step, as he had explored the *Kibalchich*. As he spoke he played the tape, letting them see exactly what he had observed. He watched Brahms fidget until he came to the part about finding the Soviets in their glass coffins.

"I took extra care to inspect them." Ramis hesitated. "I cannot be positive, but I believe they are all still alive."

He waited a moment for that to sink in. Brahms's eyebrows lifted.

"They did not end up there by chance, Mr. Brahms. My guess is that they have undergone some sort of suspended animation or hibernation."

He had walked along the rows of glass coffins, studying the masklike faces of the Soviets. He noted the coolness of the chambers, the flush of life that seemed to remain on their faces. No, they couldn't be dead. These preparations were too elaborate. It spoke of some great plan, some experiment. How had the Soviets done all this, and so quickly—within a few weeks of the War?

Unless they had been working on it all along.

"I cannot understand, though, why they did not leave prominent messages in all languages in every corridor, directing me where to go. This process must have taken some time."

Brahms frowned, thinking. "Unless the one body you found was a guardian of some sort—a monitor to watch over them, so they wouldn't need to leave any kind of signs. It sounds strange to leave only one person awake out of all those others."

On the larger-than-life holotank image, Brahms wore an expression of childlike delight. "Ramis, this is all . . . astonishing. I'm very proud of you."

Ramis wasn't sure he was glad to receive Brahms's pride.

"Did you try to revive one of them?"

"Sir?" Ramis nearly lost his grip on the chair, startled by the audacity of the question. "Mr. Brahms, I cannot read the Russian words on any of the controls. It appears to be very complicated equipment."

"Yes, but on the tape you broadcast I saw a hand-lettered

sign on the infirmary wall. It seemed to be in several different languages. Maybe the man you found knew he was dying, so he left instructions." His eyes had a distant look. "Though if he had time to do that, why didn't he just revive one of the others?"

Ramis swallowed, not knowing what to say. He remembered seeing the sign, but everything else had so shocked him that he had paid it little attention. He hadn't considered that he should do anything drastic.

"No, sir, I did not try. I was not sure of the instructions."

The director tapped his fingers together, masking a slight scowl of disappointment. He stared down at something out of the holotank's view, apparently recalling part of Ramis's tape. "Come now, Ramis, these are simple instructions—pushing a few selected buttons and monitoring some numbers. Do you realize how important that discovery could be? It is vital for us to learn if their suspended animation process actually works. Perhaps we can adapt it for our own survival."

Ramis's face must have shown a puzzled expression. Brahms put on a mask of exaggerated patience. "The Soviets have found a way to survive, apparently even without any supplies from Earth. They can just lie back and wait until someone comes to rescue them. Now, if you could revive them, and they could share their knowledge, you could single-handedly eliminate the need for any further RIFs aboard *Orbitech 1*."

Ramis kept eye contact, even under the penetrating stare of the director. He had thought the wall-kelp had already removed any need for further RIFs. Or was Brahms just looking for an excuse? He tried to make his position firm.

"Perhaps I have not described it clearly enough, Mr. Brahms. The hibernation apparatus appears to be extremely complicated. I cannot understand any of the other writings left here. Perhaps they are emergency procedures. I cannot read the Russian—not even the alphabet. What if something goes wrong with the process?"

Brahms seemed to quash a flare of anger. "Ramis . . . Ramis, you underestimate yourself. Just look at what you've done already—you Jumped all the way over there and you figured out how to open the emergency hatch by yourself, without being able to read any Russian."

He paused, as if trying to remember what else Ramis had described. "You worked the lift-shaft elevator, you explored the whole station."

His voice softened. "Now, think about it. If the Soviets were going to put themselves completely under suspended animation, waiting for someone—someone like yourself, Ramis—to come find them, don't you think they would make it simple and obvious how to go about reviving them? They can't be sure that whoever finds them will know. It must be straightforward."

"A person's life would be at stake if I fail."

"I trust your abilities, Ramis. I want you to go and look again. Maybe you missed something. It's very important that you try."

Ramis started to lose his patience with the director. "Is Karen there?" he asked.

Brahms frowned, as if wondering about the point of the question. "Dr. Langelier? Don't worry. I've already informed her that you attached her weavewire according to plan. It seems to be a success."

"No, I only meant that you should—" He stopped himself, cautious, then rephrased his words. "I would not presume to make decisions for you, since you are the acting director. But I did want to remind you of Dr. Langelier's knowledge of Russian. I believe she is fluent in the language. Perhaps if she were over here, we would have a better chance of reviving one of the Soviets."

Brahms looked at him with a stony expression that melted away into one of concern and friendship. "I'll note that, Ramis. Maybe we'll need to do it. But I think that would be a greater risk than having you try by yourself. Don't you agree? Will you at least try before we ask Dr. Langelier to make the same dangerous journey you did? I wouldn't want to risk her unnecessarily."

Uncomfortable with what Brahms had just said, but not wanting to give a definite answer, Ramis replied, "I will be back in touch as soon as I have something to report." He took a malicious pleasure in blanking the screen on Brahms.

* * *

Ramis stood outside the dimmed infirmary again, staring
at the rows of glass coffins. The silence felt suffocating. He
placed his hands on his hips and pressed his lips together,
trying to be firm about his decision, about his resolve. But a
chill made gooseflesh on his arms—strictly from the
cooled-down station; he didn't think it was from fear.

He wondered about the dead man he had discovered in
the command center. The last one—the captain going
down with his ship? Had someone remained behind, at the
last minute remembering to scrawl a list of steps for reviving the rest of the people? What had happened?

It looked like the people in the four cubicles just inside
the entrance had been the last four to go into the chambers. All of the Soviets wore loose, gray pajamalike outfits.

One burly man's elbows bumped the sides of the glass;
his knees were bent slightly, as if they had had to wedge
him into the cubicle. He had reddish-blond hair. Two
other men, dark-haired, occupied the coffins on either side
of him. Last he saw a slim woman with a sharp nose, deep-
set eyes, and gray-brown hair. Her face had a pinched look,
not the serene emptiness of the other Soviets, as if she
were still thinking even in her deep, cold sleep.

Ramis inspected the cubicles more closely. They were
transparent, frosted on the inside with a light sketching of
ice crystals. The *Kibalchich* workers had probably made
the glass from the leftover lunar material that orbited the
colony as a radiation shield.

This had not been done in a few days, Ramis thought.
This had been a calculated, extensive project—something
planned. He frowned.

Ramis went over to the burly man. Unconsciously he
had made his decision. Perhaps it had no valid logic at all
behind it, but he reasoned that if any of these people
would have the strength, the stamina, to survive Ramis's
clumsy attempt at the reawakening process, it would be
this man.

The glass looked sealed on all sides except for the end,
which was opaque, metal, with a control panel mounted in
the center. He placed his fingertips on the seam of metal
against glass, wondering if he should attempt to pry it open
to free the man from the chamber and let him thaw out in

the air. But Ramis realized that was ridiculous. It would be certain death for the Soviet man.

On the wall, the handwriting indicated the first button to push that would activate the sequence, the proper numbers that each readout should display—though it gave no instructions on what to do if the numbers were wrong, or the time that must elapse before the second set of controls should be activated. Brahms was right—it did sound straightforward.

Ramis peered down, noticing that thin tubes ran from a reservoir beneath the coffin to where they plunged into the inside of the man's elbows, anchored on blood vessels. A yellowish color in the tube showed him that a clear liquid was actually passing into the Soviet's body. Some sort of nutrient solution? Electrodes were mounted on his temples and another on his sternum.

He kneeled in front of the control panel. He hoped it would be an automatic process, that he needed only to activate the sequence and let the machine take over, that everything would run smoothly.

It appeared to be a three-stage procedure with separate readouts. Of course he wouldn't know what any of the numbers meant—blood pressure, body temperature, heartbeat, brain activity . . . the day of the week? If something went wrong, he wouldn't know how to adjust it. He wouldn't even know how to recognize that something was indeed going wrong! The instructions on the wall were abbreviated, with no detail.

The Soviet man lay there, eyes closed. His skin had a flourlike pallor; his eyelids showed a faint intaglio of veins. He had thick lips, perfectly round ears, a square jaw covered with pale beard stubble. Ramis wondered if the stubble had grown in the month the Soviets had been in their frozen sleep . . . or if the man had simply neglected to shave a day or two before crawling into the chamber. The man had a small mole beside his left eye and a tiny scar at the bottom of his chin.

Ramis knew the face would burn in his memory for a long time. This man was still alive. Ramis had no right to steal that from him.

He could not try it. He was not sure of his own abilities. He could not be so arrogant as to play with this man's life.

Then Ramis felt his stomach knot. He would have to go back to Brahms and tell him he refused, that he didn't feel competent.

Instructions written in Cyrillic characters covered the control panels. The walls had preprinted posters with lines of text, but he could not be sure which were inane signs about maintaining one's health and exercising in orbit, and which contained more crucial information for reviving the hibernating people.

He kneeled next to the controls once more. With the translucent touchpad controls, Ramis was not even sure which of the dimmed squares were activation buttons and which were blank readouts.

He could go back, get the portable video imager, and record every block of text for Karen to translate and interpret.

The START touchpad was in the upper left, according to the instructions. He wondered what the other controls were for—the ones not mentioned on the list. He could activate the chamber and hope everything proceeded automatically. Everything on the *Kibalchich* had been straightforward so far—the emergency hatch, the lift platform, the transceiver.

Ramis trusted technology. The Soviets wouldn't try to make things difficult—they would make it obvious. Perhaps Curtis Brahms was right: if they had put themselves into their sleepfreeze to wait for someone else to come, they could not know who would be first to arrive at their station. They could not be sure it would be one of their Soviet compatriots.

Before his arm muscles could lock with hesitation, Ramis reached forward and pressed his finger against the upper left touchpad.

The three readouts suddenly came to life under indecipherable labels, displaying numbers that meant nothing to him. All the numbers remained close to zero and then began to rise. One changed rapidly, while the others crept up a digit at a time. Low numbers. That all made sense— body temperature, heartbeat, respiration.

Yellow lights came on, embedded along the corners of the coffin. The frost on the inside of the glass vanished with little wisps of steam. Warming up the chamber, Ramis decided. He nodded. The first readout still rose rapidly. He watched the digits tick off faster than his heartbeat.

A thick red fluid—blood?—pushed up through the transparent tube from the reservoir below the chamber. The new blood entered the vein in the man's left arm. After a few moments the tube in the other arm began to carry a pinkish tinge, away from the body and draining down below. Ramis thought he understood that the nutrient solution was being replaced by stored blood.

Then the background light on that readout turned red. Ramis jumped and looked around, staring at the other dead squares on the panel. Keypads, or readouts? If he pushed them, what would happen? He stared at the instructions, but they gave no assistance for anything out of the norm.

The red light began to blink. The process was going wrong—he had to do something. He couldn't figure out what it meant. He felt sweat prickle down his back. A second blank touchpad flashed red. He stared up at the instructions again, as if something might have magically appeared there. He had to do something.

Acting instinctively, holding his breath, Ramis pushed the flashing red light. It must be some sort of signal. The control panel had sensed an emergency situation and indicated the button he would have to push.

"Please, please, please!" he muttered to himself.

The numbers on the readout continued to rise. The red alarm lights kept flashing. Another red light blinked. Ramis pushed that one, too, then pushed the other one again.

He was panicking. He tried to fight it down, but everything was slipping out of control, falling through his fingers. He didn't know what was going on. He couldn't react to it; he couldn't think fast enough and find a solution because he didn't know what he had done.

"What am I supposed to do!" he shouted.

A tiny curl of smoke spiraled up from the electrode on the man's sternum, then a minuscule blue arc popped the electrode off the skin, leaving a burned mark in the center of his chest.

Suddenly, inside the chamber, the Soviet man shivered and vibrated, bucking with his spine and banging his elbows against the sides of the coffin. His lips drew back and his teeth clenched in a seizure.

Ramis could not decide what to do. He couldn't get inside the coffin. He tugged at the control panel end, hoping he could yank it off and pull the man free, though he had no idea what he would do then.

"Help me!" Ramis called.

The *Kibalchich* had no one to hear him.

He banged on the glass, trying to break it and force his way in. "Help!"

The Soviet man lay still, rigid with a contorted expression on his face. His eyelids had popped wide open. He stared through the glass at the ceiling, but saw nothing. Tiny blood vessels had hemorrhaged, smearing his eye whites with red blots.

All the lights on the control panel had turned red. Two of the numerals fell back to zero; one remained at twenty-four.

With a hiss of pressurized air, the control panel end slid down, opening the chamber. The man did not move.

Ramis slumped to the floor and sat with his legs crossed, pressing his knees against the cold metal. He began to shiver uncontrollably.

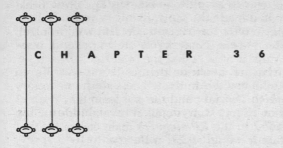

C H A P T E R   3 6

Karen Langelier put her head down and closed her eyes. She could imagine Ramis's fear, sitting in an abandoned space station with hundreds of frozen bodies—it must be like a giant haunted house in orbit. There was one dead man in the airlock, and now another in the infirmary with wide eyes, staring at the person who had killed him by not understanding the sleepfreeze process.

Or was the process itself flawed? Maybe Ramis wasn't to blame after all. But what would happen when the other Soviets did awake, only to find Ramis with their dead comrades? He wouldn't stand a chance.

If the Soviets could indeed be revived. Biological researchers had pursued suspended animation for decades, and it seemed an odd topic to be pursuing in an orbital research station. That work could have been done as well on Earth, where laboratory space was not so precious.

But Karen knew what it was like to dig into an idea, spend months or even years on a false trail, perhaps give an entire life over to a single problem, only to learn that someone else had made the same discovery weeks before. Then you had to suffer the frustration of throwing yourself back into the whole crazy cycle again with a new idea. . . .

As competent and quick to learn as Ramis was, Karen didn't believe he could intuitively guess all the necessary steps to revive the Soviets, and she was furious at Brahms for forcing him to try. More detailed revival information probably resided in the *Kibalchich*'s main computer, but she was certain it would all be in Russian.

Ramis had to have help.

Karen opened her eyes. The past few months weighed her down—her separation from Ray, her mourning for those on Earth, and now Brahms's incessant pressure to produce.

She could get out, too, just as Ramis had.

And who better than she to go to the Soviet station? She was proficient in Russian, as were other people on the scientific staff, but that was only icing on the cake. She would be the first person to test out her weavewire ferry system. And the kicker was that she knew Ramis better than anyone else on *Orbitech 1*.

One thing gnawed at her: the thought of flying unprotected and alone across the gulf of space. But if she didn't trust her weavewire, no one else would.

Fear kept her feet riveted to the floor in front of Brahms's outer office. Months ago—*days* ago—she would have lacked the courage to approach him.

Once, as a little girl, Karen had come upon her cat after it had cornered a field mouse. She had been shocked to see the monster it had transformed into as it glared down at the mouse.

Brahms wielded the same kind of power. And Karen found herself unable to turn, to hide. The door slid aside.

"Dr. Langelier. I've been expecting you. Please come in." Brahms's smooth voice seemed to waft around her, twist about and pull her into the office. Karen was determined to win his favor—but why did she already feel defeated?

A sudden image of the trapped mouse vaulted into her mind, her cat licking its chops.

Karen stopped a few feet from the corner of Brahms's desk. The director moved around the side of his desk and indicated a chair for her. He grasped her hand with both of his, wrapped his fingers around her wrists, engulfing her with his presence.

"Sit down, please."

"Thank you," she mumbled.

Brahms perched on the edge of his desk, leaning back. He slid his glasses on, as if assuming a different persona. He had repaired the broken lens. "You've come to talk about Ramis."

Right to the point, she thought. *What else does he know?* "That's right."

Brahms drummed a finger on the desk. Karen studied the man while he seemed to be pondering something. She had never noticed it before, but the glasses made him look older. He was ten years younger than she, but their lives, their career paths, had diverged wildly. Still, both were trapped on *Orbitech 1,* having to make the best of their situations.

Brahms narrowed his eyes. "Dr. Langelier, when did you first meet Ramis?"

Karen shrugged. "A day or so after he got here." A pause, then, "I guess I know him better than anyone, if that's what you're asking."

Silence. Brahms studied the holotank. "I've been going over the records. You're quite proficient in the Russian language—at least, written Russian. I assume you are competent conversationally, too?"

She nodded. He was leading her along exactly the line of reasoning she wanted.

"Dr. Langelier, I need—*Orbitech 1* needs—access to those Soviet scientists and whatever records they may have left behind. We've got to wake them. You can read and interpret all those things Ramis doesn't understand. Maybe he did something wrong when he tried to revive that first man. Do you think you could help him if you went over there?"

Karen's heart yammered at her; she kept her mouth from forming a smile. *He knows—he's got to know!* she thought. She stammered out an answer, tried to keep her composure and think straight.

He called up a memo on screen and scanned it. "Our medical staff says it would be best if someone knowledgeable in the language is actually there to help Ramis—get him to tell you what he did the first time and try to learn what he did wrong."

Brahms scowled and looked at the metal ceiling as he spoke. "Plenty of the physical scientists are fluent in Russian, but not a single one of our medical people or biologists. Apparently nobody considered new Soviet medical research worth reading about."

"The Soviets managed to come up with suspended animation before anybody else," Karen said.

"That's right." Brahms looked angry, but he laughed to himself. "Well, it hasn't been proved yet. Any moron can freeze people—it's reviving them intact that has always caused the problems."

Brahms rocked back. "Ramis was a loner here—self-sufficient and not too friendly. But I knew that if anyone was going to succeed over at the *Kibalchich,* it was him."

Karen blinked and tried to keep her expression neutral. Brahms sounded as if he had talked Ramis into going.

"But now I've got this introverted kid over there, scared half out of his wits. If I send the wrong person over, he might crack." Brahms paused for a moment. "You're one of the few people here that Ramis would trust. You've built up quite a relationship with him. He's asked about you."

Karen nodded. *He's talking me into it. But this is just what I hoped would happen—there has to be something up his sleeve.* "Ramis has become a good friend."

The acting director stared at her, his lips drawn to a tight thin line. The *Kibalchich* would give her sanctuary from Brahms.

She drew in a breath. "I'll do it. For *Orbitech 1,* of course." Karen stood. "When should I make the journey?"

"As soon as you can." He toggled down to another memo on his screen. "You had an idea about using the weavewire, without it cutting through everything?"

Karen answered tiredly. "Something like Ramis's harness. There is a way to knit the weavewire into a mesh loop —I can tie one end to a dolly and loop the other end over the line to the *Kibalchich*. That way I'll just ride the dolly over."

Brahms pushed himself up from his desk, landing lightly on his feet. He didn't seem at all interested in the technical details. "I'll throw the engineering branch at your disposal. Priority work."

"That won't be necessary—"

"Dr. Langelier," Brahms interrupted. His voice was soft, but his eyes penetrated her. "I made a mistake with McLaris—I won't do it again. Before you go, I want to have unlimited access to this new weavewire extraction process of yours, get the engineering branch up to speed on what you're doing. We can't afford to lose your technique. What if something happened to you over at the *Kibalchich*?

"Let us begin by drawing out as much of the fiber as we can. I want to have a good stockpile on hand, no matter how much storage space it takes up. The people over on the *Aguinaldo* have requested a supply of their own, and I'm happy to give it to them if they'll come get it. After all, Ramis brought us the *Aguinaldo*'s wall-kelp. We might also want to offer some of it to Clavius Base as a goodwill gesture. Maybe that'll get the Moon people to break their silence. It's starting to wear on our morale here."

"You won't need to store the weavewire—my new laser extraction technique can draw out a few thousand kilometers an hour."

Brahms smiled faintly, as if he had lost interest in the subject entirely. "Then it shouldn't be any problem. Good day, Dr. Langelier."

Once outside the office, Karen felt nauseated. Every time she interacted with Brahms, it seemed like a game of one-upmanship. She had walked away with everything she had wanted; Brahms had given her free rein to pull it off.

So why did she feel like she was being used?

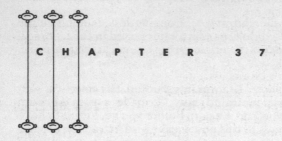

CLAVIUS BASE ■ DAY 42

The six-pack bounced over the lunar surface at twenty-five miles an hour. Dust kicked up by the wheels floated back to the ground. Metal mesh covered the passenger area, and a reinforced roll bar outlined the enclosure, permitting safe driving at such breakneck speeds to and from Clavius Base. Otherwise, the hundred-fifty-mile journey out to the telescope site would drag out twice as long as the six hours.

Clancy watched as Shen, sitting next to him, checked the radar-guided autopilot. "Forty-five minutes to cross the plain," she said. "Empty as a bureaucrat's head. All this nothingness reminds me of traveling across Nevada. Ever been there?"

"I flew into Vegas once."

"You haven't died of boredom then. There's a stretch of highway between Utah and California that goes straight for a hundred friggin' miles—no towns, cows, or anything else."

"No cows here, either."

"Good point."

They sat in silence for some moments. Clancy had a feeling Shen wanted to ask him something; she finally broke the silence. "Were you serious about needing a celestial mechanics expert?"

"Yeah."

"And you can't use my help?"

"Not for the question I have in mind. I'll ask Rockland when we get back to base."

After a moment of contemplation, Shen spoke up again. "Okay, what gives?"

Clancy chewed it over in his mind. The idea seemed so crazy. Maybe bouncing it off someone would give him a new angle to show that he was wrong.

If he was wrong.

Through the front shield he saw the flat span of crater, broken only by shuttle tracks from the once-a-day run to and from the Bigeye excavation site.

"I need a minimum-energy orbit from L-5 to the Moon."

He couldn't see much of Shen's expression behind the coated visor, but her voice sounded perplexed. "What for?"

"An orbit from L-5 to here. You know, connect the dots."

"Yeah, I heard that part the first time. But why? There's no reason for a min orbit. You can't get anything from them without a good enough guidance system, unless you're thinking of having them do the Filipino wall-kelp bit. Or we could throw rocks up at them with the mass launcher, but that method is configured to use a relay station at L-2."

"That's why I need a celestial mechanics expert. I don't even want to blab my idea until I know if it can work. But I think it will."

"Boy, I thought I changed gears fast." Shen turned her helmet to one side. "Go ahead and tell me. I'll keep my trap shut."

Clancy stared out at the lunar landscape. "Remember, I've still got to check this out, details and everything." Taking a deep breath, he started to explain.

The six-pack bounced, causing Clancy to grab onto his seat as he spoke. Shen checked the instruments to confirm they were still on course. Clancy felt embarrassed. "I know it's kind of crazy—"

"It's great!"

"But let me check it out first, okay? I don't want people to get their hopes up." *Nothing worse than false expectations,* he thought. *Especially when you're desperate for them.* It was hard enough getting the crew's morale back up with the radio-telescope project. No telling what would happen if an even larger project fell through.

Shen's voice came over the radio, sobered. "There's something even bigger on the line than people's hopes."

"What's that?"

"Your credibility."

His footsteps echoed in the empty tunnels. Light fixtures splashed shadows at angles on the smooth-bore walls. Duncan McLaris found the walk enthralling, vigorous.

He knew that walking was supposed to be better exercise than running—he'd gain the same aerobic benefits but without destroying his knees, ankles, and feet in the meantime. Not that he should worry so much in the low lunar gravity anyway. Lately, he'd taken to walking the length of the colony—five miles in all, counting the new section of tunnels that contained the wall-kelp.

Most people stayed out of the kelp tunnels, but McLaris loved the feeling of being alone in the caves. It marked a turning point in his life—a return to grace and full restoration of his inner being. The twisted path he had taken to get here, the wrong turns, the dead ends—it was a lot like his life.

He felt the thickening beard on his chin. It was stiff and prickly, but it had passed the itching stage. He couldn't imagine himself without it when he looked in the mirror now. He hadn't shaved since the *Miranda* crash.

He hadn't been able to build himself back up until now —until Chief Administrator Tomkins had showed faith in him. The crux of it all lay in the new tunnels, the paths that led in different directions away from darkness.

The sound of an electric cart came from behind him. McLaris stepped over to the edge of the tunnel and allowed the vehicle to whir past. Moments later he turned toward the administrative offices and the brighter lights.

As he entered the office complex, two people rose from their chairs to greet him—Dr. Clancy and one of his crew.

"Cliff, I wouldn't have thought you'd be back to Clavius so soon." McLaris steered them to his office.

He offered them some tea brewed from reconstituted wall-kelp. There was enough glucose in the concoction to make it pleasant.

Shaking his head at the offer, Clancy got straight to the point. "Duncan, I think we might have hit on something big. It's a crazy idea."

"No, it isn't," the woman accompanying him said. Her name tag said Shen. "Crazy, I mean. It's certainly big enough."

McLaris settled back in his chair and took a sip of his own tea. "This is bigger than the radio telescope, and you think it's possible? Let's hear it."

"Oh, it's possible," Shen said.

"I'll need some computer time. But I think Rockland can verify it."

McLaris smiled at their enthusiasm. "Do I have to guess what this is, or are you going to tell me?"

He had been the Production Division leader on *Orbitech 1*, in charge of enough incentives and bonuses to keep production moving at its peak efficiency. But Clancy's crew presented a special problem to him. The construction engineers saw themselves as only guests on Clavius Base, pulled off their "real" project of building *Orbitech 2*. Part of McLaris's effort had been to get Clancy's crew motivated into working for the benefit of Clavius Base. That meant allowing them to "hobby shop" —work on pet projects and crazy schemes. *So be it*, McLaris thought. Maybe something would come of it after all.

Clancy moved to the front of his seat. "We've found a way to get to *Orbitech 1*, if the computer models pan out. And if our experiment is successful, we could have trips from L-5 to Clavius on a regular basis."

McLaris's mouth drew out in a tight smile. "We haven't been in touch with *Orbitech 1* since the RIF. Are you serious?"

"Of course he is!" Shen said. "Dr. Rockland can verify the physics within an hour or so. His celestial mechanics group was going ga-ga when we explained it to them. They were so excited, half the group rushed off before we were finished."

McLaris continued to rock in his chair, increasing the frequency. Outwardly, he wore a smile.

Reestablish contact with *Orbitech 1*.

Damn you, McLaris! Brahms had said as they rocketed away in the stolen shuttle. Brahms was still up there.

Inwardly, McLaris's heart felt chilled.

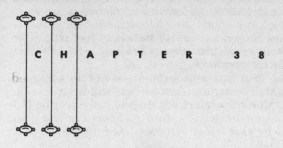

C H A P T E R   3 8

ORBITECH 1 ■ DAY 43

As she floated outside the zero-G deck for the second time, Karen thought the stars looked fixed in the dark sky. *Orbitech 1* rotated around her, its gravity quarters wheeling high above her head. A space-suited figure stood beside her with the temporary name tag that said Harhoosma affixed to his suit. She didn't know the man—Brahms had just assigned him to help her.

"Are you a hull maintenance worker or something?" Karen had asked him. Once again, she felt very aware that only a thin layer of protective clothing separated her from the vacuum.

"No," Harhoosma said in a thin, piping voice. "I am a metallurgist."

When Karen turned toward him in alarm, he continued speaking. "I specialize in vacuum welding. I have spent much time outside, testing different techniques."

That gave him some legitimacy, she guessed. But

Brahms had handpicked him to help. Maybe Harhoosma was watching her for some unknown reason.

Fifty miles away shone the *Kibalchich*. She found it ironic to want to go to a Soviet station to feel free. The weavewire bridge spanned the two colonies, fainter than the thinnest of spiderwebs.

I guess this is where you have to believe in yourself, Karen thought. Throughout her career—graduate school, post-doc, as a line research chemist—she had never had to rely so totally on herself to survive. Someone else had always stood by as a safety net—someone to ensure that she'd be all right.

Now, it was her own invention that she depended on. If something happened to the weavewire during her journey, she'd be drifting out where no one could reach her. The thought sobered her. At least Ramis had had practice maneuvering in freefall.

"Dr. Langelier, are you ready?" Harhoosma said.

Karen checked over her suit for the sixth time since coming out. Before she had left the airlock, one of the medics had injected her with a radiation-endurance drug; it would be some time before it took effect.

"All set. I guess I should get going."

Harhoosma stepped backward, keeping one magnetized sole on the metal hull. "It looks very far away."

Karen turned to the dolly apparatus she would hook to her back. In a bundle thick enough to see, the weavewire "pulley" hung over the invisible cable, then connected to the wire dolly by tungsten strands. Karen wore a package of personal items for herself and Ramis, and two spare air bottles.

Harhoosma helped her fasten onto the cable, adjusting her yaw and facing her forward, so she could watch the *Kibalchich* as it grew closer. Her months on *Orbitech 1* held no special memories for her—no pleasant ones, anyway. She felt relieved to be able to purge herself of the experience.

Karen spoke into the helmet radio. "Okay, I'm ready."

Grunting, Harhoosma pushed her away from *Orbitech 1*. She punched the forward thrusters on the MMU pack and accelerated along the nearly frictionless fiber. There was no gravity to pull her down so that she could "slide" across the fiber to the *Kibalchich*. Instead, her path consisted of long sawtooth-like motions, guided by the weavewire.

Inside the colony, she had been able to watch the festive holo coverage of Ramis's trip. But now that she participated herself, she saw none of the video, though she felt sure that holocameras mounted at various points outside the hull recorded her every move. Brahms would want to have cameras all over the place, even outside.

Harhoosma seemed to be the sole person watching her leave. She wondered if perhaps Brahms had kept this expedition quiet, just in case something went wrong. Or was he afraid dozens of people would clamor to get off *Orbitech 1* in a mass exodus?

Brahms didn't even signal to wish her good luck. One of the watchers had said that the acting director was in an important conference with someone from Clavius Base—not that Karen had wanted him to say good-bye anyway.

Harhoosma's voice came inside her helmet. "I measure you going four point six miles per hour, Dr. Langelier. At that rate," he paused, "you will have ten point eight hours of travel. You may wish to add more acceleration."

The gruff female voice of one of the monitors inside the colony broke in. "We'll give you plenty of warning to change your oxygen bottles."

"Thank you," Karen answered. She twisted her head around inside the helmet and caught a glimpse of *Orbitech 1* out of the corner of the visor. Already she could hardly pick out Harhoosma on the nonrotating end.

She caught a fleeting glimpse of something blocking out the stars, as if an object had passed in front of her. Squinting, she tried to make out the thing as it tumbled across her path. It almost looked like a person.

And then it struck her, and was gone behind her.

The RIF! It must have been one of the bodies. . . .

She breathed deeply, trying to calm herself. She pitched and swung on the cable from the collision; she used the MMU's stabilizers to stop her oscillation. Now, more than ever, she felt glad about leaving.

Trying to relax, Karen squeezed her eyes shut until splotches of color appeared in her vision. She heard her breath slowing, calming. She blinked and then stared at the open universe in front of her, still afraid of seeing another corpse.

Karen didn't admit it, but the technicians on *Orbitech 1* monitoring her elevated breathing would know how terrified she was.

The *Kibalchich* would grow larger as she approached. Now, hanging in space, she felt stranded and alone.

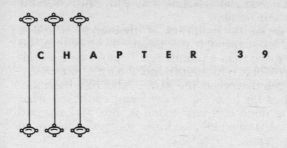

CHAPTER 39

The surprise was not that McLaris wanted to speak with him. Curtis Brahms had suspected that would eventually happen. Given enough time, McLaris would come strutting back, boasting, taunting Brahms about his escape to the Moon.

But he had not anticipated that McLaris would come humbly.

McLaris's expression remained frozen in the holotank, sagging with the light lag brought on by the signal's one-hundred-and-fifty-thousand-mile transmission path. The lag injected a one-second delay, an uncertainty, into the conversation. The image stared unflinching into Brahms's face. He saw a deep-set pain in the traitor's eyes. Good. But the emotion seemed tempered and controlled.

The office grew cold and silent. Brahms allowed a thin smile to play at his lips. He had McLaris figured out before the man could even speak a greeting. The former division leader hadn't changed—Brahms knew it, and he knew McLaris knew it himself.

Even insulated by hundreds of thousands of miles, Brahms could see through the facade now, even as he should have more than a month ago. Brahms had considered Duncan McLaris his best friend aboard *Orbitech 1*, a man whose mind worked the same, who had the same goals, who had his head on straight and could see what needed to be done and how to do it. But McLaris had turned coward, thrown his own interests above those of all the other people on the colony.

You were lucky then, Duncan, thought Brahms. *And you are lucky now.* McLaris sat fidgeting, probably looking for an opening line. But Brahms beat him to it.

"Well, well. Base Manager McLaris. The *Aguinaldo* informed us of your new position. Does this mean that Clavius Base has finally dropped that silly boycott of ConComm? It was rather a petulant reaction."

McLaris shrugged. "It wasn't my idea in the first place."

"Yes, cover your rear. I understand. You've grown a beard, Duncan." It looked thin and scraggly on McLaris's naturally boyish-looking face. "Are you trying to hide behind a disguise?"

McLaris stiffened, but ignored the comment. "We've been monitoring your ConComm link with the *Aguinaldo* all along—we just haven't replied to your transmissions." He lowered his voice. "I've called to discuss an important project between our two colonies. Strictly business."

Brahms sat back, raising his eyebrows and keeping in motion just to gain a moment to think. His walls of suspicion flew up. Out of range of the holoscreen, he gripped his fists.

"What have you done now, commandeered the Clavius Base communication center? How many people are you going to hurt this time?"

McLaris shot back, "I didn't throw a hundred and fifty people out the airlock."

Brahms glared at the image. "You would have done the same. I know you, Duncan. We're two sides of the same coin. Pressed against the wall, with all this hanging over your head, you would have taken the same desperate measures that I was forced to! Besides, Ombalal gave the order."

"Give me a break, Curtis. Ombalal had trouble getting dressed in the morning! I know *you*, too."

Brahms breathed through his nose, but didn't reply. McLaris took a long moment to continue. "I didn't call to argue with you, Curtis. I need to speak with you as an official emissary of Clavius Base."

"I'm surprised they didn't leave you out in the wreckage of the shuttle you crashed. I told them what you did."

"Yes, and they saw what you did, too. They learned what I was running away from. You legitimized my actions."

"I see." Brahms drew his lips tight.

He had expected McLaris to get his claws into the Moon base's management ranks, where he could eventually betray them as he had betrayed *Orbitech 1*. But Brahms hadn't expected it so soon.

McLaris cleared his throat, changing the subject. "I hear the Filipinos' wall-kelp has made things rather more, ah, pleasant up there."

Brahms answered in a clipped voice. "We are very thankful to the *Aguinaldo*." *If it had come sooner, or if we had even known about it, I might not have been forced into the RIF,* he thought. McLaris continued to stare at him with what looked to be an accusing expression. *Damn him,* Brahms thought. *What would he have done in my situation? Let the people riot, and have everyone die? We didn't know!*

"Down here, we're finding ways to bleach out the taste. We'll share some of our results with your people, if you're interested."

Brahms fought to control his emotions. McLaris had shown his true nature—running away, hiding his head in Moon dust, letting someone else tackle the problem. Brahms covered his anger with a vacant, placid expression. This was not the time to strike—that would come some time in the future.

McLaris continued, "Now we see that the Filipino boy has gone over to the *Kibalchich*. He's a brave one."

Brahms pushed his face closer to the holoscreen. "Duncan, what do you really want? I have no desire for chitchat. Why did you contact me?"

The one-second lag was all he needed. McLaris launched right into his proposal, catching Brahms off guard. "I don't have to give you growth statistics or projections of what will happen if our colonies remain separate, little islands slowly withering away. It could be decades before Earth sends somebody back here, if at all. Now that you've already linked up with the *Aguinaldo*—"

"I wouldn't call a one-shot trip on a sail-creature an everyday occurrence," Brahms broke in. With the light lag, McLaris continued speaking before he realized he had been interrupted.

"It doesn't matter. They did it once, it can be done again. The English, even the Vikings, beat greater odds crossing the Atlantic. Now you've sent a representative aboard the *Kibalchich*. In a few years, there could be regular trade between the Lagrange points."

Brahms held up a hand, maintaining a skeptical expression. "You didn't contact me to pump me up on space exploration, either."

McLaris drew his mouth in a scowl. "You haven't changed, Curtis. You're still a bottom-line man." Brahms didn't break his smile; McLaris knew him.

"So here's the bottom line. You will soon have access to the *Kibalchich* whenever you want to go there. Believe it or not, the people on the *Aguinaldo* are not too far behind in their access to you, if they can find a practical way to use those sail-creatures of theirs. You three Lagrange colonies are approaching a point where you don't need Earth to survive."

"You pointed that out a moment ago. We're nearing self-sufficiency right now." Brahms realized his voice remained bitter, although he should have felt triumphant about that.

McLaris brushed the comments aside. "You know what I'm talking about. The wall-kelp will keep you hanging on —*us* hanging on—barely surviving, even if we don't do anything else. But you're a closed system. If you want the colonies to grow—to expand and thrive—then we've got to do it in numbers. We've got to pool resources. You'll never achieve that critical mass on your own—not even with the *Kibalchich* and the *Aguinaldo* thrown in."

"So what?"

McLaris's face seemed to jut through the holotank. "We've got the means to help right here on the Moon: heavy equipment, ore, smelters, the mass driver. We intend to get back on our feet. Throw in with us and bring back civilization."

Brahms studied McLaris without emotion. His former division leader breathed heavily, his nostrils flared in excitement. Brahms couldn't put his finger on what had lit such a spark in McLaris.

"Dammit, Duncan, you're not giving a campaign speech. What the hell do you want?"

"I want to establish a direct, physical connection between the Moon and *Orbitech 1*."

"How? You'll never be able to get up here."

"On the broadcasts showing Ramis and his Jump to the *Kibalchich*, your commentator announced that a new way had been discovered to draw the weavewire out quickly. Is there any limit to how long you can make it?"

Brahms began to get an idea of what McLaris was going to propose. For a moment, the thoughts distracted him. "Supposedly not." Brahms furrowed his eyebrows, wondering if McLaris had knocked every screw in his head loose when he had crashed the *Miranda*. "Are you suggesting we have someone Jump down to Clavius Base? That's ridiculous."

"No, but you've got the general idea." His eyes glittered on the holotank image. "We've come up with a stable orbit from L-5 direct to the Moon. Here, I'll flash up some graphics." McLaris nodded to someone out of sight of the holotransmitter. A diagram of the Moon, the two Lagrange points sixty degrees on either side, and the Earth, replaced his image. A bright dot pulsed at L-5. McLaris's voice came over the graphic.

"If you can ballistically shoot out a line of weavewire from *Orbitech 1* with the proper initial conditions, it will be forced to follow the 'orbit' you see on the display." A bright yellow line left L-5 and began inching toward the Moon. "It'll impact the Moon, and if we can catch it, we'll establish a sort of lifeline cable between L-5 and Clavius Base—just like you've made between yourselves and the *Kibalchich*."

The graphics dissolved into McLaris's face again. He

appeared more excited. "Our original idea was to make a kind of Clarke elevator, or Artsutanov's elevator, or whoever you want to give the credit to. But we found that wouldn't be stable. If we tried to hold onto the weavewire, the impact signal would propagate back up to *Orbitech 1*, setting off nonlinear oscillations." McLaris smiled engagingly. "At least, those are the words my engineers told me to say."

Brahms had to admire him for his talent, though he resented being manipulated.

McLaris held up a finger. "But, if we caught the weavewire just after it hit the surface, we could attach some sort of capsule—a cargo container or elevator car, depending on how you want to look at it—and you could start hauling the wire back up to *Orbitech 1*."

"Like a giant yo-yo," Brahms said, getting the idea. "No, more like a fishhook—we cast the line down, you hook the fish on, and we haul it in."

He became more and more frustrated inside as he felt how important McLaris's idea could really be for their survival. Damn him again!

"Exactly! I can have some of my people talk to yours to work out the details. But the idea is so simple that even without a huge industrial base we can do this. Compared to building an actual spaceship, this would be like hammering together a wooden horse cart instead of fabricating a sports car, but it will work."

McLaris's eyes remained bright, and he kept speaking as if he was afraid Brahms would jump into the time lag. "Do you understand, Curtis? If this works, we can move between the colonies and the Moon. Think of what we can accomplish!"

Brahms felt the potentials rushing through his mind. It was the kind of idea he himself would dream up—grandiose and full of challenge, and with a huge payoff.

It would mean an end to the old ways—the thought of future RIFs could be thrown away forever. They had hope —a glimmer of a solid future, in McLaris's words.

So why did that distress him? Brahms couldn't put his finger on the anxiety it caused.

"Wait a minute. You can reel people up here, but how do you get them back down to the Moon?"

"Simple," McLaris said, answering almost too quickly. "It's like lowering a string with a bucket on the end. Well, not really, but our techies have all the details."

Brahms spoke in a low voice, gruff and businesslike, but no longer laced with antagonism. "Duncan, let me set up a meeting with my engineering group. I want a complete interchange of information—let them run their own models to make sure this thing really works. If they say yes, then we can start work right away." He lifted an eyebrow, almost as an afterthought. "If you concur, that is."

It galled him to say that.

McLaris broke into a wide smile for the first time during the interchange. "My thoughts exactly."

Now can you gloat some more because you think you've won?

"Good, we'll consider it done." Brahms paused. He felt very awkward.

A moment passed. McLaris spoke. "These are new times, Curtis. We've got to work together. Sweep away the old."

"That's the only way."

Brahms switched off the holotank and rocked back in his chair, tapping his fingertips against each other.

Before he summoned the engineering team, he grew warm with the knowledge that he might finally have a chance to see Duncan face-to-face again.

Face-to-face.

His palms felt sticky with sweat.

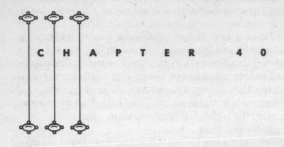

L - 5 ■ DAY 44

Karen didn't sleep the entire journey. Hooked onto
the pulley contraption, she slipped away from *Orbitech 1*.
The ride was smooth, as if on a frictionless sea of ice, even
as the pulley gently bumped against the weavewire. Otherwise, there was no sensation of movement, only the
bulky straitjacket of the space suit and echoes of her own
breathing in her ears. She could see no indication at all of
the weavewire, only the invisible line where the dolly was
attached to nothing, guiding her to the *Kibalchich*. She
felt suspended in space.

Over the hours, Karen wondered how people could ever
survive long space journeys. The Soviets had attempted
one years-long journey to Mars, and it had driven them to
destroy their own ship. Now that she thought about it,
being cramped with other people in a tiny exploratory
ship for all that time would probably push her over the
edge, as well.

She raised Ramis once, and elicited a promise from him

to meet her. She told him the time of her projected arrival, and he marked it on one of the command center chronometers.

Later, Karen flipped on her radio and trained the antenna toward the Soviet colony. "Ramis, this is Karen. Can you hear me?" Nothing. "Ramis. Are you near an airlock? I am almost to the *Kibalchich.*" She knew he could not send a reply if he had not remained in the command center.

Karen waited, then switched her transmitter off. The station loomed in front of her.

Through the middle of the torus, stars blinked in and out of view as the spokes rotated. Karen fumbled with her harness, shedding the webbing and preparing to disconnect her suit from the dolly frame. Everywhere was "down"—she seemed to be in the middle of a gigantic well that extended forever, in all directions. She flipped her radio on. "Ramis? Are you out here?" Still no answer.

She grew worried. She had told him when to expect her. The clock showed her to be right on time.

Russian letters now showed clearly on the metal hull, spelling out *Kibalchich.* She had checked out the name in the historical data base back in her quarters and remembered: Nikolai Ivanovitch Kibalchich had taken part in the assassination of Tsar Alexander II in 1881, and had been arrested and sentenced to death. In his cell awaiting execution, Kibalchich had drawn up plans for a man-carrying rocket platform fed by gunpowder cartridges. After he was executed, guards filed his sketches in police archives. In his prison cell, knowing he had no hope, Kibalchich had written on his rocket plans, "I believe in the practicability of my idea and this faith supports me in my desperate plight."

Karen wished she had the same faith in her own "desperate plight." The large doses of drugs she had taken to protect herself against radiation exposure had made her feel ill. She feared they would also slow her reactions.

"You should be almost there," said the voice from *Orbitech 1.*

"Gee, thanks," Karen muttered. She tried to wipe Ramis from her mind and concentrate on landing, going over in her head how she would come to a stop. The engineers had designed the harness with an emergency release so she could unlatch herself easily. It seemed simple enough.

But then she remembered a time in Colorado, back when she had lived in Denver, before moving to the Center for High-Technology Materials in Albuquerque. A ski slope—Breckenridge?—where she and Ray had spent one spring day schussing down black diamond runs. The sky was impossibly blue, the ground white from a late spring snow; she and Ray laughed as the lifts pulled them up, when Karen realized she had forgotten to pull the tips of her skis up. . . . She found herself facedown in a clump of snow underneath the chair lift. Because she hadn't been paying attention, a simple act had turned into disaster.

This time, if she let her attention lapse and released herself at the wrong time, Karen would suffer a lot worse than a faceful of snow.

She could make out the outer wheel's grainy surface, even small pits from micrometeors. She rotated her body around to point her feet directly at the station.

The dolly slid above composite spokes and support struts as it followed the weavewire to the *Kibalchich*'s hub. Overhead, the mirror looked flat and glistening, reflecting an image of the torus back onto itself.

Above her, a streak of Day-Glo orange marking the end of the weavewire zipped through space. *One hundred yards to go!* she thought. She had only time enough to draw in a breath before she hit the station. The suit disconnected from the pulley apparatus, and she collapsed to the hub, absorbing the shock with her feet. She wasn't sure if the magnetized soles would keep her in place. She remembered to reach up and catch the dolly support before it rebounded back along the nearly frictionless cable.

"Dr. Langelier, be # # # and to # # # # . . ." A voice broke in and out of coherence as she turned about, her directional antenna sweeping the space where *Orbitech 1* hung.

Her hand encircled the central graphite rod. It was too large for her fingers to fit around, but it served to stop her from drifting.

Karen drew in short, laborious breaths and closed her eyes, gripping the rod. If she let go she would be out in space right now where no one could reach her. She'd have only a handful of hours of air, even at one-quarter pressure.

She swung her antenna in the general direction of *Orbitech 1*. "I'm here," she said. "Have you heard anything from Ramis?"

Silence. Then, slowly, "No. Didn't he say he was going to be there to help you?"

It was her turn to ponder.

After her eleven-hour journey, she wanted to be inside —any place that had walls and a floor and a ceiling. She could find Ramis. He had found his way inside by himself; she could do the same.

Karen clicked at her mike. *"Orbitech 1,* I'm going to find one of the access hatches into the *Kibalchich.* A full report will follow." Karen clicked her receiver off. She didn't need anything from them. She could make her own decisions. She had left *Orbitech 1* because of people always telling her what to do, when to do it, and how to do it.

Karen started to shimmy along the support rod, searching for a way to get inside.

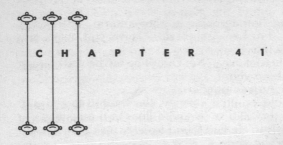

CHAPTER 41

Big Brother Moving Company.

It was precisely what Luis Sandovaal felt like as he prepared for the trip to *Orbitech 1.* This would not be just a desperate test flight, as Ramis had made. In his own typical style, Sandovaal would make this a grand procession.

He ran one hand through his shock of white hair, making it stand straight up, then surveyed all the extra baggage they would need to ensure their return, plus Ramis's. Magsaysay had insisted on that part. It had been the only way Magsaysay would even consider allowing Sandovaal to go; even then, the *dato* was reluctant.

Dobo had just returned from Mass, and Sandovaal put him to work. Since finding out he would be making the journey to L-5 with Sandovaal, Dobo had attended Mass twice a day. Sandovaal couldn't understand his assistant's actions—they had even less time to waste than usual.

Sandovaal squinted at the tanks nurturing the sail-creature embryos. The air smelled raw and wet, but Sandovaal did not notice. The thirty-six embryos nestled in the quiet sanctuary of one of the glass-enclosed wall-kelp alcoves were their only hope of returning from *Orbitech 1*. Sandovaal had no way of knowing how well the Americans had cared for the tiny embryos Ramis had brought with him, and the boy wasn't enough of an expert to tell for himself. But the embryos would take years to reach maturity; Sandovaal was bringing mature nymphs.

He and Dobo would have time to instruct their American counterparts on how to nurture the next generation of sail-creatures and make them available for sails, in case they ever wanted to come to L-4. Magsaysay didn't think they would.

Behind him, Dobo sloshed about in a vat of nutrient solution. Synthetic rubber boots rode up to his crotch, making him look ridiculous. The bittersweet aroma of the amniotic solution mixed with the rank smell of growing wall-kelp. On the other side of the crystal windows, sunlight poured through, illuminating the alcove like a weird jungle.

Sandovaal had never before considered mass-producing the sail-creatures. In fact, he was new to the entire idea of gearing his work to assembly lines. On Magsaysay's insistence, Sandovaal had documented all his work and left dozens of assistants marginally trained to follow in his footsteps.

The wall-kelp grew by itself and needed little work, but the sail-creatures were much more complicated. With his tinkering in the lab, Sandovaal could produce one sail-creature embryo per day, at most, by cloning from the viable samples he had on hand. More than 90 percent of the clones died.

Now, though, for the trip to L-5, all the sail-creatures must be the same age when they left the *Aguinaldo*. Otherwise, it would ruin Sandovaal's plans for getting back home. He had expanded his operation, finding ways to increase production, to take shortcuts.

Dobo's feet made a plopping sound as he moved through the vat. It broke Sandovaal's concentration. He turned and opened his mouth to snap at his assistant but stopped at what he saw.

Dobo was kneeling in the vat, leaning over a pocket of

sail-creature embryos. Hands cupped, he delicately directed some of the amniotic fluid into the sac. It would dry sticky on his dark boots.

Memories flooded Sandovaal's mind. The rice paddies, and the loving care the Filipinos gave to each seedling as they planted the sprouts in the flooded marsh. The Filipino culture was still here, present even in this giant rotating drum in space. And now, for the first time since the War, Sandovaal was certain that the old ways—the important aspects, at least—would still survive. Magsaysay had nothing to fear about that.

He composed himself and slipped from the chamber, leaving Dobo alone. Dobo hummed to himself—probably one of the hymns he had sung at Mass.

The viewport veranda afforded a view of the sail-creatures they would use. They were strung out in a line with their sails oriented at right angles to the sun, like gigantic, wispy butterflies. The creatures seemed to explode in growth, transforming from puttering, clumsy-looking animals into beautiful organic sails. They stretched out their skins to catch every photon within reach. They were relatively small now, but Sandovaal knew that in a short time they would be ready for the trip. The imagined sight made him draw a deep breath—an array of sail-creatures, clustered as a mighty armada of old, carrying Dobo and Sandovaal into new territory.

And if they were successful with their request, they would return with Ramis and enough weavewire to scale their next obstacle: *Orbitech 2.*

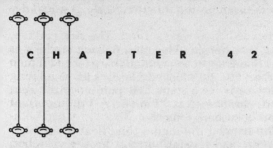

C H A P T E R   4 2

When the inner airlock rotated open, Karen saw only darkness. She removed her helmet and stared into the shadows.

"Ramis?" she called in a quiet voice, but the word sounded as loud as a gunshot. He would be somewhere inside, but she had no idea where, or why he had not met her. She was glad she had not been the first to enter the silent station.

A dark hallway curved up ahead and behind her. Wetting her lips, she stepped out of the airlock into the *Kibalchich*. She tapped a toe on the floor in an instinctive gesture, to make sure it remained solid. She dragged her pack of personal belongings just inside the corridor and plopped it to the floor. She started to set her helmet down, but decided to put up with the inconvenience of carrying it.

The *Kibalchich* was dead quiet. She could hear the blood pounding in her ears. All the lights were dim.

The airlock hissed shut behind her.

Karen drew in a breath to stop herself from shaking. *Ramis is here somewhere,* she thought. *Nothing is going to happen.*

"Karen?"

She whirled, then her shoulders slumped with relief. She had not heard Ramis approach with his bare feet. Soft light outlined his face. His eyes looked bleary with sleep.

"You are very early. Two hours." He pointed an elbow at one of the wall chronometers. "I am sorry I did not meet you. Have you been here long?"

"Early?" She noticed the digital time next to an intercom, a flatscreen, and several buttons. Frowning, Karen glanced at her own suit watch. "This clock is two hours fast." Then she rolled her eyes in a ridiculous expression.

"They're on Moscow time! Why didn't they standardize, like everyone else? *Orbitech 1* is on Greenwich Mean." She sighed. "We should have synchronized clocks, but who would have thought?"

She shook her head, still puzzled. "But why are you two hours late, and not early?"

Ramis tried to brush her question aside. He blinked his eyes again. "I must have gotten mixed up and subtracted the two-hour difference instead of adding it. I was sleeping, for the first time in days, but I planned to wake up before you arrived. I still needed some time to . . . to get something."

He looked at her with his dark eyes, hesitating. "I was not certain it would be you. It could have been one of the other Soviets, or someone else that Brahms sent over . . ." His voice trailed off.

On an impulse, Karen wanted to hug him, but in the monstrous padded suit that would have been more comical than poignant. "The important thing is that I'm here." She threw a glance at his loose, comfortable clothes. His space suit was conspicuously absent. "Where are you staying?"

"I have found several private chambers."

"Sounds like a good start." Karen handed him the helmet to carry. "Lead on, Ramis." She hooked her belongings on the crook of her arm.

Ramis took her through several cubicles and down to a second deck. Karen felt as if she were in a three-dimen-

sional maze. "You will learn your way around quickly,"
said Ramis. "It is a monotonous arrangement."

At first the station's layout confused her, but after only a
few minutes, she discovered a pattern: the three decks
were all arranged identically, but offset from the decks
above them. An octagonal pattern of compartments surrounded each staircase, holding emergency supplies of air,
food, and water. One could travel straight up or down the
decks if needed, but the main thoroughfares were staggered to break the monotony.

As they walked, she noted few displays of artwork or any
kind of decor. In recreation areas, she saw murals depict-
ing larger-than-life characters with a central hero, usually
standing in a field or a city, looking toward the stars.

Ramis stopped before a row of eight cabins with doors
open. Karen dumped her helmet and satchel onto the
floor. The rooms were not all clustered together; several
blank spaces separated the doors at random intervals.
Looking closely at the bulkhead, Karen ran her hand along
a hairline seam.

"There are doors all along here. I wonder why some of
them are closed?"

Ramis turned away. "Most of them were open, or at least
activated, when I arrived. They close behind you after you
leave the room."

"And how do you open them again?"

"That I do not know," Ramis said slowly. "I have tried to
get back inside."

"I see." Karen suppressed a smile. She lounged back
against the polished bulkhead and crossed her arms. Ramis
stared back, unblinking. She nodded to the row of closed
doors. "If they used to be all open, then I bet you did some
experimenting, trying to find out how to open them."

Ramis nodded.

Karen pushed away from the wall. "And I suppose you
slept in one of these last night?" She could not stop her
smile from growing. "And I suppose you took your helmet
and suit with you. It's in one of these rooms, and now you
can't get the door open again?"

Ramis flushed and nodded stiffly. *No wonder he didn't
meet me outside,* she thought. Though the time lag on the
chronometers had distracted her for a while, he was obvi-

ously too abashed at losing face, and had needed to make
up an excuse that would not leave him appearing stupid.
Losing his helmet because he couldn't get the door open
again! He probably thought he'd be stuck here forever.

Already, being away from *Orbitech 1* had improved her
mood. The situation wasn't funny, but if worse came to
worst, they could always smash the door in with a Soviet
forklift.

"Why don't you help me out of this suit so I can move
like a human being again? We'll leave it right here in the
hall. Then take me to the control room. That's where you
kept in communication with *Orbitech 1,* isn't it?"

"Yes, I will show you."

Over the next fifteen minutes, she struggled with the
fastenings and seals of her suit. Ramis seemed patient and
enjoyed being with her; they chatted about meaningless
things. She realized he must have been terribly lonely.

The helmet and harness lay on the floor. Karen
squirmed out of the bulky protective suit and stood
hunched over in her cotton jumpsuit, breathing hard. She
wiped a palm across her forehead and stared at the sweat
glinting off the dim corridor lights.

"How can construction engineers live in those things?"

Ramis furrowed his eyebrows. "All the body functions
are taken care of. You know how to activate the glucose
tablet dispenser? That would give you energy. Vitamin
supplements can keep you going for several shifts."

Karen shook her head. "That's not really what I meant.
Right now I'm still a little dizzy from all that antirad junk I
had to take."

Kneeling on the floor, she dug through her bag and
opened a mylar satchel. It hissed when she broke the seal,
indicating that air pressure on the *Kibalchich* was lower
than what she had left behind. "I brought you some personal effects. I went into your quarters and took anything I
thought you might want, since you left in such a hurry."
She looked into his eyes. "I hope you don't mind?"

"No, of course not."

Karen handed him a clean set of clothes, his St. Christopher's medal, and—with a smile—a pack of jerky made
from unprocessed wall-kelp. "I thought you might miss
this."

"How can I ever repay you?" he asked, then made a wicked smile. "Or is the correct American phrasing, I'll get you for that?"

She laughed, then stood up again. "Control room?"

"This way." Ramis motioned her up the corridor. He bit into the wall-kelp and winced, but chewed. He tore off a chunk and extended it to her. "For such a good friend, I will share." Ramis glared at her. "I insist."

They walked up the curving hallway. A low hum pulsed through the station, hovering at the edge of her ability to hear. Karen breathed deep. The air remained stale and metallic from the reprocessers, but it didn't have the smell of anxiety and fear hanging in every lungful. It seemed refreshing to a certain degree.

Unlike *Orbitech 1*'s low- and zero-gravity decks, depending on their configuration in the colony, the *Kibalchich* kept gravity throughout its torus, except for the zero-G command center at the hub. As Ramis activated the lift platform to take them toward the center, she felt weight dropping away from her.

The ceiling opened overhead. She felt no gravity at all, but a room appearing above her knocked Karen's orientation off kilter. Ramis kicked off the lift platform and rose into the chamber. Karen drifted up after him.

"The control room. As you requested." He made a little bow, which caused him to spin in a somersault in the middle of the room. He started to laugh.

Pinpoints of red and green light burned from control panels. Data screens and attached chairs jutted from the curved walls. A central column surrounded by a holotank extended from floor to ceiling—the light pipe, or whatever it was that connected the shield and solar collectors below the station to the tilted mirror above. The holotank was a standard Hitachi, state of the art in resolution and contrast, but appeared to lack a tactile option.

"Everything is here." Ramis spread his hands. "One person could seal himself up in this room and control the entire station. I wonder if that is what happened. It would explain the man's body I found."

Karen looked around, snagging the nearest chair as she floated by. "Are the computers voice activated?"

"I was able to transmit a message to *Orbitech 1*." Ramis

floated over to one wall. "Beyond that, I do not know. I cannot speak Russian, remember?"

Karen stared at the holotanks and the various input pads. "Well, let's try it. First off, we should learn how to unlock all those doors. We'll get your helmet back."

Selecting what appeared to be the command chair, Karen strapped in. Clearing her throat, she tried to enunciate her words clearly. It had been years since she had last conversed in Russian, and the computer would have enough difficulty interpreting her odd accent anyway.

"Computer, present a map of the colony," she said in Russian.

Nothing.

"Computer, respond."

Karen looked puzzled. Ramis hovered beside her. "What did you say to it?"

Distracted, she glanced at him. "Maybe I told it to calculate the value of pi or something. But I thought I said, 'Computer, present a map of the colony.' "

"{{AFFIRMATIVE: ALL USERS VALIDATED BY ACTING COMMANDER TRIPOLK.}}" The computer-generated voice, in English, startled both of them.

A sketch of the rotating wheel came to focus in the murk of the tank. The lines continued to add detail, forming a dense blueprint image, overlapping and growing solid as the computer reconstructed the *Kibalchich* from the inside out. The computer exposed sections to show how the inner core rotated inside the stationary outer layer of Moon rubble.

As she thought about it, Karen realized the computer responding to English instead of Russian made sense, too. "They must have found it simpler to use validated algorithms for speech recognition than to invent new ones for a whole different language."

Karen placed a finger over her lips. "Ramis, when you were trying to get back into the sealed cabins, did you ask the computer to open the doors for you—out loud, I mean?"

Ramis turned away, looking angry at himself.

"Don't be embarrassed," Karen said. "I'm not here to compete with you—or to show how smart I am. We're in this together.

"Remember, I'm a good fifteen years older than you, and I've worked in control rooms and labs most of my life. It's only natural that I'm going to hit on some things quicker than you. But I automatically thought this computer would respond in Russian—I make mistakes all the time, too."

A smile tugged at Ramis's lips. "I will remember that."

"Okay. Let's try this one more time." She cleared her throat. "Computer, open all the doors to the sleeping areas."

"{{AFFIRMATIVE: ALL USERS VALIDATED BY ACTING COMMANDER TRIPOLK.}}"

Karen grinned. "According to this, all the doors are open again. Thanks to Commander Tripolk, whoever he is. I should check in with *Orbitech 1* and let them know I got here. Too bad this is the only place you can send or receive outside transmissions."

"They can monitor them better that way," Ramis said. He waited beside her. "Let me take you to the commissary. They left many supplies."

"You didn't mention anything about supplies in your transmissions!"

Ramis raised his eyebrows at her comment. "What do you think would happen if Brahms found out the *Kibalchich* had supplies left? What he does not know will not hurt him."

Ramis ducked into one of the open rooms and retrieved his helmet, looking relieved. Before departing, he bundled the rest of his gear together and hauled it out to the open. As he stepped away from the door again, it slid shut and vanished into a flat wall.

"Now, let's see that food," Karen said. She felt her stomach roiling with anticipation, eager to gobble food that was not rationed or guarded by Brahms's watchers. She wished the preradiation treatment hadn't left her so queasy.

Karen soon discovered that commissaries remained the same no matter who ran the station. Drab and clunky, the eatery provided the Soviet equivalent of the high-protein diet she had grown used to. She chewed black bread so stale it reminded her of crackers.

Karen had purposely avoided the nicer company dining

facilities on *Orbitech 1*; she liked to eat undisturbed in the commissary there. Now, with strict rationing and specified eating times, that luxury had slipped away.

Here on the *Kibalchich*, though, Karen wondered if she might have more solitude than she could stand.

The middle deck looked similar to the other two, but lacked the clusters of small rooms. Instead, large chambers filled the space: meeting halls, a gymnasium, and even a swimming pool. Karen later discovered three more pools, located at ninety degrees to each other. She supposed they doubled as water storage and ensured an even distribution of mass around the torus. Though the *Kibalchich* held only about 15 percent as many inhabitants as the American industrial colony, it seemed to have more total water in storage. Karen wondered why the Soviets were so paranoid about supplies. Whatever the reason, they had proved better prepared for this disaster.

As they walked the corridor, Karen detected another smell in the metallic staleness in the air. An impulse made her want to open a window somewhere and get the air to circulate.

"This is where I found the Russians," Ramis said.

Karen drew in a breath, knowing what to expect—she had looked at the visuals he had transmitted to *Orbitech 1*. She imagined lines and lines of frozen bodies, like stacked cordwood.

Might as well face it before that stink gets any worse, Karen thought. She remembered a story she had heard about an old Coast Guard vessel coming upon an abandoned ship. The Coast Guard first mate entered the freighter's hold and never returned. He had been overcome by noxious fumes from decaying bodies. The tiny ship had carried Central Americans seeking asylum, stuffed together like sardines. The smuggler had abandoned his cargo, leaving the refugees to bake to death in the merciless tropical sun.

Karen spoke loudly for fear she might lose her will to enter the chamber. "Show me where the lights are." Ramis found a panel on the wall and increased the illumination in the large, dark room ahead.

Row after row of machines filled the place—crystal cof-

fins like boxes in a warehouse. The nearest coffin had one
end open, the control panel moved away to allow the re-
awakened man to emerge. But this man would never
emerge—not under his own strength. Ramis had done
something wrong in the process, and the test subject had
lain here, dead and unthawed, for four days now.

Karen walked alone to the open chamber, ignoring the
smell. Ramis hung back, reluctant. She didn't blame him.

Karen stared down into the dead man's slack face. His
eyes were closed and peaceful. She suspected Ramis had
closed them himself. *This man didn't have a clue he was
dying,* she thought. Just closed his eyes and expected to be
awakened when the time was right.

Karen turned her head and moved to the adjacent working units. A steady green glow from three monitor lights
on the control panel showed everything apparently normal. No pulsations or vibrations came from the machine,
only a faint tracing of frost inside the glass, dusting the
view of the compact middle-aged woman frozen inside. In
Cyrillic characters, the LCD name panel spelled out TRI-
POLK, ANNA.

Tripolk—the computer had said something about an
Acting Commander Tripolk.

On the walls and engraved onto the control panels, reasonably clear instructions and warnings described how to
revive the sleepfreeze subjects—all in Russian, all in Cyrillic characters. Apparently posted as an afterthought, the
handwritten English list on the wall covered only the most
basic procedure, with no details and no contingencies.
Karen muttered to herself about the arrogance of assuming that any rescuer who might stumble upon the *Kibalchich* would be able to understand. The process appeared
complicated enough that Ramis's mistakes did not surprise
her at all.

But Karen thought she could do it. She might be able to
query the control computer to enlighten her on specific
details. The computer seemed accessible to outside queries, through "validation by Acting Commander Tripolk."

Behind her Ramis coughed, bringing her back to reality.
"I was hoping you would help me remove the body. His
name was Grekov." He swallowed. "And there's the other

body in the command center airlock. The smell is going to get worse, otherwise."

Karen stared at him, realizing he was right, but finding it difficult to work up enthusiasm for the task. "You've been all over the colony?"

"I found a cold-storage compartment on the lower deck, near the waste-recycling pool. I think it was supposed to be used for storing food and specimens. We should put the bodies there, but I cannot carry them by myself. Not that I would want to."

Karen pressed her lips together. The waste recycler would be on the lower deck, of course, so gravity could help waste diffuse through the filters. "We need to go back to the sleeping quarters first and get some sheets."

"Sheets?"

"We can knot them into a body bag."

Fifteen minutes later, Karen and Ramis worked together to haul Grekov's burly body out of the sleepfreeze chamber and lifted him onto a sheet spread out on the textured metal floor. They folded the sheet over and knotted the two ends.

"Let's move him out of here. One, two, lift!" The two of them moved in small stutter steps, carrying the stiff, sheet-wrapped corpse between them.

They slid the body down the stairs, opting not to use the direct chute to the waste-recycling unit from the commissary; she could just imagine the body getting stuck there. Karen thought it best that they store the two bodies and let the *Kibalchich* inhabitants decide what to do with them. Perhaps the Soviets would want to recycle the body, or maybe they would have some sort of ceremony and eject him out the airlock.

As Brahms had done in his RIF.

They found the large cold-storage chamber next to the slowly circulating pool of waste, which was mostly clear now after a month of inactivity on the station. Ramis stood watching the pool for a moment. Karen saw steel teeth just below the surface that would grind the waste into a more manageable form before it was leached and broken down by dissolvers.

The steel teeth in the recycler brought home the detailed planning for the colony back when it had been constructed. People were going to die up here, and unless they were ferried back to Earth, which was too expensive, or ejected into space, which was a waste of valuable minerals, they were going to have to face the reality of living in a closed system.

A gust of frosty air poured out of the cold-storage chamber when Ramis opened it. On the right-side wall stood a tall bank of tiny drawers apparently filled with various samples, like an old-fashioned library card catalog. Piled metal canisters and boxes cluttered the back wall. The other side of the chamber remained empty.

Karen and Ramis placed the dead Soviet on the floor, straightened the sheets, then stood to leave. Ramis mumbled some sort of prayer to himself, looking deeply guilty.

Then they sealed the man back into a frozen sleep from which he would never awaken.

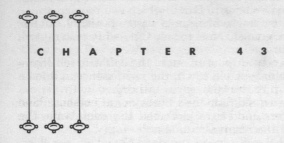

C H A P T E R 4 3

The white dream surrounded her like snow, an icy blizzard coming from inside.

Anna Tripolk saw herself standing alone in a howling void. The cold had gone beyond numbness into a tearing pain. She couldn't tell if she had opened her eyes.

Anna tried to call out, but the wind snatched her voice away and scattered the words, freezing them as they flew by. Stepan Rurik should have been there with her. He was always there when she needed him. Anna searched for him, but she saw nothing in the coldness.

Had they finally reached Mars? Was this the colony, their first winter there? How had she gotten lost outside? Where were the others?

Then she wondered, in the crazy rationale of dreams, whether she and Rurik had somehow been thrown back in time to the end of the Tsarist days. Perhaps someone did not approve of a relationship between the ranking researcher and the commander of the station. Anna Tripolk and Commander Stepan Rurik had been exiled to old Siberia, left without shelter in the snow.

Anna realized she had begun to shiver violently, but her body seemed a great distance away. The whiteness muted, faded, and focused into low lights reflected off glass walls.

Her teeth chattered with such force that it felt like a seizure. Her fingers clenched and unclenched, and she could not stop them. Her eyes were dry.

Hearing returned, but the sounds made no sense. She fought with her mind to focus things, to remember as the sounds sorted themselves out. Words.

". . . Hello . . ."

She tried to concentrate, comprehend.

"Welcome back. Can you hear me?"

The words were clearly Russian, but with an odd accent —a woman's voice. Anna blinked her eyes, afraid that she might crack a thin film of tears frozen into ice.

"I hope this one doesn't die, too." This was a different voice, male. Anna needed a moment to realize that these words had been spoken in English.

Then the wall between herself and her memories popped like a balloon. The sleepfreeze, the War, the long wait in suspended animation. The Soviets had come to rescue them. Earth had gotten itself back to its feet.

She wondered how many years had passed. Everything would be fine now. They were all saved.

A woman's face came into view—thin, with green eyes that were bright, intelligent. A pale cobweb of wrinkles flared out from the side of each eye. A few dark freckles dotted her cheeks and arms; she had red hair. She wore no uniform that Anna Tripolk recognized.

Then a young man pushed his face overhead. Dark hair and dark skin made him appear Asiatic. Mongolian? He could not be older than twenty.

He had spoken in English.

Something had changed drastically since the War. Anna's body continued to shiver. It became very important for her to know how long she had been under sleepfreeze. She tried to speak, but her vocal cords wouldn't work. Where was Rurik? Her tongue lay sluggish and still asleep inside her mouth. With exhaled breath, she managed to form words.

"When . . . how long . . . ?"

The woman and the young man seemed delighted at her question. They clasped each other and then moved their hands inside Anna's glass sleepfreeze chamber. She felt pressure as they removed the needles from her arms, peeled off the electrodes. She noticed no pain; her nerves had not fully awakened either. Pushing the young man away, the woman removed a catheter from her urinary tract.

Working together, the two of them pulled Anna Tripolk from the chamber, as gently as they could. Anna tried to help them, but her muscles would not function. Her limbs flopped. She could barely keep her gaze focused. The room spun around.

The strange woman spoke to Anna as she and the young man held her up. "It's been forty-five days since the War, and about a month since we lost contact with you."

As they helped Anna to a vertical position, all the blood rushed to her feet. *Only a month?* she thought. *What could possibly happen in only a month?* Disappointment began to well up inside of her.

But vertigo from the outrush of blood brought down a blanket of unconsciousness instead.

They had taken her to quarters that were not her own, but they didn't know that. They didn't know many things.

Anna Tripolk sat propped on the bed, covered with a crinkly insulated blanket, still shivering. A full day had passed since her awakening. She sipped strong tea, avoiding the gazes of this Dr. Langelier and Ramis Barrera.

Anger seethed in her now, swelling and falling away when she found no suitable way to express it. Her voice remained hoarse, but that only suited her roiling emotions. Anna glared from one to the other as she spoke, using English so the young man from the *Aguinaldo* would understand everything.

"So, you have no solutions? Nothing has changed. These Lagrange colonies are still practically as desperate as they were before, yet you saw nothing wrong with trying to awaken us, merely to see if you could! Why did you not heed the warnings we broadcast? The signs we stationed in

the command center?" Anna raised her voice. "Where is
Commander Rurik?"

Karen and Ramis exchanged puzzled looks. Karen
frowned and said, "There was only one warning broadcast,
then silence. We found no signs posted."

"You did not know what you were doing, yet you decided to tinker with our lives! How many people have died
because of your ignorance?"

"Only one," Ramis said. "The English instructions on
the wall were not complete. The process should have been
more intuitive. You could not know who would come to
rescue you."

Anna saw that his scorn was only misdirected anger at
himself. "Only one? Is that an acceptable number?"

Karen Langelier interrupted. "It was from a fault in the
apparatus, I think. You can check the system out. You know
it better than we do."

Anna scowled at them. "Thank you for that concession.
Why did Commander Rurik not stop you, or at least assist
you? He knew the process well enough."

Karen and Ramis looked at each other. Karen spoke in
Russian. "Who is this Commander Rurik?"

Anna frowned. "If it has been only a month. . . . He and
another officer, Cagarin, remained to watch over us, to
keep the colony intact. They did not go under sleepfreeze
with the rest of us. They had enough supplies to last them
for years."

Ramis looked puzzled, then swallowed. "We found—I
found—another body, in the command center. It was a
man. He was large and had brown hair. He was wearing a
dark uniform with many medals and insignia. He had been
dead several weeks when I arrived."

The blow was too much for Anna. She closed her eyes,
but did not lie back on the bed. Karen took the cup from
her hand.

Rurik dead? But how? He had said he would stay, for all
of them. Some kind of accident?

Anna recalled his quiet strength, how the others had
looked up to him and listened when he spoke, how he had
drifted along the edges of the Soviet bureaucracy and
somehow retained a clear perception of what he wanted
and how to dance around the ineffective political machin-

ery. He could ignore orders from his superiors and all the while convince them that he had done exactly what they'd meant to ask him.

She remembered holding Rurik, feeling warm next to his skin. Warmth seemed like such a foreign feeling to her now.

"Leave me alone," she whispered. She kept her eyes closed as she heard them leave her quarters.

Rurik was dead.

Let us not debate who is making the bravest choice, he had told her in their last few moments together. *I do what I must, and you do what you must.* She looked at the empty walls around her, but saw nothing to tell her whose quarters she was in.

Without me, you would be considered the acting commander of this station.

She gave a quiet moan.

Anna Tripolk stood in the infirmary, looking at the rows of glass cases, like baubles in a china shop. The hundreds of other *Kibalchich* inhabitants still slept unaware, peaceful . . . as she had been, just a day before.

Ramis Barrera and Karen Langelier left her alone, perhaps ashamed of themselves, or perhaps just afraid of her. This suited Anna fine. Every time she saw the two of them, she resented what they had done. She thought of Grekov's wasted life and the arrogant ignorance that had led these outsiders to believe that Soviet technology and scientific prowess was so trivial they could decipher its nuances by pushing random buttons and keeping their fingers crossed.

Anna inspected both of the newly empty cubicles— Grekov's and her own. The first cubicle had indeed malfunctioned. The awakening steps had occurred out of sequence, and the Barrera boy hadn't known how to react to the warning signals.

Grekov's body remained down in the lower deck, in the cold-storage locker by the recycler pool—frozen again, but this time, only as so much meat. Rurik's body lay there, too.

She needed to know why the commander had died. She felt a knot in her throat. She would have to do an autopsy on him.

She remembered Rurik's bravery, his charisma, his presence. He was like a legend to them all, so different from the manipulative, bureaucrat director on *Orbitech 1*. Karen Langelier and Ramis Barrera had led her to the command center. There, Director Brahms had spoken to her.

Anna had listened, repulsed by this slimy little man who rubbed his hands together, prattling his empty welcomings and congratulations and babbling shallow words through his image on the tall central holotank. But Anna drew herself up.

"Mr. Brahms, I want to assure you that under no circumstances will I allow you to revive any more of the people on this station. You have nothing to offer us. You are ruining our sacrifice. We were to go into sleepfreeze until conditions had returned to normal. You should not have directed your lackeys to waken me. Now that my commander has died, I am in charge of this station."

Brahms appeared taken aback, but then he smiled at her. "The rules have changed, Ms. Tripolk. Lines of authority and nationality no longer mean the same thing. Your sleepfreeze process could save the lives of many people on *Orbitech 1* if our food continues to run in short supply. I will not allow your petty indignation to ruin our future." He paused. "Think of it as evolution in action."

He folded his hands, appearing to thrust them through the walls of the holotank.

"But this is too heavy a subject to be discussing right now. I'm sure you're still recovering from your ordeal. We will speak again later. We are proud to have you back among the living." He smiled, then signed off before she could say anything.

In fury, she launched herself across the zero-G command center to one of the lift platforms on the opposite side. Ramis and Karen tried to be placating, but Anna had closed her ears. She rode the lift-shaft down alone.

Now she stood among the sleepfreeze cubicles with a liquid-crystal input pad in one hand, inspecting each of the chambers, verifying that everything remained stable. In her research, this was the long-term, large-scale test they had not been able to conduct ahead of time.

Before the War, Anna had located a volunteer among the station inhabitants to test the sleepfreeze chambers, when their work had proceeded rapidly and the Mars program had been a gleaming dream on the horizon. The volunteer was to be given a medal of honor, extra pay, extra leave, special privileges for himself and his family.

But after the War had cut the *Kibalchich* off, they all had to go under sleepfreeze, with survival being the biggest benefit of all.

She ticked off the cubicles on her input pad, taking inventory, checking—until she came upon one in the fourth row that sat dead. The monitoring lights remained gray and dim. The maintenance systems had been disconnected from the main power supply.

Anna bent down and found two of the wires intentionally severed with a neat cut. She stared in shock. Inside the sealed chamber, the waxen-faced man appeared different. He looked dead. His skin showed the wrong color, sagged in the wrong places. Because of the airtight chamber she could smell no decay, but this man was dead.

The severed wires could not possibly be an accident. Someone had sabotaged the sleepfreeze chamber.

Anna stood, narrowing her eyes. Outrage and confusion smoldered behind them. She made a fast check, walking briskly up and down the aisles. She wore a stiff white uniform that rustled against her legs—it felt more proper than the gray pajamas she had worn in the sleepfreeze cubicle.

She moved quickly through the large room and below decks, where the first wave of frozen colonists had been put under. She found eleven dead cubicles—each sabotaged, intentionally shut down, the wires cut.

She ran through a roster of inhabitants. Everyone except Rurik and Cagarin was accounted for. And Rurik was dead.

Cagarin.

He was missing.

Then she remembered Rurik warning her about State Security, the open secret that some of the people on the station were actually KGB. Why had Rurik picked Cagarin, of all people, to remain awake with him? Had Cagarin killed Rurik? Then why was he missing? It did not make sense.

She stared around at the walls. Everything seemed oppressive and silent. Anna felt alone and uneasy, but she would not show it, for Rurik's sake.

The *Kibalchich* hung empty, except for herself and the two outsiders. She hesitated to think of them as her enemies, but as she looked at the senseless death, the intentional executions in the sleepfreeze chambers, she began to change her mind.

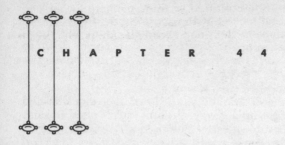

C H A P T E R   4 4

The specter of Tim Drury stood glaring down at Brahms as he cowered beneath the blankets on his bunk. Instead of rattling chains, Drury bore the shackles of his own obesity, towering over the acting director as if to smother him.

"You didn't have to kill me," Drury said. "You didn't have to kill any of us." His voice felt like the cold of space.

Brahms woke in a sweat, shivering, though he knew the temperature in his quarters remained a constant 70 degrees. He blinked and forced his eyes to adjust to the dimness, half expecting to see a bulky phantom with blazing eyes in the corner.

Brahms had had the nightmare several times before, and he forced his rational mind to combat the knee-jerk primitive fear. He felt angry at his psychological weakness —he was haunted by a guilty conscience! He recognized that, and he could live with it. He had chosen his actions; he had to face the consequences. No excuses.

He had acted swiftly, decisively. He had chosen the RIF before it was too late to do any good.

But now, other factors—unexpected factors—had changed their situation. The wall-kelp from the *Aguinaldo*, the lifeline to the *Kibalchich*, the "yo-yo" down to Clavius Base, and now the Soviet sleepfreeze technology—all provided less drastic means to help them survive.

Brahms had made the wrong choice.

He stood up and climbed off the bunk. The clock flashed 3:17 A.M. He got up anyway. Brahms didn't need to raise the illumination to sidestep the molded furniture, to find his closet and remove a soft, single-weave robe. Made on *Orbitech 1*, of course.

He kept kicking himself, damning himself. He had acted too soon. Brahms realized how the people on *Orbitech 1* were growing more and more dissatisfied with the memory of the RIF, even though Ombalal had ostensibly been responsible.

Brahms had been wrong. All those people out the airlock, ultimately for no benefit.

Their efficiency ranking had been too low. And now Brahms had proven *himself* inefficient. At the moment of greatest crisis, he had made the wrong decision—a disastrous decision—and forced it upon the others. While still cowed by shock after the murder of Ombalal, the colonists had caused no serious trouble. Now, though, they were beginning to think of other paths Ombalal—Brahms!— should have taken, options to be tried first.

In his daily broadcast to the colony at large, Brahms continued to emphasize the gravity of their situation— how the wall-kelp was helping, but they could not depend on it too much; how their plight still remained grim. But Brahms knew he was just blowing smoke to keep them distracted. The words sounded hollow. He could only maintain a facade of fear in the face of success for so long.

"To continue our policy to pursue every means of improving our chances for survival, I have directed a team of seven experts in biology, electronics engineering, and cryogenics to go to the *Kibalchich*. Apparently, nearly a dozen of the Soviet sleepfreeze chambers are empty. They will dismantle the chambers and ferry them back here to

Orbitech 1, so our people can learn how the Russians have done it.

"We hope to receive every cooperation from Dr. Anna Tripolk, the Soviet researcher who helped develop the process."

Brahms worked the stereotank controls himself, freezing the image for a moment while he glanced down at the script he had prepared. The people watching would see only a second of motionless silence on his face; few would suspect any interruption at all.

"These times are too desperate for petty national boundaries. We need the sleepfreeze process. It appears that we can now see a light at the end of our tunnel. But we cannot allow ourselves to grow complacent. Thank you for all your efforts on our behalf."

In the daily routine, Brahms also tried to make amends, or at least concessions. He listened to Allen Terachyk's complaints about the ranking system, about the mistakes the Efficiency Study might make. Brahms had scanned back over the case of Sigat Harhoosma, the man Terachyk had pointed out. Brahms considered that maybe the man did need a little more slack, some more opportunities to prove his worth.

So Brahms had chosen him to assist Karen Langelier in her Jump, though many of the other engineers had heftier credentials. He wanted to give Harhoosma a chance to earn more points, to improve his position. He was making every attempt to be fair.

Even in the most brutal decisions, Brahms insisted on being fair and just. It was the only anchor he had.

But at night, Tim Drury continued to haunt him in his nightmares. Brahms could not fool his own conscience with rhetoric.

Tim Drury had been an adequate manager. His crime had been an underactive metabolism. Brahms had watched him eat—he took no more than his own share. He also exercised. But his genes had determined that he would be obese, and he had died for that.

It was only now that he realized that, of all the division leaders, Tim Drury had perhaps been the most worthy to remain alive. Something had not shown up properly on the scores from the Efficiency Study—some factor had not been accounted for. How does one measure ultimate loyalty?

Drury was dead. Arnando had turned traitor and was now dead. McLaris had turned traitor and was still alive, now trying to worm his way back. Only Allen Terachyk remained with Brahms.

Terachyk did his best, but he did not seem to support his director as enthusiastically as he should. At times, Brahms caught him looking sidelong, a veil of accusation lifting from his eyes before Brahms could challenge him.

Tim Drury had only wanted to play checkers with everybody.

"I'm sorry, my friend," Brahms whispered. He slipped on his robe, listening to the soft rustle in his dim quarters.

He opened the door, startling the two armed watcher bodyguards outside. They looked at him, raising their eyebrows in question. Both seemed tense, afraid, and uncomfortable.

"Something wrong, Mr. Brahms?" the woman, Winkowski, asked.

"I need to go for a walk. Follow me."

But he merely went halfway down the corridor until he reached Tim Drury's old quarters. He unsealed the door using the pass code he knew.

The Filipino boy, Ramis, had lived in these rooms for the few days he had stayed on *Orbitech 1*, but he had been merely a guest there. The presence of Tim Drury still hung in the quarters.

The two watchers remained discreetly outside as Brahms walked into the darkened cabin, activated one reading-light panel, and stood in the glow. He looked around the dimness and found the metal-topped courtesy table. Tim Drury had painted a red-and-black checkerboard on its surface, making the lines himself.

Brahms leaned over and ran a hand across the pattern. It showed faint, jittery imprecisions, but that gave it charm. He turned around slowly and felt under the table surface for the small storage compartment. He opened it and removed the packet of red and black magnetic checker disks.

The guards outside watched, but Brahms got up and closed the door on them. This was none of their business.

Brahms spread out the pieces on the board, red and black, and looked down at them. He glanced up again, uneasy, as if he sensed Tim Drury's presence there, neither approving nor disapproving.

Brahms stared down at the pieces, then moved one red disk diagonally. He waited, squeezed his eyes shut, and got up. He went to the other side of the table and moved a black piece.

"I'll play for you, my friend," he said to the empty room.

Brahms proceeded to play checkers with himself deep into the night, making kings and sacrificing them. He lost track of how many games he won. And lost.

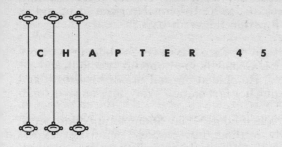

CHAPTER 45

CLAVIUS BASE ■ DAY 50

Gray cliff walls jutted up against the black sky, miles from where Clancy stood. Behind him, Rutherford Crater closed together, offering a sight not unlike the view from Clavius, but an order of magnitude smaller. Razor-sharp black shadows and intense splashes of sunlight made the landscape look like a high-contrast photograph.

With his chin, Clancy kicked up the coordinates on his helmet. Soft red numbers glowed on his visor: minus 61 degrees latitude, minus 8 degrees longitude. Right on the spot. He felt as if he were standing in the middle of a giant bull's-eye with somebody else playing at target practice.

He remembered his revelation as an undergraduate, when he had first discovered that Newton's laws of physics required corrections when applied to orbits—either because of a planet's oblate nature, or from its rotational wobbling, or from inhomogeneities in the planetary density. In fact, it seemed a miracle that Newton's laws worked at all.

The thought haunted him now. The test projectile from *Orbitech 1* was due to hit the lunar surface soon, and its orbit was well within the error bars.

Error bars.

The universe in practice was never so obliging as theory wanted it to be. Clancy flipped open his radio link.

"Hey, Shen." He chided himself under his breath and tried again, using her first name. "Wiay, let's move up onto the wall."

"We've got a half hour." Wiay Shen clumped into view, leaving slowly settling dust clouds behind her as she walked. Her footprints would remain there for centuries. "And we're ten miles from the impact point, so we're plenty safe."

"We're nine point seven miles away, if our radar fix is correct. And the impact point is only an approximation, anyway. Let's go."

"What's the hurry, Cliff?"

Silence. Then Clancy spoke in a measured voice. "I said, let's move it."

"Okay, you're the boss."

Clancy swung himself around in the big suit and made his way up the rocky incline, putting one foot in front of the other and trying not to fall asleep just because moving took so long. He frowned at himself for being so impatient.

They left the six-pack below them at the base of the crater wall. Shen helped him negotiate the jumbled terrain, pointing out cuts in the rock that he missed. They circumvented boulders that looked larger than *Orbitech 2* would ever be. For a moment Clancy longed to be back up in space, at the L-4 construction site, watching his crew welding girders, sealing habitats, putting together the largest closed environment ever made by man. If the "yo-yo" really worked as Clancy imagined it would, they might be able to go back there—someday.

They reached an outcrop of lava rock jutting hundreds of yards straight up. Turning, Clancy looked down onto the crater bed, now two hundred yards below them. Pieces of ancient ejecta lay where they had fallen after the impact millions of years before. Clancy knocked loose a small rock and watched it roll down the slope in slow motion and silence. Now he had left his mark here as well. Little actions had such permanent consequences.

They paused to catch their breath, when Shen spoke. "Are you all right, Cliff?"

"Fine."

"You galloped like a mountain goat coming up here."

He answered her with silence for a few seconds. "I didn't think I was moving that fast. Just in a hurry, that's all."

Over the radio he heard her breath stop as she prepared to say something. "Clifford Clancy, are you worried about the weavewire harness hitting us?"

Clancy nodded to himself, which of course she couldn't see behind the polarized golden visor. "It's *Orbitech 1* I'm worried about. We're so close to Clavius Base—what if some celestial mechanic desperate to earn 'efficiency points' miscalculates the orbit, trying to plant the harness too close, and misses? Imagine a kilometer per second projectile hitting us."

"The *Aguinaldo* didn't have any problem. The wall-kelp package they sent us was right on the money."

"They hit Longomontanus. They couldn't have missed that with their eyes closed. This is different. No one can be this accurate—not with a ballistic trajectory."

"So, what's the chance of the weavewire package hitting us standing here? Pretty darned small, I'll bet. My grandma once told me about how paranoid people on Earth were when Skylab burned up in the atmosphere. And we laughed at how ridiculous they all were. We have a better chance of killing ourselves by falling up here."

"Well, Skylab wasn't aimed right at us," Clancy muttered, but said nothing more. Shen had a point—the terrain was rugged where they were standing, and the canister shot from *Orbitech 1* couldn't be too far off. But standing still and waiting in the middle of the crater for the canister to hit would be a lot tougher on the nerves than trying to find it after it landed. He cleared his throat. "We'll have a better view up here, that's all. We can see where the package hits."

"Oh, give me a break, Cliffy. I won't tell anyone you're chicken. Now I'll have something to hang over you. You're going to have to ask me out or I'll tattle."

Thanks a lot, he thought, not sure if she was joking. He decided to ignore it. "We're already here, so let's stay put. As soon as the canister lands we'll get back down."

"Fair enough." Shen twisted a backpack off her shoulders, looking graceful in her bulky suit. He realized it was just his imagination filling in details. Rummaging through the pack, Shen withdrew a tripod and set it up, extending the telescopic legs to their full length.

Clancy followed her lead, but he had trouble slipping his own backpack off over his air bottles. When he finally broke out the charge-coupled diode, Shen was ready to mount the detector.

"Ready with the CCD?"

Clancy grunted. "As soon as it's calibrated." He ran the CCD through a self-test. With its enclosed iris slowly shutting out the light, the solid-state device verified sensing a light change down to a single photon.

Satisfied, Clancy pushed to his feet and handed the CCD to Shen. Since the Moon had no atmosphere, the harness streaking to impact would make no trail across the black backdrop of stars. But the CCD could find it.

They worked in silence setting up the detector, finishing with plenty of time to spare, according to the digital clock on Clancy's heads-up display. Once Clancy ensured that the CCD's view angle covered the entire crater floor, he positioned himself out of the detector's field of view. Shen joined him, lounging back against the outcropping. They waited for the smooth ocean of rock and dust on the crater floor to be marred by another impact.

After some minutes Shen broke the silence. "You really think it'll work—the yo-yo, I mean?"

Clancy chewed on the question as he continued to scan the crater floor. "If everything cooperates."

"You mean, like *Orbitech 1*?"

"How about celestial mechanics itself? We've got a lot of 'ifs' that have to be satisfied—*if* our part of the harness gets here; *if* we can finish the yo-yo; *if* the weavewire is really strong enough; *if Orbitech 1* can land the wire and reel it back in. . . ."

Shen's comment filled the inside of his helmet. "All we have to do is attach the weavewire to the harness and let

Orbitech 1 pull the yo-yo up. I thought this had all been worked out by the Clavius and Orbitech eggheads."

Clancy smiled to himself. Shen believed her practical experience as an engineer placed her far apart from the wild-eyed celestial mechanics.

"Well, *Orbitech 1* can reel out a few hundred thousand miles of weavewire in a precise orbit, exact enough to land on the Moon—but even if the wire has a locator beacon on it, can you imagine how tough it's going to be to find that sucker falling out of the sky? And remember, we won't have much time to connect it, either—probably only an hour or so. Dr. Rockland and I were arguing this morning about what the speed of sound in the weavewire is."

She turned toward him. "What does that have to do with anything?"

"That's how fast one end of the wire knows what the other end is doing, which tells us how early *Orbitech 1* has to start reeling it in. Rockland thinks sound would propagate mechanically through the fiber, which means they would have to start reeling it back almost a day before the end even gets here. But I think because of the binding potential and the chemical bonds in the weavewire, a signal will travel almost at c—probably a third the speed of light.

"You certainly know how to throw a wet towel on a hot idea, Cliffy." Shen sounded disappointed.

"I'm just playing devil's advocate—"

"Incoming! Look!" Shen's shout rang through his helmet. Clancy spotted the light flashing on the CCD unit. Across the crater floor a thin line plowed across the lunar dirt. It looked like a giant mole racing just under the surface, creating a tunnel miles long.

Shen read from the CCD, picking off impact coordinates from the matrix of light-sensitive diodes. "Impact point: nine point six nine two three miles; preliminary velocity parameters indicate it was moving at one point oh oh four klicks. That's pretty darned close for government work, huh, Cliffy?"

Clancy was floored. The impact was well within even theoretical error, much less experimental bounds. "Got the final location?" He gathered up his backpack to tear down the sensor.

"Roger dodger over and out." He heard a click as Shen switched to the open channels. She turned to find the relay transmitter on top of the crater and spoke. "Clavius Base, we've got our Christmas present. Going to pick up the package and we'll come on home."

Clavius Base acknowledged them, and Shen started talking to Clancy again. "I think *Orbitech 1* has nailed down the delivery system, wouldn't you say?"

"Let's get this stuff packed and go after the harness."

"Right." Shen bumped up against his buttocks. He felt the pressure through all the thick padding. It didn't go away.

Clancy turned and noticed that she was patting him with her hand. He flinched and decided to ignore the exchange, not sure how else to react. Thank God she had at least picked one of the most private spots in the solar system.

Once the CCD and tripod were packed, Clancy led the way down the crater wall. Dust floated behind him, kicked up by his feet as he scrambled down the rocky incline. The dust drifted reluctantly back to the surface. The other jumbled debris looked frozen, delicately balanced.

His thoughts turned to Shen. If things were different—if he weren't in charge of the whole blasted construction crew—he might work up enough courage to see whether her blatant flirtation meant something, or she was just being brash—Was she getting even for all the good-natured but rough comments most women construction engineers endured on the male-dominated crew.

He felt a surge of emotion from deep inside, a need to explain to her, to hold her and experience all the things he had been holding back for the past year . . . but he knew it could never happen. His position as construction boss demanded unwavering obedience, and if she were to take advantage of his authority. . . . Best to leave things be and not make a move, much as he wanted to.

He stepped over a section covered with loose gravel and turned to check on Shen. He felt his feet start to slide as the ejecta debris, undisturbed for centuries, broke loose and flowed under him. He waved his arms, trying to keep his balance on the steep wall.

Clancy managed to twist his body and cover his helmet

with his padded arms as he fell. He bounced against rocks
on his way down. Screams came over his suit radio. Clancy
slammed into a boulder and heard a *crack!*

Shen's shouts in the ear speakers seemed drowned in
static as he lost consciousness.

Wiay Shen watched in horror as Clancy tumbled down the
rocky slope. His space suit slammed off boulders, leaving
tiny gravel slides where he struck. Clancy rolled end over
end as if falling underwater; he kept his arms wrapped
around his helmet.

It took Shen a full three seconds to react. When she
realized the screaming came from her own mouth, she
silenced herself and started scrambling down the incline
after Clancy. The sluggish suit and the low gravity made
her effort exaggerated and slow.

Clancy came to rest by the base of the crater wall two
hundred yards below, the top half of his suit hidden by a
boulder. He lay a hundred yards from the six-pack.

Shen bounced down the steep grade, taking long, careful jumps. She couldn't see Clancy moving. "Cliff, can you
hear me? Clifford!"

She reached the boulder, knelt by Clancy's body, and
ran a gloved hand over his space suit. It was still pressurized—at least he hadn't popped a leak. She felt a rush of
relief at the discovery. The only sound she could hear was
her breathing.

"Cliff, say something, you klutz!" The joking tone
seemed limp.

She shook her hands out and wriggled them underneath
Clancy's body. If his neck was broken, she shouldn't try to
move him . . . but if he was dying, it wouldn't matter
anyway. With a grunt, she rolled his body over. *How could
anybody be hurt through all that padding?* she wondered. Through his helmet, she could see that his head
hung to one side. She scanned the vitals on his chest-moni-
tor unit:

BLOOD PRESSURE: 163/80
TEMPERATURE: 99.6
RESPIRATION RATE: 93

Shen couldn't tell if he had been injured. She made a quick decision to give him a sedative. She punched the emergency code into his chest unit, fumbling to hit the right buttons with her thick-gloved fingers. She swore at the red light that started blinking. She tried a second time, making sure to enter the medical override code correctly. This time the light burned a steady green.

Clancy's suit began to pulsate as the lower part constricted, then expanded around his legs. Based on the old-fashioned "G-suit," the movement prevented blood from pooling at the lower part of his body due to inactivity. A tiny needle on the inside of his suit pricked Clancy's neck, injecting a sedative. It also withdrew a small amount of blood, so the automated diagnostics could make a white-cell count and a blood-sugar test.

Shen watched the diagnostics flash on the chest unit.

Minutes passed as she radioed to Clavius Base, explaining her emergency. Clancy's respiration rate lowered. Satisfied that he wasn't going to die on her, Shen straightened and looked around.

A milk run, she thought. *It's a twenty-minute drive to the crater—something we could do ourselves.* She had talked Clancy into doing it, looking for another excuse to get him alone. It should have been a piece of cake—watch the weavewire harness impact, scoop it up, and get back to Clavius Base within an hour.

Her eyes lit on the six-pack a hundred yards away.

She'd better start moving. She took the distance at a lope. Once the electric motor started, she backed the six-pack to within a few yards of Clancy.

Clancy moaned into his suit radio. At least it was some sound. The ones hurt really bad didn't make any noise. Shen bent over him and pressed her helmet against his. She could not make out his garbled words.

She bent to pick him up and looked for a place to hold on. Clancy was a full foot taller and outweighed her by eighty pounds. Once the space suit was thrown in, she was dealing with a hundred fifty pound differential in normal gravity. Even though he only weighed about fifty pounds on the Moon, inertia still made a difference.

Shen got her hands under his armpits and pulled him off the ground. It seemed as if she were tugging him through thick jelly. "I thought you were slim and trim, Cliffy!" She coughed with the effort and staggered to her feet, trying to balance Clancy's bulk without jarring him too much.

Carrying him in her arms, she felt like an absurd parody of an old Frankenstein movie—a petite female monster hauling a big lunk of a victim. She felt her suit straining to combat her exertion and keep her internal environment regulated.

Clancy's suit continued its constricting motions. The sedatives seemed to have taken effect—his blood pressure was down, as well as his respiration rate. At least he was stabilizing.

Shen gingerly placed Clancy on the six-pack's flatbed and secured him there with a cable. She didn't plan to follow the speed-limit signs on the way back to the base, and she certainly didn't want her cargo to fall overboard.

She scrambled to the operator's console, keeping an eye on Clancy as she started the engine. She moved the six-pack forward and started for the steep pass through the crater wall.

Only fifteen minutes had passed since the canister from *Orbitech 1* had landed. Shen had a fix on its location, but that was far in the back of her mind as she pushed the vehicle to its limits toward Clavius Base.

Duncan McLaris absently tapped a dual-end pen on his desk. One end contained carbon ink for writing on paper surfaces; the other was a magnetic scribe for use on a flatscreen. Tomkins's once-cluttered office looked organized; it gleamed. McLaris had removed and stored the stacks of computer readouts and pictures of radio telescopes. The noise from the pen's tapping bounced through the room.

McLaris focused his mind on a single topic—a burning question to which he already knew the answer. And the answer made him feel sick inside.

In the excitement following Clancy's proposal of the yo-yo, and Brahms's agreement to try, no one else seemed worried about the most important question of all—who would risk their lives in the attempt? Who would have to go to *Orbitech 1*?

Part of the answer was obvious—Tomkins and many of

the others were so immersed in their work that they didn't want to be disturbed. But others, especially Clancy's engineers, ached for a chance to get off the "Rock." It would indeed be an experience of a lifetime.

But who really would get the most out of being sent? Clancy himself was the first obvious choice, since it was his invention—if he wanted to go. Someone else in his crew would go next. But yet . . . they couldn't send just engineers; they needed someone who would make the event meaningful, an emissary—someone who could make this joining of the colonies truly memorable. Someone to make speeches and give good holotank footage.

McLaris stopped tapping his dual-end pen and bent it between his fingers.

He knew who else should go—someone who had ties back on *Orbitech 1* . . . someone who had the vision to pull the separate colonies together and ensure the survival of the colonists.

Someone who needed to face up to the fact that he had stolen and destroyed the last regular means for the colonies to visit each other.

McLaris's pen broke in half. He looked at the two pieces, bewildered, thinking how foolish it would be to try and put them back together again.

Once the six-pack climbed through the pass, Rutherford Crater sloped down to the monotonous plain where Clavius Base lay. Shen pushed the vehicle to its full speed, driving without relying on its inertial navigation system to find her way back. She turned on the emergency beacon, and she knew Clavius would be standing by with help when she got in. But until she came within line of sight of a receiver, she couldn't depend on anybody else.

Clancy's suit diagnostics were tied in to the six-pack through a light fiber; Shen kept his vital signs flashed on the vehicle's heads-up display across the front screen. The numbers shimmered in a ghostly image from the holographic projection. Looking at Clancy's life signs, she didn't want to think about ghosts.

Two other six-packs appeared as dots across the plain, growing in size as they raced toward her. *What good are they supposed to do?* she wondered. *I'm already trucking as fast as I can.* She ignored their radio calls and drove on, not slowing down for fear of cutting Clancy's time.

The low mounds and transmitting towers of the base showed up on the flat pan of the crater floor. Wide tracks from the other six-packs looked like the marks of a giant doodlebug around the center of the settlement. Not until she pulled up to the main airlock at Clavius Base did she allow anyone to help her—and then only to carry Clancy into the clinic.

Shen didn't leave his side as they cycled through the big doors. Three medics hauled Clancy's bulk between them, pushing her aside.

As he was carried away, Clancy mumbled something unintelligible. *If those are his last words,* Shen thought, *he damn well better be saying how much he loves me.*

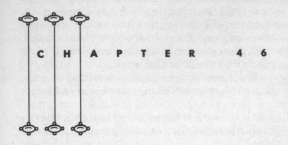

C H A P T E R   4 6

Harhoosma's lab space would not be private enough. Other people, other listeners, were dangerous things to have nearby.

Allen Terachyk recalled the lesson shown by Linda Arnando's mistake: privacy could no longer be assumed on *Orbitech 1* unless one took elaborate precautions beforehand. Terachyk wanted no eavesdroppers, no way for sharp ears to hear his words and report them back to Brahms.

He entered the vacuum welders' zero-G lab space without announcing himself. The smell of feed chemicals and raw materials hung in the air. Smoke floated near the burns; without gravity, it could not rise to the ventilator filters. Large fans on either side of the room kept the air stirred. On the wall, a cheery red sign reminded them that *Orbitech 1* considered "Safety First!"

Three men and one woman floated at the far wall of the chamber, pressed against a transparent shield with their hands thrust into gloves that extended to a vacuum chamber outside. In the cold and microgravity of space, they tested welding techniques, different filler metals or base alloys. The welders did not need to worry about heated metals absorbing oxygen or nitrogen in the vacuum, which would have made a weld brittle and weak.

Other workers practiced simple zero-G welding at several modules, spraying argon or helium shielding onto the metal, trying new flux compositions that would not separate in the weightless environment. Some of the operations hissed and sputtered with plasma arcs and molten metal; others used silent electrical-resistance welding, while the workers chatted in forced conversation.

Terachyk could call to mind most of the projects here, since he inspected them in his assessor duties. Much of the bustle and conversation involved repeating experiments, verifying results, gaining proficiency in techniques—and appearing busy for Terachyk's benefit. Other watchers reported to him daily with summaries of work performed by the nontechnical personnel on *Orbitech 1*, but Terachyk considered it his responsibility to be familiar with all the major research.

He had taken special interest in the vacuum welding shop since pointing out Harhoosma's situation to Brahms.

Terachyk looked around, placing his hands on his hips. His spring-green jumpsuit had not been washed in days, but the bright fabric looked fresh as new.

He watched the conversation and movements take on a different character, like a ripple moving through a pool, as they noticed his presence. They knew the chief assessor had come to see someone in particular.

"I need to speak with Sigat Harhoosma," he announced. At first he didn't see the man, dressed in his protective clothing against the glove-box wall.

Terachyk thought he heard a collective sigh of relief from the others, and then an intense curiosity . . . but no one would dare speak out loud until well after he had gone.

Harhoosma pulled his arms out of the dangling gloves and switched off the hydraulic-assist waldoes outside. He turned, straightened his uniform, and pushed off toward the door where Terachyk waited. Harhoosma was short and compact, with dark eyes and skin, thick salt-and-pepper hair. He held himself in closed body language. He avoided looking at anything except some imaginary fixed spot on the floor.

"Relax, don't worry," Terachyk said under his breath; he felt flushed. He was expected to do random inspections and interviews, but it made the co-workers nervous, wondering what Harhoosma might say about them in confidence. *What if somebody hears us?* Terachyk thought.

"Let's go into the conference room," he said, extending a hand. Harhoosma nodded and pulled himself along the corridor toward a room with a red-enameled door. Inside, a glossy-surfaced table occupied most of the space, with fixed chairs mounted to the floor, each with restraining bands so people didn't drift out into the room with every conversational gesture they made. LCD screens and contact noteboards were embedded into the table surface. A large holotank took up the opposite wall.

Terachyk sealed the door behind him, cutting off all outside noise. In the silence, he wondered if Brahms had rigged listening devices into any of the rooms.

Now who was getting paranoid?

Harhoosma moved over to one of the chairs, pulled himself down, and slipped the restraining loop over his thigh. He waited in silence. Terachyk sat beside him, close enough to make the other man uncomfortable.

Terachyk didn't know where to start. "This isn't what you think," he said. "Brahms does not know I'm here, and I must have your word that you will repeat none of this conversation to him."

The sharp stab of danger raced up Terachyk's spine. He knew he could be killed for this. Brahms would have no qualms about it. Terachyk was risking his life to talk to a man he barely knew.

Terachyk remembered Harhoosma's report, about his invalid wife who had come here to live in the lower gravity, who had been one of the victims in the first RIF. Terachyk had never seen the woman, though he had looked at her image in the files, wondering what she was like.

Harhoosma looked up at him, puzzled. "I do not know what you mean. Is this perhaps a trick of some kind?"

The thin, accented voice quavered. Terachyk decided to

continue, even without securing Harhoosma's promise. He had already committed himself to his course of action.

"Mr. Harhoosma, there is something I am going to tell you—no one else knows about this. Your name is on the list, a new RIF list. Brahms has decided to keep you in the bottom ten percent of people on this colony. You know what that means."

He met Harhoosma's glittering, dark eyes. The man seemed appalled, disbelieving.

"Brahms and I disagree about this. I pointed out your extenuating circumstances, the trauma you've undergone, the . . . loss of your wife." He paused. "Under the circumstances, I think you're performing remarkably well. My own family was killed in the War. But Brahms insists that we perform up to the same standards as before."

Several times, Harhoosma began to say something, but the words seemed unwilling to fall into place. Terachyk waited for him. Finally, the other man said, "But Director Brahms chose me to help Dr. Langelier on her Jump to the *Kibalchich*. He selected me out of every person on this place to assist her! Is this not true? I believed this was some kind of reward. Why would he do this thing?"

Terachyk shook his head. "Brahms has already made up his mind that you're expendable. You weren't really qualified to do that task, although I think you did an admirable job. Why would Brahms send you out like that, when he had plenty of more experienced people to choose from?"

Terachyk raised his eyebrows before giving his answer. "I think he was hoping you would slip up. Of course, he would never admit that. But I think he sent you out there, placed you in danger, because if something disastrous happened, then he would not lose anyone he considers valuable. Does that make sense to you?"

Harhoosma nodded slightly.

Terachyk lowered his voice, as if that would do any good. "I don't think he has any right to make these kind of choices. And I am tired of being an accomplice to his twisted decisions. Did you know that he was behind the first RIF? It was Brahms, not Ombalal. Ombalal taped a speech that Brahms himself had written."

Harhoosma's eyes went wide, but he sat speechless.

"The mob killed the wrong person." Terachyk drew a

deep breath and closed his eyes halfway. His throat grew
dry. "Now, please listen to me carefully. . . ."

As he listened, Harhoosma looked even more frightened
than Terachyk felt.

When the wife of Daniel Aiken opened the door of her
living quarters, she saw Allen Terachyk standing there.
Terachyk started to mumble some sort of greeting, but
Sheila Aiken met him with a hateful look of such intensity
that it made him cringe.

"What?" she asked with no further preamble. "Do you
want to throw me out the airlock, too? See if I've been
falsifying some of my own results? Maybe I'm not dusting
our quarters as often as I should?"

Terachyk breathed deeply. He had been prepared to
deal with something like this.

"I didn't execute your husband. Your husband wasn't the
first, and he's probably not going to be the last. I need to
talk to you." Gently, "Your name is Sheila?"

"I suppose Mrs. Aiken isn't really meaningful anymore."
She turned aside and said nothing, but left the door open,
implying that she had no choice but to let him come in.

When Terachyk sealed the door behind him, Sheila
Aiken looked uneasy. Terachyk stood, uncomfortable at
not being asked to sit.

"I know Curtis Brahms," he said. "I've been forced to
work with him ever since he came here. I do not like him.
And contrary to what everyone thinks, he is not my
friend."

That seemed to soften her a little, turning her anger to
suspicion. Terachyk still felt uneasy.

"I have told this to very few people: Brahms was behind
the first RIF that killed a hundred and fifty people. It was
all his idea, not Ombalal's." She sat down in surprise. "He
has rationalized in his own mind that he needed to do it.
Now, though, when things are getting better, when we
have all sorts of different ways to survive—new techniques, new hopes—Brahms isn't interested. It means he's
proved himself wrong.

"I think he's going to order another RIF. He believes he
has to, just so he doesn't look as if he made a mistake with
the first one. He can't afford to let us think things are

getting better. He's going to distort reality. He's going to
. . . sabotage things so that we remain in this horrible
situation.

"He killed your husband, and Linda Arnando—" he saw
her wince at the woman's name "—just to keep everyone
afraid. To make them cowed, to keep them shocked. It's
for his own protection."

Standing, Sheila Aiken twisted her hands together, staring at him, then sat down without breaking eye contact.

"So?" she said, but the words carried little defiance.

"Doesn't that mean anything to you?" Terachyk asked.

She sidestepped the question. "What do you want me to
do about it? Brahms killed my husband. He made a spectacle of him in front of all the other people on the colony. I
think that was the worst part—Daniel hated being humiliated more than anything else."

"It doesn't matter what I want you to do about it. What
do *you* want to do about it?" He held up his hand to keep
her from answering. "Just think about that."

He turned to leave. She remained sitting, looking at him
as if she were about to be sick. He had stirred up things she
had obviously been trying to hide.

Allen Terachyk left her quarters.

There had been a hundred and fifty names on the original RIF list. Many of those had left loved ones behind as
well.

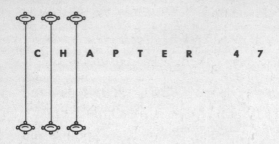

C H A P T E R   4 7

Fidgeting, Curtis Brahms leaned back in the control room of the *Orbitech 1* docking bay. He hadn't felt so eager or optimistic in a long time. The rotating light inside the docking bay changed from green to red as pumps bled the air from the chamber, cycling the bay doors. An image of the wasteful, explosive openings of those doors—from the RIF, from when Duncan McLaris had stolen the *Miranda* —flashed through his mind.

Beside him Allen Terachyk remained silent, sulking again. Brahms was getting disgusted with the way Terachyk moped all the time. This should be a good time. With the *Kibalchich*'s help, they had hope again.

"Almost here, Allen," Brahms said.

"I know." Terachyk's voice carried no emotion at all.

Brahms threw him a sideways glance. "Come on, snap out of it. This is going to be broadcast."

After another five minutes, the docking bay lights signaled that the chamber had been drained of atmosphere.

Brahms, trying to give Terachyk something to do, motioned toward the controls. "You want to run the show?"

Terachyk raised his eyes, then shook his head. "No, you do it." His voice dropped. "You have more practice than I do."

Brahms blinked, stung by the remark. He decided it would be better to ignore further comments than to encourage Terachyk's anger. What did he want? Brahms had bent over backward and was doing everything he possibly could for the good of *Orbitech 1*.

With stiff fingers, Brahms jabbed at the controls and watched through the bay window. The large doors puckered to break the seal and drew apart, showing stars.

"Okay, send the retrieval crew out," Brahms spoke into the intercom. Against the starry background he could make out the glinting light of the cargo ferry they had rigged up between *Orbitech 1* and the *Kibalchich*.

Brahms had ordered a crew to go out and move the weavewire pulley from the point where Karen Langelier had first attached it to the outer hull, mounting the terminus above the docking bay doors instead. The original line had been extended, allowing a pulley, protected with weavewire, to be installed. The pulley's testing phase had ended—Brahms had insisted they put it to use.

All six members of the team he had sent over to the *Kibalchich* to investigate the sleepfreeze chambers went together in a single large cage framework. Pushing the newly installed weavewire pulley to its limits, the investigation team had made it to the Soviet station in a little under three hours.

Now, on this end, the *Orbitech 1* workers waited for the incoming cargo cage. The pulley slowed the weavewire as the cage approached.

As Brahms watched, four space-suited figures emerged from one of the spoke-shaft airlocks and drifted into the open docking bay. They wore bulky MMU packs and moved together toward the gaping hole of space.

"Is the receiving team ready?" Brahms turned to Terachyk.

"Yes, Curtis."

Brahms felt annoyed at himself. He didn't usually let

impatience bother him like this. Terachyk knew what needed to be done, of course. So did the crew.

The investigation team had made its preliminary report to Brahms, raising his hopes. On the *Kibalchich*, Anna Tripolk had refused any cooperation in describing her sleepfreeze process. She had refused even to talk to Brahms, to let him reason with her. In disgust, he dismissed it as archaic Soviet paranoia.

He had no sympathy for that. The human need was obvious. This discovery was something that could benefit all the space colonies—and former nationalities be damned. Earth and its political boundaries were a thing of the past. He would not allow Tripolk's petty jealousies to ruin things for anybody on *Orbitech 1*.

So Tripolk had withdrawn and remained to herself on the *Kibalchich. Fine,* Brahms thought. The people on *Orbitech 1* were going to find a way to bring the human race back to its feet again. He couldn't imagine anybody wanting to sleep through that—it would be like hiding their heads in the sand. Tripolk could do all the sulking she wanted to do, as long as she didn't get in his way.

Brahms told his team to be courteous, but to disconnect three of the empty Soviet sleepfreeze chambers and ignore any protests from Anna Tripolk.

A voice came over the intercom in the upper control bay. "The ferry has slowed to a little less than ten miles an hour—Doppler shows it's five hundred yards away." The seconds seemed to draw out.

The voice started a countdown on the last fifty yards. "Three . . . two . . . one, and that's it! We've got it. Looks like smooth sailing now—the pulley has stopped and the cage is secure."

Brahms watched the space-suited figures grapple with the cage. He could see the bulky containers packed inside the cage, watched the figures handle it along the weavewire.

The recovery team opened up the cargo cage just outside the docking bay doors. Working together, they removed three coffin-sized packages and pushed them into the bay, looking like space-suited pallbearers. Techs used their MMU's to steer the containers to straps on the floor.

Brahms focused his entire world on those containers. He smiled, elated.

After the giant bay doors closed and the chamber once more filled with air, Brahms pulled on a sweater and pushed down into the echoing docking bay. The heaters had not had time to warm up the chamber—that would take a while after the chill of vacuum.

The recovery team began to unsuit, taking off their helmets and detaching MMU packs. Floating next to the chambers, they talked among themselves and watched Brahms; a few nodded to him, unsmiling. He greeted them back, acknowledging the good job they had done.

He drifted to the first of the two sleepfreeze chambers, staring at it. The investigation team on the *Kibalchich* had encased it in insulating vacuum foam on the chance that the delicate controls might be damaged by the harsh space environment.

Brahms touched the spongy, cold surface. Steam puffed out of his mouth into the chilly bay. Ignoring everything else, he clawed at the foam, tearing away hunks of insulation until he saw the glass cover of the Soviet sleepfreeze chamber. He pulled aside the foam until he cleared away a hand-sized area. His breath fogged the glass.

This was something his own people had not been able to create—a kind of technology sought for generations. But now it worked. His people could learn from it. *Orbitech 1* need have no doubt of its future from now on. He felt as if a weight had been lifted from his shoulders—*Orbitech 1* had a way out.

Above, in the control bay, Allen Terachyk looked down at them behind the glass. Brahms glanced up at him, then turned his attention back to the sleepfreeze chamber.

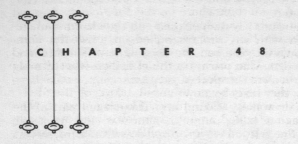

C H A P T E R   4 8

The room in the *Kibalchich* felt cold, sterile, and dead. Anna Tripolk had never needed to designate a specific place as a morgue before, but now she had thirteen dead bodies to deal with.

And one of them was Stepan . . . Commander Stepan Rurik.

With grudging help from the others, Anna had stacked the bodies in the freezer chamber. She had felt no need to perform autopsies on the twelve from the sleepfreeze cubicles—the physical details of their deaths raised no questions.

But she did wonder what she was expected to do with the corpses. Keep them? For what? They would never be shipped home again. Burial in space, perhaps? No, feeding them into the reprocessor made more sense, to save precious minerals and proteins sorely lacking on the colony now that the supply lines had been cut off.

Cagarin was not among the bodies. His disappearance

still mystified Anna. She wondered if perhaps he had died in a sealed room somewhere on the *Kibalchich*, daunted by the pressures put upon him—by whatever had destroyed Rurik. He could never keep up with the Commander's pace. She had checked Cagarin's cabin and found no sign. That proved nothing, since it was still a big station, but Anna suspected the Americans would have found another body by now.

The room was icy around her. Though not part of the cold storage unit, the outer chamber was kept just above freezing. She felt gooseflesh up and down her arms, shivers along her back; the sweater she wore did not ward off the chill. She should have brought a container of strong hot tea with her.

She hadn't been warm since she had awakened nearly two weeks before.

Alone in the lower decks, Anna sealed the doors to the frigid chamber, insisting on her privacy. There could be no telling when one of the Americans might come barging in, nosing around. Though it was none of their business, they seemed perfectly happy to grab whatever interested them. But Anna wanted to be left alone right now. She demanded it. She had every right.

This was much too personal a matter.

Stepan's body lay spread out on a portable metal table she had hauled down into the storage room. It had taken a day for the body to unthaw enough for her to straighten his limbs, to make sure that the body cavity and organs were soft enough to do a full autopsy.

Ramis Barrera and Dr. Langelier had thrown him into the freezer compartment—another disposable person aboard the Soviet station. Oh, they intended to be careful, they meant well—but they had ruined many things for her.

Anna gazed into Stepan Rurik's face, his Viking jaw pushed into a peaceful expression. They had closed Rurik's eyes, straightened his grimace. Part of her felt relief at that, but another part resented all the detail lost. The look on his face and the position of the body could have told her many things about how Rurik had died—whether it had been sudden or with prolonged agony. Perhaps even if it was a disease, or poison, or simply a cardiac arrest. But men like Rurik did not die of heart attacks.

Now, with his body frozen, stacked, and thawed again, tiny details could have been damaged. Anna would have a more difficult time learning why the commander had died.

Rurik. Stepan Rurik.

She stared down at him. Even in death his thin brown hair fell back toward its neatly combed style. The eyes were closed and sunken. The skin had blotched and blackened with the onset of decay.

Anna tried to look around that, holding up a shield of memories instead: seeing his face as he slept peacefully beside her, eyes closed, a smile on his face, content after making love. But it didn't work. She ached inside. She took a deep breath.

Using surgical scissors, she began to remove his uniform. Rurik's medals and insignia glinted in the light as she pushed his tunic aside, exposing his sunken, grayish chest.

Anna inspected him externally first, seeing no obvious signs of death, no heavy blows or major wounds. She removed the rest of his garments. He looked unreal to her.

Anna forced herself to put on her professional mask. She muttered to herself, imagining that she was talking into a recording device to transcribe the autopsy. But she had purposely shut off all recorders so that the Americans could not steal this information as well.

"Still no sign of external injury." She took one more deep breath and bent closer to the body. Using her fingertips to mark her passage, she inspected his skin, combing for tiny injuries, marks of injections. The skin felt cold and rubbery, like a chilled chemical protective glove. It made her feel detached, cut off.

"After close inspection of the skin, I have still found no indications of injury."

Here, Anna Tripolk ran into a barrier she was not yet willing to cross: she would have to draw coagulated blood; would have to run tests on his remaining body fluids. She would have to cut him open, rummage around his insides, and pluck into his most private corners.

She pictured Stepan holding her, whispering to her. Or standing there with all his silent strength. *I do what I must, and you do what you must.*

She couldn't do that to him. She stiffened, telling herself to don the professional facade again, to fit the mold of objective doctor and do what was expected of her. It just wasn't fair.

Life isn't fair. As Anna hesitated, she remembered how the crew of American engineers had come over, the second wave from *Orbitech 1* to pry into her sleepfreeze process, to dismantle her transparent chambers. Even though she had refused to cooperate, told them they could not have the Soviet technology, they had taken it anyway. They didn't care about what was right or honest. They had no qualms. They had stolen three of her sleepfreeze chambers and shipped them over to Brahms.

The rage this evoked made Anna Tripolk forget all thoughts of Rurik for a moment. Finally, she wrapped his discolored, naked body in a white sheet and wheeled him back into the frozen storage compartment. Steam wafted in the air, swirling with the disturbed air currents.

She had one other thing to do, in Rurik's private quarters. He must have left a personal log somewhere. Anna had looked at the official *Kibalchich* logs in the command center, as had Ramis Barrera and Karen Langelier, and no doubt all those other engineers from *Orbitech 1*. But there had been nothing out of the ordinary—the log entries had simply stopped.

She suspected that Rurik might have kept a diary of his own, though she had failed to find it when she had first combed his quarters. With the questions she had, finding his recorded voice was more important than performing an autopsy.

Anna Tripolk sterilized her hands in the sonic dryers, then unsealed the hatches from the storage chamber and went to search her lover's former quarters.

She managed to avoid bumping into anyone on her way there. That wasn't too difficult, since the *Kibalchich* had so few inhabitants. But when she entered Rurik's private chambers, she closed the door behind her and engaged the locking mechanism.

"Lights, half illumination please."

The glow rose in the chamber. She looked around at the

silken purple coverings on the bed unit, neatly made. To the end, Rurik had maintained careful order, even in his own quarters. A few papers lay stacked on his desk. The terminal screen was folded into the desk and shut off. It was just the way she had left it, days ago after awakening, when she had had to satisfy herself that this wasn't all some sort of trick, a scheme, mind games the Americans might be playing on her.

She paused at a sudden thought: it seemed as if Stepan had known he would not return to this room again.

On the holocube on his desk was a picture of Anna Tripolk's head. It was a bad image, lifted from her personnel file—her heart ached to think that he had used it to keep his memories going.

She wondered if Rurik had come down into the infirmary and stared at her through the transparent case of the sleepfreeze chamber. Had he touched the glass? Had he talked to her in his loneliest times? What had he been thinking about?

As she studied the holocube, she noticed that her image looked distorted. Frowning, she inspected it closer. Her face looked odd, bloated. There was something just inside the image that caused her features to bulge out. Switching off the holocube, she watched a d-cube appear in the center of the device. He had disguised it with her image. Was it meant for her—something only she would discover right away?

Anna didn't think Stepan would hide his personal log, but maybe he would make it more likely for her to find it before anyone else. What had he been thinking about?

Switching the holo back on, she picked up the cube and stared at an image of herself, several years younger, when she had just begun the background work that would be the keystone of her mission aboard the *Kibalchich*. She had been searching for ways to make a Soviet Mars colony viable—the sleepfreeze process for the long journey, for the colonization of a new planet.

Anna had been younger then, more idealistic. The future was bigger and brighter, before so many opportunities had turned into dead ends.

She pulled the d-cube from the image and inserted it

into Rurik's terminal. The screen fuzzed and projected an image of the commander. He had left the lights too low to capture a good image of himself, and he had lain on his bunk as he spoke. This kept him partly out of view of the recorder so that his image wavered, shifting from clarity to indistinctness. But his voice came in clearly. She couldn't see the expression on his face, but the tone of his words let her know the emotional wringer he had apparently gone through. She swallowed, afraid of what he might say.

"I suppose someone will find this record, eventually. Anna, I hope it's you, but I have no guarantee of that. It could be centuries before anyone comes back here. I hope the sleepfreeze process protects our people for that long. We certainly couldn't test it under such extreme conditions.

"I am all alone." His voice suddenly sounded tired. "I have killed Cagarin and dumped his body in the materials reprocessor." Rurik leaned forward and smiled tightly. "He always wanted to be of service to the State."

Anna stood up with a sharp indrawn breath and stepped backward from the image. Rurik had killed Cagarin? But he was the political officer! She continued to listen.

"I am a traitor, I suppose. I refused the last order my government on Earth issued to me. I have questioned orders before, but this one I could not rationalize. And in refusing, I aroused the suspicion of Vice Commander Cagarin. It should be no surprise that Cagarin had approval and veto power on the *Kibalchich*—but that is all on paper. There is no more government, and I remain commander of this station."

Anna Tripolk sat back down on the bunk, confused even further. *Vice Commander* Cagarin? Stepan had hinted that Cagarin was KGB—but even then, she had thought he was just some bureaucratic flunky.

She had wondered why Cagarin had remained awake with Rurik, what special position he had. It made no sense. She felt as if the tip of the iceberg was rising out of the sea and showing more and more that she had never suspected.

"You see," Rurik continued, "the *Kibalchich* has much more to it than most of us realized. State Security had its own plans for this 'strategic position' at L-5. Not the straightforward idealistic challenge that you had, Anna, though that's too bad—a successful mission to Mars was such a nice goal, the perfect cover story.

"There's no place for KGB at L-5 or in humanity's future. Their paranoia—along with equivalent paranoia on *Orbitech 1* and our entire world—is what caused the downfall of Earth. They seem to forget that human beings are supposed to be an intelligent species. We have to prove that now.

"I refused my final orders from Earth; I could not destroy *Orbitech 1* and murder fifteen hundred helpless people. Cagarin and his people would have killed me, taken over the station, and followed the instructions without question. I could not allow that. I knew that in order for us to survive, most of us had to go under sleepfreeze, to wait for help. I convinced Cagarin that I had every intention of following the government's directive, but that people here would riot if they knew about it. I told him I would carry out the instructions after everyone had gone into the chambers. No one would know.

"Cagarin was suspicious, but he agreed. I put him out of the way before he discovered what I was planning to do. Then I disconnected the sleepfreeze chambers of the other eleven KGB people. The remaining survivors on the *Kibalchich* have clear consciences and true forward-thinking minds. They are the hope for our future. I have removed the tainted ones.

"Anna, if it is you listening to this, don't resent me. It will all work out for the best. If someone else is hearing my words, I can only hope mankind has matured a little in the years since I recorded this."

Anna breathed heavily. She stopped the recorder. Stepan, a traitor? She allowed the shock to sweep over her. Stepan, a murderer?

She played the recorder through at fast forward, catching snippets of Rurik's message. His entries became more disjointed, day after day, as he remained alone on the silent station.

"I have no idea how long it will be before someone comes. I hope it will be time enough for our wounds to heal. I have cut off all communication with the other colonies and warned them to stay away. I cannot guess how long that will remain effective. I do not intend to wait and see."

Anna Tripolk closed her eyes, not wanting to hear what he was going to say.

"Anna, you must understand. I cannot put myself into sleepfreeze—there is no one here to operate the chamber." He looked around the room. "I do not know how long I can stand this." He lowered his voice.

"And the transmissions I have intercepted from the other colonies—on *Orbitech 1* I watched them kill ten percent of their population. . . . Their new director, Brahms, executed two more. Things are getting very bad all over. I have had no contact with anyone on Earth. I begin to fear we will never come away from all this. What is the use?

"It may be a hundred years until the madness has been wiped out." He was silent for some minutes. The d-cube recorded only the sound of his breathing. When he spoke, the words sounded forced.

"Using the medical computer and the pharmaceutical dispensary, I have found an appropriate and supposedly painless poison. After I record this, I am going to the command center. I will adjust the computer to recognize Anna Tripolk as commander of this station."

She saw Rurik's image sit up from the bed and walk over to the screen before the picture blanked out.

She felt angry to discover tears running down her cheeks. She brushed them away. Her fingers felt cold. Her confusion and grief funneled together into anger. How could Rurik do this? What did he mean he was ordered to destroy *Orbitech 1*—that was nonsense! How could he make her commander of this station? She wasn't ready for that; she didn't want the responsibility.

Commander Tripolk. She snorted at the sound of the title. There must be another reason—he had acted more as a coward than a commander.

She stood up and ejected the d-cube from the terminal. In Rurik's holo her own face looked back at her, a younger face, before her dreams had been shattered. One thing she did know was that Rurik was a traitor—and a murderer.

Anna put the cube on the floor and crushed it with her

heel. Then she brushed at her jumpsuit, searching for her own dignity, and walked stiffly out the door.

A commander belonged in the command center.

Very well. She would see just what she could do there.

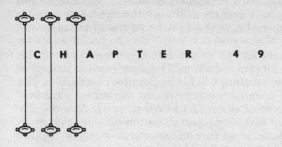

C H A P T E R 4 9

From the *Aguinaldo*'s observation blister, the array of sail-creatures looked like a gossamer armada, ready to skim the Earth and crawl back up the gravity well to L-5. Techs had arranged the sail-creatures in a staggered two-dimensional mosaic, sails oriented perpendicular to the Sun.

Luis Sandovaal could barely make out their full outlines, the stubby central bodies with only a hint of the enormous cell-thin wings.

President Magsaysay stood with Sandovaal, Dobo, and Dobo's wife. Sandovaal thought Dobo's wife looked puffy —probably from living in low gravity for too long, or perhaps she had just been crying a lot lately. She should feel proud of the great adventure her husband was about to undertake, not whimper about it.

Outside the colony, space-suited Filipino techs swarmed over the score of metamorphosed sail-creatures, attaching fiberoptic lines between the sails—wires that connected each creature to its nearest neighbors. The middle two sail-creatures were being readied to house Sandovaal and Dobo. Hormone capsules and a patchwork of electrodes had been inserted into the cavities of the other eighteen giants.

Sandovaal started to speak, but felt a lump rise in his throat. What an odd sensation! The sight outside looked so beautiful; it was a climax to his bioengineering career. The mosaic of sail-creatures was no doubt the largest cluster of life-forms the solar system had ever seen. He found it impossible to say anything—and the intense emotion embarrassed him. Sandovaal turned away and spoke in clipped sentences so his voice would not crack.

"Dobo. It is time for us to go."

Dobo continued to stare out the crystal blister. He kept an arm around his wife's plump waist. The *Aguinaldo* rotated, giving the group an encompassing view of the sail-creatures, the stars, and the vast distance they would have to travel.

Sandovaal began to grow cross. "Dobo—"

"Luis, Luis." Magsaysay put a hand on Sandovaal's shoulder and nodded toward the exit. "You have to go." Sandovaal grunted and led the way from the veranda toward the airlock end of the *Aguinaldo*.

When they arrived, Magsaysay studied Sandovaal's ice blue eyes. "The techs are not through checking your sail-creatures. You want to make sure everything will work, do you not?"

"We tried it on one sail-creature. Ramis was successful. The neural network will ensure that it works for all of them."

Magsaysay replied with uncomfortable silence.

What was taking Dobo so damned long? Sandovaal fidgeted and tried explaining further.

"Once the electrodes are implanted in the sail-creatures' cysts, I can apply the same pressure to each one and steer them all as a group. The effect is the same as having one vast sail. The additional sail-creature nymphs we are carrying will provide more than enough means for us to return—unless the blasted American colony eats them or something." Sandovaal felt annoyed—back to normal after that dangerous flirt with emotion.

Magsaysay sighed and turned to face him. "I know you

think you must go to *Orbitech 1* to get the weavewire for
our own use. But we could likely use MMUs to get over to
the *Orbitech 2* construction site. Ramis proved that Jumping is possible, though it is not as efficient for transporting
supplies." The *dato* pursed his lips. "At least this way you
will be able to bring Ramis back. But I do not want your
confidence to blind you to danger."

Indignant, Sandovaal drew himself up, though Magsaysay stared out one of the viewing windows. "I am a big
boy, Yoli. I know how to take care of myself."

"You are too crusty sometimes." The voice came from
behind him. Sandovaal whirled to find Dobo and his wife
in a tête-à-tête.

"What!" Sandovaal squinted at Dobo, but he and his wife
stood preoccupied, holding hands like juveniles. When
Dobo failed to look at him, Sandovaal snorted and turned
back to President Magsaysay.

Magsaysay suppressed a smile. "This has greater implications than just bringing back the weavewire, Luis. You are
going to determine if we should continue these trips, bring
the colonies together." He hesitated. "I never thought I
would see the day this would really happen."

"This trip will never be an everyday occurrence," Sandovaal said, wondering if Magsaysay was trying to lessen
his accomplishment.

"Maybe not now, but it will happen. I assure you."

"That is not my main concern. If we do not get moving,
the sail-creatures will die before we reach *Orbitech 1*." He
snapped at his assistant. "Dobo! Finish kissing her and let
us get out of here!" Sandovaal pulled on his helmet.

Dobo dabbed at his wife's face with a tissue. Sandovaal
started to admonish his assistant again, but realized that
Dobo couldn't hear him with his helmet on.

Sandovaal grumbled to himself and started checking his
suit status. The antiradiation treatment he had taken was
already making him queasy, or maybe it was just anxiety
about the long journey.

Minutes later a voice in his helmet transceiver interrupted him. "Dr. Sandovaal, are you ready?"

Dobo stood by the airlock, fully suited. At the other end
of the room, his wife forced a smile. Sandovaal grunted

something meant to be unintelligible and met Dobo by the airlock. "Well, what are you waiting for?"

As the airlock door swung shut, Sandovaal forced himself to wave. The holocameras would be recording all this for the daily intercolony broadcasts, suitably embellished with the appropriate Filipino patriotism. At least he had managed to avoid being present while the bishop blessed his space suit.

Magsaysay stood outside the chamber with his hand on the shoulder of Dobo's wife. She held her chin up high, proud. Sandovaal felt a twinge of guilt that he had yelled at his assistant—it might be the last time that either of them saw the *Aguinaldo*. Dobo remained silent, much to Sandovaal's relief.

The external door cycled open and left them staring at empty space. Outside, three techs moved forward, outfitted with compressed-air tanks for maneuvering. They steered Sandovaal and Dobo by the arms toward the waiting sail-creatures.

The magnitude of the fragile mosaic became evident to Sandovaal as they drew near. The delicate wings, extending scores of kilometers, could not withstand much more than the solar photon pressure that would push them on their journey.

A glimmer of light brought Sandovaal's attention to the array of wires connecting the sail-creature bodies. With them, the sails would be somewhat limited in their ability to turn, but the increase in weight the array of creatures could carry more than made up for the limitation. Ramis's trip had been by the seat of his pants; by comparison, this one would be a walk in the barrio.

Two of the techs turned and jetted off with Dobo to one of the central sail-creatures. Sandovaal allowed himself to be taken to the other. The cavity in the core of the creature widened like a womb, into which the techs inserted him. Sandovaal tried to cooperate and help them, but he soon lost his temper and yanked his elbow away from a too-persistent tech.

Before he pulled his helmet inside the organic darkness, he looked up at the universe; the *Aguinaldo*'s huge silvery cylinder; the broad, fragile wings of the sail-creature.

The cavity was just as he had imagined it—cramped, but

pliable enough so that he could move around and push out with his legs. The techs had embedded a small flatscreen teleceiver in the cavity wall, allowing limited communications with the *Aguinaldo*. At the bottom of the cavity he found a computer wedged against one of the curved organic walls.

As part of the "payload" of the sail mosaic, a dozen sail-creature nymphs had been anesthetized into dormancy and packaged outside, sealed to keep them from being exposed to the vacuum. Wall-kelp made up the remainder of the cargo.

Wires ran into the back of the battery-powered computer. Since Ramis's initial trip, a team of electrical engineers had worked out a method of controlling the sail-creatures' movements through tiny electric shocks. The boy's method of using a knife to prick the inside of the cavity was much too imprecise for any additional trips.

The computer controlled a neural network that coordinated the array's movements. Sandovaal felt satisfied that most of the uncertainty was gone from using the sail-creatures, but plenty of things could still go wrong. He settled back into the cavity, pushing against the pliant walls so that he was firmly embedded and somewhat comfortable. He suspected he would grow to hate his space suit over the next week or so.

He watched the techs seal the cavity outside, closing off the dim wedge of starlight. Good thing he wasn't claustrophobic. The most frustrating part was that he would have to spend days with no one but Dobo for company.

It would only take a few hours for the wall-kelp inside the sealed cavity to generate enough oxygen so he could remove his helmet. He would have nothing but his own wall-kelp to eat during the entire journey, and that suited him just fine. Sandovaal thought briefly about suggesting that the techs double-check the outside sealant, but dismissed the idea. They had thorough checklists, drawn up by Sandovaal himself.

All communication lines checked out, and the electrodes were responding to the periodic queries. The sail-cluster appeared ready to launch.

He reached up and flicked on the flatscreen. They would want him to make some sort of speech, of course. After working with holotanks on the *Aguinaldo*, the primitive two-dimensional image seemed weirdly different.

President Magsaysay appeared on the screen. "Luis, Dobo is having some last words with his wife. Then you will be ready to go. We will switch to open broadcast."

Sandovaal watched a tiny window lined in red at the top of his flatscreen. Dobo had blacked out his private channel, keeping Sandovaal and everyone else from eavesdropping.

"Tell him to wrap it up. I do not want this mission to fail because he cannot say good-bye in less time than it takes to make the entire journey!"

Magsaysay grinned. "Would you like me to do anything else before you go? Have the bishop say a prayer, perhaps? With your batteries, you will not be able to keep communicating with us for long."

"I realize that—I just have to convince Dobo that we must only use them in an emergency."

Magsaysay ignored Sandovaal's complaining. "We and *Orbitech 1* will be beaming an open channel to you. We are broadcasting this over ConComm, making this an international voyage, Luis. The people on Clavius Base are attempting to send someone to L-5 using a new technique of their own, and they intend to arrive about the same day you do. It is truly an exciting time." Magsaysay paused as he looked offscreen. He turned back to the camera and spoke again. "The techs are showing that you are free to launch."

Sandovaal shot a glance at the computer. The network readout showed complete communication between all the sail-creatures. Sandovaal muttered to himself about Dobo once again when the direct window blinked green. "It is about time, Dobo."

"What was that?"

Sandovaal cleared his throat. He switched the flatscreen from Magsaysay to the outside view, but kept the audio channel to Magsaysay open. A small solid-state transmitter was affixed outside Sandovaal's cavity, showing a wide-angled view of space. The Earth hung in one corner, half lit by the Sun. They were near the optimum time for launch, when the sail-creatures could take best advantage of the solar photon flux.

Sandovaal felt a rush of adrenaline. For a moment he imagined the array of sail-creatures as a pack of snails straining at the starting gates. . . .

In front of him lay the grandest adventure of his life, made possible only through his years of research in developing the sail-creatures. Nothing else seemed to matter—the Earth beckoned him onward, enticing him to dance in a dangerous ballet of gravity.

Sandovaal reached out and initiated the command that would send a tiny voltage jolt to the electrodes embedded in the array. Imperceptibly, the sail-creatures began to recoil from the irritating sensation. Their bodies moved scant millimeters as they started to swing their vast wings around, until they were fully exposed to the light pressure from the Sun.

Minutes passed before Sandovaal could detect any sensation of movement by watching the image of the *Aguinaldo.* The acceleration process had begun, and they continued to gain momentum from the solar photons. In a week's time they would be skirting the Earth.

When he first noticed that his armada was moving at a crawl, Sandovaal whispered into the audio channel. "Yoli, is the recorder on? I wish to say something for posterity."

After a short pause, Magsaysay's tinny voice came over the speakers in his helmet. "Go ahead, Luis. We are anxious to hear you."

Sandovaal smiled and drew a deep breath. *"Aguinaldo,* do not fear for us. This is another triumph for all Filipinos. And, in the immortal words of the great General MacArthur—I shall return!"

CHAPTER 50

A cluster of people milled just inside the main airlock. Tomkins had always felt uneasy in groups. He also hated going outside, where he had to devote 99 percent of his attention just to stepping in the right place with the right speed, constantly checking his gauges and monitor lights, responding to incessant chatter through his suit radio.

It was crowded as everyone suited up and checked connections. Tomkins pushed away an elbow that bumped against his side. He was amazed at the chaos in which Clancy's engineers worked together, packed in and moving with a dizzying choreography, but somehow they all suited up faster than any of Tomkins's Clavius Base personnel did.

In the prep room, McLaris moved to him and groped for his hand, pulling off his thick glove for a firm handshake. "Dr. Tomkins."

McLaris searched Tomkins's eyes; he seemed at a loss for words, frightened. He had shaved off his patchy beard, and one of the other assistants had helped him trim his hair so that he would be a presentable ambassador to *Orbitech 1*. His gray eyes looked wide and glittering.

Tomkins returned McLaris's grip, clasping the smaller man's hand in what he thought was a warm and paternal gesture. "Three days from now you'll be there, Duncan."

McLaris set his mouth. "I know."

"Who am I going to get to run this place? You're always welcome back. You know that."

"Thank you. I appreciate that. This place has become my home—I feel useful here. I'll miss it."

Tomkins laughed. "And I'll miss you. I've gotten more research done in the past few weeks than in the first three years I've been up here. You've got a gift for administration, Duncan."

"Some skills are more useful than others, but not all the time." McLaris pressed his lips together, letting the uneasiness show again.

Tomkins squeezed his shoulder and stepped back. "The yo-yo will work just fine, if our Mr. Clancy says so—*Dr.* Clancy, I mean." He laughed. "You'll be safe."

"That's not what I'm worried about," McLaris mumbled.

"I know." McLaris had his own ghosts to chase, and until he confronted them, Tomkins knew that no words would put the man at ease.

Standing a full head taller than most of the people in the prep room, Tomkins searched the crowd with ease. Clancy stood trapped in a corner, surrounded by eight members of his construction crew, all of whom insisted on checking his suit seals to make sure he would be safe. Glued to his side was his deputy, Wiay Shen.

Shen had done fine emergency work hauling him back to the base after his fall. Clancy seemed almost disappointed that he had sustained no greater injury than a minor concussion, which was what had knocked him unconscious. Shen still took every opportunity to mother him. Since the accident, everyone else on Clavius Base had noticed how inseparable the two were.

Tomkins made his way to them, flexing his arms in the tight suit. Few of the standard-issue garments fit his tall frame, and he was unaccustomed to the restricted movements. He held his helmet in his hands, ready to seal it into its collar.

Shen and Clancy turned away from the rest of the crowd. Clancy flailed his arms to get the crew away from him. "All right, already! I know how to put on my own blasted suit!"

Shen added her own admonishment. "Didn't you guys ever hear the one about too many cooks spoiling the microwave dinner? Or whatever it was . . ." Regardless, she took a moment to check all of Clancy's connections herself.

"You take care of yourself," Clancy told her in a quiet voice.

"Look who's talking, hotshot." Shen ran a hand up and down his side. Her glove made a crinkling sound against his suit. "You sure you're going to be up to this trip? There's no one to get you out of a jam if something happens."

"Besides bruising my leg, all I got was a bump on the head. Dr. Berenger gave me her blessing. This'll be just like riding an elevator—a heck of a lot safer than riding in a six-pack with you."

"Knowing you, you'll find a way to get in trouble."

Tomkins cleared his throat to interrupt their private discussion. "Dr. Clancy?"

"Dr. Tomkins?" Clancy swung around and shook Tomkins's gloved hand. He moved with a slight limp, but seemed no worse than before the accident.

"I can't think of two better people to make the first trip on your yo-yo. Good luck, Clifford. I'd like to stay, but I need to get out to Clavius-C if I'm going to watch your ascent."

"That's all right," Clancy said. "Duncan and I need to be ready for the weavewire when it arrives. We should move out the same time as you do."

Shen interrupted. "*Orbitech 1* plans to start reeling in the weavewire less than an hour after it arrives—whether you're hooked up or not. That doesn't give you much time."

Tomkins smiled. "Very well. Have a good trip and all that. Best of luck, and I expect to see you back in one piece. The radio telescope project will certainly need your guidance when you return."

Clancy nodded to Shen beside him. "Wiay can manage the crew while I'm gone. In fact, she might kick a few more butts than I do. Now that they've got this fire lit under them for the project, you'd better take advantage of their willingness to work." He grinned and looked at his crew jostling around in the prep room. "If I get back—"

"*When* you get back," Shen chided.

"Okay, when I get back, and if this yo-yo method of getting to the Lagrange colonies turns out to be feasible, the whole crew is going to be antsy to get off here. They want to work in space, you know—not with rocks between their toes."

Tomkins nodded. "You're right, of course." He turned to Shen and bowed, bending down to her height. "And my apologies if I doubted your competence, Ms. Shen."

"You couldn't offend me if you tried."

"That's what I was hoping you'd say." Tomkins rubbed his big brown hands together. "Would you like to accompany me to Clavius C, Ms. Shen? We'll have the best live view you can get of the ascent. Or would you rather see the official broadcast that goes out to all the colonies?"

"I can watch the recording any time I feel like it. I'd rather have a front-row seat."

McLaris stepped up to join them. "Clifford?"

"Let's do it."

Tomkins stood back as the two started for the airlock. McLaris turned for one more wave, then pulled his helmet over his head, sealing it down around his collar.

Clancy grinned at his crew as Shen held his helmet for him. She reached over with one hand, pulled his head down to hers, and kissed him. He blinked and put on his polarized helmet quickly, as if to cover up a blush. Two other people from Clancy's crew followed them into the airlock, ready to escort them out to the yo-yo capsule, which they had dubbed the *Phoenix*, where they would help attach the harness falling down from the American colony.

The big airlock door swung shut and began its cycle. Shen stood watching it with a fixed expression.

"Ready?" Tomkins asked.

"Uh? Oh, yeah. Just a minute." Shen blew her nose. "The six-packs over in area two should be ready to go."

"After you, then." They waited for the airlock to cycle.

Shen insisted on driving the six-pack and seemed to make a point of not using the inertial guidance system. Tomkins sat in silence, occasionally acknowledging Shen's conversation, other times just listening to the hollow echo of his own breathing. They rode out, leaving tracks in the lunar surface, swinging past the *Phoenix.*

Spotters were staggered across the plain of Clavius, some up on the rise of the crater wall. Nearly every holo-transmitter on Clavius Base scanned the sky overhead, searching for the harness preceding the weavewire. On the open channel, one of the other base scientists, bored with his regular duties, took a turn giving the commentary for the event. Tomkins decided he would listen to it all later.

Out here, on the sterile lunar surface, he pictured the vast radio telescope, the shining accomplishment that showed how human beings could still construct their own wonders, even when everything else had been taken away from them. Arecibo II. He knew it was pretentious to include it among the grand monuments of mankind—the pyramids, the great bridges, the tall buildings, the giant dams—but perhaps Arecibo II would last longer than all of those. The project would show how people continued to strive, even when they had lost so much. The Earth might have fallen silent, but the universe would not be able to hide its secrets much longer.

Their six-pack rolled over the lunar dust. Tomkins craned his neck to look up into the starry blackness, but only ended up straining it inside the helmet.

"You've got to bend your whole body backward," Shen said, seeing what he was trying to do. "Like this." She leaned back in an exaggerated curve. "Otherwise, you'll just see the inside of your helmet."

"I hope we can spot the harness before it lands," he said.

"Visually, not much chance of that." Shen stared straight ahead at the unbroken crater floor. "But *Orbitech 1* coated it with radar-reflecting paint. That should make its cross

section a hundred times bigger on radar than it actually
is."

Tomkins thought for a moment. "The Moon is still a big
place for it to land."

Shen turned toward Tomkins, but her gold-coated visor
blocked off any view of her face. "You didn't see how close
that first harness hit where it was supposed to. Dead on.
It'll get here."

"Then everything should go as planned." He sensed
some other worry in her. She didn't seem to want to talk
about it.

"Yes, it should, shouldn't it?"

Tomkins started to reply, but he kept quiet. Shen's sar-
castic tone left him puzzled. It seemed out of place, especially on such an important occasion. He could understand
her feelings for Clancy and her concern for his safety. Yet
the sense he was getting was more than just "my lover is
leaving."

Tomkins sighed. Much as he had disliked his years in
management, they had left him with a few rudimentary
processes for dealing with human problems.

He asked softly, "Did I miss something about the journey? I was under the impression that the yo-yo was
straightforward—once the weavewire hook arrives, it'll be
attached to the hook already in place. It's a thousand times
less complicated than building and piloting a spacecraft."

He heard Shen snort at him. He hated these helmets—
he could not see her expression. He continued, "Well, a
constant tenth of a G acceleration isn't going to harm
them, either. So what's up?"

The six-pack bounced over a rock Shen didn't bother to
avoid, jarring Tomkins. The vehicle seemed to have sped
up during his conversation, and the textured ground
flowed along beside them. They began to climb the side of
the crater wall. He heard a long sigh over the helmet
speakers.

"Dr. Tomkins, I know you wanted to stay out of the
details once you let McLaris take over the base administration stuff, but—" She paused. "Well, I'm surprised you kept
yourself so completely in the dark. Four days from now,
McLaris and Cliff will be zipping along at more than two
thousand miles an hour straight toward *Orbitech 1,* with

nothing to stop them but a couple of revamped engines from a crashed shuttle. They won't have any gravity to slow them down, no weavewire pulling in the opposite direction to halt their progress. If those engines don't fire exactly when they're supposed to, and for exactly as long as they need to, the *Phoenix* will smash into *Orbitech 1* like a meteor. I'd have to be crazy not to be worried."

Tomkins looked straight ahead without seeing the outside view. He hadn't even noticed that Shen had stopped the six-pack. She lifted one of her legs over the seat and eased out onto the lunar surface. Tomkins followed her, planting his feet on sturdy ground with a clear memory of Clancy's fall a few weeks before. Two miles away and a thousand feet below their level, Tomkins could see the activity in the center of the crater, where the skyhook would hit.

Below, McLaris and Clancy would be strapping themselves into the compartment where they'd remain for the next several days, if all went well.

It had been so easy to hand over the operation of Clavius Base to McLaris. He had been so efficient, so methodical in his work. Shen was perfectly right—Tomkins had divorced himself entirely of management responsibility. He had not even taken time to review what was happening on the base. McLaris took care of everything while Tomkins was wrapped up in the radio telescope—his true love. He prayed he wouldn't have to give that up.

Shen stood on an outcrop jutting from the crater wall. Tomkins joined her. The *Phoenix* looked alone and unhindered out on the flat plain, like a hitchhiker waiting for a ride. Once the hook fell out of the sky, the crew would have to scramble to hook it up before their time ran out. The old patched hull of the *Miranda* looked contorted by its airtight welds and grafted metal plates. While Clancy's engineers had begun to restore the manufacturing facilities on the Moon, they had not yet rebuilt the industrial facilities enough that they could construct a new vessel.

With the salvaged hull of the crashed shuttle, and extra materials dismantled from unnecessary equipment on Clavius Base, they had turned the *Miranda* into a completely new kind of vehicle, a true phoenix. The rocket engines had been removed and mounted on top, test fired

once to make certain they could provide braking thrust.
The thing looked like a bastardized hodgepodge of leftover parts.

Which it was.

Now that Tomkins was in line of sight of the operation, a
voice crackled in his helmet. "We have a visual on the
skyhook, everybody. It matches the radar echo. Give us
five minutes and we'll have you linked up and ready to
go."

Clancy's voice came over the *Phoenix*'s radio. "Just stay
clear of that weavewire. I don't want anyone getting sliced
up."

"Everything's under control out here, Clifford. You two
just make sure you're strapped in. You'll be in for quite a
yank when that cable starts hauling."

Tomkins and Shen watched the scene without speaking.
Though they couldn't see it themselves, they learned that
the tiny package had indeed struck the far side of the
crater. A specially modified six-pack racer sped across the
floor to retrieve it. Tomkins realized ironically that no one
would ever be able to see the fine thread tying the colonies
together.

Tomkins waved a hand to the yo-yo assembly below.
"When Duncan explained this trip, I naturally thought
everything was well known—very little risk and all that. I
guess it's a naive way for theoreticians to view the world—
just assume that things are 'engineering problems.'"

Shen let out a short laugh. "'Engineering problems' can
really screw you up bad if your survival depends on everything working just right." She continued with vehemence:
"Once Cliff got it through people's head that it didn't matter how fast the yo-yo was pulled up, everyone bought it.
Escape velocity doesn't mean beans when you've got a
constant force pulling you up."

Excited voices filled the radio. The six-pack racer returned to the *Phoenix,* and suited figures scrambled over
the top. Tomkins wished he had some sort of binoculars,
but the curved faceplate would have made them useless.

Once the hook was attached, the figures jumped back
down to the crater floor and rolled away in their six-pack.
The vehicle wheeled a safe distance away, then turned and
waited.

"We don't really know how long it's going to take," Shen said. "It should be soon now."

"Clavius Base and *Orbitech 1*, we are ready to go!" Duncan McLaris's voice broadcast. Since the sound speed in the monomolecular strand approached the speed of light, as Clancy had predicted, once *Orbitech 1* started reeling in the weavewire, the *Phoenix* would start moving.

"See ya later, Cliffy!" Shen broadcast.

Before he could reply, the *Phoenix* suddenly jerked up, hauled off the surface of the Moon in a puff of lunar dust. The modified hull of the *Miranda* pulled away. From this distance, it looked to Tomkins like it was levitating. The yo-yo shot up into the black soup of stars at an angle to the horizon.

Clancy's voice came over the radio. "We're off! The acceleration is less than lunar normal, so we don't feel too bad. But boy, we are getting a sight you would not believe!"

Whoops from a dozen different microphones filled Tomkins's helmet. Down on the crater floor, where dust still settled to the surface, he could see tiny figures outside the six-pack making superhuman leaps in the lunar gravity.

The *Phoenix* ascended into the deep blackness. Shen stood staring down at the launch site.

"If you bend over like this, you can see better!" Tomkins said to Shen, bending backward as she had shown him. "Are you still worried?"

Shen continued watching for a moment, then turned to their six-pack. "Now it's that guy Brahms who concerns me."

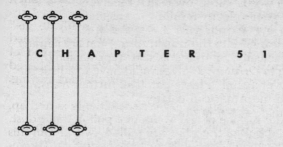

C H A P T E R   5 1

Luis Sandovaal tried to keep the antenna pointed toward the incoming signal, beamed from the *Aguinaldo* over three hundred thousand kilometers away. The computer-driven servo had failed and he had a hard time manually steering the delicate controls.

Cramped in the sail-creature cyst, he felt his impatience simmering into anger. He tried again to adjust the antenna, overshot the mark, and hissed at himself before making another attempt. Back in the lab he could maneuver the microwaldoes and juggle chromosomes one at a time in the nucleus of a single cell. He couldn't dare admit that he was having problems now.

Hourly news updates, beamed from the *Aguinaldo* on the open channel between the colonies, gave Sandovaal and Dobo some respite from worrying about their trip. As bored as he sometimes felt, Sandovaal wondered how young Ramis had endured it. Dobo spent most of the time sleeping.

A burst of words came over the receiver. "# # # # showing that your velocity is falling as calculated. You will soon need to # # # your sails # # # # # # #."

Sandovaal leaned into the transmitter. "You are coming through sporadically, *Aguinaldo*. Next transmission time I am switching to *Orbitech 1*." He would have to adjust the antenna all over again! "Please patch all further transmissions through the American colony."

"Rog# # that. # # # # out."

Remembering the difficulty he had had before, Sandovaal decided to take a short nap and then begin trying to direct the radio dish toward *Orbitech 1*. The sail-creature mosaic had passed through the side lobe for inter-Lagrange point communications and could not pick up anything from Clavius Base, but he would try anyway.

Eight years before, when he first had arrived on the new *Aguinaldo*, full of enthusiasm, things had been much brighter.

As he had disembarked from the first shuttle-tug, Sandovaal still couldn't feel his own weight. The shuttle had docked at the *Aguinaldo*'s zero-G core, and after six days of transit, he was getting tired of floating around. He wanted to move to the rim and feel the artificial gravity pull on his legs, even if it was only a seventh of Earth normal. He wanted to feel solid again.

He drifted with the other new arrivals down the passageway, bumping into walls. Coming into the gleaming *Aguinaldo* at its axis, he saw the ten-kilometer length unfold before him—a gargantuan cylinder broken only by the lightaxis running straight down the center. The dizzying edges rolled up, encircling his view. Other new colonists milled around him, gasping and muttering to each other.

He had not envisioned the colony quite like this—nothing of such . . . magnitude. Sandovaal felt embarrassed at his awe and tried to hide it. It was only engineering, after all—on a large scale, yes, but still just pieces of metal welded together.

He let his eyes rest on all the broad open space. As he had feared, he saw distressingly little green. How did they expect to make themselves independent from Earth without devoting most of their effort to intensive agriculture?

Someone prodded him from behind. A bored American attendant standing off to the side seemed more interested in his nails than in helping anybody. "Hurry it up, ladies and gentlemen. Other colonists are waiting to disembark."

A slidewalk covered with stickum held Sandovaal's feet to the floor as the crowd moved along. He could feel himself growing heavier as they traveled along the sloping end toward the cylinder's edge. Looking back over his shoulder, he felt dizzy from the sight: back at the zero-G core, the slidewalk moved almost straight up to the axis; toward the rim, the moving belt sloped until it was tangent to the ground.

"Ladies and gentlemen, if I may have your attention, please."

The crowd quieted as the attendant moved from his position and perched on one of the slidewalk rails. "When we get to the rim, chasers will direct you to your housing units. We have to process five thousand people in the next week, so please be patient with us. The housing units have all been certified, but something could have slipped past us. Please remember that the transition staff is extremely overloaded and we're doing our best to make sure everything runs smoothly. Any questions?"

The speech came out rapidly, without inflections, as though the attendant had said it dozens of times. Sandovaal wrestled with the American colloquialisms.

The slidewalk came to a stop at the rim. The new colonists swarmed to the lines. Attendants yelled over the din. "A through D, this line—if your last name starts with A through D, please wait in this line!"

Sandovaal drew in a breath and tried to control his impatience. He made his way to the "Q thru T" line and deposited his bags in front of two young women. He fidgeted and clenched his jaw as he waited, slowly moving toward the head of the queue. It reminded him of a crowded registration line at the university in Manila.

"Your last name?" The dark-haired woman didn't look up from her table.

"Sandovaal."

A moment passed. "To the left and down three kilometers; Luzon block." The woman pointed without looking up. Her hair was offensively stylish.

Sandovaal stood his ground. "Tell me, where are the biogenetic laboratories?"

The woman looked up, puzzled. "Move on to your apartment, please. A map of the *Aguinaldo* is posted in your quarters."

She paused. Sandovaal kept his temper in check. "The biogenetic labs—where are they?"

"Sir, I told you—"

"You did not answer my question." Sandovaal pulled himself up and glared into the woman's face. "Young lady, I am Dr. Luis Sandovaal, the *Aguinaldo*'s chief scientist. Now, you will show me the biogenetic laboratories or you will not find your name on the seating list for any shuttle back to Earth. Do you understand?"

The woman tapped a stylus on her desk, looking around for someone to rescue her. Finally, she summoned a steward to direct him. Sandovaal ducked behind the barricade; he heard other people in the line grumbling at him.

The steward eased Sandovaal away from the crowds, leading him to an electric cart. He refused to let the steward help him stuff his bags into the cart's cargo bin.

Within moments they sped azimuthally up the rim, past the orderly fields of crops, the fish pens, all the empty, wasted space. Sandovaal saw offices and maintenance buildings, parks, ponds, and row upon row of housing areas.

When they arrived at the laboratory complex, Sandovaal cut off the steward's insincere apologies. He dragged his luggage from the cart. "Which one?" The American pointed to a low prefabricated building, then sped off in the cart before his passenger could say anything further. Sandovaal admonished himself for not having noted the man's name.

Without entering, he already knew how artificial the lab would look. He hated it when other people "designed" what was best for him. At least with modular construction, he could uproot a wall or two and fix things.

Sandovaal entered the empty research complex, calling out as he entered each lab area, "Dobo! Where are you?"

Dobo Daeng had arrived on an earlier shuttle; he should have been here setting up.

The research buildings looked like a geometric progression of identical laboratory areas, reflected endlessly upon each other. With each empty room, closet, and bay he found, Sandovaal's blood pressure inched up. Nothing had been set up, nothing prepared, nothing ready to go. Some crates had been piled in the halls, marked with stenciled words in English. None had been opened.

Getting to work was the only way Sandovaal knew how to settle down. Without Dobo here, he would have to unpack and set up the laboratory materials himself. He attacked the task, flinging open cupboards, glancing at the facilities. He located the main supply room and hauled out brown boxes of test tubes, sketchboards to be linked into the computer, special pipettes that would work properly in the low gravity.

After a few hours, the magnitude of the task wore at him. He couldn't get started until everything was in its proper place, in order. In frustration, he ignored the tedious jobs and decided to set up the computer. He had already planned his analysis of the *Aguinaldo*'s ecology, and now he wanted to see how bad things might be.

The mainframe's crates weren't hard to find, though the components fit together into a computer only as large as a suitcase. Sandovaal usually left such work to the hardware people, but he had little trouble assembling the computer himself and running two simple diagnostic routines. . . .

Sandovaal immersed himself in a study of the *Aguinaldo*'s resources, running simulations, variable checks, and endless projections. Over and over he graphed out the results and discarded them to try again.

He left only to relieve himself or to scrounge some instant coffee from an aluminum packet he had included in his file drawer from Scripps. He uncovered some prepackaged food among the supplies when he noticed he was hungry. He found himself nodding asleep, but splashed cold water on his face and went back to work.

Persistence. It felt good to be doing something again.

The laboratory lights came on by themselves when the lightaxis dimmed for the colony's nightfall. He had no idea how much time had passed when Dobo finally arrived at the laboratory.

Sandovaal whirled from his chair as the assistant walked in. "Dobo, look at this." The words came as a command.

Dobo rubbed his hands as he approached Sandovaal. "I just got unpacked and did a little exploring. My wife and I are still settling down." Dobo slowed as he looked at Sandovaal, then raised his eyebrows. "Work has not been scheduled to start until tomorrow, but I decided to check in at the laboratory. They said you were brought here after you disembarked. Have you located your dwelling yet?"

"Look at this." Sandovaal jabbed his fingers at the display.

Dobo squinted at the holoscreen. He pondered for an unacceptably long moment. "It appears to show—"

"It leaves no room for doubt. With the *Aguinaldo*'s current agricultural plan using only Earth crops, a catastrophic shortage of food will occur if any imbalance is brought into the system, even years down the road."

"What system?" Dobo squinted at the screen, puffing out his pudgy cheeks and muttering to himself. "Crop yields, animal offspring, population growth. And the figures are for fifty years from now. What does this have to do with molecular biology? I thought we were setting up a new genetic institute—"

With an exaggerated sigh, Sandovaal said, "At one time I thought you were bright, Dobo." He gestured across the graphs, indicating nothing in particular. "Use your imagination—or did you forget to pack it? If this colony is to survive, this data shows we must design special *new* crops tailored to this environment, not Earth's."

Dobo frowned. "A new ecological system—ah, so that is where our work comes in."

"I just said that. Now, pull up a chair and help me with this design matrix. Or better yet, finish the unpacking."

Sandovaal attempted to plug a fiberoptic cable into the monitor but was quickly frustrated by the maze of cable ports in the back. "Where does this go?"

Dobo didn't seem to notice Sandovaal's harshness. "The second port. But my wife, Dr. Sandovaal—she is waiting for me outside. We were going to mass."

"Your wife is an adult, old enough to take care of herself.

You did come to the *Aguinaldo* to assist me, correct?"
Sandovaal turned back to the screen.

Dobo looked lost in thought for a moment and then
shrugged. He pulled up a chair next to Sandovaal. . . .

After closing his eyes and listening to his breathing in the
closed cyst, Sandovaal gave up trying to sleep and sat up.

Unlike Ramis, who had continued to accelerate until the
end, Sandovaal wanted his armada of sail-creatures to arrive at *Orbitech 1* intact. So they had tacked a carefully
calculated course, allowing their kinetic energy to evolve
into potential (or whatever the nuts-and-bolts people
called it), and steered for a spot in the middle of the
L-5 gravity well—between *Orbitech 1* and the Soviet *Kibalchich.* He dismissed the insignificant danger of running
into the weavewire strung between the two colonies, but
nevertheless they had plotted the sail-creatures' course to
bring them in above the ecliptic plane.

Satisfied that the *Aguinaldo* transmissions had indeed
ceased, Sandovaal turned his attention to inspecting the
sail-creatures. He flicked on the external flatscreen camera. From his vantage point in the center of the array,
everything appeared to be all right. He swiveled the exterior camera around and tried to pick out the individual
cores dotted among the huge wings. Only his nearest
neighbors were visible, since the tiny camera could not
resolve features more than twenty kilometers away.

Slapping at the controls, Sandovaal activated the direct
fiberoptic line to Dobo's sail-creature. The vision segment
on the flatscreen showed only a gray-white storm of static.
A deep, rumbling sound buzzed out of the speakers. Sandovaal jerked upward and pressed at the volume control.
Listening for a moment, he raised his white eyebrows.

"Dobo!" No answer. "Dobo, wake up, you imbecile!"
Nothing.

"Dobo—you are to keep on the schedule. Now, wake up
immediately!"

Sandovaal grew angrier with each passing second until
he felt as though he might explode. He was glad the doc-
tors on the *Aguinaldo* could not monitor his blood pressure. Dobo must have turned off his receiver, as well as the
visual portion of their communication link; only the audio

came through. Inexcusable! "Probably left the transmission line on just to intimidate me."

Sandovaal had kept in constant contact, making sure Dobo didn't sleep too much, that he kept his mind challenged by listening to Sandovaal's theories on bioengineering. Someday Dobo might have to carry on the work.

But it seemed that as soon as they had pushed off from the *Aguinaldo*, Dobo had become difficult—adhering to his own schedule, switching Sandovaal off in the middle of a conversation, only to apologize later for "accidentally" bumping the television controls. You would think the man had a mind of his own.

Sandovaal snorted. A mind of his own! A preposterous thought for anybody who knew Dobo Daeng.

He stopped abruptly, wondering if Dobo had actually been trying to intimidate him. A moment passed before Sandovaal snorted again, wondering if the cramped solitude was beginning to give him delusions. *No*, he thought, *not Dobo.*

Twenty kilometers away, in the core of his own sail-creature, Dobo stopped making his snoring sounds into the microphone and pushed away from the transmitter. With a grin on his face, he watched the flatscreen image as Sandovaal switched off the monitor. As before, Sandovaal had forgotten to turn off his own transmitter.

Dobo watched in quiet amusement as Sandovaal threw a fit but found no target for his outrage. Finally, after all these years of being an unappreciated assistant . . .

If nothing else, Dobo was having the time of his life.

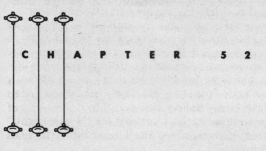

CHAPTER 52

The shock did not wear off, as Anna Tripolk had thought it would. Instead, the secret left behind by Commander Rurik unlocked many doors inside her, unleashing outrage, betrayal, anger, despair. She had never felt like this before.

Instead of healing, for more than a week Anna's emotions had festered, twisting, depriving her of sleep. Without realizing it, she had somehow descended into a personal hell.

Anna remembered going into the command center ten days before, or was it eleven? She had lost track of time. Her attention had been elsewhere. After hearing Rurik's personal log, his excuses, the rationalization of his suicide and the murders he had committed, she had gone up to the weightless command center alone. She had never felt so alone.

The corridors were empty, echoing. Part of her feared encountering *Orbitech 1* technicians, but the Americans had seemed interested in stealing only the sleepfreeze technology, and had left the command center alone.

But the command center was the only place they could radio back to their American colony; they would have to come here eventually. She knew they gathered every day to listen to the inane propaganda broadcasts from the other colonies, cheering for some kind of "spacecraft on a rope" being reeled in from Clavius Base to *Orbitech 1*; that and more talk of those sail-creatures.

She had to act while she had her privacy. Whatever the Americans were doing could wait. The weightless room stood empty now.

"Computer," she said, feeling the alien English words roll off her tongue. "Verify my identity. Anna Tripolk."

She waited a moment as the computer digitized her voice and compared it with the pattern it had stored.

"{{VERIFIED.}}"

"Did Commander Rurik leave any instructions concerning me? Did he designate me as commander?"

"{{YOU ARE COMMANDER OF THE KIBALCHICH.}}"

She felt her insides go watery at the affirmation. What Rurik had said was true. But what had he meant? "Computer, seal all access into the command center. I do not wish to be disturbed."

The open door from the lift platform slid shut. She heard no bolt-locking mechanism on the other doors, but that didn't matter. The computer would refuse to open them for anyone else. She floated, lost in her own confusion.

"Computer, the last order transmitted from Earth was received by Commander Rurik. Recall the file and play it for me."

"{{COMMANDER RURIK DELETED THAT FILE.}}"

That didn't surprise Anna. In consternation, she held onto one of the fixed chairs and let her legs drift out from under her. She set her mouth.

"Computer, did you store the content of that message— the substance, if not the exact words? Piece together peripheral files if you have to."

"{{WORKING.}}" Then, "{{COMPLETE.}}"

"Summarize."

"{{YOU HAVE INSUFFICIENT ACCESS AUTHORIZATION.}}"

"Computer, I command the *Kibalchich*. Authorize access."

"{{WORKING . . . COMPLETE IDENTIFICATION REQUIRED. PLEASE PLACE YOUR HAND ON THE GENETICHECK.}}"

Anna searched out the geneticheck pad, then placed her hand on the device. Seconds later she felt a sharp prick as a minuscule sample of her skin was taken.

"{{IDENTIFICATION CONFIRMED, ACCESS GRANTED: DETONATION SEQUENCE ALEXANDER. COMMANDER RURIK WAS ORDERED TO USE THE KIBALCHICH'S DIRECTED-ENERGY WEAPON TO DESTROY ORBITECH 1. VICE COMMANDER CAGARIN WAS TO ENSURE THAT THE ORDER WAS CARRIED OUT.}}"

"What directed-energy weapon?" Anna demanded. "The *Kibalchich* is a research station. We have no directed-energy weapons here."

"{{THIS STATION WAS BUILT FOR THE EXPRESS PURPOSE OF BASING A DIRECTED-ENERGY WEAPON. ALL OTHER CONCERNS ARE SECONDARY.}}"

Appalled, Anna Tripolk pulled herself down into the chair and stared at the holotank in the center of the room.

"Explain. Display graphics. What weapon? How could that be?"

A diagram of the *Kibalchich* appeared in the center of the tank, etched in glowing green lines against a black background.

"{{A CACHE OF NUCLEAR DEVICES KEPT IN WATER STORAGE IS DESIGNED TO SLIDE DOWN TO THE END OF THE ROTATIONAL AXIS BENEATH THE SHIELD AND DETONATE, ONE DEVICE AT A TIME. X-RAY CONVERTERS EMBEDDED IN THE AXIS FOCUS THE ENERGY TO THE REFLECTING MIRROR ABOVE. THE MIRROR CAN BE TILTED TO DIRECT THE X-RAY LASER TO A SPECIFIED TARGET.}}"

On the image, a small doughnut-shaped disk slid down the central axis to its end. A slow-motion simulated explosion went off and a bright purple ray shot through the center, ricocheted off the overhead mirror, and stabbed out into space beyond the fringe of the holotank image.

"But those nuclear devices were supposed to be for thrust!" Anna whispered. "For *thrust*! The overhead mirror was going to be our primary solar collector!"

"{{THAT IS A POSSIBLE SECONDARY APPLICATION.}}"

"Secondary application!" Anna screamed, realizing that her emotion would be completely lost on the voice-recognition software. "It was supposed to be the *only* application! That's what the *Kibalchich* was put up here for!"

The computer waited for her to ask a direct question, but she didn't feel like speaking. Instead, sobbing, Anna let herself drift in the command center. Though her body was weightless, she felt as if a planet-sized brick had been hung around her neck.

Nightmare demons kept rearing up at her in her quarters, jerking her conscience back and forth. Her grief and dismay at Rurik's death had changed into outrage at him and his betrayal. He had known all along that her work was only of secondary importance to the people who ran the *Kibalchich*—the ones who *really* ran it. Her work, her dreams, had been just a cover—something to distract everyone.

Stepan Rurik had known all along, and he had held her and caressed her and let her tell him about her ideas. All the while he had allowed her to go on thinking those things, knowing they would never happen.

Yet he was so devoted to that brutal little secret about the colony that he had refused the last order from Earth. Rurik had, in effect, forced them all to go into sleepfreeze so he could avoid that one command. It had turned him into a murderer, driven him to suicide. There were eleven KGB representatives aboard the *Kibalchich*, and Rurik had taken it upon himself to dispense justice. Didn't he trust the other two hundred people aboard to have some sense? Even if Cagarin had taken over the station, he wouldn't have lasted. Everyone else aboard had come for the same reason that had called Anna Tripolk.

As the days went by she watched the people from *Orbitech 1* take away her sleepfreeze chambers—another step in dismantling her hopes for a Mars colony. She remembered the other people who had died, how Ramis and Dr. Langelier had awakened her from deep sleep on a whim, though they had no better future to offer.

This would not have happened if Rurik had followed his damned orders and gotten rid of *Orbitech 1*. The anger

and betrayal made her want to lash out, and she had so
many targets to choose from.

Now she entered the command center again. After the
computer had verified her identity and again sealed all the
access doors, Anna Tripolk strapped herself in the command chair that had once been Rurik's.

"Computer, I am commander of this station, correct?"

"{{AFFIRMATIVE.}}"

"Commander Rurik had access to the directed-energy
weapon, did he not?"

"{{FULL IDENTIFICATION NEEDED TO ACCESS THAT IN-
FORMATION. PLEASE PLACE YOUR HAND ON THE GENE-
TICHECK.}}" Anna complied and the computer responded,
"{{AFFIRMATIVE. COMMANDER RURIK WAS GRANTED AC-
CESS TO DETONATION SEQUENCE ALEXANDER.}}"

"And since I am now commander of this station, do I also
have such access?"

The computer checked through the chain of logic. "{{AF-
FIRMATIVE.}}"

Anna Tripolk closed her eyes and let a breath out between her teeth. "Good. That is very good."

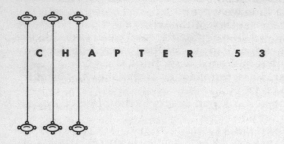

CHAPTER 53

The *Miranda* held dark memories for him. Duncan McLaris had thought he would never see the ruined shuttle again, but now he was riding inside it. This time, instead of fleeing death at *Orbitech 1,* he was voluntarily going back to the L-5 industrial colony—going back to Brahms.

This time he rode with Cliff Clancy. For the first half day, Clancy kept peering out the restored portholes, overjoyed to be back in space. He reveled in the triumph of his yo-yo invention, which appeared to be working exactly as he had imagined. Clancy kept clapping him on the shoulder, full of anticipation.

McLaris remembered Stephanie Garland, the pilot who had not been able to land on the Moon. He had a flash of memory, picturing Garland's body torn and impaled by jagged strips of the *Miranda*'s hull. He had only been half conscious then—why did he remember everything with such cursed clarity?

Cliff Clancy had been there at the crash, too. The construction engineer seemed to know what McLaris was thinking. "Last time we were both here, Duncan, seems to me I was pulling you out of the wreckage."

McLaris forced a smile. "I was in pretty bad shape. And one of the things that confused me to no end was wondering what in the hell an *Orbitech 2* construction jock was doing on the Moon." Clancy laughed at the comment. But in truth, McLaris had been concerned with that for only a moment. He didn't like to remember. It had been a dark time—something best left to nightmares.

It made him think of Jessie too much.

McLaris pushed up from his seat and peered out one of the ports. Above them, mounted with heavy support struts and jury-rigged controls through the hull, the *Miranda*'s rocket engines would fire and give them braking thrust so they wouldn't smash into *Orbitech 1* like a bullet.

McLaris tried to force himself not to think about the absurdity of it all. *A giant yo-yo.* And being so close to Clancy in the cramped compartment made it unwise for him to worry about the situation out loud. He could not see the long weavewire hauling them in. He wondered how they would ever know if the fiber somehow broke and left them to drift forever in a distorted orbit around the Earth. He tried to push the thoughts from his mind. It was too much like arguing about how many angels could dance on the head of a pin.

Clancy kept in touch with his people at Clavius Base through the communications interface. He looked for any excuse to call down to them, especially Shen. But he seemed to be accomplishing a lot, still managing his crews, even at this distance.

Wiay Shen's voice came over the link. Her responses were beginning to lag, indicative of the small but noticeable light delay. "Our last Doppler reading confirmed your acceleration, Clifford. You haven't deviated one part in a million. Pretty steady machinery they got up there. How's it feel to be a fish on a line?"

"Don't know. I never went fishing."

"Never?" Shen's voice sounded surprised. "Clifford, you're culturally deprived. I'll have to take you, next time we're back—" She cut herself off, as if realizing what she had been about to say. The awkward silence lasted for a moment.

McLaris interrupted, calling across to Clancy. "Ask her how *Orbitech 1* is taking all this. Is Brahms setting up a reception or what?"

"There hasn't been this much excitement since construction on *Orbitech 2* began. Remember, the Filipinos sent out their own representatives almost two weeks ago— that Dr. Sandovaal character and his assistant. They're practically on top of L-5. The *Aguinaldo* has declared a national holiday. When you all get there it'll be like a family reunion."

McLaris remembered how bothersome he had always found family reunions to be. He turned away from the flatscreen. Shen and Clancy's constant communication sometimes gnawed at him—it reminded him how he would never talk to his wife Diane again. But that was only part of it. Now that he had been traveling for two and a half days, now that they were almost to *Orbitech 1*, the self-doubts began to bubble into his consciousness. The last thing in the world he needed was time by himself to sit and think. That proved far more dangerous than Clancy's engineering problems. He kept asking himself why he had volunteered to come.

It's easy to sign up for the Foreign Legion when you're sitting in an armchair.

McLaris tried focusing his eyes on the two holes in the wall opposite him. Only two and a half days ago the acceleration chairs had been fastened to that wall, secured to the *Phoenix* by protruding bolts. Soon after the weavewire had yanked them off the lunar surface and *Orbitech 1* had started reeling them in, he and Clancy had moved the seats to where they were now for the gut-wrenching deceleration when the *Miranda*'s engines blasted one last time.

He kept picturing Jessie in her enormous space suit. *I am brave!* she had said.

McLaris let his arm fall to his side; a startling jangle of musical notes rang out. Clancy glanced over his shoulder, smiled with amusement, then returned to speaking with Shen.

McLaris lifted Jessie's battered old "keeburd" from the deck. Besides a few changes of clothes and the d-cubes he had accumulated at Clavius Base, the programmed keyboard was the only personal item he had brought with him to *Orbitech 1*. It was useless, sentimental . . . and absolutely necessary to him. There were too many memories, too many demons to slay once he got back aboard *Orbitech 1*. He needed every tie to the past, every tangible object that meant something to him.

The fresh start on Clavius Base had brought him back from personal damnation. His horror and guilt had abated in the last two months, once Philip Tomkins had given him important work to do. He had rebuilt a defensible wall of self-esteem, brick by brick.

He clutched Jessie's keyboard close to his breast. He activated one of the preprogrammed routines, and listened to "Twinkle, Twinkle, Little Star," conjuring up visions of his daughter plinking along and trying to chase the lighted keys with her fingers in an imitation of playing the song. Clancy ignored the music as McLaris closed his eyes and drew in a deep breath of the warm, recycled air. The Moon was no place to leave the only link he had to his past.

He would need all his strength to confront Brahms.

Even Hitler had executed less than 10 percent of his own people. By that criterion, Brahms stacked up against the worst of them. McLaris wondered if anyone really thought Roha Ombalal had been responsible for the RIF.

Damn you! Brahms had shouted to them as Stephanie Garland had pulled the *Miranda* out of the docking bay and launched it toward Clavius Base. McLaris couldn't imagine that Brahms would ever forgive him.

A cold thought struck McLaris. Had he been the factor that had forced Brahms over the edge? Had he pressed Brahms into a no-win situation by taking the only shuttle, the last hope of *Orbitech 1*? McLaris did not feel strong enough to shoulder any more blame.

But Brahms would be waiting for him, nevertheless.

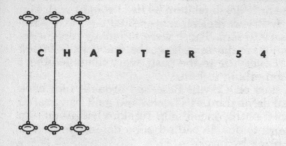

CHAPTER 54

The command center around her was empty, comforting. Anna Tripolk closed her eyes, letting relief mask her fear. The decision rested strong in her—the one path out of her maze of contradictory thoughts.

When the callous thieves had come on board the *Kibalchich*, Anna realized more than ever the implications of the remaining colonies joining forces. The technicians had already dismantled three sleepfreeze chambers and hauled them back to Brahms. The weavewire yo-yo from Clavius Base was hurtling toward *Orbitech 1*, and she had heard a message about Filipino emissaries from the *Aguinaldo* riding solar sails and bearing down on L-5 even now.

Without pause for discussion or even consideration, Anna Tripolk felt left out on the fringe, brushed away while everyone else made decisions for their future. Things were getting away from her, moving too fast and out of control. She clenched her hands so that the fingernails bit into her palms. Her arms felt cold. "Computer, raise the temperature in the command center!"

Anna was thankful that only Dr. Langelier and the Barrera boy still remained on the *Kibalchich*. Brahms had recalled the other techs to work on the stolen sleepfreeze chambers over there, but Anna knew they would return to take more. She had no doubt that if *Orbitech 1* needed them, Brahms would pull out the sleeping Soviets and leave them to die on the infirmary floor.

Brahms had shown his ability to justify anything he required.

Barrera and Langelier had insisted on staying here, though. Brahms had asked them to return, but they had both requested to remain longer. By now they had been on the *Kibalchich* for weeks, eating Soviet supplies, reveling in their complete freedom. No wonder they did not wish to return, and Brahms did not seem inclined to press the issue. As commander of the *Kibalchich*, Anna felt well within her rights to send them back—even toss them out of the airlock if it pleased her. But she knew what would happen—a swarm of Americans would then ransack the Soviet station in vengeance, all with the approval of Director Brahms.

Anna drifted around the control room, pushing against the bulkhead to change directions. She reached out and grabbed the back of the command chair to pull herself down. Once strapped in, she turned to the holotank surrounding the station's massive central axis. Consoles were set into the curving walls. Green ready lights outlined the dim screens, indicating their dormancy. The voice-activated main computer made it unnecessary for her to identify each separate station. When other people filled the command center, each working their own tasks, they used the old-fashioned direct-input method. But Anna Tripolk was alone now. The computer heard only her voice.

Alone.

She drew in a deep breath. She was alone with everything that had shaped her life, all her memories.

She spoke toward the holotank. "Computer: flashback image sequence from catalog—Novosibirsk, two years ago, spring. Display outside, then laboratory views. Whatever you have on record."

Instantly the scene appeared in the holotank, the three-dimensional image overflowing into the control room. A flat river plain extended for miles about; squat buildings dotted the horizon; a crisp, cloudless sky seemed to envelop her; the lead-gray Ob River did not appear to be moving at all. She saw the buildings, the industry, the *Akademgorodok* where all the researchers had settled.

The image swept Anna into the main physics laboratory —scores of people milled around a new-generation tokamak, talking and smiling with excitement. But this was a standard image from the computer's library, emphasizing the powerful magnetic fusion prototypes. She didn't expect to see any highlights of her own biochemical work.

Anna spoke again, in a whisper. "Computer, same time, display Moscow, then dachas."

The scene transported her to the center of Red Square. Graceful minarets, impossible arches, colorful Tatar-inspired onion domes. . . . Thundering footsteps pounded past her as if she stood in the center of a parade—standard images again, May Day, crowds of bright uniforms. She could almost feel the cool spring air, but she realized it was just the chill in the command center.

Tears streamed down her face as the holotank transported her across her homeland. Everywhere she saw the same scene: hard-working Russians, or Estonians, or Kazakhs, or Belorussians, or any of the other nationalities, proud of their work and unwavering in their values . . . at least according to the documentary films the *Kibalchich* had stored for years to come.

She drew back from the holograph, allowing it to play in front of her, instead of being immersed in its progression. *What is left of it all, then?* she wondered. *And what's to come of us with all this activity on the other colonies?*

She knew the answer—she only had to look at the demise of the Third World nations before the War. Entire cultures swept away, integrated into the superpowers' way of life, run over by an economic steamroller.

Orbitech 1, with Curtis Brahms at its head, was setting itself up as the center for a new order, a new America to swallow up all the other colonies. With Clavius Base and now the Filipinos joining forces, nothing would remain of the old ways, the dreams she and others like her had had. She would not allow her dream of the Mars colony to be stolen away once again.

Who could know what Brahms's new order would decree about what remained on the *Kibalchich*, the assets that could be distributed to the highest bidder? Her station at L-5 would become nothing more than a salvage yard to fuel the collective power of the other groups that were even now joining forces.

Tears flowed down her face.

Orbitech 1. She had an out.

Now Anna knew that from the first construction of the *Kibalchich*, the designers had prepared for the possibility of outside aggression. They had taken advantage of the *Kibalchich*'s configuration to include their weapon.

The other colonies could not be permitted to join forces against her. Earth still smoldered by itself as a testimonial.

She had a chance to prevent that from ever happening again.

She couldn't.

But yet . . . she had to.

Anna's voice wavered when she spoke again. "Computer: begin detonation sequence Alexander."

"{{AFFIRMATIVE. PLEASE PROVIDE AUTHENTICATION.}}"

"Authentication phrase *Narodnaia Volia.*"

"{{GIVE CODE NUMBER.}}"

"Eighteen eighty-one."

Anna allowed herself a small smile at the quaintness of the procedure. The *Narodnaia Volia,* or "the People's Will," was the radical group to which the original Nikolai Ivanovitch Kibalchich had belonged—the group that had assassinated Tsar Alexander II in 1881. Which had led to Kibalchich's arrest and imprisonment. Leaving him free to dream of rockets carrying people to the stars. . . .

"{{DETONATION SEQUENCE ALEXANDER INITIATED. PLEASE STATE SPECIFIC OPTIONS.}}"

Anna's voice tightened, but she swallowed and kept going, reciting what she had planned after studying the specifics of the weapon. "Prepare for a one-burst sequence, use normal procedure. Limit yield strength to seventy-five kilotons. Firing coordinates to follow. For now, prepare a radar lock on the object approaching *Orbitech 1* from lunar orbit."

"{{AFFIRMATIVE. ALEXANDER SEQUENCE IS ACTIVE. WEAPON PREPARATION ACTIVE AND PROCEEDING. DETONATION IN TWO HOURS.}}"

A warning siren ran up and down the scale, startling Anna. As she recovered her position, she kept her eyes riveted on the holotank as an image of the yo-yo vessel came into view, reconstructed by Doppler radar imagery. The craft's image shined a false hue.

As she watched it hurtle toward *Orbitech 1*, she imagined the sequence of events occurring deep within the *Kibalchich*: robot arms removing a thermonuclear warhead from storage at the bottom of one of the pools of water. The nuclear devices had been undetectable, their characteristic neutron and gamma emissions hidden by the water that covered them, and masked by the tons of shielding rock that filled the outer, nonrotating hub. The preprogrammed robot arms automatically prepped the warhead—a two-hour sequence necessary to activate its detonation mechanism, set the yield to seventy-five kilotons, and perform other detailed checks. And after the warhead had made the journey down the central core to below the massive solar shield, it would detonate, channeling its awesome energy up the *Kibalchich*'s core to power an x-ray laser. The *Kibalchich*'s mirror would provide the final link. Even as the mirror itself melted under the huge energy flux, it would direct the coherent radiation toward its target. Down at the opposite end of the core, the solar shield would provide partial protection from the nuclear explosion; the tons of lunar scrap rock in the outer hub would provide the remainder. The system was designed to be used only once—it was worth the two-hour wait.

The approaching yo-yo vessel from the Moon would be stopped by the x-ray laser, vaporized by gigajoules of radiant energy. *Orbitech 1* would probably survive the burst. This action was to stop them from their grandiose plans—a warning shot—not to destroy them.

"History," Anna whispered to herself. "I must make a record for future generations. For what they do not remember, they are doomed to repeat."

* * *

The warning siren reverberated throughout the station. Speakers set into the bulkheads rang out words that at first made no sense. Karen recognized Anna Tripolk's voice.

"There is nothing you can do—I control the command center. Do not attempt to communicate with *Orbitech 1*."

Ramis bolted upright from his nap. "Karen!"

Karen met him outside his cabin. "I don't know what she's doing."

Though he had shorter legs, Ramis passed her by springing up steps three at a time to burst onto the first level. The command center hung above them, up the connecting shaft. Ramis waited for her as she joined him on the lift platform. But when he pushed the controls, the lift refused to function.

"She's deactivated it," Karen said. "And probably the doors up top, too." She felt concern and fear growing in her. Anna Tripolk had never adjusted to her new situation, but kept herself isolated, begrudging any contact. She seemed a bitter woman. But now Anna was apparently doing something that would endanger all of *Orbitech 1*.

Ramis decided to forego the lift platform, and raced up the hand rungs instead. Karen watched him ascend, then hauled herself, rung by rung, feeling her weight drop away as she climbed toward the zero-G center. Ramis floated outside the sealed command center door, banging against the black plasteel while holding a hand grip to keep himself steady.

Karen arrived, panting. "Do you know what's going on?"

Ramis pressed his ear against the metal doors. After a minute, he pulled it off again. He, too, was out of breath from the climb. "I can hear the vibrations through the metal, most of the words. She is deploying some sort of weapon that will detonate in a hundred and twenty minutes. She's going to destroy the yo-yo."

"How can they have a weapon? This is a research station! They're not supposed to—" Karen began to pound on the door, feeling hysterical herself.

Ramis gasped under his breath. "If she is going to fire a weapon at *Orbitech 1*, Dr. Sandovaal and Dobo and the sail-creatures could be hit! They are on their way!"

He spun himself around in a way that made Karen dizzy, then scrambled back down the rungs. He shouted up at her. "I will suit up and go outside. Perhaps I can do something there. Stay here and try to talk to Anna! You must stop her if you can."

Karen interrupted, listening to her voice grow shrill. "She is locked inside, Ramis! She controls all *Kibalchich* communications from there! And this weapon—my God, Ramis. If she can destroy *Orbitech 1*, then it's probably powered by a nuke."

"Then I must get outside and contact *Orbitech 1* and Dr. Sandovaal directly. I'll use my suit radio."

Karen put her fingers against her forehead. She wasn't good at making snap decisions. She had never seen herself in a leadership role. "Ramis, if she hears you radio a warning, then she'll target *Orbitech 1* instead of just the yo-yo. What are we going to do?" Panic grew like a living entity in her. She bit her lips, using the sharp pain to focus her thoughts.

"Get back inside as soon as you can. If the weapon detonates in two hours, you'll be unprotected from the blast— you'll fry if you're caught out there."

Ramis crooked one elbow over a rung and called back up at her; Karen had to strain to hear his voice. "Dr. Sandovaal was very . . . important to me, and to everyone on the *Aguinaldo*. What good is living if my family dies?"

Karen pushed back, speechless. The command center door pressed unyielding against her back, sending her drifting in the shaft. "Ramis . . ."

But he turned down the corridor out of sight, back into the torus. Karen wasn't sure if he was ignoring her or if he hadn't heard her.

But he had left her alone to try and reason with Anna Tripolk.

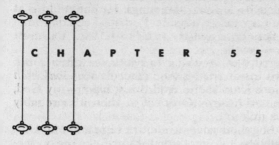

CHAPTER 55

ORBITECH 1 ■ DAY 72

Brahms stood with his arms crossed, staring down at the sleepfreeze chamber. Someone had cleaned the lab room, making everything ready for his inspection. Overhead, an air-recirculating vent whirred to life. The black technician saw that Brahms was smiling, and smiled back. The tech placed his hands palms-down on the surface of the chamber.

"So, you think it's all ready?" Brahms asked. He squinted his eyes and poked a hand inside the chamber, feeling the rough material of the resting area. It didn't seem a very comfortable place to spend a great deal of time.

"Well, we repaired the electronics that were sabotaged. That part was easy. Everything else seems hooked up properly, as far as we can tell. That Soviet doctor lady was as much help as a disease. Wouldn't tell us anything. But with Dr. Langelier's help translating some Russian records, we figured it all out. The technology is straightforward." The technician spread his hands, still smiling.

Brahms was annoyed that the tech did not wear an ID tag, and even more annoyed at himself for not being able to remember his name.

Nancy Winkowski scowled at the tech. "So, it's ready then? That's what the director asked."

Brahms glared. She did well in her duties as watcher, but sometimes she got carried away. Cowed, Winkowski fell silent. Brahms looked at the technician, waiting.

The man raised his eyebrows. "It's ready as far as I can tell. We were able to bring back a few vials of the serum they used to put themselves under. I'm not a biochemist, but the lab tells me it's something to slow down the metabolism. We brought along the low-freezing blood substitute and hooked everything up. Of course, people aren't standing in line to volunteer for testing it." He let out a nervous laugh.

Brahms nodded. "We may not need it after all. If everything else works out right." He extended his hand to the tech, who shook it uncertainly. Brahms glanced up at the chronometer on the wall. "Good work, but I have to go now. The *Phoenix* is due to arrive soon. And who knows when the Filipino solar sails will get here." He realized he was talking to himself.

"Please keep me informed." He gestured to Winkowski. "Come with me." They left the lab space at a brisk walk. He saw scrub marks on the walls—fresh patches where more graffiti had been removed. Winkowski knew enough to remain silent as he pondered.

Everything was happening all at once. The yo-yo arriving from Clavius Base, bringing McLaris back. The sleep-freeze chambers ready for testing. The Filipino sails coming around for their rendezvous to take a package of the weavewire.

"Is the weavewire ready for delivery to the *Aguinaldo* representatives?"

Winkowski looked filled with her own importance, which made Brahms think less of her. "It is easier to let the Filipinos take a weavewire unit back with them than to store the unbraided strands. They can use their own raw materials. They don't have the capability on their colony to construct a new unit—"

"Yet."

"That's right, not yet. According to their transmissions, it will take a few weeks to mature enough sail-creatures for their return trip. During that time we should be able to query them about bioengineering techniques so we can duplicate their efforts. The staff insists it would be too difficult to learn through holotank transmissions. Besides, Sandovaal wants to check on the embryos the Barrera boy brought with him, to make sure we're taking care of them properly."

Brahms cut her off impatiently. "The colony has been informed of the arrival time for the *Phoenix?* Broadcast ready for the PA holotanks and for transmission to the other colonies? You don't know how I hate to have everybody watching all the moves I make!"

"It's ready. My sense is that we're all getting pretty excited about the arrival."

Brahms pondered that. "Yes, won't it be wonderful to have McLaris back?" He clamped his lips together to quell further sarcasm. "Have you tracked down Terachyk yet?"

Winkowski averted her expression. "Nobody seems to know where he's gone. All I get is a bunch of people who can't remember if they've seen him or not."

Brahms felt the anger overwhelming his anxiety again. "It sure would be nice if I could find out where my own chief assessor is. I hope he's not hiding under the covers at a time like this."

He picked up the pace toward the docking bay. "Come on. We've got a lot happening today."

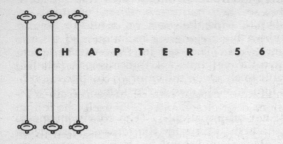

CHAPTER 56

Ramis ran over a final suit check as the airlock hissed and cycled. He felt the suit ballooning around him, the soft sounds of outgassing. The airlock seemed to take forever.

Through his helmet, he heard a muffled voice coming from the PA system—maybe Karen had learned how to use the intercom—but the words faded into silence as all the air left the chamber. He had cut himself off. Karen would have to come outside and use her own suit radio if she needed to contact him, or else get inside the command center.

The outer airlock swung open, leaving him with a dizzying depth of stars in front of his faceplate. The view spun around as the *Kibalchich*'s torus rotated. The broken rubble shield cast flickering spots on the hull, like leaf shadows on a forest floor.

Breathing shallowly, Ramis pushed out of the chamber and worked his way over the *Kibalchich*'s hub. The graph-

ite axis rod extended from the mirror above to the massive
solar shield below.

Ramis could feel a strange sensation in his suit, against
the hull where his feet were anchored. It seemed as if the
Kibalchich vibrated to a new motion; the central graphite
rod seemed to jitter with the resonance. Anna Tripolk had
activated some sort of weapon, whatever it was. He
whirled around, then caught himself to keep from spinning. The airlock door closed and sealed itself—he felt an
enormous "click" through contact with the hull. Ramis
bent forward and punched the Cyrillic OPEN switch above
the airlock.

Nothing.

Undaunted, he flipped the manual override switch.
Again nothing. Anna had locked him out.

Ramis felt cold, and his stomach tightened. As Karen had
reminded him, if he couldn't stop the weapon, or at least
get back inside before it detonated, he would fry from the
radiation.

Ramis flipped up his radio options and began to key in
Orbitech 1's emergency frequency, but the clipped voice
of Anna Tripolk burst in over his suit radio. "Ramis Barrera, I have sealed open all the inner airlock doors on this
station. You can not reenter. If you issue any sort of warning, I will destroy *Orbitech 1*. The blood of more than a
thousand people will be on your hands."

Ramis thought rapidly. He still had the weavewire to get
back to *Orbitech 1*—but without the dolly to ride over, he
might as well have nothing. Which left him with Jumping.
He quickly shelved that idea. He had full air tanks, but it
would take him too long—the weapon would detonate
before he got there. He had less than two hours.

Ramis ground his teeth together, but he didn't bother to
respond to Anna. Nothing more came over the radio. He
boosted himself up over the hub and steadied himself
against the rod holding the mirror. Everything seemed
serene. The stars burned as ice-cold pinpoints; the great
wheel of the *Kibalchich* rotated underneath its rocky
sheath.

Across the depth of space, he looked toward the bright
spot of *Orbitech 1*. Something hung in his way, eclipsing

the stars. It seemed like a thick fog, a thin film blocking the view—

Dr. Sandovaal! The sail-creatures!

Ramis squinted and tried to find the sail-creatures' stubby bodies in the gigantic cluster—that would tell him how near they were. But it was like trying to find a rice husk at midnight in a soccer field. They were floating in, oblivious to what was about to happen, and he had no way to warn them. Anna would be listening to any transmissions.

Until it hit him that he had an easier way.

One hour and twenty minutes remaining—it seemed an eternity to her. But nothing could stop her now, not with Ramis Barrera locked outside, and Karen Langelier banging on the sealed doors to the command center and whimpering into the intercom.

"Anna, please! You don't know what you're doing." Langelier's voice echoed through the command center.

Because of emergency safety programming, the computer refused to shut off the intercom during detonation sequence Alexander, claiming that it must remain open. Anna tried to ignore Langelier's whining. "Don't you have any respect for other lives?"

That angered her. Any respect for other lives? She snapped, "I am not the one who murdered a helpless man in sleepfreeze through simple incompetence! Think of all the people dead on Earth. I am not the one attempting to band together with the remaining survivors in space to wipe out the people on the *Kibalchich*. This station had a grander purpose than anything your people will ever attempt. I will not let you ruin it."

Anna shuddered and ignored everything else the other woman shouted back at her. The discussion would sap her strength, redirect her anger, and possibly raise some doubts. She could not afford that.

Anna checked the tall central holotank, keeping a close eye on the progress of the yo-yo vessel making its way up from the Moon. It sped onward, its acceleration constant, less than two hours from its destination. The delicate tracking mechanisms on the *Kibalchich* kept the target in focus.

If she timed it right, the *Phoenix* would be destroyed with minutes to spare.

She tried to imagine what the people of *Orbitech 1* would think. Would they realize her position? Would they find that her decision was the only way she could prevent a corrupting system from rising again? She fought for her own future, to keep the *Kibalchich* from becoming expendable. Generations from now, the Soviets might herald her as their savior.

They were nice thoughts, but she knew the Americans would never see it that way.

The computer interrupted her musings. The command center diagnostics blinked, catching the side lobe of a radio signal being broadcast from just outside the *Kibalchich*. Anna snapped at the control system, "Increase the gain—subtract all noise." She hissed under her breath. "I warned him!"

Ramis's voice came over the speakers for just a few seconds. She could not make out what he said—he spoke gibberish, babbling nonsense words. Then he fell silent. "Computer, translate!" she said. "Is he speaking some sort of code?"

"{{WORKING.}}"

A minute passed. Ramis did not rebroadcast. "Computer! What did he say!"

"{{UNABLE TO TRANSLATE. UNDERGOING HEURISTIC PROGRAMMING—}}"

"Computer, what was the target of his broadcast? *Orbitech 1*?"

"{{NO KNOWN TARGET. ANGULAR PARAMETERS ONLY: 0.006 RADIANS AZIMUTH, NEGATIVE 0.8226 RADIANS POLAR.}}"

"Display!" she said, growing frantic. How was she supposed to make sense out of some coordinate numbers? The computer showed a three-dimensional grid emanating from the *Kibalchich*, with a narrow cone of Ramis's broadcast extending away from the station, nearly straight toward Earth.

But why? Nothing on Earth could help him. If he was lucky, some amateur radio operator might pick up the signal, but to what purpose? Had the Filipino boy gone crazy? Did he hope that someone on Earth would relay the message to *Orbitech 1*? Not if he spoke nonsensical gibberish.

"Anna, please listen to me!" Karen Langelier's voice burst out of the intercom speakers.

"Be quiet!" Anna shouted.

The sudden stillness in the control room closed around her, making Anna feel the churning anxiety. Her head pounded, and she found herself breathing shallowly. Why was it so cold in here?

"Computer, raise the temperature in the command center!"

Ramis Barrera's transmission had upset her. She didn't know how to respond. Anna struck the arm of the command chair with a fist. "Who is it? What is he saying?"

C H A P T E R 5 7

L - 5 ■ DAY 72

It was not the hissing sound of static that brought Luis Sandovaal out of his sleep inside the sail-creature's core. He had been dreaming of airships flying over Baguio City in the summer heat. But he immediately snapped awake upon hearing the clipped, high-pitched sounds of a message being shouted in Tagalog.

Tagalog!

It seemed like a dream. Sandovaal blinked open his eyes, not quite believing that he was hearing his native Filipino tongue.

"—if you can hear me! Dobo, Dr. Sandovaal—this is Ramis. Steer away from L-5! Somehow, you must get away. The *Kibalchich* plans to destroy *Orbitech 1* with some sort of weapon. Save yourself and warn *Orbitech 1*! Please hear me—I cannot risk transmitting again. Holy Mother Maria, watch over all of us."

The transmission cut off.

Sandovaal drew in deep breaths. It was not a dream. He

glanced at the radio, bringing his head up from the soft wall of the sail-creature's body. His helmet distorted the view, but he did not dare sleep without his suit, since even a small leak in the sail-creature's cyst would destroy the fragile internal environment.

Sandovaal yanked off his helmet and listened to the radio speaker, raw and unfiltered from the bone-conduction circuit in his helmet. He heard little hissing or static. That was nothing unusual, but still . . . had he really heard Ramis's voice?

Holy Mother Maria . . .

The boy had never much embraced Catholicism, but Sandovaal remembered the day that his parents had been killed in the accident. The boy had stood with his head bent down, President Magsaysay holding his shoulders, and had wiped a single tear from his face. It seemed to usher in the era of rebellion, his assertion that there was nothing on the *Aguinaldo*—or in the universe—that could stop him in his quest to prove himself.

Holy Mother Maria.

Sandovaal punched up the direct communications link and discovered that it was already on. "Dobo, wake up!"

"I am awake, Dr. Sandovaal," came Dobo's reply. "That was Ramis on the radio. What are we going to do? We will be over the center of the Lagrange well in an hour."

If Dobo had heard the transmission, too, then Sandovaal was not imagining things. He scowled, already burying himself in the problem. "Let me think, Dobo."

He did not bother quizzing his assistant on the consequences of possible decisions. He would have to decide for himself. Dobo would look to him for answers—and Ramis himself was obviously hoping that Sandovaal could rescue them all. The boy would never expect a proud and brave Filipino like Sandovaal to heed the warning he had issued.

Sandovaal drew in a deep breath and smelled the humid musk of wall-kelp. He reached out and switched on the outside monitor. The sail-creatures moved slowly enough that he could not risk a rash decision—any alteration in trajectory would take a long time to correct. He pondered what he could do that would have a suitable . . . flair.

At the moment, the cluster of sail-creatures were headed for a point just above the ecliptic plane, where they would perform a final tacking to stop their motion relative to the L-5 gravity well. The movement was programmed into the flight computer that controlled motion stimulus to the mosaic of creatures. *Orbitech 1* would be ready to send out its emissaries with MMUs to help the two of them exit from their sail-creatures and to package up the dormant nymphs for the return journey.

Sandovaal swung the exterior camera around and surveyed the broad armada of sails. They were oriented perpendicular to the Sun, already slowing in their journey, converting kinetic energy to potential. Soon, the computer-generated signal would initiate one last command, to tack to a slow drift. Sandovaal inched the camera to a view of *Orbitech 1* and panned across to the torus of the *Kibalchich*. Everything seemed tranquil and unmoving.

Save yourself and warn Orbitech 1! Ramis had called. The boy was not one to make up fanciful stories. Sandovaal knew he could take him at his word.

He bumped the radio around the different bands, but found no sound of danger, no other cries of alarm. Everyone seemed unaware of the *Kibalchich*'s plans, and no one else could have understood Ramis's warning in Tagalog. He heard only the banter between the colonies over Con-Comm—news about the ascent of the *Phoenix* and the imminent arrival of the Filipino sail-creatures. He thought about *Orbitech 1*: innocent victims. They didn't even know what was coming. Once again, Luis Sandovaal would save them all.

He stared at *Orbitech 1* and the *Kibalchich* for some time. What he was about to do had worked for his forefathers, many years ago, when they had placed their own feeble longboats between those of two warring nations. He was taking a chance that it would still work now.

Sandovaal punched a new set of directives into the flight computer. Light coursed its way through kilometers of optical fiber, taking the message to sensors in the other nineteen sail-creatures in the mosaic. Sandovaal began to sense the slow, lumbering rotation as the sail-creatures turned away from the irritating shocks. Over several minutes, the sails would reorient themselves, forcing the armada to drift five kilometers below their intended rendezvous point.

Directly into the line of fire.

After three days, the yo-yo vessel seemed hot, claustrophobic, cramped. Outside the thick ports, *Orbitech 1* shone like a bright star, unwavering without atmospheric distortion, and growing closer by the second. The counterrotating wheels on either side of the colony blinked with various service and guidance lights in a well-timed sequence.

The image burned in Duncan McLaris's mind—so much like what he had seen when fleeing the colony more than two months before, stealing the *Miranda* and taking Jessie with him. The memory brought a heavy feeling to his stomach, but he pulled in a deep breath of stale air, focusing on an inner strength he had found over the past couple of months. In less than an hour he would be on board, back where he had started. He didn't know whether to think of it as home or not, but it was a place where he could face his fears and move his life forward again. He tore his gaze away from the port.

Clifford Clancy hummed to himself, checking over the *Phoenix*'s diagnostics. McLaris forced himself to watch the construction engineer as the man prepared for the final maneuver that would slow them to a halt. At times, Clancy's optimism and enthusiasm grated on him; now, though, it gave him strength.

Clancy shot a glance over his shoulder and grinned. "Ready for the big splash?"

McLaris frowned. "Excuse me?"

"Big splash. We'll be going down in history either way, Duncan. If those reconditioned rockets fire enough to bring us to a stop, we've established a way to get from the Moon to L-5. If they don't," he said, shrugging, "we'll take out *Orbitech 1* like a cannonball. We're going over thirty five hundred miles an hour, which is enough to ruin everybody's day." He grinned. "Kind of exciting, isn't it?"

McLaris tried to keep a calm expression on his face. "Most fun I've had in years."

He knew it would get even worse when he finally faced Brahms again.

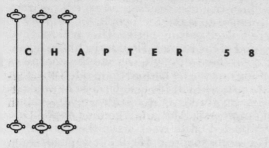

CHAPTER 58

The hallways were free of people, as Brahms marched with his escort to the docking bay. The watchers had been thorough for the last few days. The usual graffiti and petty vandalism confirmed a general aura of unrest, but Brahms had set up maintenance teams to be even more rigorous in cleaning up any sign that all was not well on *Orbitech 1*. He had to put up a good show for Duncan McLaris's return.

He suspected McLaris's arrival had something to do with the growing restlessness of the people. Plenty of other colonists probably felt as he did, still angry at the man who had stolen the *Miranda*. No wonder people were getting worked up, letting off steam. But Brahms had insisted that the watchers maintain order. A sweep of the halls ahead of him removed any chance of an incident.

However, another mood seemed to bubble through the colony over the past few days—one that pleased him. A good director kept in touch with the attitudes of his people, and now he sensed a feeling of enlightenment, of hope. The joining of the colonies again, the sleepfreeze chambers, the *Phoenix*, and even a second expedition from the Filipinos, seemed to show the people on *Orbitech 1* that things were indeed getting better. They had reached the light at the end of the tunnel. They had a future again.

Brahms had seen them through. Despite the enormous decisions weighing on him, he had led them safely through a time of great crisis. He felt his face flush as he smiled.

A yell made its way through the corridor, reverberating in the unusual emptiness. "McLaris is coming back!" One of the watchers peeled off to track down the woman.

"Leave her!" Brahms snapped. He didn't want anything to spoil the triumph of this day, but he wondered why the voice had sounded relieved instead of angry.

Brahms purposely ignored it. When he arrived at the spoke-shaft elevator, he punched the controls himself. He wondered why he felt afraid of McLaris. He held all the cards; McLaris was little more than a sacrificial lamb.

But Brahms still had not decided what he was going to do.

He stepped inside the waiting cubicle and allowed three watchers to follow him. The group remained silent during the ascent. *What does McLaris really want? Why is he coming here of his own free will?*

When they reached the shuttle bay, Brahms pushed out into the huge, weightless chamber. Other people worked at the edges of the bay. They were his people; he trusted everyone here completely. A team of workers waited outside, out of sight, inspecting the other end of the weavewire and the machinery used to reel it in.

He let a smile flicker across his face. All he would need to do was have someone dissociate part of the cable, snip the thread to leave McLaris and the yo-yo floating nowhere for all eternity. But he dismissed that thought as the coward's way out. He would face his enemy in front of all the watching eyes on *Orbitech 1*. McLaris would have to make an accounting for his actions.

As he drifted up into the hanger area, Brahms swiveled to view the control room. A cadre of watchers in green jumpsuits manned the boards. Allen Terachyk was not among them.

Brahms called down to Nancy Winkowski. "Dammit,

track Terachyk on the intercom and tell him to get up here. This is important!"

She nodded and pushed off to the communications console on the wall.

As he floated in, Brahms looked around with a sudden flashback to one of the other times he had been here—the time he and Linda Arnando and Allen Terachyk had watched the recording of a broken and terrified Roha Ombalal reading the speech Brahms had written.

It had been less than three months since the RIF, since an angry mob had killed Ombalal. Luckily, the uprising had not spread, and the watchers had maintained order through the dilemma.

Now the people had hope again. Everything was coming together for them all.

Except for Duncan McLaris; he was the unknown factor. What would the people do? Brahms had kept the colonists occupied, working at their normal schedules. But he didn't want order to break down, especially not now.

Adrenaline rushed through his body. He thought briefly of ordering McLaris executed when he arrived, so the people would have no clear center for their anger, no one to rally around. . . .

No!

Brahms drew in several breaths to calm himself. Despite the risk, he simply did not do cold-blooded acts like that. His action would not have great enough justification—it would look like a personal vendetta, to get back at the man who had humiliated him.

And worst of all, Brahms did not want to leave the people with some sort of a martyr. The Filipinos at L-4 had given him a lesson with their own history—he didn't dare give them an Aquino to rally around. McLaris's situation already reminded him too much of Douglas MacArthur returning to the Philippines: an emancipator.

Inside the bay, the other workers did not notice his mental gymnastics. Brahms decided he would let the people decide what to do with McLaris. After all, if *Orbitech 1* contained the remnants of the American system, he should at least give some semblance of a democratic process.

And if another mob formed, as with Ombalal, they would take care of McLaris anyway. Maybe Brahms would even quell them and once again come across as a voice of reason, a peacemaker, a true leader they could all depend on.

Brahms snapped at the nearest watcher. "I have decided on a change of plans. This is a truly historic occasion. Broadcast a general announcement that anyone who wishes to be present up here for the recovery of the *Phoenix* is welcome, space permitting. They may join me down in the shuttle bay."

Nancy Winkowski's eyes widened. "Mr. Brahms, the security—"

"Do it. Now." He felt suddenly tired, and wiped a hand across his forehead. Exhaustion clung to his bones. Too many things were happening—there were too many decisions, too many memories, but he could not rest yet. *Orbitech 1* depended on him. "Those who cannot attend are urged to view the ceremony on the holotanks."

Winkowski blinked at him, but couldn't seem to form her concern into words. Brahms sighed with tired impatience. "You heard my orders?"

"But, sir, you can't—"

"Do it." He felt exasperated.

Winkowski stood her ground. "Mr. Brahms—you have our allegiance. You know that. But this is suicide. What if the people rally around McLaris and try to overthrow you!"

Brahms laughed, astonished. "McLaris stole the *Miranda* and ran away from us at our time of greatest need."

She looked around and spoke quickly. "Am I allowed to call in reinforcements? Arm the guards—"

"Absolutely not! This is not an armed camp. If we begin to do things like that, people will grow restless. It will become a self-fulfilling prophesy."

Brahms glanced around the shuttle bay, struck by the relatively few watchers present. Winkowski might indeed have cause for concern, but he decided to stick to his beliefs. He had been strong; he had made tough decisions before. But all the time a nagging thought in the back of his mind kept questioning. Was he slipping, after all?

Brahms forced a whisper. "All right, limit the number of people in the shuttle bay to fifty. First come, first served. Get maximum coverage of the arrival over the holotank."

Looking somewhat relieved, Winkowski turned and pushed off for the elevator.

Brahms floated in the bay, waiting for word of the *Phoenix*. The holotank above the main access projected a visual from ConComm. Holocameras displayed the yo-yo as it approached *Orbitech 1*.

Any moment now Brahms expected to see the awkward rockets ignite. He could make out more and more of the old *Miranda*'s hull. It seemed ironic that McLaris would return in the same vessel he had fled in. But instead of a gleaming new spacecraft, the *Phoenix* looked like a broken body—just as McLaris was returning a defeated, broken man.

Anger began to glow in Brahms again. Seeing the wrecked shuttle would probably stir the people up even more. McLaris wouldn't have a chance.

A sudden noise caught his attention. He searched the shuttle bay, saw everyone turn at the same time toward the elevator. Three limp bodies, surrounded by blood spinning in red globules, were pushed into the hangar area. Seconds later a crowd poured from the exit. They must have climbed into the shaft—

He heard more shouting, then a figure pointed at Brahms up in the control bay. The man bent his knees and shot his body upward, followed by a shouting crowd. Brahms froze, unable to understand what was happening.

As they drew close, he recognized Allen Terachyk leading the way.

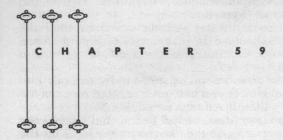

CHAPTER 59

Karen punched at the intercom controls, trying to get *anything* to work, to open up the control room. She ran through different combinations of buttons on the tiny panel. No response.

"{{NUCLEAR DEVICES INTERLOCKED, READY FOR PRIMARY AND SECONDARY DETONATIONS. AUDIO OVERRIDE NOT REQUESTED, COUNTDOWN PROCEEDING. ONE THOUSAND SECONDS TO DETONATION. ANNOUNCEMENTS WILL CONTINUE AT INCREMENTS OF ONE HUNDRED SECONDS UNTIL THE FINAL ONE HUNDRED SECONDS.}}"

Karen kept pounding at the panel; still nothing. She pleaded into the intercom.

"Anna, please don't do this—you can stop it! Think of all the people who are going to die. Think of how that'll harm the future of the entire human race. You're someone who looks toward the future. Don't you believe anymore? We can all work together and make our dreams real."

Karen fell silent for a moment, then continued, this time

with an angry, exasperated tone in her voice. "That's right, don't answer me! If you don't respond, you don't have to justify your actions. Just stay locked inside there and hide. That's what you're good at, isn't it, Anna? Hiding! When the War happens and things look grim, instead of trying to work with the rest of us, you and everyone aboard the *Kibalchich* just go to sleep and wait until somebody else solves the problem. If you hide under the covers, maybe it'll get better all by itself. You're a coward!

"What about your Mars colony? I know that's what your work was about. It can be more than a dream if all the colonies come together. Don't throw everything away!"

The intercom remained silent. Anna Tripolk ignored her. Karen looked wildly around. *What else can I do? Come on, think!*

Were there any other access doors? Was there another master control panel, or a hidden air vent? She swept her eyes around the curving walls. There was nothing. The command center remained sealed.

In the command center, Anna's eyes widened at the appalling stupidity of the Americans. She couldn't speak in her astonishment, but then everything broke through and she screamed into the intercom speaker.

"This is the Mars colony! The *Kibalchich* itself!" Anna sucked in a deep, gasping breath. "How could you be so blind? All the sleepfreeze chambers were here for testing *and deployment!* As soon as we were certain they worked, all two hundred of us were to go into hibernation, except for Commander Rurik and a few monitors."

She pounded her fist on the arm of the command chair. "The warheads we carried were supposed to be used for *thrust*—detonated against the shield to accelerate us out of Earth orbit on a long, slow journey to Mars! Why else would we prepare for such a long period of isolation? Or strengthen our equipment for lateral accelerations? Think!"

The words rolled out. She had always loved talking about her dream, but now the words wounded her as she spoke them. "When we got there, an initial team of colonists would be awakened to set up base camp on the surface. Our reflecting mirror was designed to detach and go into Mars-stationary orbit, where it would focus sunlight onto our colony and down into a power substation. We were going to revive more of us as rapidly as the colony could handle them."

She laughed. "It was beautiful, beautiful! All the while, the rest of you thought we were just a research station here. Mars was going to be ours."

Anna realized she had begun sobbing. At least Langelier had stopped talking. "But now, that will never happen. You have stolen our sleepfreeze chambers. You are ganging up on us. Even my own people had other plans for the *Kibalchich*—as a weapon against your colony! And now I have no choice but to use it, to save the future."

Anna drew in a breath and closed her eyes, shivering with the cold in the room. *Orbitech 1* held seven times as many people as the *Kibalchich* . . . but numbers held no weight. If the death of two people in the yo-yo would pave the way for her dream, then how was Rurik's situation any different? If one death is justified, then why not two? Three?

Or even more? What makes the measure of an ideal, a lifelong dream? Her mind crunched through the rationale, sounding like a different voice in her head. Can a true dream be measured by any number of souls? And how is one death any different from a thousand? *But she was only going to stop the Phoenix.*

It would be on the Barrera boy's conscience then. It was his fault the others would die—not hers.

Anna's head pounded. Her throat felt raw. Her breathing came faster. She was hyperventilating. She was a doctor; she should know what to do. But her vision grew fuzzy with the crushing weight inside her head.

"Computer, display *Orbitech 1* from exterior monitors."

Once again the holotank flashed. *Orbitech 1* appeared as a wavering blob, blurry. Anna wondered if tears had ruined her vision, but after knuckling her eyes she realized the image itself was distorted.

Something big blocked the view.

"Computer, focus! Center on any debris between the *Kibalchich* and *Orbitech 1* that might cause a visual distortion. What is it?"

The holotank blur grew sharp, showing a long dark-green object like an old Havana cigar but with stubs on the side, expanding out to a translucent matte that extended past the holotank's edge. The computer drew back the view. A vast cluster of sail-creatures, like leaf butterflies, all hung together, gracefully settling down into the center of L-5. She saw dozens, connected in a mosaic pattern, immense and graceful.

She had never seen anything so awesome, so beautiful. So fragile.

And as they drifted between the *Kibalchich* and *Orbitech 1*, directly in her line of fire like an impossibly delicate shield, they seemed to stop, to break apart.

Tears streamed down her face as she let out a moan, trying to block the nightmarish vision from her memory. Her lips trembled and she whimpered Rurik's name to herself. She collapsed back into the command chair, shivering, and squeezed her eyes shut, swallowing herself in blackness.

"{{NINE HUNDRED SECONDS TO DETONATION.}}"

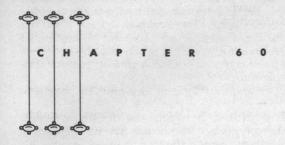

CHAPTER 60

The sight from the external monitor showed the sail-creatures barely moving with respect to the rotating *Kibalchich*. Luis Sandovaal held his breath out of anticipation. The cluster of sail-creature bodies showed as glimmers against the starry sky. Sandovaal caught only a wisp of the organic sails as they extended across the gravity well, aiming for the heart of L-5.

The armada reached past *Orbitech 1* and the *Kibalchich*, like a giant piece of tissue separating two armies. The sails would not appear to be a formidable foe, but the symbolism in the gesture should be clear to everyone on the two colonies. Any act of violence between the *Kibalchich* and *Orbitech 1* would have to destroy the sail-creatures, and would thus be directed against the Filipino people as well.

Sandovaal pressed his lips together in a grim line. "Dobo, I hope you are ready to be brave," he said into the direct communications link. "We will show these people that no one can stake a political claim again. Our actions affect all of the survivors away from Earth. We cannot behave like children on a playground."

It was the only way they were going to survive, he knew. If anyone went against the unified body, then the human race might not survive. *United we stand, and all those other patriotic sayings,* he thought to himself.

Dobo's voice came over the speakers. "I am glad you are here, Dr. Sandovaal. I hope Ramis will be all right."

Sandovaal wondered why Dobo put up with so much from him here, so far away from the *Aguinaldo.* "I am glad you are here, too, Dobo," Sandovaal whispered, but he kept his voice so quiet that he doubted Dobo could hear. Which was what he had unconsciously intended anyway.

Sandovaal watched the monitor. The *Kibalchich* and *Orbitech 1* continued to orbit around L-5. The sail-creatures slid between them, a wall of passive resistance.

Luis Sandovaal switched the monitor from external back to the open intercolony ConComm. *Orbitech 1* personnel yammered about the armada of sail-creatures being off course, but admitted that sails were difficult to steer anyhow. Sandovaal snorted. A separate window on the channel remained devoted to the ascent of the *Phoenix.*

The *Aguinaldo* had done its part in bringing the colonies together. And now Clavius Base had joined in the task. Sandovaal envisioned all the colonies connected by a lifeline of sail-creatures and weavewires. He felt confident that his ploy would work in preventing the *Kibalchich* from any aggressive act—if, in fact, it could be prevented.

Sandovaal felt warm, satisfied that his life's work had played an integral part in the unification. The rest of the journey, and even the remainder of his career back on the *Aguinaldo,* would be spent tying up the loose ends of his work. He punched off the ConComm and moved to transmit a message that he had altered his course on purpose.

But as he reached for the control, his right arm went numb, ice cold. All feeling stopped. He tried to flex his hand—nothing. No pain, no feeling. He started to twist and felt a stab across his rib cage, through his stomach.

Heart attack, he thought. *Strange that I feel no chest pain. I must contact Dobo and let him know. . . .* He felt tired. Thoughts flashed into blackness, as if they were leaking out of his head. *Dobo. Yes, Dobo can carry on.* He had, after all, studied under one of the greatest biological engineers of all time.

Sandovaal coughed. Blood came out of his mouth, bubbling, boiling in tiny swirls and globules in zero-G. He had trouble breathing. Air whooshed past him. His eardrums pounded.

He noticed a small slit in the sail-creature cavity, growing wider. Air rushed out, water vapor crystallized, leaving a thin sheen of ice covering everything in the cavity.

They had flown into the weavewire. . . .

Unlike MacArthur, he knew he would never return.

As he died, Sandovaal cursed himself for his idiotic incompetence.

C H A P T E R   6 1

ORBITECH 1 ■ DAY 72

Brahms exited the control bay with as much grace as he could muster to face the uprising. He held himself rigid to quell his anger and astonishment. His expression was like a mask of ice. The watchers in the control bay had bolted out into the maintenance corridor upon seeing the attackers—mutineers?—charge out the spoke-shaft elevators.

Two bodies drifted in the docking bay, surrounded by droplets of blood. The had murdered two of his watchers! They had *killed* two people.

Brahms forced his outrage down. He wished he had his eyeglasses to hide behind, to make him look dignified.

Allen Terachyk floated up to Brahms. A mass of his supporters followed, and dozens more emerged from the elevator shaft. Terachyk wore a defiant, victorious expression.

Allen Terachyk—his only remaining division leader. They had all failed him—McLaris, Arnando, and now Terachyk. And Brahms himself had RIFed Tim Drury, perhaps the only one worth keeping.

As Brahms watched the approaching group, he drew himself up. He grasped the handhold on the wall, but found it slippery with his sweat. He would not—could not —allow the mutineers to know they had frightened him. It was the easiest way to lose control. He had come so close to bringing things back to normal, and now Terachyk was going to ruin everything. Brahms took a moment to center himself, to clear his thoughts. This was going to be the most difficult negotiation of his life.

The people behind Terachyk pushed off from each other. Brahms recognized a few of them, but couldn't pin down names. The motion sent them spreading out in a pattern that surrounded Brahms, above and below. Two women hit the bulkhead and bounced back out into the shuttle bay, coming in over his head. They must have practiced the effect.

Brahms scanned the faces. Some had their eyes open wide with fear and uncertainty, others carried a righteous anger, some just stared back diffidently. He realized that Terachyk must have contacted the low scorers on the Efficiency Study and convinced them that another RIF was in the making. Perhaps he had also banded together those who had lost friends or family in the first RIF. What most surprised Brahms was that Allen Terachyk had actually done it. And he had chosen a time when the entire colony would be watching.

Brahms had never expected to see Terachyk, who moped about and did nothing but complain and wallow in misery, adopt any kind of cause—especially not one like this.

Terachyk hung in midair, facing Brahms, but a few inches below eye level. In the back of his mind, Brahms faulted him for that—as a psychological advantage, he should have tried to tower over the director. Brahms decided to use it to his own effect.

Terachyk waited until the shuttle bay became silent before he spoke. "It's over, Curtis."

Brahms's mouth twitched. He debated how to play his own hand. "Before the fat lady sings? I appreciate your concern, Allen, but until the *Phoenix* arrives, we don't know for sure we can connect the colonies. Your timing is a little off."

"Nice touch, Curtis—but it isn't going to work this time. Everybody here knows you were responsible for the RIF. It's time to pay the piper."

Brahms widened his eyes in a condescending expression. He used his position to glare down at Terachyk, ignoring the others around him. He felt so weary of all this. "I was responsible? I seem to recall you were there, too, Mister Division Leader Terachyk, and you did nothing to stop it. If you're going to dump blame on me, you'd better take your own share."

Terachyk blinked, caught off balance. "It wasn't me who—"

Brahms pressed his advantage. "Shall we call up the minutes of the meetings and show all these people exactly how much you were involved?" He raised his voice so it would carry to all the other people in the shuttle bay, but he kept his tone even, conversational. He knew the minutes of the meetings would show little or nothing, but the gathered people wouldn't realize that.

He didn't let Terachyk answer. "Why do you insist on harping on the one bad decision and ignoring everything else? Do you think you would have been able to get the wall-kelp from the Filipinos? Do you think you could have gotten the sleepfreeze chambers from the Soviets? Do you think you could have established a weavewire link between us and Clavius Base?"

Brahms knew he was taking more credit than he deserved, but his life was on the line. "Really, Allen. Do you honestly think the other colonies are going to help us, unconditionally, if push comes to shove? What's in it for them? Think! What does an alliance mean if everyone is not a player? The *Phoenix* is on its way, and so are the Filipino solar sails. We've got to have them in with us; otherwise, it will be one Lagrange colony against another—"

"At least we won't have to worry about another RIF, dammit!" Terachyk was losing control.

Brahms felt confidence surge up in him. He tried to make his voice soothing. "Of course not. With everything I've done to help us survive, we'll never have to worry about a RIF again.

"Allen—" Brahms turned to face the other mutineers.

"All of you. We're so close. I can't tell you how sorry I am for the bad decisions that were made in the past. But if we're going to bring in a new civilization, at least make sure we've got all our players in place."

He set his mouth and waited. He hoped he had stalled them long enough to defuse the mob psychology Terachyk had whipped up in them.

The loudspeaker broke the mood. "Attention in the shuttle bay. ConComm reports one minute until *Phoenix* deceleration. We have lost contact with the *Aguinaldo* emissaries, and a salvage crew has been dispatched to recover them. They will rendezvous with *Orbitech 1* shortly after the *Phoenix* arrives. ETA is five minutes."

Brahms spoke up even as the PA clicked off. "Well, Allen? Can you afford five more minutes, or will you bow to anarchy? Why don't we wait and see how this all turns out?" Terachyk set his jaw; Brahms could see the muscles working in his cheeks. Around him, dozens of eyes glittered, staring, angry, uncertain.

Brahms sensed them faltering and tried not to show his relief.

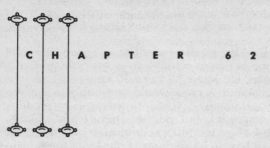

CHAPTER 62

PHOENIX ■ DAY 72

Cliff Clancy rubbed his palms together. His eyes shone with excitement. "Ready, Duncan?"

Duncan McLaris took an instant to whisper, "What if I'm not?"

"Ha, ha—funny man," Clancy said.

"Shouldn't we put our suits on or something?" McLaris asked. He remembered clambering into an unfamiliar space suit once before, watching Stephanie Garland to make sure he completed all his checks properly, helping Jessie into an oversized suit. *Diddy, it's too big!*

"If these engines don't fire like they should, all the suits in the world aren't going to make one whit of difference. May as well stay comfortable." Clancy shifted his position in the deceleration seat. "My suit always smells like dirty socks anyway."

"Huh?" When Clancy did not answer, McLaris checked the straps on his seat. He pulled in a lungful of the stale air. Clancy kept his eyes on the monitor that displayed the countdown. An hour before, *Orbitech 1* had stopped pulling in the weavewire, allowing the yo-yo drift in, but keeping the slack taut for the backward blast of the braking engines.

McLaris felt helpless, dependent on a dozen different people, any one of whom could destroy everything with a careless mistake. He knew all too well how easily people could make mistakes. A crew would be waiting to receive them outside *Orbitech 1,* ready to salvage or rescue—though if the engines failed, neither operation was likely. If nothing else, the "reception committee" would get a grandstand seat to watch the *Phoenix* plow into the shuttle bay.

Clancy cracked his knuckles, as if to distract himself from nagging doubts about the hydrogen rockets he had helped install.

McLaris didn't react, though the noise increased his own anxiety. In his mind he kept playing over possible scenarios of his upcoming reunion with Brahms. Would the man greet him with a handshake, or with an execution squad?

Less than three months ago he had stolen the *Miranda.* Ten percent of the *Orbitech 1* population had been sent out the airlock in a reduction in force. Much had changed.

He tried to keep his mind open, optimistic—both deeds had been done, McLaris had suffered for it, and no doubt Brahms had suffered for his own actions. That was the past. If they wallowed too much in the past, they would never find their future. Now, with the *Phoenix* from Clavius Base, and the Filipino delegation arriving at *Orbitech 1,* he could sense an entire new era about to burst forth—a second stage for human civilization.

Surely Brahms could not hold anything against McLaris for so long.

A voice came from over the ConComm. *"Phoenix,* this is Orbitech 1. We have you at two hundred fifty miles. Begin your deceleration now. You have a ten-second window."

"They're right on the money, Clifford." Shen's voice came over the open circuit. "Do it."

"There are going to be a lot of fireworks in five minutes if this doesn't work." Clancy moved to punch at the screen, ready to override the computer-driven command if ignition was not accomplished.

Hydrogen–oxygen rockets kicked in just as he reached out.

McLaris felt as if he were being squashed by a giant hand —months of lunar gravity had deteriorated his stamina for undergoing acceleration. He rolled his head to one side, and it pushed against the deceleration seats they had mounted on the "ceiling." Clancy continued to stare straight ahead, trying to fix on the control monitors. His face seemed drawn back in a weird mask, a grin twisted all out of proportion by the pull of gravity.

It took an effort to breathe, but somehow Clancy grunted out a comment that McLaris heard even over the roar of the engines.

"Nothing's gonna stop us now!"

CHAPTER 63

Karen pounded on the sealed door to the command center. "Anna!" A smear of blood marked the surface where her raw fists had beaten against the metal. She heard nothing from inside. Anna Tripolk refused to respond at all.

"{{FOUR HUNDRED SECONDS TO DETONATION.}}"

"Please, Anna! Open the door!" Her voice broke as she became frantic. She waited and listened, but heard no other sound from the command center. She had to get inside.

Karen felt trapped. She could not possibly get her suit on in so short a time. Four hundred seconds, less than seven minutes. Ramis was still outside.

"{{THREE HUNDRED SECONDS TO DETONATION.}}"

The computer's voice filtered through the intercom, so she knew she was hearing the inside of the command center. What if Anna had passed out? Had some sort of breakdown? Karen knew the other woman was unstable.

"Anna, answer me! Are you all right?"

She felt like a hypocrite. Anna would not believe any show of concern from her, but Karen at least expected a response. She pounded on the door again.

Karen tried to calm herself, to think of any way possible to get into the room. Anchoring herself against the power lift floor, she pressed her raw palms against the metal and tried to push it aside, hoping it had some sort of emergency override system. But nothing happened. She saw only the intercom, no door controls. And she knew nothing of electronics anyway, nor did she have any tools, even if she could find a way to jury-rig some way to break in.

Okay, think! She ran a hand through her hair. Her reddish curls were straight, soaked with sweat. She found herself breathing faster. There had to be a way to get inside, a back door. . . .

"{{TWO HUNDRED SECONDS TO DETONATION.}}"

In about three minutes, some sort of weapon was going to go off beneath the *Kibalchich* and destroy the *Phoenix.* Or maybe Anna had set it to destroy all of *Orbitech 1* instead.

And Ramis! Anna had locked him outside, left him unprotected. Karen had no way to contact him. He was going to be roasted in the detonation. He was going to die, along with all the other people Anna Tripolk had targeted.

"{{ONE HUNDRED SECONDS TO DETONATION.}}"

"I know what time it is! Stop reminding me!" she screamed into the intercom.

After a brief pause, the computer voice spoke again. "{{AUDIO OVERRIDE ACCOMPLISHED. VERBAL COUNTDOWN DISCONTINUED.}}"

Karen blinked in astonishment and choked with sudden hope. She had to act fast. If the computer was voice-activated, she might be able to communicate over the intercom. The computer would not know, or care, if she was physically inside the room or not.

"Computer, confirm access to command controls!"

"{{AFFIRMATIVE. CONFIRMATION AUTHORIZED BY COMMANDER TRIPOLK.}}"

"Continue verbal countdown! In one-second intervals."

She didn't want to hear how little time she had, but still, she needed to know.

"{{EIGHTY-EIGHT. EIGHTY-SEVEN . . . }}"

Karen pressed her lips up against the speaker. The descending numbers seemed to roll through the lift-platform corridor, washing over her.

"Computer, stop the detonation sequence!"

But the computer did not acknowledge. "{{EIGHTY-ONE. EIGHTY. SEVENTY-NINE . . . }}"

"End the detonation sequence! Cancel! Abort! Halt! Quit! Stop!" Computer language semantics—she had to use the right word. Or perhaps only Anna Tripolk could stop what she had started.

"{{SIXTY-EIGHT. SIXTY-SEVEN . . . }}"

Karen screamed, "Computer, open the command center door!"

The outer elevator door slid open. Karen pushed inside, slammed at the control panel, and floated up from the floor. The door in front of her face hissed open, leaving her to stand weightless on the threshold. The air smelled stagnant with sweat. Inside, the command center was silent, daring her to enter.

Karen grasped the lip of the door and pulled herself forward, finally noticing tiny drops of blood from her battered fists smearing the outside wall. She flexed her hand, not yet feeling any pain in her adrenaline shock, but knowing it would come.

She pushed outward and sailed into the room. Anna lay slumped in the chair. The holotank in the center of the room showed a three-dimensional graphic of the nuclear weapon sitting behind the solar shield.

"{{FIFTY-ONE. FIFTY . . . }}"

"Anna! Stop it!"

Karen hit the opposite wall and bounced back toward Anna. Reaching out, she grabbed at the command chair, and the motion set her feet spinning. She stopped her rotation. "Anna!"

Anna Tripolk's head hung limp.

"{{FORTY-FIVE. FORTY-FOUR . . . }}"

She shouted one more time at the walls. "Computer! Stop the countdown!" Then she added, for good measure, "That's an order!"

The computer answered, "{{ACCESS DENIED,}}" then continued its countdown.

Karen breathed deeply through her nose. The War. And now, the end.

She wondered how much she would be able to feel or sense when the warhead went off. She squeezed her eyes shut.

What if Dr. Sandovaal does not make it? thought Ramis. *He has pulled too many rabbits out of his hat—perhaps he cannot maneuver the sail-creatures fast enough to escape.* Ramis remembered how sluggish Sarat had been at the end of its journey. Ramis didn't even know if Dr. Sandovaal had received his warning.

He tried to open the sealed airlock door one more time, felt the vibration rippling up his arm. Anna Tripolk had locked him out, leaving only Karen inside to reason with her.

The superstructure did not look any more formidable to Ramis than when he had first arrived—had it been three weeks, already? The graphite-composite rod that held up the giant dish mirror jutted above him. *Orbitech 1* gleamed a hundred kilometers away, its details masked by the distance. Ramis turned around and scanned the stars—he could make out the sail-creatures only dimly.

But that did not stop him.

If he had heard Anna correctly through the muffled bulkhead door, then this mirror was the key to the weapon system. It might aim the destructive beam and reflect it to the target, pinpointing either the *Phoenix* or *Orbitech 1.*

Ramis stared at the mirror, bending backward to see better over the curve of his faceplate. His magnetized soles clicked against the *Kibalchich*'s hull as he tested his stretch. He would have to add extra strength in his jump, extend himself to compensate for the brief tug of the magnet's grip.

And if he missed the mirror, he would go flying off into space.

His time was running short. The weapon would detonate within seconds if he believed the clock on his heads-up display. He had no other choice.

The Jumping on the *Aguinaldo,* the trip to *Orbitech 1,* the hundred-kilometer Jump to the *Kibalchich*—all seemed minor compared to this task: a mere twenty-five-

meter hop, no farther than the length of a small rice paddy
. . . yet he was now truly alone: no hull to catch him, no
sail-creature to nudge him, no weavewire to send him
bouncing back if he missed.

Ramis aimed his body carefully, bending deep to get the
most push possible, and jumped as hard as he could. He
shot up and reached out. The ring mirror seemed to be just
beyond his grasp.

He snagged the edge with his curled fingertips and
jerked himself around. He felt his muscles strain with the
sudden change; his arm was nearly yanked from its socket.

"Booto!" he cursed, coughing from the pain and surprised at his own profanity. Wincing, his eyes shut, he
hauled himself to the surface and crawled to the unfin-
ished side. From the impact the mirror bent, rocked
against its support, and began oscillating. He tried to increase the rocking motion by crawling and swaying across
the mirror.

Ramis felt like laughing. Anna would never be able to
aim her weapon now.

Red lights blinked in the *Kibalchich*'s command center. A
siren shrieked up and down the scale, making Karen jerk.

Dozens of windows opened up in the central holotank,
displaying a visual of the giant mirror from different external cameras. Oscillation rates, yaws, periodicity, and pitch
angles all flashed in red. The mirror rocked back and forth,
held in the center by the single graphite rod. The carefully
configured parabolic shape had been bent from some kind
of impact.

"{{UNABLE TO OBTAIN TARGET LOCK. MIRROR WILL RE-
MAIN UNSTABLE FOR SEVENTY-FOUR POINT SIX TWO MIN-
UTES. UNABLE TO DETERMINE AIMING ABILITY OF NEW
MIRROR CONFIGURATION.}}"

The computer fell silent; a second passed.

"{{DETONATION SEQUENCE ABORTED.}}"

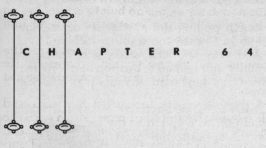

CHAPTER 64

Two minutes of stomach-knotting blasts from the hydrogen–oxygen rockets seemed like an eternity. The *Phoenix* roared in Clancy's ears; he vibrated like a man at a jackhammer. He prayed to himself, all the while thinking about how a transposed digit in the computer codes, an impatient worker affixing one of the gaskets with too little sealant, a measured exhaust angle offset by a fraction of a degree—any trivial mistake could make everything fail.

Visions of catastrophe filled his head, until the burn ended with explosive silence. Tugging back against the connecting weavewire, the *Phoenix* counteracted all the velocity they had built up over three days.

Then they hung still.

The port showed a glowing—unmoving!—vision of *Orbitech 1*. The industrial colony filled the view, only a short distance away. They had stopped themselves with their cobbled-together engines.

Clancy ripped the restraining straps from his chest and

pushed away from the acceleration chair, bellowing like a madman.

Orbitech 1 began pulling the weavewire again, slowly hauling the yo-yo in toward the waiting docking bay.

McLaris looked gray and sick, shaky. Clancy clapped him on the shoulder and helped to unstrap him. "We made it, Duncan! Have that keyboard of yours play something triumphant!"

Clancy felt ready to tackle anything, but McLaris didn't look in any condition to respond to the humor. After rebounding from the opposite bulkhead, and performing a spontaneous jerk-worrble from a popular punk ballet, Clancy managed to reach the communications console. He whistled as he established contact with Clavius Base and *Orbitech 1* on the open channel.

"Howdy, howdy! This is the, ahem, successful pilot of the one and only orbital yo-yo in history! Braking rockets have fired and we are home free. Forget all that stuff about 'the Eagle has landed'—the *Phoenix* has risen!"

Wiay Shen manned the comm unit. Her almond eyes lit up when she saw Clancy's face intact. The full second of light delay burned her image in Clancy's mind. He grinned at her.

"You made it!" she cried. He heard cheers in the background from his crew. "I mean, of course you did. We weren't really worried about you hitting *Orbitech 1*—"

A massive brown face moved into view. Tomkins grinned and gave them a thumbs-up. "Congratulations, you two! Cliff, you can take a rest now, but Duncan's work is just starting."

The *Orbitech 1* ConComm broke in, overriding the transmission from Clavius Base and pushing Tomkins's face off to the side of the screen. *"Phoenix*, we have you positioned and our intercept crew is ready to receive you. We are still having some difficulty contacting the Filipino emissaries—"

"Wiay, do you know what this means?" Clancy smiled smugly as he pushed his own override back to Clavius Base. The *Orbitech 1* people knew what they were doing; inside the *Phoenix*, Clancy and McLaris could do nothing but wait anyway.

Shen's face reappeared in the center of the screen. "Cliff, Dr. Tomkins wants to talk to Duncan. Let him—"

But Clancy couldn't stifle his own enthusiasm. "Once we get aboard *Orbitech 1* and get everything arranged, I'm coming right back home to you. Back to Clavius, I mean—"

"Cliff!"

Wiay's tone forced him to get hold of himself. He sighed. "Uh, go ahead. Put Tomkins on." He swiveled in the cramped compartment. "Hey, Duncan, come on over."

McLaris needed a moment to reply. He hadn't even left the acceleration chair yet. His eyes seemed focused on something imaginary behind the walls of *Orbitech 1*. "Sure, just a minute."

It took an unusually long time for him to move into range of the monitor.

When McLaris began to talk with Tomkins, Clancy noticed that the base manager could not keep his mind on the conversation. He looked very worried.

Outside the viewport, *Orbitech 1* waited for them.

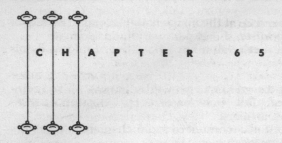

C H A P T E R   6 5

Karen stretched out her hands and cried, "Yes—oh, God, yes!" She reveled in the feeling for uncounted moments. The weapon had not gone off.

Anna Tripolk sat unconscious, still strapped in the command chair. Her face was slack, her eyelids drooping and unaware. She had drawn her knees up to her chest.

The immense shaft jutting through the command center stood before Karen like the cage of a giant monster. The cylindrical holotank hid the central optical fibers that would have driven the x-ray laser. Green lights on control panels burned all around her, bathing the room with a serene glow. Everything had stopped, as if holding its breath. A solitary window in the holotank showed the image of Ramis hanging onto the *Kibalchich*'s mirror, like a fly on glass. What was he doing up there?

She had to tell *Orbitech 1* what had happened. They would be retrieving the *Phoenix* even now. They didn't realize how close to death they had come. Ramis had saved them.

Karen looked up at the image in the holotank. Ramis! Of all other priorities, she had to get him inside first.

"Computer, close all inner airlock doors. Inform Ramis Barrera that he may reenter the station."

"{{CONFIRMED. ALL INNER AIRLOCK DOORS HAVE BEEN SEALED. OUTER AIRLOCKS NOW FUNCTIONAL.}}" The computer paused, then spoke once more. "{{EXTERNAL PERSONNEL INFORMED.}}"

"Computer, access external radio channel."

"{{CONFIRMED.}}"

Karen drifted past the command chair, watching Anna Tripolk but avoiding her at the same time. She called out toward the walls, hoping the computer would broadcast her words.

"Ramis, can you hear me?"

A tired voice came back. "Karen? Has it stopped? Are you inside the command center?"

She perked up. "Yes, I am."

"I am on the mirror. I jumped up here to spoil the aim of the weapon. The mirror is still oscillating, but slowing down. I am getting dizzy. Please tell me the weapon has been deactivated."

Karen wanted to laugh. Of course he would have tried to do something like that. "Yes, we're safe now. Can you get off the mirror?"

"I am near a strut. A minute more and I will be back inside. The computer spoke to me a few moments ago, telling me the airlocks were working again, but I could not move any faster."

After a moment of silence, he spoke again. "Karen, have you heard any word from Dr. Sandovaal?"

She felt exhausted. She wanted him back inside, telling his own story to her. But that could wait. She had forgotten about the Filipino emissaries and their sail-creatures. "No, Ramis. Not in the excitement. Can you see them out there?"

He paused. Karen looked down at the motionless Anna Tripolk, certain that she had had some kind of breakdown.

Ramis's voice came back over the speakers. "I can see the sail-creatures, but they did not go away as I warned them to do. Instead, they seemed to come closer." He made a clicking noise into his radio. "If you have not heard from Dr. Sandovaal, then something must be wrong. I am afraid they might have sailed through the weavewire."

Karen didn't know what to say. She was going to offer to send a message, to try and contact the Filipinos, but Ramis would have been able to do all that with his suit radio.

"I am going to reenter the station to get an MMU. I will go to them."

"Ramis!" The idea sounded crazy, but Ramis would try it anyway. "How much air do you have?"

"I will get a new tank. If I use maximum thrust and forget all about safety factors, I can either get there and back here, or return to *Orbitech 1*. Yes, I can do it."

"Ramis, don't—"

"Do not stop me, Karen."

She waited, hoping he would change his mind, but she knew he wouldn't. "Ramis, be careful—"

"I will be."

She could do nothing to stop him. Not now. After his first flight to *Orbitech 1*, his Jump to the *Kibalchich*, and his leap up to the overhead dish mirror, Ramis made his own decisions. He was too headstrong to listen to anyone else.

Karen relaxed, letting a weight of responsibility drop from her shoulders. She couldn't shoulder so much blame. Everyone did the best they could, in whatever way they found possible. She had done a damned fine job herself, she thought.

Behind her came a small animal cry. Anna Tripolk began to wake up, shivering.

The emotion of the last three months welled inside Karen. Everything seemed to cascade back: her separation from Ray, the War, surviving the RIF, Ramis arriving and becoming her friend, the journey here to the *Kibalchich*. . . .

Karen drifted to Anna Tripolk and grasped her shoulders. Anna looked devastated and helpless. Karen held her close and stroked the woman's hair. Tears came quickly. She didn't know what to say, but she said it anyway.

"You poor dear. It's all right now. Everything will be all right."

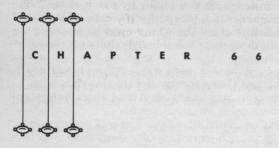

C H A P T E R   6 6

The crowd watched the *Phoenix* in the holotank above the shuttle bay doors. The five minutes it took to bring the craft into the shuttle bay seemed an eternity.

Brahms felt surrounded by dissipating anger as *Orbitech 1* prepared to receive visitors. Terachyk simply didn't have the charisma to keep the mutineers whipped into a frenzy—not when Brahms used all his abilities to sidetrack them.

Terachyk had no doubt planned his revolt to occur at a time of greatest tension, but he had not counted on the spark of hope even the mutineers would feel. The arrival of the *Phoenix* and the simultaneous appearance of the sail-creatures carried a kind of majestic awe. In their minds, they would give Brahms credit for this, no matter what Terachyk had told them. Their attitudes reminded Brahms of the euphoria that had filled the station when Ramis Barrera had first brought them the wall-kelp.

On the holotank overhead, the recovery team, outfitted in the red-and-silver space suits bearing the Orbitechnolo-

gies logo, grappled with the hulk of what had been the
Miranda. Brahms saw a hodgepodge of retro-rockets, vac-
uum-welded fixtures, and the airtight living area—pieces
attached at random over what had once been the shut-
tlecraft.

Brahms had a flash of a memory, recalling how the *Miranda* had docked there shortly before the War, with its
pilot requesting to stay a few days and relax before returning to Earth orbit for another run.

McLaris was on board that vessel now. Coming back.

The look of the *Phoenix* bespoke desperate acts, the
Clavius people piecing together whatever they had available. Desperate acts—like McLaris stealing the shuttle in
the first place, or Brahms proposing the RIF. Or now Terachyk and his revolt.

Desperate times called for such desperate acts. Sometimes they succeeded, and sometimes they failed.

He turned to look at Terachyk, and the other man glared
back at him.

On the three-dimensional view, the recovery team positioned themselves around the *Phoenix,* avoiding the
weavewire linkage. The radio crackled over the open
band; ConComm refrained from adding irrelevant voice-
overs.

"Start pulling them in again! Caterpiller speed—don't
jerk 'em too much!"

"Reeling in. Doppler has them constant at twenty feet a
second."

The image jittered as the *Phoenix* moved and the holocameras tried to maintain their focus.

"Don't increase speed. Coming along just fine."

"Holding steady."

"We've got five MMUs on this side of it. A few good blasts
should slow this baby right down to a stop."

Brahms was struck by the irony that no one else on
Orbitech 1 even seemed aware of Terachyk's mutiny, but
instead remained intent on the yo-yo situation. He realized that this meant Terachyk's revolt must be relatively
tight-knit and small. He had probably brought every one of
his supporters with him.

Now if Brahms's watchers got together and burst in
here. . . . He swallowed, afraid of the thought and pray-

ing they wouldn't try anything after all. He had no doubt
that if the crowd grew any bigger, he would never survive.

His thoughts were interrupted by the blast of the PA.

"Clear the shuttle bay—I say again, clear the shuttle bay.
Prepare to bring *Phoenix* on board. Airlock opening in two
minutes. Clear the shuttle bay."

The wall of people still surrounded Brahms. He felt
someone grab his arm, but he did not resist. Terachyk
turned to him, wearing a thin smile. "Well, will you join us,
Curtis? Or do you prefer to remain here when the airlock
doors open?"

Someone snickered. Brahms ignored the sea of faces
that turned to stare at him. He wondered if Terachyk
would really seal him in the shuttle bay with the doors
about to open. He answered quietly, "I'll follow you, Allen."

But Terachyk persisted. "You would have sent me out
the airlock if I hadn't measured up to your damned Efficiency Study. You did it to Tim Drury!"

Brahms felt very tired of all this. He met the stares of the
crowd. "If we don't get out of here soon, we'll all go out the
airlock just because you talk too much. Everyone knows
what I did, and everyone knows you helped me."

"I didn't have anything to do with the RIF—"

Brahms spoke sharply but quietly, to keep his voice from
projecting. "Later, Allen. Complacency has never been a
valid excuse under the law. If you want, and if they
want—" He swept his free hand around. "I'll release the
results of the study, right now, and let everyone see how
they were ranked. We'll tell them what criteria *you* used as
chief assessor to rank them. The numbers on that list are
more your doing than mine. Let's show them all. Then
there'll be plenty of time to discuss this—even for a trial, if
that's what you want."

Terachyk looked angry and frightened. The people
nearest him frowned; one looked Terachyk up and down
and seemed to move away from him.

"One minute to airlock doors. Clear the shuttle bay.
Final warning."

"Right now the *Phoenix* is coming," Brahms said. "Let's
get out of the way so the crew can come aboard." He

waited a moment and then, in disgust, clapped his hands and shouted, "Everybody, clear the shuttle bay. Now!"

People moved to obey. Terachyk grew red and started to retort at the director's audacity, but then seemed to think better of it. Instead, he snapped, "Let's move out. Keep hold of the director."

A few people grumbled, but the dissident crowd kicked off from the wall toward the series of airlock doors to storage rooms and the observation areas. Two large men roughly tugged Brahms along with them. He wondered where Winkowski and the other watchers had gone. He couldn't quite believe they would desert him so easily.

The two escorts shoved him through an opening to the observation deck, but they never allowed him to be alone. No one spoke. Within seconds they had sealed themselves behind sheltering doors, watching as the magenta warning lights flashed, reflecting light off the airlock doors.

A murmur rippled through the crowd, a rising excitement. A loud "clunk" came from just outside the colony. The PA sound reverberated throughout the observation deck.

"Prepare to open shuttle bay doors. The *Phoenix* has arrived. Everybody give the crew a welcoming hand."

The airlock doors yawned open and spread wide to show the vessel drifting in, flanked by five people in space suits, pushing it along with the force of their combined MMUs and nudging it into place.

The ConComm announcer on the PA broadcast cheers from random sections on *Orbitech 1*. Clavius Base sent up congratulations. In the observation deck the mutineers' eyes were wide. A man next to Brahms began crying openly, his tears coming off his cheeks and floating in front of his face as tiny spinning water globules. A woman moved among the others, pounding people on the back.

The change felt instantaneous to Brahms—the anger and righteous dissatisfaction among the mutineers was defused; despair was diluted with a new burst of hope.

"Full pressure in the shuttle bay: seven point five psi and ready for visitors. We should be seeing the reception committee from Director Brahms any minute now."

Terachyk stiffened, and Brahms turned to him. "Well,

Allen, should we go greet them? Maybe you'd like to shake hands with McLaris for the cameras?"

Terachyk gestured toward the door, but said nothing. He wore a stormy expression. The airlock doors opened, allowing them all to spill out into the cold shuttle bay. Their breath steamed into the chill air.

Brahms noted that it was the first time since the War that people passed him by without acknowledging his presence. Only one of the big men held onto his arm.

Through the main front window port of the altered *Miranda,* Brahms could see two men inside, working at the hatch. One of them would be McLaris.

When Terachyk reached the metal hulk of the *Phoenix,* the mass of people in the weightless bay moved Brahms up alongside him. Someone called, "Stand back, they're coming out!"

The *Phoenix*'s airlock door crept open. The metal moved, a gap opened. Brahms saw a hand.

The crowd began to cheer. The reaction was so unlike anything Brahms had heard in a long, long time, it overwhelmed him.

Clifford Clancy pushed out from the airlock and floated into the middle of the shuttle bay. He grinned, holding his helmet in his hand, and gave a thumbs-up signal. People spilled toward him. Some of them collided with each other, but no one seemed to notice.

Brahms caught Allen Terachyk's eye. A voice from inside the *Phoenix* barely made it over the other sounds. "Hello, Curtis."

Brahms turned his head to see Duncan McLaris floating just inside the yo-yo. He pulled himself out into the light.

Then the spoke-shaft elevator doors slid open, and this time dozens of green-clad watchers emerged. Nancy Winkowski led the cadre. They all carried clubs—long rods and pieces of pipe. Winkowski pushed into the crowd and started clubbing people, swinging her instrument as she flew through the bay. One woman let out a scream as a pipe struck her in the leg.

Brahms watched Duncan McLaris's expression click like a slide show through a series of emotions—fear, betrayal, disappointment, outrage. McLaris seemed to think he was the target for assassination—that Brahms was trying to kill him for returning.

Brahms saw Terachyk's men fly from the *Phoenix*, scattering throughout the bay. Terachyk himself cringed back against the vessel's hull in helpless terror.

Nancy Winkowski propelled herself in, brandishing the club in front of her.

"Stop!" Brahms screamed over everything, hauling the deep voice up from the center of his chest. "Stop it! Put down your weapons! Winkowski, I order you to cease!"

He felt all the clubs aimed at him, ready to fly. He wondered why he wasn't seeing his life flash in front of his eyes. He cringed, waiting to hear one more crack as a pipe found someone's head.

Instead, after a brief pause, Brahms turned and said, "Welcome back, Duncan."

McLaris held onto the *Phoenix*'s hatch. Had he not been in zero-G, he would have collapsed to the floor. A moment of awkward silence hung in the shuttle bay, leaving only the injured woman's cries and scattered shocked murmurs. Clifford Clancy looked astonished and confused, but he did not move. No one else seemed to understand what was happening.

"Oh, put down your weapons, you idiots!" Brahms shouted. "Bloodshed is not the way to solve problems! I thought you would have figured that out by now."

Terachyk shouted angrily, "Only if you answer publicly for what you have done, Curtis."

Brahms sighed, trying to exaggerate how weary he was of all this. "You can have your trial. And then we will get on with doing what we need to do." He felt very calm, unafraid now: the colony would survive.

He looked up and met Duncan McLaris's eyes. The other man had shaved off his beard; he looked older, but stronger. McLaris seemed to comprehend the power struggle that was going on between Terachyk and Brahms.

The crowd broke into uncertain murmuring. The watchers and the mutineers warily eyed each other and lowered their clubs. Terachyk tried to make himself heard, but his voice sounded weak and broken.

"Everyone is invited to the assembly hall. We will broadcast proceedings against Director Brahms. We will divulge

the files of the Efficiency Study for everyone to see. There
will be an open discussion of what action *Orbitech 1* should
take against him." He turned to stare at Brahms.

"If any," Brahms added.

McLaris interrupted, directing his words to Terachyk.
He spoke in a low voice. "I think you just may find that
sometimes people are forced to make difficult decisions
under extreme pressures, and sometimes they make the
wrong choices."

He paused. "But you'd better look pretty deep into your
own heart before you cast the first stone, Allen."

Brahms blinked, amazed that McLaris had stood up for
him. Or was McLaris perhaps talking about himself and his
own decision to steal the *Miranda*?

"Allen," McLaris continued, raising his eyebrows,
"aren't you at least going to welcome me back?"

Terachyk blinked at him, as if he could not bear to deal
with another variable at the moment. He started to say
something, but McLaris motioned with his head toward
the exit. "Save it for later, Allen. I've been cooped up in a
yo-yo for three days."

The people diffused toward the separate doors of the
spoke-shaft elevators that would lead out of the docking
bay to the toroidal hub of administrative offices, conference rooms, and business areas. Nancy Winkowski drifted
past, perplexed but adamant. The pipe in her hands looked
unwieldy, yet she held onto it.

Several of the other mutineers stayed with Terachyk.
McLaris tried to remain among them, as if he thought he
could defuse tensions further. "I want you all to meet Cliff
Clancy. Dr. Clancy is the one who came up with the idea
for the yo-yo, and he was also head of the construction
engineers working on *Orbitech 2* before the War."

Clancy started shaking hands, moving out to the people,
who seemed eager to embrace him and talk with him. He
glanced back at McLaris, who nodded for him to go ahead.
Terachyk waved his supporters away, indicating that they
should move to the assembly hall. Others began to leave,
thinning out the bay.

Brahms maintained his wooden smile, waiting his
chance. When he finally saw most of the attention directed
away from him, when much of the fear and anger had died

down among the people in the docking bay, he grabbed Nancy Winkowski around the waist and snapped a whisper into her ear. "Follow me!" He clamped his grip down on her and gave an enormous push against the side of the *Phoenix*, propelling both of them across the bay, toward the bank of spoke-shaft elevators standing open on the opposite wall.

Brahms heard shouts; clubs whistled overhead as they flew past them, only to bounce off the far wall. To her credit, Winkowski followed along, adapting without the slightest idea of what Brahms was trying to do. The two of them slammed against the inner wall of the spoke-shaft elevator. Brahms's wrist stung from the impact, probably sprained. He hit the elevator door control and watched the people boiling toward him, shouting and cursing. The last thing he heard was Allen Terachyk ordering the others to stop.

"Where's he going to hide, anyway?" Terachyk yelled.

Where indeed? Brahms thought.

They would figure it out sooner or later.

C H A P T E R 6 7

ORBITECH 1 ■ DAY 72

When the rescue crew hauled Ramis into the *Orbitech 1* shuttle bay, his low-air indicator on the heads-up display had been burning for some time. He didn't care. He didn't waste time or energy talking. His vision remained fuzzy; his skin felt flushed and overheated.

He was numb with shock at what he had seen.

The rescue team had hauled the remnants of the *Aguinaldo* expedition, some supplies, and four intact nymphs still packaged and dormant for the return journey. Dobo Daeng, flailing in his space suit, seemed not to know how he could best cooperate with the crew.

Ramis had arrived too late.

As he had approached the sail-creature mosaic, he had seen that it was severed in half, with one huge section cut off from its controls and drifting away on a new orbit. He had seen Dr. Sandovaal's body in the central sail-creature that had flown straight into the weavewire.

They had planned a beautiful maneuver, jettisoning the dead sail-creatures and slipping gracefully into position at the center of the Lagrange well. But now the mosaic was ruined.

The rescue crew from *Orbitech 1* had reached them while Ramis was still trying to contact a frantic Dobo in the other sail-creature cyst. Ramis had felt such a tremendous sense of loss that he could barely see to assist the team. He had found it impossible to talk on the radio. He didn't even want to speak to Karen.

The rescue team assisted them into the shuttle bay. Dobo chattered over the suit radio, directing the salvage crew to hurry with the dormant sail-creature nymphs. Ramis moved without enthusiasm, feeling as if the world had fallen away from him.

As they floated across the threshold into the docking bay, he saw the hulk of a weird-looking vessel moored to one bulkhead. The yo-yo had arrived intact from Clavius Base. Anna Tripolk had tried to destroy this vessel. He had helped save it. He had protected all of *Orbitech 1* with what he had done. Ramis stared at the *Phoenix* as the massive door to the bay closed behind them.

All the colonies had found ways to tie each other together, even without the safety net of Earth. Seeing the *Phoenix* gave him some freedom from his grief.

Sandovaal would have complained about how clunky it looked.

After the shuttle bay had filled with air, medics appeared, checking him and Dobo. Someone twisted Ramis's helmet off. He felt detached, and let them do what they wanted. Several people came forward in greeting, but they moved in a haphazard group, without the formal control Ramis had expected. He recognized Allen Terachyk and a man who looked like Duncan McLaris from the ConComm broadcasts, but he did not see Director Brahms among them.

Before the men could say anything, the PA clicked and a voice came over. "We've located the director. I think someone official should come and deal with this. Mr. Terachyk?"

In the lab room, the black technician looked baffled. He shrugged, looking up at Terachyk and McLaris. "Seems like he did everything right."

Nancy Winkowski stood huddled in a self-protective stance. Her wide eyes harbored an amazed expression, tinged with a bit of defiance. "He made me help him. I did the best I could."

They stared down at Brahms in the sleepfreeze chamber.

The director lay motionless, with a serene and empty expression. Through the curved glass of the cubicle, he seemed to be deep in the sleep of exhaustion.

Terachyk looked upset. "That bastard!"

McLaris allowed himself a smile, which he covered before anyone else could see.

Terachyk glared at the motionless face behind the glass and slapped his hand on the surface. "He thinks we'll forget about it if he hides his head under the covers!"

"Stop that, Allen!" McLaris spoke sharply. He picked up the d-cube left lying on the surface of the chamber. "Let's listen to what he had to say."

Nancy Winkowski turned away, as if she didn't want to hear Brahms's words again. McLaris stared at the d-cube, sighed, then walked to the reader in the lab room. He pushed the cube in and stood back, pursing his lips. They all turned toward the small holomonitor.

Brahms appeared, looking haggard, but with an odd inner peace behind his expression. Off to the edge of the image, McLaris could make out a blurry figure that must have been Winkowski.

"Duncan, Allen—and all of *Orbitech 1*—I place myself in your hands. Right now a long trial would be divisive and destructive to our fragile balance. It would sap our energy and our attention, which would best be directed elsewhere. And I am too tired to go through with it."

The image of Winkowski mumbled something at the edge of the screen, but Brahms made a dismissive gesture with his hand. He continued.

"I leave the decision to you. You can take the easy way out and just disconnect me—throw my body out the airlock to join the hundred fifty-two people lost in the RIF. But do not allow yourselves to forget that I acted in what I thought was the best way to ensure our survival.

"Punish me or forgive me, as you see fit. We all do what

we must do. Right now I want nothing more than to rest. I leave you to determine how long that rest will be."

The holographic image dissolved into static, then nothing.

Winkowski had started to cry. McLaris took a deep breath and pulled his lips tight. "That's it. We've got a new start." He turned to walk away. "Let's try not to screw it up this time."

Terachyk slammed a hand against the chamber. Spinning, McLaris saw the man trembling with anger.

"I hope he's having nightmares!"

In the depths of his cold sleep, Curtis Brahms dreamed of playing checkers.

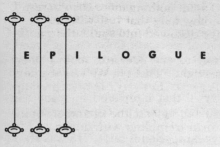

EPILOGUE

ORBITECH 2 ■ YEAR 3

Ramis watched as Clifford Clancy boosted his daughter up on his shoulders, letting the giggling girl survey the open spread of the newly completed *Orbitech 2*. The girl's face had an Oriental appearance, muted and mercifully free of Clancy's own craggy features. Wiay slipped an arm around Clancy's waist and beckoned for Ramis to take in the view with them.

As Ramis drew close, Clancy nodded toward the girder webwork of the outer, larger torus still being assembled. "Another two years and we'll be finished. *Orbitech 2* will give us enough growing room for fifty years."

"A lot will change in that time," Ramis said, watching the silvery figures moving around in space. Most of Clancy's construction crew had left the Moon the first chance they could, though some had agreed to stay, apparently to Clancy's chagrin.

Ramis knew he was being too quiet on his first tour of *Orbitech 2*, but other thoughts kept him distracted. He remarked on how the colony looked enormous—especially without any growing foliage. Bare steel decks gave the impression that the huge station was naked and cold. But that would change. Several species of Dobo Daeng's modified wall-kelp would cover the decks in only a few months.

"I wish Father Magsaysay could have seen this," Ramis said in a quiet voice.

"I thought he wasn't all that interested in space construction," Clancy said. "He seemed pretty wrapped up in the *Aguinaldo*."

"That is not what I meant," Ramis said. "He was afraid that once the Americans and the other colonies got over their period of crisis and did not need us anymore, you would treat us as 'little brown brothers' all over again."

Ramis took a deep breath. "But the last time I saw him, he took me to one of the viewing verandas on the *Aguinaldo* and pointed out to *Orbitech 2*. He told me his worries were wrong—that we had learned not to focus on the survival of the Filipino race, but on the human race. He was very proud of all of us. I think he felt fulfilled. He was happy to see us growing again."

Wiay patted her swollen belly. "Cliffy and I are doing everything we can to help. We'll have Lang Ti's little brother running around soon."

Ramis looked away from the viewport, blinking. "Huh? Excuse me, I did not hear you."

Clancy frowned, rubbing his fingers against Wiay's shoulder blade. "You've been absentminded lately, Ramis. I thought this tour of *Orbitech 2* would get you out of the doldrums."

Ramis shrugged, pulling himself away from his thoughts. "I am sorry, but I am considering too many things at once. Director McLaris has offered me a very good position working with the sail-creatures if I wish to return to *Orbitech 1*. It is either that or join Mr. Terachyk and Dr. Tomkins on the radio-telescope project. But something makes me uneasy. It all seems so permanent."

Clancy laughed. "I can't imagine why a nineteen-year-old wouldn't want to settle down and choose a course for the rest of his life! You've still got wanderlust. You're looking for some grand challenge; otherwise, you're not going to be happy."

Clancy flipped his daughter off his shoulders and over his head. She shrieked as he caught her and held her upside down. Wiay spoke over the child's laughter. "No one's going to blame you if you join the *Kibalchich*, Ramis. That does seem more like your style."

"I was afraid someone might point that out to me. I thought I was the only one crazy enough to consider the possibility," Ramis said, looking away.

"I hope Brahms's trial isn't held until after I leave. I don't want to testify."

Clancy snorted. "I wish they'd get it over with. They've had a team of guards by his sleepfreeze chamber for the past three years."

"Mars may be the best thing for all of us," Wiay answered.

"Not me," Clancy said. "I had enough dirt between my toes on Clavius Base. But if the Soviets can make a go of anything, it'll be getting that colony established. Anna Tripolk seems to be fully recovered now, but a lot of people would still be happy to have her a bit farther away. Once she's got her mind focused on something, I'm not going to get in her way."

Wiay sounded wistful. "Cliffy, you can't tell me you didn't have any fun on the Moon."

Clancy snorted. "Our daughter is not going to grow up speaking Russian—okay, so call me a throwback to pre-War patriotism. But I don't want to miss a day of her life, not even in sleepfreeze. She'll grow up and lead a normal life here on *Orbitech 2*."

Wiay stuck out her tongue. "Spoilsport."

Ramis turned his thoughts back to the *Kibalchich*. Mars! If he could talk Karen into going. . . .

He said quietly, "I must get back to the *Aguinaldo* and inform Dobo of my plans. Since Father Magsaysay died, Dobo is the last family I have there."

Clancy shifted his daughter and placed a hand on Ramis's shoulder. "You can always come here to visit us."

"If I go to Mars, it might be fifteen years before I come back—or never."

Wiay grinned at him and took her daughter from Clancy's arms. "In fifteen years, Lang Ti will be old enough to make you settle down."

Ramis blushed and pointedly looked out the viewport as Wiay and Clancy both laughed. Through the transparent sections of the huge enclosed greenhouse dome of *Orbitech 2*, he saw a tiny dot fluttering in the open volume. The dot grew larger, approaching one of the window sections. Stubby wings flapped gracefully as the sail-creature nymph soared in its zero-G environment.

The nymph flew free with a dozen or so other creatures, unhindered by people or structures in the core. It had no boundaries, room to do what it wanted. Ramis felt a kinship with it.

He had to go to Mars.

"Salamat po, Sarat," Ramis whispered to himself as he watched the sail-creature gracefully flap away. "Thank you, Timely One!"

ABOUT THE AUTHORS

Born in Wisconsin, KEVIN J. ANDERSON graduated from the University of Wisconsin, Madison and received a degree with Honors in Physics/Astronomy. He presently works as a technical writer for the Lawrence Livermore National Laboratory and has written, to date, more than a hundred short stories for magazines and anthologies as well as four solo novels.

MAJOR DOUG BEASON has lived in such places as California, Canada and the Philippine Islands. A graduate of the United States Air Force Academy, Doug holds a PhD in physics and is currently the Director of the High Energy Plasma Laboratory at Kirtland AFB, New Mexico. He is also an accomplished short story author and has written several "high-tech" novels. Doug met Kevin while on sabbatical at Livermore, California, where the two discovered a liking for pizza, beer, and writing SF. "We hit it off fine . . . [and] we decided to try our hand at collaborating," says Doug.

"Reflections in a Magnetic Mirror"—a novelette which appeared in Bantam's *Full Spectrum*—marked Kevin and Doug's first collaborative effort as Bantam authors. *Lifeline* is their first novel together. Bantam plans to publish two additional novels by this formidable team in the near future.